Pain lanced through the shoulder of the Reven crossbowman as he rolled over and tried to crawl away. The feathered shaft dragged on the ground, ripping into his wound. A guttural snarl escaped his lips as shadows lengthened on the grass from behind him and he heard the soft approach of his doom.

"Not so fast," said the woodsman, kicking him over onto his back.

The Reven stared up into the shadows of the hooded figure looking down at him and spat.

"You are no woodsman."

The man appeased him with a nod. "And you are no longer a Reven."

Also By Anthony Lavisher

With Jamie Wallis
Vengeance

Anthony Lavisher

Whispers

of a

Storm

ry

For my beloved Amy
You are the beat of my heart.
Thank you for sorting out the bubbles.

Acknowledgements

Thanks must go to all of you who have helped me on this road, you know who you all are and without you, I would not have got here...finally.

I would especially like to thank the pop master, Gill Hollis, for helping Khadazin and Cassana on their way. Also to Ted Sherborne, for pointing me in the right direction and making sure that the old ways never die.

My love and thanks must also go to Amy, for showing me the right path when I became lost in the forest and for helping me with the electronic edition.

Special thanks must also go to my great friend Jamie Wallis, for his superb cover and to Helen Smith, Frances Jessop and Catrin Collier for their invaluable guidance and kind assistance.

And to David Gemmell, for bringing my imagination to life and inspiring me to tell my own tales.

CHAPTER ONE

Fortunes

The two men watched him from the concealment of the alley's shadows, motionless amidst a dark night's backdrop of rubbish and broken fencing. The man, their prey, leant against the dark doorway of Mason's Inn and retched heavily, the alcohol he had consumed at the bar that day apparently keen to find its own way home. Their target was tall and broad-shouldered, a local stonemason of some note in the city of Karick, and his skin as black as the dark night sky. The heavy cloak he wore shrouded his true frame in a vain attempt to ward away the fierce chill in the early summer night air.

Wiping the spittle from his bearded mouth, the stonemason pushed himself leadenly away from the inn's porch and almost fell out into the street beyond. Fortunately for him, the dry cobbles underfoot steadied his feet and gently nudged him on his way as he stumbled across the quiet street towards the cluttered alley that cut through a row of dark, silent houses, which would save him at least an hour's worth of swaying and stumbling home. Groaning and trying to focus on his footing, he began weaving his way down the treacherous alley, commonly known by the locals as Cutpurse Way. Mumbling away to the night, he stumbled over an unseen object and began cursing as he passed blindly by the two shadows, who watched him patiently from their hiding place and shared swift hand signals.

Both of the men knew what to do. The stonemason's name was Khadazin Sahr; he owned a popular workshop in Marble Plaza no more than four streets away and had made a name for himself some years back by saving the life of a well-respected merchant called Savinn Kassaar. The merchant, Savinn Kassaar, had been checking up on his business interests in the south of the city when three men had overpowered his bodyguards and chased after him with knives drawn. Armed only with his masonry hammer, Khadazin had put down two of the assailants and chased away the third before a passing militia patrol had come to his aid. Savinn Kassaar had handsomely rewarded the stonemason for his help and had used his connections and persuasion within the city to buy the workshop for him in the prosperous plaza that the stonemason now called home.

For a week now the two men had watched the stonemason's movements and traced his familiar journey from his workshop early in the afternoon, to the Mason's Inn and then back home again via Cutpurse Way, late at night. Their strict orders had come through to them with the warning not to underestimate his strength. Taking heed of this reputation the two would-be assailants moved cautiously after their target, aware that another two of their companions lay in wait further down the alleyway. Their strength would have to come from their numbers.

Oblivious to the two figures creeping after him through the darkness, the tall stonemason stumbled on his way. Unaware of the danger, he lost himself deep within the muddle of events that had haunted him so badly over the past few weeks... He had been so full of pride a month ago when he had received an official looking letter at his workshop from a well-dressed messenger. He had turned the letter over and hesitated, his hand shaking as he noticed the red waxed seal bearing the mark of an eagle in flight, clutching one half of a straight, broken sword in each talon. It was the crest of the noble High Duke Stromn of Karick, voice of the Valian Council and presiding ruler of the Four Vales. Nervously he had broken the wax seal and torn open the letter. His hazel eyes had widened in amazement as he saw the message in beautiful, elegant handwriting. It was from the high duke's chancellor Relan Valus. Slowly, he read aloud the message, frowning. Somewhere in amongst the lyrical words which only served to confuse him, he comprehended that, out of all of the masonry samples submitted recently to the chancellor's office, it was his workmanship that had been chosen to carry out some maintenance repairs about the gardens of the high duke's keep. Wiping his brow, the stonemason read the letter again and again, and it wasn't until the following morning that the words had finally sunk in. Full of pride, he had paid a local scribe to acknowledge his receipt of the letter and of his joy at having being selected. Allowing the scribe to

3

choose the humble and flattering tone of the letter, he said that he would start work without fail at the required time, four days later. Khadazin left the scribe with a spring in his giant step and cancelled any other jobs that he had been booked to do later that day.

His work had begun four days later as directed and was progressing nicely without any setbacks, other than the distraction of the splendour and majesty of the high duke's keep. He had even received a congratulatory note from Savinn Kassaar, which left the mason wondering how the merchant knew about his great stroke of good fortune.

On the third day, however, the hottest of the early summer so far, Khadazin had fallen asleep in a secluded corner of the gardens whilst having his lunch. Some hours later he was woken by the sound of voices on the other side of the hedgerows behind him. It was already early evening, the shadows of the blossom trees shading the grounds beginning to lengthen and reach out to cool the garden's beautiful flowerbeds and marble pathways. The stonemason remained where he was, not wanting to be caught sleeping on the job. If he was discovered, he would have been flogged for his stupidity and laziness. The shame of his incompetence would have left any esteem he held around the city in tatters.

But as he listened to the voices close by, fear stirred in his rapidly cramping body; what was he overhearing?

"No, I can assure you, the high duke suspects nothing," an anxious voice replied in defence to a previously unheard question.

I should not, by the storms, be listening to this! Khadazin had panicked silently.

"He had better not, my friend. We have worked

undetected for many years now. Our plans must not fail before we have ever truly begun. Our brother has already managed to distract the Seventh and the fool has obligingly agreed to send his daughter here to attend the Valian Council on his behalf."

Even in hushed tones, the speaker's abrasive voice was edged with warning and, despite the fear building inside him, the stonemason couldn't help but strain to eavesdrop on their conversation.

"If our brother's report is well founded, she will leave within the fortnight," the second speaker had continued. "This will be our first chance to seize the puppeteer's strings and the girl must be taken long before she and her entourage arrive."

Seventh? A girl? Khadazin was trying to piece together the information and make some sense of it.

"And you, I trust, can arrange this?" the first speaker had enquired, unconvinced.

"Of course! We still have a hunting party at our disposal, do we not? We will have our brother *suggest* that the girl's party travel a less worn road, where she can easily be taken without drawing the attention of any Valian patrols. Once she is ours, we will be able to influence matters on the northern borders a lot more easily than we can at the moment, will we not?"

There had followed a long, still, heart-rending silence that left the stonemason fearing he had been discovered. He was slowly beginning to move his position to help ease the cramp biting into the muscles of his lower back, when the first speaker started again, tension laced in his words.

"This had better be opportunism and not recklessness that leads us to this course of action. After all, we have many better-placed pieces on our board and we would not wish to risk our queen at such an early stage of the game."

What is going on here? Khadazin had screamed silently, terror eating away at his thoughts. He screwed his eyes shut, hoping it would help to block their voices out of his mind.

"True," the other man had mused thoughtfully. "But if we take his daughter now, we can keep her at our disposal until we see fit to use her. We may not get this chance again for a very long time, my friend."

"Hmm...Yes, you are right. We must act swiftly if we are to catch the girl on her journey here."

One of the speakers rose and slowly smoothed down his crumpled clothing. Subconsciously, Khadazin had tried to sink lower into the flattened grass beneath him, to avoid being spotted.

"I will contact you in the normal way. Return to your duties brother and think no more on this matter for the time being. Soon all will be as our lord would wish it. I shall talk to him on the stars this very night and set the pendulum in motion."

"Wait, when will I hear from you?" the first voice had demanded of the now retreating speaker.

"You will." Had come his cold, assured reply and then all was silent.

For some time the other man had remained, his thoughts trapped deep within the turmoil of his own treachery. Then, with startling abruptness, his footsteps could be heard retreating hurriedly away into the distance, leaving the shadows behind to lengthen out ominously across the silent gardens.

The stonemason had remained flattened into the soft lawn, his heart racing as it beat on the drums of panic in his ears and drowned out the oppressive silence of the gardens beyond his hiding place. His mind had tumbled with a multitude of questions that whispered back at him with a myriad of different answers. Whoever this girl was she was in great danger and her father must have been someone of great importance for these men to go to such lengths to capture her! And what was that about the Valian Council (the annual meeting that took place in the city between the rulers and politicians that governed the Four Vales)? It sounded as if the girl's father had been coerced into sending her to attend the council in his stead, so that she might be used as some kind of bargaining tool. And who were the two men? Were they from some secret organisation working in the shadows of the high duke's household, planning dark mischief and strife? They had referred to each other as *brother* and hinted at other members of this brotherhood! Who were they? And what were their goals? Khadazin had no answer to his maelstrom of questions and above his rising panic, the only things to be heard in the gardens that evening had been the loud thump of his terrified heart and the distant calls of the birds, as they sang their farewells to the glorious day.

Breathing deeply, the stonemason had sat up, sweat drenching his body and running in rivulets down his furrowed brow. Shaking, and bemoaning his sudden change of fortune, he pounded his fists on the grass and, drawing his knees up to his chest, he buried his head in his hands.

He had stayed hidden for at least another hour before pulling himself up from the dampened grass; leaving his large frame imprinted in the well-tended lawn beneath him. By this time the last feeble rays of the sun had slowly begun to dry the fear from his clothing and, eager to be away from the keep, he had gathered up his tools and hurried from the gardens as innocuously as his fear would allow him. He was hurrying across one of the many courtyards of the old keep, and nearing the guarded gatehouse, when a voice from behind had called him to a stop. A man was striding purposefully towards him, his elegant velvet blue robes dancing over the cobbled courtyard. The nobleman's harsh features narrowed critically as he studied the tall man subconsciously cowering before him.

"What are you doing here alone at this unsanctioned hour, peasant?" the nobleman had demanded angrily. His neatly groomed greying eyebrows had arched up with irritation over piercing green eyes that were flanked with lines, creased by middle age. It was one of the speakers from the garden and Khadazin had been unable to keep the fear from stealing into his eyes.

"I asked you a question! Are you ill? What's wrong with you?"

"Oh, forgive me my lord. Your sudden appearance startled me, that is all," the stonemason had blurted out, trembling.

It was Relan Valus, of all blessed men. The very man whose office had hired him to come to the keep in the first place! The same man who not an hour before had been meeting in secret in the high duke's gardens, plotting foul deeds with an unknown accomplice. Until that day Khadazin had not been able to put a sure voice to the face of the man who was always at the high duke's side, when he attended matters of state and public events. The events unfolding before the stonemason were becoming more terrible by the minute. He needed time to think, but, as the chancellor stood before him, growing increasingly more impatient, time was the one thing he did not have.

"I was on my way home from my duties here at the keep this day, my lord," he had managed.

"Who are you, man?" the chancellor had asked, his irritation rising.

"Why, I am the mason, Khadazin, my lord. It was you who commissioned me to work here at the high duke's keep," he had answered, noticing the terror that crept briefly into the chancellor's eyes.

"Oh yes, I recall now, of course I do," Relan Valus had spluttered indignantly. "Well perhaps I shall check on your progress tomorrow. For now, be on your way and do not expect to receive pay for your extra work."

The stonemason had backed timidly away, bowing his forgiveness. "Oh no, my lord, I do not and would not consider it."

Turning, Khadazin had hurried away, the chancellor's baleful eyes following his every faltering footstep.

That night Khadazin had locked himself away with a bottle of Valian Dark. His fear had chased after every heartbeat, his breath catching at every noise from the world outside. Would the chancellor seek to silence him? Surely he now knew that his meeting had been compromised?

The mason did not sleep well that night and had struggled through the early hours, deciding whether or not to return to the keep that morning and continue his work. After tussling with his fear and his conscience, he had finally decided that to not return to the keep would have sent a clear message to the chancellor that he had, indeed overheard his meeting and would have probably signed his own death warrant.

So Khadazin had returned to the keep and the gardens he so desperately wanted to avoid. He had spent the next three days hurrying a week's worth of work and had not seen anyone except the four gardeners who tended to the grounds in the morning and were always gone by midday. Once he had finished his work, he had wandered about the courtyards looking for the chancellor's office, in a hurry to receive his payment and be off. Confused, he stopped a passing chambermaid. The pretty, dark-haired lass was carrying a basket full of linen and after jumping at his sudden, foreign appearance, she had kindly directed him to the chancellor's office. Fortunately for the stonemason a bespectacled old man had slowly opened the door. The aide acknowledged his completion of the maintenance work and announced that payment would follow within the week, once they had inspected and were satisfied with his workmanship. If they were not, he would not get paid for his work. Khadazin had thanked the man and hurried home, via Mason's Inn.

As the week slipped away slowly into the next he had begun to worry over what he should do. The chancellor could not be certain if he had been in the gardens during their secret meeting. If he had been sure, the stonemason knew he would no longer be alive. Should he tell someone? He didn't possess many close friends, if any at all. Those who knew him well tended to be his customers and they could often tell the stonemason's mood by the thunder in his face, or the acid on his tongue. He was not sure he could trust anyone at the keep, other than the high duke himself and he, a mere mason, would have never been granted such an audience. And what should he say to him if he was granted audience? What was he to do?

As the pressure over his dilemma increased and another week slipped by without payment from the keep, he had turned to seeking all of his answers in the bottom of a wine glass and, as of yet, had found nothing there that had pleased him...

Further down the dark alleyway Khadazin stumbled again, snapping his thoughts from the past and dragging himself back to the present. His surroundings spun about him as his inebriated vision swung in and out of focus. Blindly he reached out a huge hand and gripped a fence post for balance as he fought to keep down the remaining contents of his stomach.

"You are not in control anymore," he slurred to himself, nearly falling through the rickety fencing. Somehow he caught sight of the two faceless figures, as they moved from the shadows to block his intended path home. For the first time now he became vividly aware of how silent the city night-life was and a chill bit into the nape of his neck, warning him of the threat these cloaked figures represented.

Breathing raggedly he shot a furtive glance back the way he had come and, to his horror, he could see two more hooded figures, stalking him through the rubbish. His mind spun in tandem with his swirling vision as he held on to the post and struggled to steady the alley dancing seductively around him.

"Not here for my purse then?" he complained, looking about for something to defend himself with, anything...

The two assailants approaching to his left suddenly came charging towards him, knives glinting faintly in the pitiful moonlight. Grunting, Khadazin let go of the post he was vainly trying to free from the ground and threw himself recklessly to meet them; his senses sharpening slightly from the anger building up within him. Blind to, or accepting of the danger he faced, he met their rush head on.

Somehow he managed to sidestep a knife thrust and, grasping the offered arm, he pulled the attacker off balance and hurled him into the fencing. The man collapsed in a broken tangle of boards and splinters and somewhere a dog began to bark in irritation. As the stonemason recovered from the first attack, he felt the burning of a knife wound that tore through his robes and slid painfully across his ribs. Fortunately for him the pain was dulled by the alcohol rampant within his body and, growling, he smashed one elbow into the depths of the attacker's dark cowl, connecting with bone and breaking a nose with the impact. As the attacker reeled back, Khadazin dealt a huge blow to the man's stomach and then brought both hands down on the back of his neck as he doubled over. Footsteps dragged his attentions away from the man as he dropped without a sound. Both of the other assailants were close enough now to charge at him and, as he met them, a cudgel slammed into the side of his head, the impact exploding in his ears and sending him reeling. A second blow to the stonemason's left shoulder put him onto his knees and, as they leapt upon him, he lashed out desperately, connecting with one of their chins in the thrashing melee. The other attacker bore him to the ground and they rolled about, flailing madly. The attacker's breath rasped in his face, a vile concoction of garlic and rotting teeth and pain shot through Khadazin's injured side, as the man somehow managed to bring his weapon to bear amidst the tangle of robes and thrashing limbs. Snarling gutturally, the stonemason closed his huge hands about the assassin's neck and pulled him onto a head-butt. Oblivious to the pain in his building frenzy, Khadazin flipped the man to one side and scrambled up drunkenly to meet him. Jilting his stance, the stonemason caught the man's wrist and, as he twisted it violently, wrenched the cudgel deftly from the man's grasp with his free hand. Movement from his left also announced the return of the third ruffian, a knife raised to strike. With one desperate motion, Khadazin smashed the cudgel into the face of the man he held and inadvertently parried the thrusting assassin's blade as he pulled his weapon away from the man's bloodied and pulped face. Letting go of his captive, the stonemason allowed him to crumple to the floor and turned to face the new threat. Again the man slashed the knife at his face, forcing the mason to back away and stumble over a body behind him.

"Well the odds seem to be with me now, brother," he grinned, his teeth flashing mockingly in the moonlight.

The barking dog had now found a partner and together they snapped their disapproval at the commotion coming from within the alleyway. Somewhere off into the night, a woman also screeched her anger at the disruptions from an upstairs window. As Khadazin spoke, the man at his feet groaned weakly and without taking his eyes off his opponent, he stamped down on the man's neck, silencing him immediately with a sickening snap. This did not bring the reckless attack that the stonemason had hoped for however; as the last assassin stood back guardedly, the blade he held poised menacingly before him.

Hurry up! Khadazin groaned inwardly as he fought down the pain beginning to seep through the veil of his intoxication. His side burned painfully and his left shoulder was going numb. The blow on the side of his head throbbed terribly and was probably swelling up like a second face by now.

His vision blurred slightly as the man suddenly attacked, feinting right and then leaping towards him across his fallen comrade. Again the stonemason met his attacker boldly, purposefully taking a vicious wound to his left forearm as he blocked the strike and hammered a furious blow to the man's midriff. An explosion of air burst from the attacker's lips as he curled over and, hurling down his weapon, the stonemason moved behind him. Wrapping one huge arm about the struggling man's neck he crushed the life from his windpipe.

Dropping the limp body to the ground he stepped back and clamped one hand over the wound in his side. Blood flowed freely through his shaking fingers. His heart pounded furiously with the adrenalin and nervous anger at large within him as he swayed dizzily, the night coming quickly in and out of focus. Dumbly he surveyed the alleyway. None of the attackers moved and the night was deathly silent once again.

So, the chancellor had indeed known that he had been overheard and had become paranoid that the stonemason would unmask his traitorous little scheme. Oh he wanted to! But a mere commoner such as he would have no friends at the high duke's court and with no hard evidence he would probably be thrown into the city dungeons for hurling about such ludicrous accusations.

Another wave of pain shot through his body and he

collapsed to his knees, biting at his lower lip to try and divert the agony.

"Lady, give me strength," he growled through clenched teeth, staring pleadingly up at the stars glinting in the impenetrable black night sky. Fumbling for the fallen cudgel, he forced himself onto his feet and began stumbling his way down the alleyway. Eventually the end of the alley spat him out into the adjoining street beyond and he swayed there for a moment, breathing in deeply, glad to be free from the suffocation of his supposed death trap.

Then a new terror overcame him. Once the chancellor heard of this failure, he would send more assassins. Khadazin knew he could not hide in the city forever; he would need to get out and away before it was too late. But the chancellor would be expecting him to flee! What now? He would need help to escape the city, but the only person he trusted enough to help him was the one person he did not want to drag down into this mess. No, it was best if he kept his only real friend out of it for now, and he had already taken decisive actions, should something happen to him, anyhow! And what about the girl? If what he had overheard in the high duke's gardens were true, then the girl and her entourage would have left for the city a couple of days ago. If only he had found the courage to report what he had heard, he may have been able to help the girl. If only he had not fallen asleep. If only this, if only that! It was too late for regret now, and far too late for him to start attributing self-blame. The past was already lost to the stonemason, stolen away by the heat of a summer's day. If he was going to survive this, he would have to look to the future and for now, look after his own affairs. He needed to find a militia patrol and get them to help him across to the west side of the city, so that his wounds could be tended at the militia hospital. Once there, he could plan his next move. If the esteemed Chancellor Valus wanted his silence, then he was going to have to work that little bit harder for it from now on.

Steeling himself, he stared away down the empty street to his right and spied the faint tongues of flame licking at the night sky from the torches of a familiar militia patrol heading down Scoundrel's Lane, away from him. Wincing in pain, he forced out a weak smile and, clinging onto the lifeline of hope that the patrol offered him, he hurried after them as fast as his injured body would allow.

Moments after his passing, a shadow stirred in the darkness of a doorway. Unbeknown to the stonemason, his problems went with him.

CHAPTER TWO

Dark Pursuits

The beautiful forest was little more than an ancient bystander as the woman raced madly through her surroundings. Leaping over ditches and barely avoiding tree roots and vines she crashed, without thought of her own safety, through overgrown pathways of bramble and thorn, which reached out to grab her and pull her from her flight. Her breath was coming in gasps and her fear was rising as she ran into the unknown. Behind her she was sure she could hear faint sounds of pursuit, getting ever closer and bringing with it the death that she had earlier so narrowly avoided.

Her heart was pounding furiously as she fled into a small clearing, and it was here that the forest finally managed to bring her to a stop. A sound somewhere off through the trees had tempted her to glance behind and it was then that she stumbled, her coordination failing and her luck finally running out. Surprisingly there was no pain, only the sudden wrench of breathlessness that dragged her from the depths of her fear and left her lying face down in the soft dewy grass. Moaning, Cassana rolled over onto her back and lay there, staring up at the beautiful azure sky that gazed down upon her through the treetops of the forest clearing. Breathing in deeply, perhaps properly for the first time in many minutes, she watched a single cotton-white cloud trek unopposed across the sky. She closed her eyes, focusing her attention on the sounds of the land. Birds heralded the morning, welcoming its glory, unaware of the massacre that had occurred not more than a mile away. As she listened, Cassana could hear somewhere over to her left, the humming of an unknown insect as it foraged a wild flower for nectar.

Her heart still raced and, although the sun's rays kissed at her cold body it could do little to warm her, sweat-drenched as her clothing was.

"A little early to be catching the sun, is it not?" observed a soft voice suddenly, splitting the serene quiet of the small clearing.

Cassana's fear kicked her into motion and she rolled up onto one knee, her hand whipping forth the slender dagger concealed in her left, deerskin boot, as her eyes searched for the newcomer.

I am dead. They have found me! Cassana looked around in panic, the thumping of her heart blotting out all other sounds. For a moment she could see nothing and then, just as she was beginning to think her erratic mind was playing tricks, she spotted a figure at the edge of the tiny clearing, watching her quietly from under the shade of a large, gnarled oak tree. The hairs on the back of her neck tensed and the blade she held shook visibly in her hand, as she fought to maintain control of her nerves.

The figure moved slowly out into the sunlight,

18

empty gloved hands held out to show that there was no threat intended.

"You won't need that, my lady," a man's voice stated, as the figure looked cautiously to the north and did not attempt to make eye contact with her.

Cassana rose shakily, still holding the weapon guardedly towards him.

"W-who are you, sir?" she stammered, trying to retain some composure. The man ignored her and moved away towards the tree line to the north. He was silent for a time as he listened intently. He was dressed in soft woodland green and brown leathers, a long hooded hunting cloak of dark embroidered cloth cascaded about broad shoulders and swept to the heels of his soft leather boots. Cassana watched him move along the fringes of the clearing, colourful anger filling her cheeks at his continuing avoidance of her question. He moved silently and with a grace that she was all too familiar with, having grown up amongst many skilled warriors and knights back at home. The man turned, as if sensing her eyes upon him and he reached up to lower the hood concealing his features.

Cassana slowly let out a breath as the man regarded her with his deep green eyes. He was in his late thirties possibly, his weather-beaten face creased by the early ravages of age. He had brown, unkempt hair, his several-day growth of beard flecked with grey and his broad forehead furrowed as he stared almost critically down a crooked sloping nose at her.

"Have you finished staring?" Cassana demanded, rapidly losing patience now.

The man's eyes sparkled briefly before he looked away again, much to her annoyance.

"What are you doing out here?" he asked, cutting

the breath from her next angry question.

She couldn't find the words to explain what had recently happened as the images of her fears rose up yet again and came crashing back at her crumbling wall of composure. The blade in her hand began to tremble and she stuffed it falteringly back into her boot.

"Are you from the caravan that took shelter in Fox Glade last eve?" he asked. Cassana quickly nodded, unable to reply.

"What happened to you, girl? Where are your companions?"

Cassana, relieved by the gentleness in his voice, began to sob uncontrollably as she dropped to her knees, her legs giving way. The man sighed and moved over to her, studying her closely as he put a gentle, comforting hand on her right shoulder. She was trembling like a leaf, caught up in an autumn storm. She was no more than twenty summers by her looks and her long shoulder-length glossy black hair was tousled and wild. She started suddenly at his touch and her pale tear-stained face looked up at him through the veil of her hair. Even in her current predicament and condition she still had a beauty about her, her features, although plain, held something captivating in them. Her glistening blue eyes steeled as she met his pitying gaze above her small up-turned nose and her full lips parted, ready for some kind of remark.

"Where were you headed?" he asked, removing his hand and stepping back as she made to rise.

The girl smoothed down her once-fine travelling clothes; a dirtied silk blouse and a soft leather riding skirt. She was tall and lithe; her boots reaching just below her knees with a green sash wrapped about her slender waist. She wore a plain silver band on her left index finger and a pair of golden bangles on her wrists.

"Where are you headed girl?" he repeated firmly.

"Karick," she whispered, staring at him. "I, I mean we were heading to the great city. We camped in the glade you spoke of last night and were to begin the remainder of the journey today."

"What happened to your friends, miss? What are you running from?" the man pressed, glad to be finally getting some sense from her.

"Reven," she breathed the name as if she didn't truly believe it herself.

The man showed little reaction and Cassana blinked in disbelief.

"Did you hear me, sir? There are Reven in the Moonglade Forest. They attacked us at dawn. I barely escaped with my life!"

The man looked to the north thoughtfully and then turned his attentions back on her.

"Who are you?" he demanded abruptly.

"My name is Cassana," she answered, stepping back from him slightly.

"I asked you who you are, girl?" he was suddenly very menacing and Cassana tensed.

"Reven don't come all this way just for a bit of raiding, miss, and you are not dressed like some common traveller, no matter how many scratches you now bear. Most who pass through here are not escorted by eight knights either, travelling through the forest to avoid the open roads!"

Cassana shrank from him, pulling the blade from her boot once more. For the first time now the scratches she had endured began to burn and the pain somehow brought her to her senses.

"How did you know that? Were you watching us?"

The man stood quietly for a moment before replying.

"I always make a point of surveying strangers to these parts; I did the same with your little party last night, as the tall knight prepared a meal for you."

Cassana felt a spark of anger ignite as she detected a hint of disdain in his voice.

"That is my business and as I do not know your name sir, it remains none of yours," she snapped, immediately regretting the lack of courtesy in her tone.

The man smiled, shaking his head ruefully. "Where are you from lady? If you want my help, you had better start talking, as we will be fast running out of options."

Something in his voice suggested to her that he had dealt with Reven tribesmen before and her truculent defiance began to buckle.

"Forgive me, sir." She bowed her head slightly as he nodded in acceptance.

"My name is Cassana Byron," she began, lowering her dagger. "My father is Alion Byron, the Lord of the North Vales. He has had much to occupy him of late and was unable to attend a meeting of the Valian Council in five days time, so he decided that it was time I became the daughter he had always wanted me to be. I was to attend the meeting in his place and act on his behalf."

Cassana knew she shouldn't be telling him this, but she had nobody else to turn to now. This woodsman knew the terrain better than she and could probably help her to safety.

The man showed no reaction to her revelations and watched her steadily, his arms folded across his chest. He arched his eyebrows, signalling for her to continue.

"We left Highwater five days ago and my

bodyguard, Elan, decided that we should take the forest road to save time and shield any suspicions our group may have aroused."

Cassana faltered. "They attacked us this morning at sunrise, cutting through us before we knew what was happening. E-Elan protected my escape and was to follow me if he could... I haven't seen him since!"

"It appears that the Reven knew about your journey, miss. Perhaps it is you they want..."

"My father surrounds himself with loyal friends; they would never have betrayed his trust." Cassana bristled.

"I know of your father, Cassana. He has powerful friends, but equally powerful enemies and his lands border that of the Reven's tribal lands. There will be no shortage of people lurking in the shadows, plotting his downfall. Maybe you are the target of such an attempt."

Cassana blinked in slow disbelief and then, with realisation, wiped away tears with her free hand as she stood defiantly before him.

"Then they must not have me, sir, and I would beseech you to aid me to safety, if you can?" She held his eyes with her own, refusing to blink.

Without a word he nodded and motioned for her to follow him as he turned and began walking across the clearing to the south.

"We must hurry, my lady," he told her quietly. "I can take you to the edge of the forest, as close to safety as possible, from there a local militia patrol will hopefully find you and escort you to the city, if we are lucky."

Cassana ran to catch him up.

"Who are you, sir? Might I know your name?" she asked him.

He turned to her to speak and then stopped. Glancing behind her shoulder he growled softly. Cassana followed his gaze and felt the hairs on her neck and arms stand up, as they warned her of an impending danger. Several hundred yards to the north above the treetops dozens of crows had launched into the sky, as if disturbed from their roosts by some unseen sound or presence.

"Move," he hissed urgently.

Together they hurried from the clearing, the man stopping briefly to retrieve a sturdy dark bow and a quiver of black feathered arrows from the gnarled protective embrace of an ancient oak.

"You *can* shoot?" he asked passing her the bow, sunlight aglow in the weapon's lovingly tended wood.

"Yes," she answered, defiance returning to her voice. She slung the quiver over her left shoulder as he passed that to her as well. "I had –,"

Turning in disinterest he strode away, wrapping his cloak about his tall frame as he left. Glowering in barely contained frustration, Cassana followed him deeper into the shadows of the forest's welcoming embrace.

It soon became evident to the man, however, as they raced through the forest, that they were not going to be able to outrun their pursuers. Cassana's flight through the forest earlier that morning had already taken its toll, the girl had run the breath from her lungs but was still fighting determinedly to keep up with him, hinting further at the spirit he had seen smouldering in her eyes on more than one occasion since they had met.

Finally, after nearly an hour of fleeing through the thick forest, he was forced to call a halt and the girl collapsed to the leafy ground with an exhausted whimper of relief. The forest was alive. Sunlight knifed through the thick leafy canopy overhead, showering the dewy foliage beneath with its reawakening kiss. Birds chattered and flitted amongst the boughs of the tall oaks, their ancient knotted trunks coated with moss and insects. A squirrel scampered about its treetop domain, foraging for food as it leapt from branch to twig, unperturbed by the presence and the problems of those gathered below.

Cassana's lungs were on fire as she gasped for breath, her body burning with fatigue as her muscles tightened painfully. Panting, she lay on the floor, her face resting on a pillow of leaf-carpeted grass. The dampness helped to cool her as it clung to her sweat-drenched body and the pungent smell of the forest calmed the wild beating of her heart. After a time she peered up through her snake-like, tangled curtain of black hair and pushed herself up onto her knees. Brushing the thick strands from her eyes she looked about, marvelling at their surroundings. The giant oaks and birches stood apart, an army of grim sentinels with sinewy branches that seemingly reached above their heads to block out the sun and shield them from prying danger. Saddened by a subtle breeze that combed through the forest, they wept silent occasional tears of leaves and late blossom that fell gently to the floor and blanketed the forest with a beautiful carpet of natural colour.

Her rescuer stood several feet away; a mysterious shadowy apparition who surveyed their surroundings silently, his arms folded patiently across his chest.

"It is so beautiful, so peaceful here," Cassana whispered in awe.

"That it is, my lady," he agreed, turning to her with

a faint smile. He moved to her side, offering a hand and helping her to her feet. She nodded her thanks and then frowned as she took in the further deterioration of her once resplendent clothing. Sighing, Cassana reached back down to recover the bow at her feet, wincing as her calf muscles tugged with the effort.

He was watching her as she looked to him for guidance and she felt the broil of anger rising up within her once again.

"I am afraid that we are running out of time," he stated simply, holding his hands out honestly. "You are clearly exhausted and I am certain that our pursuers will soon catch up with us." His face softened almost apologetically.

Cassana visibly paled, the colour of exertion draining from her face as her heart began to race once again and her glistening skin began to prickle with fear.

"C-can't we reach a settlement? I heard tell of a few here in the forest, we might find refuge there?" she asked forlornly, but he was already shaking his head.

"We are several hours in the wrong direction from a lumber village," he admitted, tossing his head over his left shoulder in the general direction. "They would not thank me for bringing such a taint to their doorstep and I would not palm our problems on to those who do not warrant it!"

"But the Reven are many. At least twenty! They will easily cut us down."

"The Reven would not undertake their mission with such large numbers, my lady," he said, almost casually, "we are probably being tracked by five, or six of them at the most."

Cassana's expression told him she didn't believe a word he was saying and he turned, moving away from her dismissively.

"How can you be so certain?" she pressed on. "Unless you have met with them before?" she paused, triumph stealing into her eyes. "You have, haven't you?"

He ignored her, stepping over a jutting rock as he made his way to the south once more, the fury of Cassana's glare burning into his back as she strained to catch him up.

"Why won't you just give me a straight answer?" she demanded, trying to draw level with him, but he moved ahead with a quickening of his step.

"Because *we* don't have the time or I the inclination right now, miss," he said with an impatient look behind him. "We have to reach higher ground before they catch us, so why don't you use some of that air you are wasting and put it to good use for once?"

Turning from her he lengthened his stride and, in trying to keep up with him, Cassana lost her angry retort in amongst her near-futile gasps for breath.

With her head bowed in concentration and all of her focus fixed upon putting one foot in front of the other, it took Cassana another several seconds to realise that the woodsman had stopped and she barely avoided stumbling into the back of him. He glanced back at her, Cassana following his gaze as he looked away once again. Up ahead a brook bubbled across their path, its cool clear waters glistening with the sun that spilled unchallenged through the break in the tree canopy in golden curtains of radiant light. A solitary willow dipped its limp branches into the refreshing brook and Cassana caught the brief glimpse of a tiny bird fishing from its branches, before it sped away from her scrutiny to safety further down the stream. Across the shallow waters, the land began to elevate slightly and she looked quizzically across at the man as she stepped up alongside him.

"Yes, Cassana," he nodded, answering her silent question. "We will make our stand here and on our terms."

The girl's eyes flashed with terror and he placed a comforting hand on her trembling shoulder.

"See that tree over there?" he asked her and pointed up the rise to a thick oak, standing twenty feet from the stream, which still managed to shadow the bank with its reaching branches. Cassana nodded.

"Well I want you to position yourself behind there and cover me with your bow when they come for me."

"But what about you?" she baulked, casting a furtive look behind them. The forest was thankfully quiet and her hopes leapt momentarily.

Perhaps they have lost our trail... she thought to herself unconvincingly.

"Where will you be?" she asked again, as he had refused even to acknowledge her previous question. The grim look he dealt her made her wish she had never asked.

Wordlessly he moved ahead, splashing through the stream and across to the bank on the far side. Cassana followed his lead; the clear water cooling the scratches on her legs as she waded across, the ripples of her passing sending tiny silver fish darting away to find safety among the stones and plants of the stream's silt bed.

"Be ready, Cassana," he told her, watching thoughtfully as she moved quickly by him and positioned herself behind the gnarled oak.

Turning back, the man stared to the north, waiting for the coming storm.

"We are close," promised the Reven tracker to the three hunters impatiently gathered behind him. The tribesman was kneeling, smiling confidently to himself as he examined the thorns on the broken branch of a bramble bush. Tiny fibres of cloth fluttered there, caught on a breeze that whispered to him, seducing him on with a promise of the prize that was soon to be theirs. The girl had been lucky! Had the knight and her guard not intercepted them, they would easily have caught her and would now be stealing away back across the border to the glory and rewards that awaited their successful return. It was a temporary setback, of course. Her entourage was dead; the foolhardy knight's head stuck on a spear as a warning to any other Valian bastards that came between them and their prey. She would not escape them a second time…

The Reven paused, calming his blood lust slightly. There was still the unanswered question of the mysterious *friend* who had met with her back in the clearing an hour or so before. Judging by the weight of the footprints they had found, it was a he. But as to why he was helping her, none of the hunting party knew. None of them really cared. Two Valians against four Revens was not really a battle worth considering. It was almost too easy. The fight would be over swiftly and they would finally claim their prize and be able to return home to receive the adulation of their clans.

Well, three of them anyhow.

The Reven rose, ignorant of the blood running from the slight wound in his right shoulder and turned to his comrades. The two members of the Raven Clan met his smooth gaze, with knowing eyes. They had agreed long before they had set off on this mission that the two members of the Great Bull and Black Bear Clans would not make it back, no matter what the outcome. Fortunately for them, however, the knight had deftly removed the Great Bull problem in the initial ambush and that only left the Black Bear clansman to dispose of now. Once they had captured the girl, they would kill him immediately and be rid of his disdainful tongue and offensive presence. It was rare to find members from different clans working together these days, but they had been promised many riches by their employer, if they managed to put aside their differences long enough to complete their mission. Across the Great Divide mountain range to the north, the Reven tribal feuding was worse than ever now. Since the defeat by the Valian armies some fifty summers ago, the Reven people were a splintered nation. Constant fighting between rival clans had plunged the once-united nation into disarray and, as its people starved, the different clan elders sought only to increase their stature by crushing their rivals and taking their lands from them. Should the Valian armies have wished it, they could quite easily have crossed the mountains into the tribal lands and finished the Reven race off, once and for all.

The tracker turned his attentions back to the man in question and smiled at him, his mind filled with images of torture and dismemberment.

"Let's get on with it then, Vulture," the Black Bear clansman snapped at him, misinterpreting his smile for glee at picking up her trail once again.

The tracker nodded a couple of times, masking his

hatred, and wordlessly the hunters continued on with their pursuit.

An hour later they finally noticed their prey up ahead of them, silhouetted by the sun which filtered through the tree cover and revealed their location. The hunters slowed to a halt and shared triumphant glances as they began striding towards their prey. Weapons slid slowly from sheaths and scabbards as they approached and one of the Raven clansmen fitted a bolt to the small *Punch Jacker* crossbow he carried.

As they closed in, the tracker began to feel uneasy. A hooded figure stood weapon-less on the far bank of a brook, silently watching their approach. He had chosen his ground wisely, the sun was at his back and there was some killing ground between them. Looking around, the tracker could not see the girl, but he was sure she was here somewhere. He guessed she was up the rise somewhere, possibly behind one of the trees, cowering in fear with the rabbits and the butterflies. He felt some of his confidence return. The noble bitch had probably never even left the embroidery room, and that meant that her protector would stand and fight alone. They closed upon the brook and came to a halt on its bank, waiting in a line as they listened to the silence that came upon the forest; as if the ancient place sensed the bloodshed that was to follow.

"Give us the girl, woodsman – no point in everyone dying today," the tall bare-chested Reven bluffed, as he tested the grip on his huge sword. His scarred body bore an impressive tattoo of a snarling black bear that rose up menacingly on his chest. The creature's two clawed forearms were spread ready for battle as each one swept down the man's arms, the claws coming to a

31

stop at his wrists. His head was bald, save for a black ponytail that grew from the base of his skull and dangled limply over one shoulder. A row of skeleton's teeth pierced both his eyebrows and a bone finger earring dangled from each of his lobes.

The woodsman remained stoic, hands at his side as he watched them from within the shadows of his cowl. As they faced each other, the Reven tracker caught a glimpse of the girl in a shaft of sunshine, peering from behind a tree, not far up the incline from them. He smiled wickedly as she noticed him watching her and ducked quickly from sight.

The woodsman watched the four Reven intently. Three of them carried hand weapons, but the real worry was the crossbowman; a short powerful looking Reven whose fierce face was covered entirely by thick streaks of black and grey war paint. He could also see glimpses of a raven, tattooed roughly on his chest underneath his tattered, black, animal-skin waistcoat. The one who was bleeding, the Vulture clansman, was looking past him to where Cassana was hiding and he could see the Reven smile confidently.

"The girl stays," he replied, diverting the Reven's attention. At his words the four of them tensed, their eyes glaring at him malevolently.

"Turn back while you still can and go back to the flea-pit you crawled from," he ordered them. "This forest is sacred and your presence here offends me!"

The Reven began laughing, one of them spitting into the brook with distaste.

"You are insane, woodsman," the Vulture called out. "Why not give us the girl and go back to your deer; I'm sure they are in season now."

Cassana fitted an arrow to her bowstring with a shaking hand as the Reven began laughing. She pressed her back against the rough trunk of the tree and tried not to breathe as their mirth began to filter away. For a moment all was silent but for the babbling water of the brook, and slowly she edged a glance from behind the left side of the tree. The Reven were still waiting on the far side of the stream, all of their attentions now fixed upon the woodsman. He stood calmly across from them, hands still loose at his sides. Cassana cursed, he was standing in her line of sight and she could not get a clear shot at the Reven holding the crossbow. If he didn't get out of the way, they would shoot him down where he stood.

Move damn you!

Suddenly the distant caw of a crow echoed from the treetops, shattering the brittle silence and she could see the Reven tense. Her breath died on her lips and she drew back the bowstring, the feathered shaft pressing against her cheek. The Reven to the right of the group edged forward and the woodsman's hand whipped forth, pointing at him to stop. He obeyed instantly, staring blankly ahead and dropping his broad axe on the ground. To Cassana's shock, he dropped to his knees and fell forward into the stream with an audible splash, the sunlight revealing the ivory hilt of a knife jutting from the bird tattoo on his neck. Cassana blinked… and the forest came alive again as the Reven roared their battle cries and surged across the brook.

The woodsman stepped swiftly to his right, throwing another knife at the tall Reven as he moved. Catching her wits before she lost concentration, Cassana sent the arrow arching towards the crossbowman as he raised the wicked device and trained it on her protector. He must have sensed the danger however, as he turned his attentions towards her, just in time to catch the arrow deep in his left shoulder. As he fell away, she reached for another arrow and chose a target.

The woodsman's second throwing knife took the Black Bear clansman high in the chest, slowing his advance as he splashed through the water towards him. Throwing back his cloak, the woodsman drew the sword belted at his waist and leapt towards his attackers. Ducking low past the Vulture's wicked lunge, he cut through the man's throat as he moved past him and spun away from the huge sweeping attack from the other Reven, turning to face him from the far bank of the stream, his blood red sword raised in salute. The Black Bear clansman turned slowly in disbelief, barely aware of the tracker collapsing at his side into the water, awash now with the blood spilling from the Reven's grasping hands.

"It seems we have underestimated you, woodsman," he grimaced, pulling at the knife embedded in his chest.

"Not just me," the man replied.

Pain ripped through the Reven's mind, as a black-feathered arrow pinned his ponytail to the nape of his neck. The Black Bear clansman toppled forward, blood bursting from his mouth and staining the look of confusion painted upon his face. The woodsman looked beyond to see Cassana standing before him, no more than ten feet away, the bow raised before her as she reached back for another arrow.

The man smiled grimly and turned away from her.

Pain lanced through the shoulder of the Reven crossbowman as he rolled over and tried to crawl away. The feathered shaft dragged on the ground, ripping into his wound. A guttural snarl escaped his lips as shadows lengthened on the grass from behind him and he heard the soft approach of his doom.

"Not so fast," said the woodsman, kicking him over onto his back.

The Reven stared up into the shadows of the hooded figure looking down at him and spat.

"You are no woodsman."

The man appeased him with a nod. "And you are no longer a Reven."

Cassana winced and looked away as the man plunged his blade into the Reven's chest before turning towards her, the blade swaying behind him like a steel headstone.

"Gather your weapon, my lady," he told her calmly as he moved back to the brook to retrieve his knives and make sure the other Reven were dead.

Cassana stood where she was, an arrow still fitted to her bowstring. The battle had not lasted more than forty seconds. All that tension and posturing before and it had been finished off with a swift, lethal flash of a sword and a taut snap of a bowstring. It was all over so very quickly...

She trembled and gasped, realising she had not drawn breath since loosing her first arrow. Returning the arrow to her quiver she shouldered the bow and stepped into the stream. The man sheathed a sword at her tentative approach and handed it to her, a comforting smile creasing his bearded face.

"You fought well," he admitted. Turning, he began

dragging the corpses from the water.

"How did you know which way to step, sir?" she wondered, trying to think of something to say as she tied the sword to her waist, using her sash.

He turned slightly as he dropped the Reven with the black bear tattoo onto the grassy bank.

"When you pulled your knife on me back in the clearing, I noted that you were left-handed," he stated, searching through the dead man's belongings. "This meant that you would probably hold the bow with your right hand and the safest shot you could take, would be from the left side of the tree."

Cassana arched one eyebrow, nodding. *Of course. How silly of me!* She chided herself sarcastically.

"Do you think there are more of them?" she asked, looking about their surroundings worriedly.

"I don't think so," he admitted honestly. "We should be safe, for now at least. So we had better get you to safety before nightfall, my lady."

Striding away he pulled his sword from the Reven's body and cleaned the blade on the corpse's fur clothing. Sheathing the weapon he wandered back, regarding her curiously.

"Are you going to stay in there all day?" he enquired.

Cassana looked down to find that she was still standing in the stream, the waters clear once more. The Revens' blood washed away on the gentle current. Stepping out, she waited for him to cross.

"Where did you learn to fight like that, *woodsman?*" she enquired, failing to disguise the capricious tone in her voice.

He walked past her and began heading up the incline. "Come on, girl, we still have several hours to go before we can fully relax," he told her, failing to hide his irritation.

"Evasive as always," she said under her breath, casting a final look behind her at the bloody bodies soaking the forest floor. Breathing a sigh of relief, she followed him up the rise and into the sunshine.

It was late afternoon by the time the forest began to thin out and Cassana sensed they were reaching the end of their journey together. The last few hours had passed in silence, allowing Cassana to mull over what had happened that day. She had lost her friends, slain by the Reven hunting party as they descended out of the mist and onto their camp. For whatever dark purpose, they had dared to cross the border and try to steal her away. If her rescuer was right, that meant that there was a spy in her father's camp and, in saving her, he had given her the chance to get back home to Highwater where she could try to expose the traitor. But first she had to reach Karick and get help. She didn't really know anyone there and with Elan probably dead... with him gone, there would be nobody to advise her now. She fought down the emotions threatening to overwhelm her and blew out her cheeks. She could almost hear the thunder that would bellow from her father, when he got to hear what had happened. It was not quite what he had planned, when he said that he had wanted her to finally become her father's daughter. She looked ahead to her saviour, setting a brisk pace through the shade of the trees. It was funny, she no longer felt tired any more. Just alive! Gathering her courage she ran to catch him up.

"Who did you serve, before you came to the forest?" she demanded, her voice calm and resolute.

"Nobody," he said unconvincingly. "I serve only myself and the land that I have made my home."

"I do not believe you, sir," she pressed on. "We all serve somebody; you must have fought for someone at some point. You move like a knight, you have perfect balance and the swordsmanship to complement it. You did not learn those skills living in the forest!"

"Don't profess to tell me about myself girl," he snapped, rounding on her. "I have served many people in the past. I have bled for them; I have even been willing to give up my life for them."

Cassana recoiled, shrinking from the vehemence and the spittle flying from his lips.

"Forgive me, I did not mean to anger you," she said, holding her hands up. "You have saved my life this day and will not even tell me your name! I just wanted to find out something about you – that is all."

After a moment he visibly calmed before her eyes, the bitterness draining from his twisted features.

"The apologies should be mine, Lady Byron," he admitted, kneeling at her feet, taking one of her hands gently in his own and kissing it. She looked down her scratched arm at him, as he peered up over her hand at her.

"Apology accepted, sir. I will say no more on the matter," she promised him, as he released her hand and straightened.

Nodding his thanks, he motioned for them to continue and she fell in alongside him, her thoughts hooded and her tongue chastised.

The Moonglade Forest fell away from the two weary travellers as they stood within the shadows of its branches and watched the sunset staining the cloudless blue sky. For a time they stood beside each other, each lost within their own thoughts as they stared across the rolling flatlands and marvelled at the tranquillity and serenity of the area.

"If you follow the tree line to the south-west," he said, pointing, "you can just make out the town of Havensdale on the horizon."

Cassana nodded with relief. Civilization, at last! She turned to him and dazzled him with a smile. "I cannot thank you enough for what-,"

He held up a finger to her lips to silence her. "At least for today I can say that I have served a lady of Highwater," he smiled sadly. "You should be able to find safety at the town. They have strong ties with Karick. You must find Dekan Ardent, the mayor, and explain to him what has happened. I am sure he will see that you are guided to safety."

"You could come with me?" she hoped, but he was already shaking his head.

"I have swallowed enough of the politics and been on the wrong end of the *justice* that rules the capital. I have stomached as much of it as any man could take!" he told her, ignoring the spark of curiosity that lit up her eyes. "I will not go back to those marble halls, I cannot." he finished sadly.

Pressing a finger to his lips, she leant up to kiss him on one cheek. Free of the forest now, she could smell the woodland on him.

"Thank you," was all she could say. Shivering, she went to give him back his bow, but he waved it away.

"Keep it, my lady. You use it better than I anyway," he told her ruefully. Beaming, she stepped back from him and curtsied.

"I must go, Cassana," he said, bowing gracefully. "I

will look to your friends and grant them the honours they deserve."

"My thanks, sir," Cassana whispered. "I will not forget you." Turning, she walked falteringly away, her head pounding, her heart racing.

When she turned back to look for him moments later, the man was gone.

CHAPTER THREE

A Brief Respite

Cassana was on the brink of exhaustion by the time she finally reached the outskirts of Havensdale some hours later. The sun had already sunk beneath the horizon by then, painting the darkening sky's canvas with beautiful brush strokes of deep orange and blood-red gold. The fields that belonged to the town's surrounding farmsteads were empty of workers now and yet full of golden crops that waited reluctantly for the coming harvest. Cassana stopped briefly to catch her breath, marvelling at her peaceful surroundings. With the heat of the day now gone, she could feel the fresh breeze that stole across the plains from the east and left the crops swaying rhythmically with each gentle passing. As far as her eyes could see, the plains swept away to the south; luscious flatlands of vibrant grass, interspersed with abundant meadows of colourful wild flowers. Beyond the town of Havensdale she could also see the glistening waters of a river, sweeping up from the south and swinging past the town into the forest to the north-west. If her tedious geography lessons had been worth the effort and she was correct, it was the River Haven. Closing her weary eyes she let out a deep sigh, allowing the refreshing breeze to pass over her, cooling her cuts and blowing her tangled hair into her eyes. Brushing the thick strands away she ignored the tightness of her stomach and the rising hunger knotting there. She could wait a little longer to feed her hunger and, until now, she had not even considered it, such was the maelstrom of emotions raging away within her young mind.

It would take her a very long time to sift through her scattered thoughts and assemble them into some sense of order, so that she could analyse what had actually happened to her that day. If she ever managed to recover from the horrors of the early morning attack on her camp by the Reven, she knew that she would never be able to shake the memory of Elan from her heart, as he urged her to escape…

"You must flee, Lady Byron," he had ordered her, as they ran from the battle raging around them.
Cassana had protested, as she always did when told what to do. "I-,"

"Not this time, my lady," Elan had growled, cutting into her words and ignoring the truculent gleam in her eyes. "Your father entrusted you to my care. I must see you safe, before all else."

The battle in the glade was being lost behind them, as Elan moved them further into the protection of the forest. Screams rose above the clash of steel against steel, as the frenzied battle cries of the Reven began to chase through the forest after them.

Cassana's heart was racing madly as she hurried further away from the glade and it took her a few more moments before she realised that her protector was not following her any more.

"What are you doing?" she had cried, turning, although she had already guessed what his answer would be.

The knight was standing several metres away from her, his silver ring mail suit glinting in the early morning light. His long Valian sword was gripped loosely in his left hand and he was looking back over his shoulder towards the distant glade. When he turned back to her, she had seen the regret and then the determination that had flashed in his steely blue eyes.

"Go, my lady," he had told her gently, trying a smile that failed miserably. "I will buy you time to escape and rejoin you if, when, I can."

"No!" she had protested, cold fear freezing any further words on her trembling lips. But before Elan could speak another word they had heard shouts of glee coming from the glade behind them, as the sounds of battle faded. Before Cassana could say anything further to him, the knight had raised his bloody sword in salute to her. Kissing the blade he had turned and run silently back the way they had come. Cassana had taken two faltering steps to go after him as he disappeared through the tall trees, before her fear got the better of her. Sobbing, she had turned and fled away through the forest towards the south, leaving the sounds of fresh battle behind her...

Blinking back tears Cassana drew in a deep breath, her nostrils wrinkling as the heady smell of the crops assaulted her senses. The thoughts of the sacrifice made by her entourage were too raw to deal with just now. There would be time later, when the dust of the day's events had settled, when she could truly mourn their loss and show them the honour they deserved. Shaking her head sadly, she ran a trembling hand through her tangled black hair, regretting it immediately. Arching her back, she felt her muscles tighten as she sought to stretch the aches from her body and she rolled her neck to ease her tension. After many hours of travel, the string of the dark bow bit deeply into her shoulder and the strap from the quiver of arrows left her opposite shoulder red and raw. To round off her misery, the sword taken from the Reven and given to her by the woodsman had already badly bruised her right thigh and she had almost discarded it a few miles back. If Cassana was honest with herself, she had never felt so exhausted before in her whole life.

Blowing out her held breath, she gathered up her self-pitying thoughts and placed them at the back of her mind for now. Her immediate goal was to report to the mayor of Havensdale, although she had forgotten the name that her saviour had told her. Hopefully he would be able to find sympathy in her plight, as she had no coin to buy food and lodgings for the night. Although she was not entirely sure how she would ever manage to convince the mayor to help her, when she looked like the wretch she did now. If her luck held, and he believed her, she would need to get to the city and report to the high duke what had befallen her party. As from there… Cassana shook her head blankly. There would be time aplenty to plan her journey home once she had reached the sanctuary of Karick, and standing in the middle of a corn field all night was not going to help her one bit. Snapping herself upright she forced herself onwards through the tall crops towards the protection of Havensdale and the promise of a warm meal and a soft bed.

The town of Havensdale was surrounded entirely by a wooden palisade that formed a viable defence to any threats towards its inhabitants. As she left the cornfields, she stepped onto a well-worn pathway that snaked around the eastern side of the town and meandered away into the forest to the north. Stopping momentarily, Cassana looked into the shadows of the Moonglade forest and shivered. Quickly forming a mental palisade of her own she beat back the raw emotions that rose up in her mind and headed away down the path. As she rounded the eastern side of the town's defensive wall, she heard the welcoming sounds of life coming from within. Muffled conversation, punctuated by laughter; a dog barking its annoyance at some disturbance; a mother calling for her children to come in for the night. These everyday sounds lifted her spirits, drawing her on and offering her new hope. Above her now she could also hear the sound of booted feet, as a guard patrolled along the wall. Cassana was sure that she would have already been seen skulking about in the fields and guessed that any strangers to the region would be met at the gates when they arrived. As she wandered along the wall, Cassana could now clearly see the River Haven. Its sedate waters were aglow with the last embers of the day and a tiny fishing boat was making its way back to a small makeshift dock, its two occupants hopefully satisfied with their efforts. Although there was no visible bridge, Cassana guessed that there must be one on the western side of the town to allow its denizens access to the far shores, where she could now see the buildings of two large farmsteads. Tendrils of curling black smoke rose from the chimneys, as the farms' occupants cooked their suppers and sought to provide a foil for the cold of the coming night.

A girl met Cassana as she finally reached the high, yet open, double-gated entrance to Havensdale.

"Welcome to Havensdale, miss," the girl greeted her with a bright smile. "What brings you to our town this lovely evening?"

Cassana was slightly distracted by the girl's youthful appearance and did not respond at first. Possibly no more than fifteen winters old, the girl was dressed in a full suit of leather armour that was peppered with metal studs, in the hope that they would offer better protection and perhaps blunt, or turn aside, a blade or an arrow. A short sword was belted at her waist and a small shield hung off her back. The girl had long black hair; much the same colour as her own and the thick lustrous locks were tied back in pigtails. She had a pretty face of unblemished skin, a small nose and wide, full lips. Her tired green eyes flicked about Cassana's face as she, too, took in the other's appearance.

"Are you well, miss?" she asked when Cassana failed to answer her, genuine concern lighting up her eyes.

Cassana forced a smile. "I am now, thank you," she managed. "I seek shelter for the night and hope to have a meeting with your mayor, if possible?"

The girl looked her up and down again. "The mayor is away on business for the week, miss, but we can certainly offer you shelter for the eve. And if you need to speak to someone, I am sure his daughter would oblige you."

"That would be wonderful." Cassana replied quickly, her voice choked by relief.

"If you follow me then, miss, I can take you to her if you like," the girl replied, stepping to one side to allow her a tantalising glimpse into the town beyond.

"You are too kind, thank you," Cassana said, stepping forward. "My name is Cassana," she stated, offering her a scratched hand.

"My name's Sara," the girl replied, taking her hand in a brief, timid shake. "If you follow me, miss, I shall lead you to Captain Ardent. She is the leader of the Havensdale militia and the mayor's daughter."

"Thank you, Sara." Cassana replied and followed the girl guard into the town.

To Cassana, Havensdale was more a walled settlement, than a town. It was a welcoming community of stone and wood buildings that stretched away in clusters, rather than rows, and surrounded a wide cobblestoned marketplace in the heart of the town. The permanent market stalls were empty now however, erected near to a large stone well in the centre of the marketplace. Here, a red-haired woman fetched pails of water from the depths below by cranking up a winch, and a young girl hopped about her heels, tugging impatiently at the hem of her long skirt.

Sara led her in silence towards a small building on the southernmost fringes of the cobblestones, allowing her charge to take in her surroundings. Cassana could see several dwellings to her left, two-storey homes, all with thatched roofing. Near to them were two slate-roofed buildings with signs above their windows. She could not make out what was painted upon the signs at this distance, but by their look she guessed them to be stores of some description. Away to her right she could make out a similar arrangement of homes and premises of work. One of the larger of these was clearly a blacksmith's, and the large sign hanging above the wide double doors that led to the forge beyond read *Farlow's Smithy*. All was silent for the end of the day now, but Cassana could still see the glow of heat coming from the furnace within. Further up on her right, she noticed a large inn, with stabling at the side of the establishment. Lights flickered from behind its curtained windows and she could hear the sounds of laughter coming from inside. A man sat out on a bench underneath the inn's porch, quietly smoking a pipe as he relaxed from a day's hard labour with a tankard of ale or cider. A large sign hung like a noose from a tall gibbet-like post outside the inn and had a painting of a well upon it. Someone had expertly painted a 'The' above the painting in bold black letters. Many other buildings surrounded the market area further to the north and beyond the inn, but they were indiscernible now as dusk continued its purposeful march towards night.

"If you could just wait here a few moments please, Cassana?" Sara asked her; shy now for some reason. Cassana nodded, fighting against her desire to head for the inn as the girl stepped forward and knocked on the door of the small building. The stone and slate structure had only one barred window on its front and, after a moment, Sara opened the door, stepped into the room beyond and closed the door gently behind her.

Alone again, Cassana looked behind her. The south gate's walls had wooden steps, allowing the guards access to the ramparts above. One such guard, Sara's companion perhaps, was watching her intently and boldly taking in her bedraggled appearance. He was around the same age as Sara and dressed in similar armour. However he carried no shield and wore two short swords, belted on both hips with a confident swagger. His blonde hair ruffled in a breeze up there and he took in Cassana's appearance with unreadable dark eyes. Cassana nodded to him briefly, then turned her attentions back to the doorway. Around the town people were still making their way home for the evening and any townsfolk who came near to Cassana as she waited, took in her filthy appearance with looks ranging from sympathy to brazen curiosity. After a futile attempt to make herself look presentable, Cassana gave up. It would take a hot bath and a hard brush to scrape away the mess and reveal the woman beneath, who had started out on the long journey from Highwater, five days ago now.

The door to the stone building slowly opened, scattering aside Cassana's thoughts of home before they could surface completely. Sara stepped outside again and smiled timidly.

"The captain will see you now, miss," she announced, moving aside as Cassana subconsciously adjusted her hair, making it even worse.

"I must return to my duties now," Sara stated. Without waiting for a response, she hurried off towards the steps that led up to the ramparts above the south gate.

"Thank you, Sara," Cassana called after her. The girl looked back over her shoulder and flashed her a brief smile, before hurrying up the steps towards the young man who was eagerly awaiting her return. Not used to being the focal point of gossip, Cassana stepped through the open door to avoid the inquisition and glances that would have probably been coming her way in the next few moments.

As she closed the door behind her, Cassana found herself in a plain, inhospitable room furnished with a large oak desk and two opposing chairs. Behind the desk, a large barred window charitably offered the room some fading light and drew her attention to a rickety looking bookcase that heaved with parchments and books and leaned ominously off the wall, away to her right. On top of the precarious bookcase a thick candle burned low on its wick, threatening to overbalance the bookcase and send its contents spilling out across the room's dusty, wooden floorboards. To her left, a barred cell had been built into the room and was currently occupied by an empty straw pallet and a chamber pot. A woman perched on one corner of the desk and regarded Cassana's quick inspection of the room with inscrutable hazel eyes. She was dressed in leather trousers and wore soft leather boots, dusted and scuffed on the toecaps. Her vest of chain mail glinted in the candlelight and her long shoulder length auburn hair hung in ringlets. Cassana guessed the plain looking woman to be in her late twenties and watched her quietly as she uncrossed her legs and stood beside the table. Smiling broadly the woman came forward with an outstretched hand, adorned by two rings of silver and gold.

"Greetings," the woman said, as Cassana took her offered hand and shook it firmly. "My name is Fawn Ardent. I am captain of the Havensdale militia and can speak for the town in my father's absence."

She released Cassana's hand and stepped aside before she could reply, motioning towards the chair that faced the barred window across the desk.

"Thank you, captain," Cassana said cordially, as she painfully slid the quiver and bow from her aching shoulders, resting them up against the wall behind her. Drawing out the offered chair she sank onto the unforgiving cradle of wood with a weary sigh. After the day Cassana had just experienced, the hard chair felt like one of the velvet sofas her father had in his study back home. The captain moved around to seat herself across from her guest as Cassana noted the quill, ink pot and several scattered parchments on the desk in front of her. Stealing a surreptitious look at the neat handwriting, Cassana had seen enough such papers on her father's desk over the years to recognise the monthly despatches that all cities, towns and villages were required to send to the capital, by law. These despatches would detail the events and news happening in each region, ranging from births to deaths, marriages to convictions. Karick was the heart of the Four Vales, a living organ that required the veins of its kingdom to supply it regularly with the lifeblood of information it needed to keep the country running safely and prosperously.

"Now to business," the captain said, clasping her slender hands together on the parchments in front of her. "I understand from recruit Campbell that you requested an audience with my father! Might I enquire as to the nature of this request, miss...?"

Cassana quickly remembered her manners and smiled. "Of course, Captain Ardent. Forgive me. My name is Cassana," she paused momentarily, wondering how much she should divulge. "Cassana Byron," she finished swiftly, remembering that she was here for the militia's help, and lying about who she was would not help her cause. The captain's eyes flashed with momentary recognition as Cassana continued.

"I left Highwater five days ago with an entourage of

knights on our journey to the capital. I was, I mean, I am to attend the Valian Council in five days time on behalf of my father, in his absence."

"Your father being?"

"Alion James Byron, Lord of Highwater and protector of the North Vales," Cassana said flatly, keeping a lid on the unjustified irritation seeking to rise up inside her. "My father has many pressing matters back home and sent me to deputise and speak on his behalf. We were advised to take a more cautious road for safety and journeyed through the Moonglade Forest so as not to arouse any unwanted interest. We camped last night in a place I now know to be called Fox Glade. In the morning…"

The captain opened a drawer on her desk and pulled forth a small silver hip flask as Cassana stumbled over her tale. Unscrewing the small top, she passed it across to the pale young woman who was fighting with her memories.

"Here, drink some of this. It will help you to fire your thoughts," she ordered her gently.

Cassana received the flask with shaking fingers and drank swiftly without even thinking of what was contained within. She was so desperate for something to help her combat the voice of fear suddenly crippling her determination, that she trusted in the captain without really being able to detect anything of her motives beneath her formal, impartial demeanour. As the fire of the brandy burnt through her fears and chased away any building tears, she coughed and, looking up, read much sympathy in the captain's eyes.

"Thank you, captain," she said, swallowing, in an attempt to cool her burning throat as she passed back the flask. The woman smiled comfortingly as she screwed the top back on and slipped it into the drawer.

"A sip of the *Burning Leaf* often helps to blunt the fear," the captain said, her words full of concern and warmth now.

"In your own time please, Lady Byron. If you can tell me what has happened to you, I will see what I can do to help?"

Drawing in a deep breath, Cassana rubbed at her weary eyes and proceeded to tell the captain everything that had occurred to her since she had woken in her tent early that morning. The moment she came to mention the presence of the Reven in the Moonglade Forest and her terrorised flight from her pursuers, Captain Ardent sat up straight in her chair and her face took on a dreadful pallor. Finding strength in the captain's concern, Cassana continued with the events that had unfolded over the rest of the morning and that subsequent bloody afternoon. From the mysterious woodsman, to their fight at the brook, all was included in her account and nothing of significance was left to tell for another day. When she had finished, Cassana slumped back into her chair, leaving the captain to stare at her across the desk. After a disconcerting moment, the captain leant forward again.

"Are you sure, Lady Byron, that there are no other Reven pursuing you?" Captain Ardent's immediate concern was primarily aimed at protecting her people, and justifiably so.

"As certain as I can be, captain," Cassana answered honestly. "The woodsman seemed sure of it and, by his actions and kindness, he has forever earned my trust and my favour."

"Indeed," the captain mused thoughtfully. "Your mysterious guardian has certainly done us all a great service this day. I know there are many individuals who inhabit the forest, for their own reasons and purposes. But I do not recognise the description you have given me, Lady Byron. Indeed we have our own woodsman, who protects our immediate borders in the forest. But he is very old now and does not match your man, I am afraid."

"Please captain," Cassana pleaded, holding up her hands. "Cassana is fine; I am not comfortable with the etiquette of title amongst friends."

Captain Ardent smiled and after demanding the same from her guest, she rose, excused herself momentarily and hurried for the door. Opening it wide, she called up to the guards on the gate, ordering them to close the south and west gates as a precaution. Without explanation, she asked Cassana to follow her. Obediently Cassana rose, gathering up her bow and quiver as she followed the captain outside.

Carrying her weapons for her, Captain Ardent led her across the deserted market area towards a large inn on the north side of the cobblestones. The large three-storey building was a fine looking establishment with large stables at the rear. As they approached, Cassana scanned her surroundings again, noting many more homesteads before her. To her right was a small, newly-built chapel, dedicated to the worship of The Lady. The modest stone building was surrounded by a cluster of simple homes. To the north-west of the chapel, Cassana could see a large manor house. The elegant building was hidden behind a stone wall, yet visible through the wrought iron gates that prevented access to the grounds within. To the right of the estate, she could also see a large house of some note. It too had extensive grounds, surrounded by a wooden fence that protected a paddock inside. As they neared the inn, Cassana could just about make out the two large barns at the rear of the paddock and the young man who was leading a horse towards them. The captain noted her interest.

"That place is probably known to you, Cassana," she guessed. "Ward's Livery Stables?"

Cassana thought for a moment. "Of course!" she said, clicking her fingers in recognition. "I had forgotten all about it. The stables are well known to all in the North Vales. I hear tell that the quality of the stock bred there is second only to the high duke's livery in Karick."

The captain nodded her head in agreement. "The stables have indeed put our humble town on the map for many a year now. People come from all corners of the country to purchase their mounts from the owner, Darin Ward."

"Including my father," Cassana admitted. "Storm is the finest mount he has ever owned and has carried him safely through many border skirmishes with the Reven."

Captain Ardent's eyes flashed with obvious pride as she led her charge up the three wooden steps to the porch of the inn. "Welcome to the Arms of the Lady Inn, Cassana," she said, as she pushed open the double doors to allow her entrance into the light beyond. "I will see to it personally that you are cared for this night, Cassana. A warm meal, a hot bath and the softest bed the proprietor Joseph Moore can offer you."

Cassana was overwhelmed by the compassion she was receiving from another stranger this day and she nodded her head in silent gratitude as she crossed the inn's threshold, her eyes wet with emotion.

She found herself in a large, spacious, well-lit

taproom, simply furnished and yet welcoming nonetheless. A long bar stretched invitingly along the east wall away to her right and a dozen or so stools waited patiently for customers to help them prop up the lovingly polished oak bar. Two paintings of local landscapes hung above shelves laden with bottles of various wines and spirits. A middle-aged man and a young dark-haired woman busied themselves behind the bar and both looked up as she entered. Seeing the surprise in their faces at the arrival of a newcomer to their town, Cassana felt her cheeks burn with embarrassment and looked inquisitively around the inn to escape their attentions. A dozen or so circular tables were spread about the room, four accompanying stools tucked under each one. To her left a large fireplace waited patiently for the colder nights to start drawing in and fresh logs were readily in place in the hearth, two comfortable looking chairs positioned before it. A splendid and eye-catching painting of a snowy mountainous region hung above the fireplace, perhaps to increase the effect the roaring fire would have on its patrons during the colder nights. Even though there were no customers in attendance, the room still managed to warm her and Cassana shuffled forward reluctantly, allowing the captain to step into the room behind her. Seeing the captain arrive, Cassana's hosts smiled broadly and offered her a friendly welcome.

"Take a seat, Cassana, I'll sort out the arrangements with the innkeeper and then we can talk some more."

She handed Cassana back her quiver and bow, then strode towards the bar, calling out a greeting. Moving to a table in the far corner, Cassana sat down with another weary groan, her belongings forgotten at her side. Trying not to eavesdrop on the ensuing conversation and react to the subtle looks coming her way, Cassana buried her head in her dirty hands, resting her elbows on the table in front of her.

It was some minutes later, and just before Cassana had dozed off into a welcome sleep, that a man cleared his throat politely, jerking Cassana from her rest.

"Welcome to my establishment, miss," the man from behind the bar said. His pleasant face was broad and friendly, his bald head wrinkling from the effort of his huge smile. He wore a large white apron over his blue shirt and dark trousers, a damp cloth slung casually over one shoulder.

"My name is Joseph Moore. Captain Ardent has asked me to look after you for the evening and to care for all your requirements," he stated, reaching out a large hand to greet her. Cassana shook the offered hand and smiled in return.

"Begging your pardon, miss, so as not to make offence," Joseph said, his brown eyes blinking awkwardly as he released her hand, "but you must have had a day? You look dead in your seat."

Cassana forced a bright smile, nodding. "It has been a day I will not forget for a long while, sir," she admitted, more to herself than to the kindly looking man, standing before her. "But the welcome I have received from your captain and your good self has done much to help me already."

Joseph beamed proudly as he subconsciously wiped his hands on his apron. His face widened in sudden horror, as he found some offence in his actions.

"Pardon me miss, I didn't mean that your hand – which is, I didn't wipe mine because..."

Cassana laughed heartily, and felt her spirits lift as the poor man shuffled uncomfortably and blushed away before her.

"Please Joseph, I did not take offence!" she placated him, holding up her hands in peace. The innkeeper breathed a sigh of relief and straightened himself.

"Well, ahem, back to business then, miss. We have a bed to offer you this night, no charge of course. I'll also have one of my girls' draw you up a hot bath and we will feed you up with a warm meal and water you down with a cool drink. In whichever order you prefer, of course!"

Cassana could see Captain Ardent heading over to them so she dealt a smile to both of them as she arrived.

"I cannot thank you both enough for the aid you are offering me. It gratifies me so much that I will not forget this and, when I can, I shall see that your generosity is reciprocated in kind."

Both of the townsfolk smiled humbly and it was the innkeeper who spoke first.

"The Arms of the Lady are always wide open to those in need, miss," he exclaimed. "Now how can I begin? A bath?"

Cassana thought through the choices, finally listening to a cry from her stomach.

"A meal will set me well on my way, Joseph," she admitted.

Sweeping the cloth off his shoulder the innkeeper bowed low and excused himself, as he headed away to bark out instructions to the kitchen staff, through a door behind the bar.

Captain Ardent watched him leave, and then turned her thoughts back to her charge. "I have told him only that you need our help, my lady. You have enough to deal with already, without the drums of gossip beating out their exaggerations around the region. For now you are here as my guest, expenses met and your needs catered for."

Cassana felt the tears suddenly welling up in her eyes and the captain saw them brimming there.

"I shall leave you for an hour or two, whilst I see to my militia. Get some food inside you, relax in a hot bath and we can talk some more later this evening." It was an order, not a suggestion and, before Cassana could reply, the captain had extricated herself and was heading for the door. Cassana watched her leave and shook her head in disbelief. Things were going far too well for her at the moment...

Before the lull in the day's proceedings allowed Cassana time to dwell on past matters, the dark-haired girl from behind the bar came over to her. She was tall, slim and only a few years younger than Cassana. Her long dark hair was tied back behind the neck and pinned taut by clasps over her ears. She had a beautiful aura about her; a perfect face enhanced by alluring hazel eyes, a small upturned nose and full lustrous lips. Cassana was taken aback. At all the official functions, parties and dances she had attended with her father over the past few years, she had never encountered someone with the beauty that this young woman possessed. The rich women in their elegant mansions, magnificent palaces and breathtaking marble halls had spent many coins on their appearance for the gratification of those fawning around them, yet none of them could manage the presence, even if understated, that this young woman radiated. And to find her here, in a quiet town on the southernmost borders of the north vale – hidden away from the world and the noblemen who would surely seek to court her. Unlike the long flowing silk gowns worn by the aristocracy, this young woman wore only a plain white blouse, loosely buttoned and guarded by a clean pinafore. On her feet she wore plain sandals and, as she approached, Cassana noticed that the young woman limped heavily, relying on her right leg for strength. She carried a tankard in her left hand and, in her right, a steadying cloth was underneath, stopping the liquid within from spilling on the recently swept wooden floorboards.

"Greetings, miss," the young woman said with a sociable smile. Cassana felt compelled to like her already, such was her nature.

"Compliments of my father, miss." She placed the tankard on the table before Cassana and watched her lick her lips thirstily.

"Thank you…?" Cassana held the young woman's eyes, as she paused long enough to force a response.

"Scarlet! Scarlet Moore, miss," the girl answered, smiling. Curtseying, then blushing foolishly as she fiddled with her cloth.

Cassana smiled comfortingly and watched the girl as she excused herself and began to back away. Observing the amber liquid in the tankard, Cassana put it to her lips and sipped at it slowly. She had not had anything to eat and drink since breakfast and gulping it down quickly was not about to do her any favours.

"Hmm," she moaned, delighting at the rough hop-nosed flavour sliding down her throat. Scarlet smiled, stopping as Cassana was hit by a delicious after-taste of piquant berries.

"What is this ale, Scarlet? It is delicious." In her current condition and state of mind it felt like the finest thing she had ever tasted.

"Campbell's Own, miss," the girl said proudly. "Brewed locally by the farmer, Robert Campbell, who owns a farm yonder," she went on, nodding her head through a west-facing window.

Cassana nodded in recollection of the farmsteads she had noticed upon her arrival.

"Campbell? I met a girl on the gate as I arrived, I believe her to share the name?"

Scarlet nodded. "That would have been Sara, his second of three daughters, miss." She began to leave, eager to be on her way again. This time Cassana simply thanked her and allowed her to depart, without further delay. Licking her lips, she turned her attentions back to the local ale. Raising the tankard, she offered a silent toast to her friends, old, new and recently departed.

The next hour for Cassana was a pleasant respite from events of the day, a perfect tonic to quell the emotions that whispered from the back of her mind and threatened to pull her back into the dark waters of her own inner fear. Firstly, Joseph Moore returned, personally delivering her a steaming bowl of delicious onion soup, a fresh tankard of the delightful *Campbell's Own* and taking her compliments away with him, for the chef who toiled in the kitchens beyond. Following a fine course of poached carp and honey-glazed vegetables, Cassana received another tankard of ale and witnessed the arrival of two elderly gentlemen. Dressed in woollen shirts and wading leathers, the two old fishermen shuffled their way to their seats in an adjacent corner to Cassana and chatted amiably, as they eagerly awaited Scarlet and her delivery of two silver tankards, frothing with mead. Playfully chatting with the young woman, they proceeded to boast of the day's fine catch and even finer weather. After sharing a joke or two with them Scarlet limped back to her place behind the bar and one of the gentlemen, the one who wore a pair of bent, metal-rimmed spectacles, followed her departure with eager eyes and a rueful grin to his companion. Chuckling, Cassana raised a smile and her drink in their direction as one of them noticed her watching them and they soon returned their attentions to the tankards in front of them.

Not long after, a young woman came in from the cooling evening outside. Dressed in the familiar garb of the Havensdale militia, she wore a single sword off her left hip and wandered wearily over to the bar to be greeted warmly by Scarlet. The newcomer was shorter, considerably so and she had a fuller figure and a rounder, plainer face. Lank blonde hair tumbled about her shoulders and her blue eyes lit up as she stepped round the other side of the bar to give Scarlet a peck on the cheek. Announcing her evident weariness to her, she bade farewell and headed out through the kitchen door. Scarlet caught Cassana watching her and dealt her a bright smile, before returning to her chores. Was she her friend, or sister? Cassana was not sure and quickly forgot about the subject as Joseph Moore returned and announced that, when she was ready, she could retire to her room and take her bath. Thanking him, she announced that she would first finish her ale and then would indeed retire for the evening, once she had met with the captain again. Bowing graciously, Joseph returned to his daughter's side and gave her quiet orders. Nodding her acceptance, the young woman left via a staircase leading up to the second level, in the corner across from Cassana's table.

It was a while longer before the captain returned, however, just as Cassana was contemplating whether to order another ale or not. The captain seated herself across the table from her charge, smiling warmly again.

"I trust Joseph has looked after you, Cassana?"

She nodded in return. "Indeed so, Fawn. It is a lovely establishment here. With welcoming service, excellent food and dare I say, delightful local ales."

They shared a knowing smile before the captain nodded and her face became serious once again.

"I won't keep you from your rest for too long, my lady, as I am sure you are eager for a bath and your bed. As you are already aware, we are required to submit despatches to the capital every month and I thought that, as I was about to send them off within the next few days anyway, I could perhaps use that as a good excuse to see you safely to Karick. The Great Road is often a dangerous one for a solitary traveller, what with outlaws and the highwayman Devlin Hawke still at large."

Cassana had heard that the notorious criminal was still managing to evade the high duke's patrols and was thankful of finally receiving the offer she had come here to find.

"Captain, I do not know what to say other than to accept your most welcome offer. I have to admit that the thought of travelling on to Karick alone, after what has happened to me, was not very appealing. Even though any imminent danger to me may have passed, it would reassure me to have company on my journey."

The captain clapped her hands together in satisfaction.

"Excellent, my lady! I will have your clothes repaired and cleaned for you in time for our departure in the morning then, and I will arrange fresh travelling clothes for you to take as well. Tomorrow, when you have rested, breakfasted and collected your thoughts, we shall head out with a patrol for the capital. I have already secured promises of mounts from the livery stables and that will hopefully ensure a swift and safe journey for us all."

Overwhelmed and secretly relieved, Cassana clasped the captain's hand in firm gratitude. The Reven had released her own mount, before attacking the camp that morning.

"My thanks again, captain. I promise you that the high duke will personally hear of your benevolence and that my father will also see you well recognised in the capital. And you will always have my favour and friendship, should you wish it?"

Fawn nodded humbly, "My thanks Lady Cassana, I do."

Releasing her hands, she rose and smiled. "Rest now my lady, and I will see you in the morning. Joseph will see to the repair of your clothes and your care in the meantime. So, until tomorrow, may the Lady watch over you and keep you safe."

"And to you, my friend," Cassana replied, her throat thick with emotion as she watched her departure. When the captain was gone, Cassana drained the last liquid from her tankard, gathered up her meagre possessions and went in search of the innkeeper.

Soon after, Cassana was escorted up to her room by her host. He presented her with a quiet cosy room at the rear of the second level of the inn and asked his daughter Scarlet to prepare her bath. In his absence, the young woman brought up several pails of hot water for the brass bath and chatted to Cassana as she relaxed in a soft woollen robe that was waiting for her on the bed. During the amiable conversation, Cassana learnt that it was customary in Havensdale for the youth of the town, upon reaching sixteen winters, to be drafted into the ranks of the militia for two years service. It was hoped that during this time, they would come to learn humility amid the hormones raging within them and grow to love and respect their homeland and the people they were charged to protect. In reward for their services, they would receive camaraderie, training in arms and diplomatic skills, exemption from payment of local taxes, and a free meal and drink at the establishment of their choice every month. At the end of their two-year service, the recruits were free to leave and follow the calling of their hearts. However, most recruits chose to remain within the ranks of the militia; their lives enriched by the experience and the respect they now received.

Cassana also discovered that Scarlet had joined the militia a year ago, but had suffered a horrible riding accident whilst crossing Merchants Market, eight months previously. Her mount, spooked by a crow, had thrown its inexperienced rider to the cobbles and had then trampled on her left leg for good measure. The young woman's eyes had flashed with brief frustration as she recounted her tale and had then steadied, as she quietly admitted her determination to rejoin the militia one day. Cassana was impressed. This girl had strength as well as beauty, and she found herself thinking of the sister that she would have had herself, if her mother had not died during the birth; the newborn following soon after. Scarlet, detecting a shift in Cassana's attention and seeing her distant eyes, quickly bade her good night. Taking Cassana's filthy clothes with her, she promised to have them back at first light and quietly closed the door behind her as she left; Cassana's thanks finally chasing after her. Alone again now, Cassana sat on the soft, enticing bed for many minutes, before scattering rose petals into the steaming water of the bath. Disrobing, she scrutinised her scratched and bruised body in a long, standing mirror. Her slim body looked as bad as it felt and she stretched wearily, like a waking cat. Testing the water, she found the heat invigorating and the smell of the rose petals refreshing. After a few moments she was relaxing in the stinging water, the heat massaging her aches and warming her fears away.

After an indeterminable amount of time, Cassana rose from the now cool waters of the bath and wrapped her chilled, yet contented frame in the warmth of her robe. It was dark outside now, the town silent and the black sky pricked by glittering stars. Extinguishing the candles that lit her room, Cassana slid into bed. Before she could even listen to the thoughts tumbling about in her mind, the soft feather pillow claimed her attention above her languor and she was asleep within moments.

CHAPTER FOUR

Flames in the Shadows

It was with no great amount of certainty that Khadazin finally convinced himself that he was actually awake and no longer lost in a deep tormented sleep, scattered with incoherent memories and filled with wild imaginings of what was to come. His body was wrought with stiff agony, as he lay on a cold stone floor in a thick impenetrable darkness, his eyes wide and seeing nothing. The blackness of his surroundings did not allow him to gauge anything and his pounding head did little to settle his nerves or to calm his mood. His body was numb and naked. Kissed by a chill stealing through the smothering blanket of darkness and rigid from the pain of the injuries he had sustained during the fight. The fight!

Khadazin tried to move, but his pain held him down and the pounding of his head chided him for his self-inflicted abuses. Rising up on the back of his fear, a wave of terror smashed aside his fog of confusion as it dragged the events of his life for the last few weeks back into unwelcome focus. The secret meeting between the chancellor and his companion, and his resulting spiral into panic and drink. The ambush in the alleyway, the...

Khadazin groaned pitifully as he tried to recollect what had happened following the brutal attempt on his life. He couldn't remember! Any recollections of what happened after he left that cursed alleyway were confused and fading, as he slowly sobered up. His throat was raw and he fought down the need for a drink; although as the alcohol in his blood thinned and his senses returned they brought the agony from his wounds back with them. He could remember heading towards a patrol, but after that there was nothing. Only the blackness of confusion and the vagueness of uncertainty. Hopefully he would be able to recall what had happened in time, but for now he decided, it would be better to focus his attentions on the present and try to deduce what his future held. As he attempted to move again, his body reminded him that the future was probably blacker than his surroundings and his circumstances had not changed for the better.

It took many minutes, but eventually Khadazin managed to blindly negotiate his injured frame into a sitting position, using his right arm for balance. The stone under his palm was roughly hewn, slick with dust and wet with worse. Terrible smells assaulted what senses he had left, a nauseous concoction of rotting straw, urine and excrement. What little air he could feel was stale and oppressive, leaving the stonemason to guess that he was somewhere deep underground. Khadazin gingerly drew his knees up under his chin; pain screaming through his large frame as he felt his congealing wounds tugging and opening again.

Khadazin's fear was palpable and the fresh pain was able to settle the bile rising in his throat, as he groaned in disconsolation and hurled silent curses at the chancellor. As he shook with rage, the stonemason kneaded his temples with his hands to try and ease the pain in his head. As he did so, he ran one hand up through his tightly cropped hair, suddenly feeling the wound on the back of his head and the thick blood clotting there. With realisation, came despair. Someone must have followed him, striking him from behind. The blow must have knocked him senseless and bludgeoned any recollection from his mind. *Bastards!* Khadazin fumed, shaking with fury. He nearly got away from the chancellor's reach, thought he almost had. But the assassins must have had backup, backup who had waited until he was vulnerable and then struck when his attentions were elsewhere. It was probably not surprising though, Khadazin reasoned with himself. He had taken a terrible beating and suffered several wounds. He would not have been aware with the blood rushing through his head and the alcohol fuelled adrenalin coursing through his veins. Well, obviously! Otherwise I wouldn't be here, would I? Wherever here was?

He shook his head and sobbed uncontrollably. Life had been going so well for him, these past few years. Since his heroic rescue of the merchant Savinn Kassaar, life had changed for him in the city. He had gained a positive name for himself, one that had helped to establish his business and improve his standing in Karick. It had not always been that way of course...

His father had decided to leave his homeland in the Western Reaches of the Far Continent following the death of his beloved wife Sharina, the mother of his only child. With no family of his own left alive following a terrible plague that had decimated the continent, he had only his wife's family for company during his period of mourning. They were a bitter, divided family however, who had never agreed with their daughter's choice of husband in the first place and had only begun to accept her decision upon the birth of their first grandchild. Unsure of what to do and determined to make a better life for his child, Khadazin's father had spirited his eight year old son away from their clutches, two months after his wife's death. Still suffering from his loss Khazin Sahr sold his business, a humble stonemason's workshop in the fair city of Ashander and bought passage aboard a merchant ship that was heading across the Far Sea for the Valian lands known as the Four Vales. Leaving no trail, his father had managed to flee his war torn country and to his dying day, had never heard from his wife's family again. Success, he may have thought. But after the first few years of life in their new home in Karick, the glorious city and capital of the Four Vales, Khazin Sahr had begun to wonder if he had made a very rash decision.

The Redani people who inhabited the Western Reaches were tolerant people; welcoming of strangers to their shores and eager for the cultural knowledge the different seafarers and merchants brought with them. Since the arrival of the first explorers two centuries earlier, amicable trade began between the two continents and for those who dared the journey across the dangerous Far Sea, the profits and rewards were well worth the risk. To the greedy Valian merchants it was evident that the dark skinned people of the western lands would be a great source of trade for the Four

Vales. This friendship however, was not reciprocated by the Valian people when their neighbours from across the sea came to visit their own shores.

Unlike the welcome they received after landing at the city port of Ilithia, Khazin Sahr had met with open hostility when he reached the city of Karick, his frightened son at his side. The supposedly cultured people of this capital city treated them with more disdain than the beggars who wallowed in the poor quarters of the city, pleading and thieving their way through life. After weeks of living in shelters run by one of the city's churches, Khazin found work with a local stonemason thanks to the sponsorship of a sympathetic priest. The owner soon put aside his own prejudices when he realised the worth and skill of his new employee. Over the next few years the man's humble business prospered and with it, came a subtle change in the way that people viewed and treated the dark skinned genius, who worked for him. This charity did not stretch to his ten-year-old son however, and the tall lad was often on the receiving end of severe beatings by the local youths. Any schooling was impossible because of this and as the young Khadazin grew, gaining strength and victories of his own, his father persuaded his employer to hire the muscular lad as his own apprentice. The man readily agreed and over the next ten years Khazin taught his son all that his own father had once taught him. By this time however, their employer had become gravely ill and it was then that Khazin offered to purchase his business from him. Needing funds to pay for his treatment and provide for the care of his own family, their employer reluctantly agreed. Within a month the papers and contracts were signed, allowing the frail man to retire and be with his family. Three months after that, he was dead. The disease in his lungs too far advanced to be treated by the physicians he had spent most of his money on. Khazin had attended the funeral, offering his grieving widow his condolences and his monetary support. Her husband's kindness had allowed him and his son to find a new life in this foreign land, when it looked like there was none to be found and it was the very least he could do to repay the compliment. She had received his charity gracefully, stating that her late husband had admired him a great deal.

The widow and widower became close over the next eight years and the business, although handicapped by fresh prejudices, still managed to make some profit. By now Khadazin was a strong, imposing man in his late twenties. Skilled at the trade his father had passed onto him and running the business on his own as Khazin spent most of his days with the new love in his life. Such a union was not without trouble of its own however and the woman's two sons could not forgive her, for, in their eyes, she had tainted the memory of their father and brought shame upon their family name. Khadazin was openly happy that his father had found happiness and although he was secretly angered by the disgust from many of the locals who knew of their relationship, he kept his thoughts to himself and directed his fury into his work. He had always found it difficult to develop relationships of his own, hampered by the hostility in the eyes of the people he met. After a time, he withdrew from the public eye and the only people he ever saw were his customers and suppliers.

A year later, his father's love died. Khazin was inconsolable and after the poorly attended funeral, he hid himself away, rejecting all attempts of help from his son and finding comfort in the bottom of a bottle. Khadazin was sick with worry, eager to let his father grieve, but mindful of the abyss he was letting himself fall into. Months slipped painfully by and the stress of balancing his work and caring for his father began to take its toll on him. The priests at the local church would only help if his father sought it and when Khadazin tried to persuade him, the drunken man chased his son away with harsh words and incoherent ramblings. By the time Khazin Sahr finally drank himself to death a year later, Khadazin was already fighting with his own problems and sank deep into an even darker and dangerous depression. Ironically it was because of this that he had intervened when assassins had chased the merchant Savinn Kassaar that fateful day, three months after his father's funeral. The merchant's heritage was clearly a mix of Valian and Reven; and in Khadazin's eyes these Valian thugs were the excuse he needed to vent some of his frustration upon the people who had made his life a misery over the last two decades. He had not felt better about himself following the fight, but had inadvertently given himself the chance for a better life. Had he known then what he knew now, however, Khadazin may have stayed up on the roof of the villa and let the assassins have their man.

Khadazin shook those thoughts from his head and growled in frustration. He was supposed to be focusing on the present, not lost within the quicksand of his past. Wallowing in yet more self-pity and blaming everyone else but himself as usual, for his life and the hardships he was facing.

"Be the man in charge of your own destiny," his father had said to him one day, following a particularly bad beating by the local bullies. "Not the shadow chasing after the sun of a dream."

Khadazin had listened well that day and had never been on the end of another beating by the local bullies, again. Well, not until now, anyhow.

Focusing on the pain wracking his body, he used it to divert his attentions and concentrate on his surroundings. Drinking in the wall of black silence he closed his eyes and honed his senses. After a time, he could detect the faint and distant sound of water dropping from a height to splash on a gathering pool on the stone floor, somewhere away to his left and several dozen metres behind him. The echo reverberated through the curtain of blackness and thundered in his pounding head. Khadazin licked his dry lips; eager for the unseen liquid as the humidity of his surroundings began to seep through the mantle of pain he wore. Shifting his position, he winced and began feeling across the filthy stone with trembling hands as he blindly sought to trace out his surroundings.

"You are alive, I hear!" A brittle voice croaked out of the darkness across from him and Khadazin started in fright. For a moment he listened to the silence, turning his head as he sought to detect further sounds. Was he delirious? Were his wounds and the alcohol playing tricks on him still?

"Am I going mad?" Khadazin asked himself, speaking aloud.

"Not yet," the ancient voice croaked again, cackling. "Soon you may wish you were, however."

There was a pregnant pause, before the voice sounded again. "You are not from these lands stranger, that much I can tell."

Khadazin's mind reeled and throbbed painfully as he struggled to answer coherently.

"My birth home is Ashander, but I have spent most of my life in Karick."

"That couldn't have been easy," the voice observed bluntly. "Saw you when they dragged you in yesterday, blacker than these shadows you are."

Khadazin felt the anger broiling away within him. "Who are you, shadow?" he snapped angrily, waving his fist at the blackness in front of him. "Where am I and who was it who brought me here?"

There was silence for the next few moments, as Khadazin's words bounced away off unseen walls and faded quietly into nothingness.

"You should save your strength, friend!" the voice pointed out softly, as the stonemason was about to demand his answers again. "So whilst you listen to me, relax yourself a moment and gather your wits." Again, another meaningful pause and Khadazin sunk back into his exhaustion and remained silent.

"Good lad, well to the first. I am Cornelius Varl and normally I would say it is a pleasure to make your acquaintance – but I would not wish such an ill place on even the most corrupt of men." Silence again as the rattling, wheezing voice gained breath.

"To the next question. You are in prison of course, even that knock on your head could not have blunted your senses that much."

Such was the sarcasm, Khadazin should have retorted angrily. But the truth of Cornelius' words placated him.

"As to where, I can only hazard an educated guess. I arrived much the same as you, hit from behind and dragged into the dark, some twenty years ago now."

"Twenty years?" Khadazin baulked.

There was a long silence while Cornelius breathed heavily, coughed up his bile-filled lungs and spat into the dark. "Yes lad, twenty years at the very least. You lose track of all time down here. I was an architect. A brilliant one, if I may say so and in charge of building the high duke's keep after his inception. After the construction was complete, for my efforts I was taken from my home in the dead of night by cloaked and hooded assailants, similar to the ones who dragged you down the steps into your cell."

Khadazin's mind was pounding from the strain of concentration. "But why did they take you? I don't understand!"

Cornelius chuckled ruefully. "I know all the secret passages, I designed them. All of the listening alcoves, the spy holes, escape tunnels. All of them! Apparently some people did not trust me with the knowledge I had, have. So they locked me away from temptation."

"Surely not the high duke himself?"

"Of course not!" Cornelius snapped. "That man has not a shred of dishonour within him; but there are those who have the duke's ear and wait in the shadows, plotting to darker ends. I imagine they use these tunnels and spying devices for their own means and I expect the duke is not aware that most of them even exist."

Khadazin shook his head dumbly, as a wave of despair rose up within him. Twenty years? The poor man! How had he survived down here all this time, without going insane? Khadazin was a weak man; he knew that and the thought of spending even a month in such incarceration left his determination paralysed by fear.

"How have you survived, Cornelius?" Khadazin

whispered, shaking his head incredulously.

"Hope," came his reply. "The hope that one day I can escape and taste the fresh air one last time. The hope I have for a final walk with my wife and children along Merchant's Way and up the Valian Mile to look at the high duke's keep."

"You are a braver man than I, Cornelius Varl," Khadazin stated. "I fear that I would not be able to hold onto that hope for such a long time."

"You will have to find that courage if you are to survive what is to come, my young friend," Cornelius said, his voice quiet and ominous. "Get some rest now. Not the rest of unconsciousness, but the healing rest of sleep. You have many wounds and will need your strength. We shall talk more about you if you wish, when you are clearer headed."

Khadazin felt the hair on his body prick with fear and any further questions he put forward were met by a black wall of silence. Sometime later Khadazin could hear the rattling sounds of snoring and soon after, he gave in to his pain and joined his invisible neighbour in an uncomfortable, uneasy sleep.

When Khadazin woke some hours later, he was still wrapped in darkness and the pain from his wounds numbed his body. His head was clearer now. Still visited by pain from the blow to the back of his head, but now free from the presence of any drink. Lying on the filthy stone floor he had secretly hoped he would wake to find it had all been a dream, but the greeting he received from the darkness dispelled any hopes he may have held on to.

"Welcome back! How do you feel now?"

Khadazin mentally read his condition as he

laboriously sat up and did not like what he found. "Not good, but at least I am still alive." For now, he added silently.

He could sense Cornelius nodding, before he spoke. "Good, good!" he said to himself. "So, are you ready to tell me a little bit about yourself, Redani?"

Khadazin was taken aback by Cornelius's knowledge of his people. Most inhabitants of the Four Vales were not usually quite so respectful of his heritage, when addressing him.

"I, well yes. I guess so, my friend." He was not sure if he should, but he needed to share his turmoil with someone.

"Reflecting on the past will help you to focus on what is before you, giving you the desire you will need to fuel the fires of your instinct." Again another Cornelius pause. "You will need this instinct if you are to survive down here and perhaps one day be free of this damnation."

Khadazin nodded to himself, before speaking. "My name is Khadazin. I have lived in Karick, if that is where we still are, for most of my life. My father brought me here for a better life, from my country many years ago now. I am a stonemason, by trade. I have a workshop in Marble Plaza."

Cornelius was silent for a time, before he coughed up some words. "Must have been hard! The people who live in that part of the city are very good at using their noses to look at you, rather than their eyes." He chuckled, somewhat ruefully. "So how, by the storms, did you manage to get a workshop in that part of the city? Not by your charm and powers of persuasion, I would guess?"

Free of his hangover now, Khadazin was able to

rein in his usual short temper and calmed his breathing, before answering. "It is true, as you say. I would normally be driven from that part of the city; such is my heritage. But I saved the life of a man, some years ago. A well-respected man who holds much influence in Karick and has great kindness in his heart. He rewarded me for his life by helping me to establish myself there and used his connections within the city to put fresh business my way."

"Noble, indeed," Cornelius admitted. "Who was this man? Do not expect to find the same charity from your captors here, Khadazin!"

Khadazin had not expected to. "My friend is one Savinn…"

"Kassaar." Cornelius finished for him, a chuckle echoing from out of the dark. "Very lucky for you. I know of this man. Well-respected, as you say and owner of many trading companies. Even when I was a free man, I was aware of this man's swift rise to prominence within Karick. It was a source of much debate. Many found it strange how a mixed could become so successful, so quickly in a city brimming with prejudice."

"Mixed?" Khadazin asked.

Cornelius sighed. "Has that blow slowed your senses lad? Reven and Valian blood! It's the narrow eyes that give away his tribal side." He paused, pondering his next words. "And yet he still managed it? Hmm, I wonder how he did it?"

Khadazin had wondered that too. But he had always found Savinn to be a charming, clever and intelligent man who was open with his thoughts and honest in his dealings. Surely that must have counted for something on his road to success?

"Anyhow," Cornelius said, wheezing. "Enough history. He won't be able to help you a second time, I fear. Let's not tread in circles lad. What have you done to end up down here in the dark, with me?"

The first seeds of suspicion began to germinate in the back of the stonemason's head as he sensed urgency in the old man's words. Surely they had all the time in the vales? When he spoke, Khadazin chose his words carefully.

"I received a commission to work at the high duke's keep. I worked in the gardens, carrying out maintenance repairs on the walls and statues there."

"Ah, the gardens," Cornelius momentarily lost himself in the past. "Splendid good fortune."

"Or perhaps not!" he continued, when Khadazin did not reply. "What happened stonemason?"

"I overheard some people talking," Khadazin began, his aching mind racing. "They were plotting to have a girl taken, on her journey to the capital." The stonemason could hear Cornelius shift his position in the dark, his attention obviously piqued and when he did not speak, Khadazin continued. "She was to attend the Valian Council, on her father's behalf. They had orchestrated this, and were going to kidnap her to use her as a pawn in some dark game they have been plotting."

"Do you know who they were, who this girl was?" Cornelius asked quietly.

"I do not," Khadazin admitted evasively. "I did not see the speakers and they did not mention the girl by name."

"Hmm," again more musings from his neighbour. "Did you recognise the voices? Was there any information that they let slip, which might help you in the future?"

"Not that I can recall," Khadazin said slowly, raking his mind for ashes of information. "No wait, I do recall them mentioning 'the Seventh' – if that is of any use?"

"The Seventh?" Cornelius said hastily. "Well that is of use to you, Khadazin. The Seventh refers to the seventh member on the Valian Council. The council is made up from prominent members of the Four Vales, lords, ladies and politicians. They meet every quarter year, to discuss political matters and debate new proposals for the continuing prosperity of the Valian people. In my day the Seventh member of the council, at the time of the high duke's inception, was Lord Alion Byron. But he did not have any children back then…"

Khadazin relaxed his doubts about his neighbour slightly. Cornelius had managed to shed some light on the conversation he had overheard that fateful day and it helped him to put some of his confusion into order.

"My thanks, Cornelius," he said. "It had not occurred to me that they were referring to the seventh member of the council."

"So how did you come to be down here, though?" Cornelius's inquisitive nature was back again.

"I must have been seen as I left the gardens, following their meeting." Khadazin reasoned. "I remained hidden, such was my fear and stayed many hours after they had concluded their meeting. I-I was terrified. I did not know what to do next and lay awake through the night deciding. Finally, I decided that if I did not return the next day, it would tell them that I had indeed overheard the conversation."

"Sensible," Cornelius acknowledged. "But ultimately only delaying the inevitable, I presume?"

"Yes!" Khadazin whispered. "I was attacked by four

men. I managed to fend them off, but as you know, I was injured. The last thing I recall, was heading towards a militia patrol for help."

The dark was silent for many moments, leaving both men to shuffle their own thoughts. Khadazin felt his heart racing as the memories flooded back and his wounds began to cry out for fresh attention.

"And yet they have kept you alive!" Cornelius observed, finally. "Why did they not just slit your throat and be done with you?" Although the thought was too terrible to contemplate, Khadazin had begun to wonder that very same thing.

"I cannot tell. I can only hope that they live to regret their mistake." Khadazin said, feeling the fresh broil of determination rising up within him.

"That's the spirit, lad." Cornelius said, his voice snapping with praise. "Hold on to that, for I fear they will want to *speak* to you further. Have you confided what you heard to anyone else?"

Khadazin paused, halting any quick response. When he spoke, his voice was calm and clear. "I did not tell a soul. I have no friends in the city, not even enemies that I would wish such danger upon."

"I fear they will want to find that out for themselves at some stage, lad." Cornelius answered. "It can be the only reason why they have kept you alive, as far as I can tell. So when they come for you, which they will, you must be strong, no matter what."

"Fear not my friend, I will remain strong." Khadazin responded. "They have made a grave mistake by not killing me. I will not return the favour, so easily."

"Good, good!" Cornelius said. "Now rest some more and gather your strength. You will need it!"

Khadazin thanked him and lay back upon his stone

bed. He was beginning to like the feel of the cold stone, as it reminded him that he was still alive. For a long while before sleep finally claimed him again, the stonemason lay staring up at an invisible ceiling, his mind lost deep within a myriad of possibilities. Survival was now his primary instinct; the need to stay alive long enough down here, so that he could regain the strength stolen away by the assassins with the thrusts and slashes of their knives. The old architect had passed on his dream of hope to him now and it grew brighter with each nervous heartbeat. But unlike Cornelius, Khadazin now had a growing desire for vengeance. An all encompassing desire to escape his incarceration one day and make the chancellor regret that his men had failed to kill him and silence the secret he carried with him.

Khadazin woke with a start, shook from his dreamless sleep by the distant booming of thunder. Panting, he lay listening to the reassuring sound of Cornelius snoring as he became accustomed to the silence of his prison once again. At first there was nothing, above the beating of his heart and the ragged reach of his lungs. Then, just as he was about to resume his rest, he heard the faint echoes of booted feet upon stone and the distant sounds of jingling keys, as someone fumbled for a lock. The stonemason rose up, his pain momentarily forgotten as a door crashed open and the foreboding footsteps continued to come closer.

"Be strong, Khadazin." Cornelius whispered. Khadazin hadn't even noticed that he had stopped snoring.

Together they waited, the sounds of approach coming closer and closer. Another door opened, another crash and now, the faint echoes of whispers as their captors shared their thoughts. Before Khadazin had realised it, he began to detect the faint orange glow beginning to seep through the curtain of the dark, away to his left. As his captors came closer the hungry tongues of flame spread into the shadows, chasing them away into dark. Khadazin focused his attentions on the torchlight that was outlining a doorway now. Shadowy steps rose out of the dark to the door and the orange flames allowed him to see that he was in a rough-hewn stone cell. Rusted bars kept him in place and there were rags and straw piled up in the corner away to his left. When his captors stopped at the door, the torchlight allowed the stonemason to see the wizened apparition across from him. His beady eyes glittered in the poor light as he strained to see Khadazin in the dark. The old man looked like a withered stick. Thin and filthy, his hunched form rocked back and forth as he watched him. Long wispy hair ranged wildly about a skeletal face and his grey long beard covered up any of the decency he had left. Unlike Khadazin, Cornelius was clothed in the remnants of tattered rags and his skin was covered in scabs and bites.

"Be strong." Cornelius hissed again, nodding to him. The smile he sent through the two sets of bars looked more deranged than anything else, but Khadazin flashed him a broad smile of thanks. A key went into the lock and was then turned.

Blinding orange torchlight spilled into the large room, sending its inhabitants reeling as their eyes stung in the alien light. Blinking out the orange blotches imprinted in his eyes, Khadazin turned back to watch the four cloaked and hooded figures that moved silently down the steps and came ominously towards his cell. The lead figure was carrying the torch and its flames hungrily licked up the poor oxygen in the room. As they gathered ominously around the cell, the last figure turned its head towards Cornelius.

"Are you still alive, old man?" a man asked, his deep rough voice incredulous. The old man shied away from the figure and did not answer, scuttling back to the shadows at the rear of his heavily cobwebbed cell.

"Still winning that wager!" the speaker chuckled, turning to join his companions.

Khadazin's strength and courage was already beginning to wane as one of the hooded figures turned a key in the lock of the barred door to his cell. He was finding it hard to breathe and his body was shaking uncontrollably as he imagined phantom scenarios of what was to become of him.

With a shriek of protest, the barred door was hauled open and the torchbearer stepped aside to allow his companions into the cell. Wordlessly, they marched across to the stonemason and hauled him up roughly, by his armpits. Khadazin did not fight them. He was trying to conserve his strength and he bowed his head in submission.

"Not so tough now then, I see!" the torchbearer observed, as the stonemason was marched from his cell. The hooded party shared a chuckle as they headed back towards the steps.

Cornelius stole a look through his hands as they dragged the dark giant up the stairs. His huge black naked frame was submissive, covered in welts and wounds from his fight with the assassins. Khadazin's head turned briefly, before he was dragged from view and his dark eyes flashed like a viper. He had a strong harsh face, yet striking and memorable. There was a huge bruise on one side of his dark face and his square jaw tightened as he fought against his pain. His broad, flat nose was bloodied and his tight-cropped black hair was crusted by dried blood. His ears were small and one of them was bloodied at the point where there must have once been an earring, torn from its lobe by the man's captors. As they left the room, the hooded figure stopped at the top of the stairs and turned back briefly. He raised his torch towards the occupied cell and then turned away again. With a crash the door was closed and the choking light dragged away with it. As the orange tongues of flame faded away, the blackness gathered in eagerly behind it again.

Alone in his cell, Cornelius welcomed the solace and then smiled.

CHAPTER FIVE

The Road to Karick

The following morning after an undisturbed night of sleep it was with a heavy heart that Cassana reluctantly left the warmth and protection of the town of Havensdale. After a hearty breakfast in her room; delivered early by Scarlet Moore, she dressed in fresh travelling clothes and packed her clean clothing away in the backpack the girl had left for her. After studying herself in the tall mirror for some time, she washed her face, combed the tangles from her long scented hair and tied it back behind her neck in a ponytail. Her eyes were still haunted and ringed by the dark circles of her recent ordeal; but she felt stronger this morning, and her determination was filled with fresh vigour. Shouldering her pack, she gathered up her weapons and quiver, drank in the serenity of her sun-filled room for one last time and then went downstairs to say her goodbyes.

Joseph Moore was alone in the taproom and he greeted his guest with his usual broad and welcoming smile.

"Ah, good morning my lady," he said cheerily. "I trust you slept well?"

"Indeed I did, thank you, sir!" she replied, placing her empty breakfast plate on the bar with a bright smile.

"That pleases me, my lady." Joseph beamed. "When you feel ready, Captain Ardent asked me to direct you to the militia headquarters. Scarlet advised her that you were taking breakfast, on her way to the bakery – so she was aware to expect you shortly."

Cassana breathed deeply and smiled. "Then I shall be on my way Joseph." she said, her voice tinged with a hint of reluctance as she leant in close and kissed him on one cheek.

"Ahem, well, um yes! Thank you, miss!" he flustered, blushing. "Safe journey, miss. I hope we might have the pleasure of your company again soon?"

"Indeed you shall, my good man." Cassana promised, offering him a curtsy. Joseph offered her a clumsy bow in return and escorted her to the door. Holding the door open for her, he watched her walk through. Thanking him Cassana patted him on the shoulder and after offering final heartfelt farewells to him and his daughter, she headed back across a sun-kissed Merchant's Market towards the militia headquarters. Joseph watched her quietly for a few moments, before heading back inside.

Captain Ardent was waiting outside for Cassana and greeted her arrival with a smile and an enquiry on her night's sleep. She was dressed in similar garb as the day before but now wore a long green hooded riding cloak. She had a leather satchel slung over her left shoulder, despatches for the chancellor's office no doubt! Four horses were tethered outside the headquarters, three brown stallions and one black mare. All were saddled and ready for the journey, saddlebags full of supplies and bedrolls tied securely in place. Two male militia soldiers also waited by their mounts and regarded Cassana's arrival curiously. Meeting their gazes she offered them a nod and a shy smile in return.

"May I introduce our companions for this journey, Cassana?" Captain Ardent said, indicating and introducing the two men. The taller and older of the two men was Colbin Wicksford. Very late into his twenties the burly man had long dark hair, a plain and yet winsome face and an unkempt beard. His blue eyes returned Cassana's appraisal with slightly more relish and flickered confidently as he met her smooth stare. A Valian Longsword was sheathed on his back, its hilt and pommel visible above the neck of his dark cloak and a large wooden shield was tied to the saddle of his mount; a brown stallion with a white patch on its left cheek. He was dressed in well-lacquered leather armour and wore low, stiff-looking dark riding boots.

The second man was in his early twenties and dressed almost identically to his companion, with the exception of a hooded cloak of woodland green. He had a short sword belted at his side and his boots were new, reaching just beneath his knees. He was a handsome man with a very likeable face, short dark hair and a softly defined jaw line. His brown eyes blinked frequently in the dazzling sunlight and his thin lips parted in a welcoming smile beneath a small straight nose. Cassana blinked in return and felt a flutter of heat as the captain introduced him as Kallum Campbell. Cassana was not surprised to hear that he was Sara's older brother, such was the nature of the tightly-knit community and surmised that to run a successful farm, it made sense to have many sons and daughters to help you out.

Introductions now made, the captain announced their immediate departure. With fair weather and a favourable road, the journey to Karick would take them no more than three days, which would give Cassana a day to acclimatise to the city and announce her arrival. Directing Cassana to the third brown stallion, Colbin passed her the reins and helped her to strap her belongings to her saddlebags. He then watched helplessly as Cassana missed his offered hand and leapt expertly up into the saddle. Captain Ardent mounted the black mare and once their companions were similarly positioned, they turned their steeds towards the south gate. Two young militia recruits each held one half of the large wooden gates open for them as they cantered by. A young lad and lass, Cassana's fleeting attention was drawn to the tall slender girl. She had long, thick, curling tresses of the deepest black and her brown eyes were narrow and oval in shape, evidence of her Reven heritage. The girl caught Cassana's momentary look as she rode by and returned it truculently.

Free from the protection of Havensdale now, the tiny column of riders made good ground that day as they followed the dusty road south through the Valian countryside. Cassana had not been this far south for several years now and she was eager to refresh her memory as she drank in the beautiful plains and meadows they travelled through. The sun bathed the land in a glorious golden light, majestic in its cloudless kingdom of brilliant azure blue. They stopped a couple of times that day, once for a sparse lunch and again to rest and water their horses. Cassana found her mount very well trained and although they were unfamiliar to each other, they soon became one; testament again to the reputation held throughout the Four Vales by the Havensdale livery. The few times that any conversation was started, Cassana found her companions to be both engaging and welcoming. She warmed immediately to the boisterous and easy nature of Colbin, glad to be free from the trappings of etiquette that she had to adhere to back home. Kallum however, she found to be a quiet man who listened politely and intently, saying little but answering much with his eyes.

Any time she found him watching her, Cassana felt the heat on her cheeks rise and she did her best to excuse her attention with a polite smile. Although she was used to attention back home at the various functions and parties her father insisted on parading her at, here, out in the country, she felt more vulnerable and innocent to the bold appraising stares she was receiving. Whereas with the woodsman, she had felt angered, with Kallum, it was a different sensation altogether.

At the end of the morning's travel, the small company of riders had lost sight of the River Haven as it twisted away from them towards the south-west through a large forest. They encountered very few travellers that day. At noon they met one lone rider heading towards Havensdale from the nearby eastern village of Colden. He was known to Fawn and her companions and they sent the old man on his way with their good wishes and hopes for a safe road. Later that day they also met a tiny wagon, laden with hay. The two drivers were men in their late forties, both rough looking and yet forthcoming with their greetings. They were known to the captain and also from Colden village, having joined the road earlier to head south towards the Crossways Inn. After they had left them behind, Fawn explained to Cassana that a day's ride from here was a junction known as the Northern Crossways. This was at a point where four roads met; the Great Road heading south towards the capital and three other roads that led to the north, east and west. The roads were busy highways for the many traders who used them as a dangerous method of transport for their goods and wares to the numerous villages, towns and cities of the North Vales. An enterprising businessman had built an inn at the junction, and his establishment was a popular resting point for the many wayfarers and merchants. However this region, particularly to the south and east of the Northern Crossways, was also notorious for the activities of certain bandits and highwaymen, eager to plunder the merchants wagons for their valuable wares and rob unsuspecting travellers of their jewellery and purses. The most prolific of these was Devlin Hawke, the elusive highwayman who had relieved many weary travellers of their purses over the past few years and eased the burden of countless merchant wagons. As Captain Ardent had mentioned to Cassana the previous day, the scoundrel's activities had been thwarted more recently by the increased number of patrols along the Great Road. But the highwayman possessed a devilish courage and he still blatantly continued to operate in the area. On one occasion he had even managed to steal several mounts from a Valian patrol as they rested for the night – leaving behind a message that read 'Take a walk back where you came from, I am not ready for your noose yet,' ending it 'yours elusively, Devlin Hawke.' The reward for his capture had increased after that to ten thousand gold crowns, a princely sum indeed. But as of yet, the authorities had not managed to apprehend or kill him. Colbin declared that he wouldn't mind a share of that reward, but the look on Kallum's face suggested that he harboured more of a respect, than a loathing for the charismatic brigand.

By the end of the day's travel, when they found a small copse of trees off the main road to shelter for the night, Cassana's posterior was aching and her thighs and back burned with the effort of a long ride. After tending to their mounts, the small group looked to their own needs and shared a hot meal and a flagon of Campbell's Own around a roaring fire under the cover and protection of a misty darkness. By the time Kallum volunteered for the first watch, Cassana was full from her supper and drained from the exertions of her journey. Captain Ardent assured her of an unbroken night's sleep, waving away her protestations at not being included in the roster for the night's watch.

Weary and submissive, Cassana crawled into her bedroll and not for the first time recently, was soon asleep under a clear, black night sky.

The next morning, following a light breakfast, the companions rejoined the south road and set off towards the Northern Crossways. The morning was bright again, the cloudless skies cleared by the sun, but there was also a blustery wind that raced through the grasslands and helped to chase away Cassana's fog of sleep. The elevation of the land here was starting to incline and soon led them down into a large valley that swept as far as the eye could see. Tall trees dotted the horizon away to the east and a cluster of hills crested the valley to the far west. Several hours later they were free of the valley and once they had crested the rise and stopped to rest their mounts, Captain Ardent drew Cassana's attention to the distant forest several miles to the south-east of their position.

"It is rumoured that Devlin Hawke finds refuge in the Greywood Forest, but as of yet none have found courage to go in and look for him." she said, with a thin smile.

Cassana tilted her head thoughtfully, sweeping strands of wind-wild hair from her eyes. "Why is it called the Greywood?"

"The trees there are mainly silver birch," Fawn explained, "giving the forest a very grey, morose look in the morning and at night." Cassana nodded but did not agree, as she found the silver birches that carpeted the lower foothills of The Great Divide mountain ranges back home, to be beautiful and elegant sentinels. Colbin watched the distant trees with a wistful look on his face. Snapping his thoughts free from the promise of wild adventure and great rewards he patted the neck of his steed and moved them on along the south road once again.

Towards dusk, they began to see the distant building of the Crossways Inn – as it watched the traffic on the roads and welcomed the weary inside with the promise of a hot meal and a cool drink. Cassana could see several wagons and carts moving along the roads to the east and west, black silhouettes against the dying sun and noticed lights twinkling through the many windows of the inn. Guiding her mount alongside Captain Ardent, she leaned close.

"Are we to stay at the inn tonight, captain?" she asked quietly.

"I had planned to," Fawn answered, glancing over

at the nervous looking young woman. "Is that not your wish, my lady?

Cassana ignored the curious looks coming back her way from the two male riders in front of them and nodded. "I am uneasy, if I am to be honest. The people who organised the attack on me may have positioned lookouts here, in case I slipped their net."

"And this would be a good place to have people watch the roads!" Fawn finished, nodding her head thoughtfully. "I did not think of that Cassana. But as an insurance, I think we would be wise to avoid the Crossways altogether."

As the captain ordered the party off the road to the east, she gave the men orders to ride on and find a suitable place for them to camp for the night. Ignoring their quizzical stares, she watched as Kallum and Colbin rode off through the tall grasses of the plains away from them and shared quiet words.

"Thank you, Fawn." Cassana said, sighing in relief. "I may be paranoid, but after what has happened, I do not want to present myself to further danger until I can report to the high duke what has befallen me."

"Sensible, I would call it," Fawn said, offering her a friendly smile. "When I get back home, if it helps, I could pen a letter to your father for you on your behalf? If there is indeed a spy in your father's camp, they may watch out for any news from you."

Cassana thought about it for a moment, as both women allowed their mounts to lead them slowly across the plains.

"It might help me out, as you say. But I do not want to put you in any danger, Fawn," Cassana admitted, after a long period of contemplation. "You have already helped me more than you could ever imagine and if I let you send that letter, it might thrust you into this mess. I could not live with myself, if I brought harm to your door!"

Fawn's face wrinkled in disagreement. "Well surely that is my choice, my lady? But I can see by the look in your eyes that you will not hear any more on the subject and so I will offer you this compromise. If you have not contacted me by letter or passed through Havensdale on your way home, two weeks from now. I shall send word to your father, detailing all that has happened to you. How does that sound?"

Cassana reluctantly agreed, not about to get into an argument. Although once she reached the sanctuary of the city, she was sure that the high duke's office would see to those concerns on her behalf anyhow.

"That is a fair compromise, my friend and I once again thank you for your concern." Cassana said, smiling in relief. "I promise that I will come back through Havensdale on my way home, and under better circumstances, hopefully."

Captain Ardent smiled in return but said nothing. She could see the worry fade somewhat from Cassana's face and was wise enough to let the matter drop for now. Although she didn't openly voice her concerns there was still a faint doubt tugging at her mind, warning her that Lady Byron's problems were still far from over. She could only hope that once they delivered her safely to Karick, she would find the help and protection that she so obviously needed.

Regaining control of their mounts, the two women headed off through the long grass after their distant companions. That night they camped under the natural shelter offered to them by a grassy knoll; with a solitary oak tree to keep watch on top of it. Under the bright stars, they shared a cold meal and quiet conversation as they listened to sounds of the night and the call of the crickets that infested the long grasses of their surroundings. More perturbed by her own caution than she would care to admit and the incessant rumble of Colbin's deep snoring, it took many hours before Cassana finally drifted off into a light, disturbed sleep.

The following clear morning was spent shadowing the Great Road as it knifed south through the flatlands and crossed into the heartland of the Four Vales. Still with one eye on the safety of her charge, Captain Ardent decided it best to stay off the main road and keep to the wilds as a precaution. By now Colbin and Kallum were bursting with curiosity and any attempt to wean information from their mysterious charge or captain, was met by a wall of steadfast silence. In the end they gave up and concentrated on their surroundings, taking in the sights of the lush grasses of the plains and the wooded slopes of the Crescent Hills away to their east. With the threat of brigands more tangible now, the party travelled in wary silence.

At midday following a welcome rest for both horse and rider, the party set off again with a hazy sun high over their heads. The lush horizon shimmered with the heat and they stopped more regularly that afternoon, whenever a copse of trees presented shade for them. At one point as they rode down a steep incline, Cassana spotted a large dark bird wheeling lazily in the sky in front of them.

"What a beautiful sight!" Cassana breathed in awe, marvelling at the bird's elegance as it cried out its joy at the day and idly scanned the grasslands beneath for prey. "Does anyone know what type of Raptor it is?"

"Uh?" Colbin grunted, his sweaty face wrinkling in confusion.

"What Cassana means," Kallum interjected, as Cassana was about to reply. "Is what type of bird of prey it is! Am I right, my lady?"

Cassana nodded, seeing the look that crossed Colbin's face and the grin that Kallum taunted him with. "If you spent some time reading, rather than concentrating on my father's ale all the time – you might actually learn something."

Colbin growled playfully, as the younger man wheeled his horse out of harms reach. At a safe distance now, he flashed another mocking grin at his cantankerous companion.

"All right then, smart arse," Colbin countered. "What *Raptor* is it then?" That wiped the victory from Kallum's face and he looked away at the circling bird and shrugged.

"Damned if I know," he chuckled. "The book didn't have any pictures."

Cassana and Fawn laughed, their mirth light in contrast to the raucous guffaws of the two men.

"If I may," Fawn said, sniffing back another laugh. "By the white wing-tips and the way the bird wheels in large sweeping circles, I would guess it to be a Black Kite."

"How did you know that, captain?" Colbin demanded, as Cassana thanked her.

Fawn looked over at him and winked. "My book had pictures!"

By the time the small party of riders reached the outskirts of the city of Karick later that day, the sun was thankfully starting to sink beneath the distant horizon.

Rejoining the bustling Great Road again they picked their way through the traffic of wagons and caravans, keeping themselves to themselves. At various points Cassana could see wanted posters nailed to the trees that began to line the roadside, or under the occasional signpost that told the traveller of their last three miles to Karick. Every poster was the same. A nondescript drawing of a dark-haired man, his face covered in a black mask below his eyes; and the promise of a reward of ten thousand crowns for his capture. Cassana couldn't read the name on the posters very well, but after what Fawn had told her, she didn't need to!

The last three miles to the city was an easy affair and Cassana felt her hopes begin to rise. In silent contemplation of what was to come, she took in her surroundings with relish and bathed in its sights and sounds. People were happy! The travellers heading to and from the city were in a fine frame of mind today. Jovial banter and warm greetings between friends and colleagues were commonplace, their conversation broken only by the braying of donkeys and bleating of the sheep that the shepherds only seemed to bring onto the road to cause chaos. Closer still, Cassana began to note the farmlands that began to claim their territory. Heaving with rich crop and cattle, all of them were divided up by fencing and watched over by farmhands and distant farmhouses. Another mile closer and they also began to encounter small communities at the roadside. Small hamlets of tents, for people not willing to pay coin inside the city, or perhaps disliking the claustrophobia that they found inside the great walls. Aware of the towering high walls rising up on the horizon now, Cassana also saw a cluster of brightly painted wagons off to her right through the line of trees. She could hear children screaming merrily as they chased each other around their camp-site and Cassana spotted a tall woman dressed in a long skirt and draped in bright silks and colourful scarves. Wayfarers! Many people victimised these travellers for their way of life, branding them layabouts and thieves. But Cassana had seen them back home, when they attended the city of Highwater's solstice festivities every year. They would put on bright shows, sing fine music and perform mesmerising dances for the populace. Cassana loved the thought of travelling the free road, no two nights under the same sky. And the romanticism of their way of life, although probably harder than the illusion of their shows, was still an enchanting dream for Cassana. Colbin soon shattered that ideal.

"Hold onto your purses and keep your eyes on the road." he chuckled quietly and Cassana felt her anger rise.

"Now, Colbin," Fawn warned him, her voice laced with anger of her own. "I won't tolerate such insular attitudes from my men. We are representatives of our town here in the city and that is not the kind of behaviour I expect from the senior soldiers under my command."

"Well, the last time they were in town, thefts went up no end!" he argued, as they rode on.

Cassana nodded sadly, feeling her own anger subside. Her father had dealt with the same accusations and narrow-mindedness for many years now.

"Yes," Fawn sighed. "And we have been through this many times before, have we not? Because of this reputation, the dishonest members of our community use it as an excuse to step up their activities. It always happens."

"Reputation is a terrible thing," Kallum offered. "One bad deed can outweigh a hundred good ones."

"If I may?" Cassana said, daring to join in. "We have the very same problem in Highwater. Every year several Wayfaring communities come to the city to help celebrate the Summer Solstice. They have been for the past fifteen years now and every year the crime rate goes up."

"There you go, see?" Colbin said, clicking his fingers triumphantly and pointing at his ally. "What did I tell you?"

Cassana was already shaking her head. "You misunderstand me, sir! All of the wayfarers caravans were searched the first year this happened. Only one wayfaring community was found to be responsible and only then for several petty thefts; they were banished from the city after that. But the crime rate still rises each year and their wagons are still routinely checked. The wayfarers make good honest money from their performances, I do not think they would risk being banished from the city."

"People will always use a good opportunity for some dishonest activities." Fawn said, finishing the conversation with a meaningful look towards Colbin.

Cassana inadvertently looked over at Kallum and caught him watching her in return. Smiling shyly, she turned her attentions away again and continued the final leg of her journey in silence.

The city of Karick was a welcome and magnificent sight for Cassana, as she and her entourage dismounted on the cobblestone road leading towards the giant granite walls of the capital. Pennants hung limply from the battlements above the huge gatehouse and hundreds of people filed through the opening into the city beyond. Distant tall towers rose up into the shadows of the coming night, stretching themselves free of the choking grip of the streets beneath them. Leading their mounts by the reins, the companions joined the throng of people and allowed themselves to be driven silently on. Cassana's eyes flicked here and there, nervously wondering if anyone was watching for her arrival and then chiding herself for being so paranoid. If they were really that worried about her, surely they would have sent more tribesmen to capture her?

It took another hour in the fading light, but they finally managed to reach the city and filed into the gatehouse; their horses shoes clattering and echoing under their stone cover. The Valian guards at the gate; resplendent in their ring mail armour, flicked vigilant eyes over the crowds as they searched for smugglers or anyone who looked like they had something to hide. As they passed through, Cassana kept her eyes firmly on Colbin in front of her and finally led her horse into Karick, capital city and heart of the Four Vales.

The noise and smell of the city beyond rose up like a wave of civilization and smashed into Cassana's face as they led their mounts through the masses in the huge cobbled square beyond. Hawkers and merchants cried out advertisements for their wares. The intoxicating smell of food and spices began to filter through the body odours of the masses and Cassana licked her lips hungrily. People hurriedly crossed their path, jostling their way unceremoniously towards their unknown destination and others bumped by them as they struggled away from the gatehouse. In the centre of the square a large statue of a proud looking warrior in full battle armour rose up out of the tumult, casting a steely look towards the gatehouse and any travellers that dared bring trouble to the city. It was a statue in honour of the late Valan Stromn, the High Duke who had led the armies of the Four Vales across the Great Divide, some fifty years ago now and crushed the uprising of the huge tribal hordes gathering under the single banner of the chieftain Reven Skarl – known as The Dragon among the clans. Their chieftain had somehow managed to steal the banner of the Four Vales years before, using it as a talisman to unite the warring clans together and persuade them to march as one on the Four Vales. On the barren wastelands of the tribal plains the two nations had met and fought. For three bloody days both armies gained and lost precious ground, before Valan Stromn had led the charge that broke through the hordes lines and had met the Great Chieftain Reven Skarl in single combat. Clutching his standard of The Dragon in one hand, the chieftain had fought fiercely as the battle around them died and bitter enemies on both sides stood together as one to witness the outcome. It came in the end with a desperate riposte from Valan Stromn, as his opponent overpowered him. Cutting through the chieftain's stolen standard, his sword snapped in half, the broken length of the blade burying deep into the warlord's throat. As he staggered back, the blood and unity of his people drenching the ground, the two armies had separated in shock and silence. Wounded many times himself, the high duke had picked up the broken blade of his sword and took Reven Skarl's standard in his other hand. Waving it towards the broken lines of the tribal hordes, he took the banner and his armies back with him across the Great Divide. With the spirit of the horde destroyed and their warlord slain, the clans fragmented once again – plunging the north back into civil war as they fought for the scraps of dominance. Valan Stromn and his armies returned home to the Four Vales in triumph, beginning the next fifty years of unity and peace. A great fortress was built in the mountain pass of the Great Divide, above the city of Highwater, as warning to the clans and their aspirations of conquest. From that day on the tribal people across the mountains to the north were also called the Reven, in honour of their chieftain. Leaderless, the clans did not unite to attack the Four Vales again.

Captain Ardent's voice rose above the clamour and directed them to a meeting point, away from the bottleneck of the gates and as one they began forcing their way to her.

Ignoring the merchants that thrust their wares into her face with the promise of the '*deal of a lifetime*,' Cassana noted that Kallum and Colbin had their free hands firmly on their purses. Pickpockets were no doubt rife at this time of the day and had she anything of value, Cassana would have shared their concerns.

It took some moments, but eventually they were together again on the southernmost fringes of the huge entry plaza, besides a large signpost that pointed off towards the many adjoining streets and lanes.

"Are we all still in one piece?" Fawn enquired and grinned when she saw the looks she received. "Okay, let's get out of this madness. Follow me up the Valian Mile if you will!"

As one again, they set off along the Valian Mile. It was so named because of the wide mile long street that stretched towards the high duke's keep rising up in the distance from them on a large hill. The road was lined with shops selling all types of wares and with busy inns and taverns of differing quality that heaved with patrons in various stages of inebriation.

A particularly striking four-storey building caught Cassana's attention and she was drawn to it further by the pleasing harp music playing within. The sign above the porch read 'The Jade Eagle Tavern.'

"One of the finer establishments in the city!" Fawn observed. "If you have the coin to spare, that is." She caught Cassana's eyes with a wink.

As they passed by a militia patrol bearing torches to chase the dusk away, they noticed that other soldiers were beginning to light the candles in the street lamps that lined the mile. As they led their horses up the gradually rising street towards the keep, they could see flames springing to life ahead of them, lighting the road like a cavalcade of fireflies.

Cassana began to feel her apprehension rise again as they approached the high duke's keep and she turned to Fawn.

"Where will you be staying tonight, captain?"

Fawn looked over her saddle at her and saw the shimmer of worry in the young woman's eyes.

"We will stay at a little place I know called 'Freeman's lodge' – I am known there and can normally get good rates from the proprietor."

"Perhaps I could find you lodgings at the keep?"

"There is no need, my lady." Fawn replied, ignoring the hopeful look on Kallum's face. "We will see you safely there, deliver our despatches and be on our way."

Cassana's face visibly dropped. She had known this moment would come, but she had become accustomed to the captain's company and was going to miss her. She had few friends at home, other than her childhood friend Lysette and her handmaiden Clara. Most others, who purported to be her friend, were only currying favour with her to increase their own standing on the social ladder of Highwater. No fool, Cassana had become very good over the years at separating genuine friendships from falsehoods. With Fawn, she detected only her good grace and intentions.

Forlornly, she focused her thoughts back on the magnificent keep before them. She had seen it years before of course, but the sight never failed to impress her and with age, came another level of appreciation. Tall and elegant, the keep rose into the night above the defensive wall that protected it. Several torches moved along the battlements at different intervals, revealing the locations of the keep's sentries and candle flames flickered through many dark windows of the four towers reaching out from the keep into the dusk above them. A single, tall dark tower reached far beyond the other four, rising high towards the stars. The Moon Tower! Cassana had heard about the tower's history when her father brought her here before. High Duke Karian Stromn, the son of Valan, was a man of passion and science. He was fixated by the stars and had commissioned the tower to be constructed so that he could watch them from the open room at the top of the tower and look out across his city, sprawling away beneath him. Few people had ever been to the zenith of the tower, but it was rumoured that the floor of the viewing room was made from polished black marble and that the constellations found in the sky had been etched into the floor with silver. Apparently, when the moon was at its fullest, the constellations on the floor would glow with silvery life.

In the silence the small group continued up the steadily rising road, free now from the hustle and bustle that spilled onto the streets from the north gate. As they topped the rise, the four of them stopped under the stare of the keep to catch their breath. Four guards stood silently outside the huge open gates of the keep and watched them solemnly from the shadows and flickering torches of its entrance. A portcullis was drawn up and its sharp teeth waited patiently, seemingly ready to snap down and swallow anyone within. Cassana found herself wishing they had arrived a few hours earlier. She was safe now. By some miracle she had managed to reach the sanctuary of the capital, when the odds against her the previous day would have been very long indeed. Despite the ominous feel of the dark keep at night, she was safe. But why was she feeling so nervous?

"Come my friends," Fawn said, fondly stroking one ear of her mount as she set them off towards the gatehouse. Colbin flicked a glance at their charge as they followed the captain, reluctantly trailing behind her and he couldn't help but detect the fear in the young woman's haunted eyes.

As they neared the gate, one of the guards strode out to meet them.

"Welcome," he said, his tone formal. "Can I enquire of your business here at the high duke's keep, this evening?"

"You may! I am Captain Ardent of the Havensdale militia," Fawn replied, with a cursory handshake. "We have other business in the city tomorrow and have brought our monthly despatches for the chancellor's office with us." Fawn produced the leather despatch satchel as evidence.

The guard studied the satchel with a nod of confirmation to himself. "Welcome captain," he said, pulling his frame up respectfully. "You will find refreshments at the mess hall should you wish it and your horses will be cared for during your visit. The chancellor's…"

"Thank you, but I have been here many times in the past." Fawn said, smiling. "We shall find our way and be gone before we can be a nuisance to you."

The soldier shrugged slightly and clenching his right fist, he slapped it in salute above his heart. Fawn returned the salute and with a final word of thanks, she beckoned for her party to follow her. As they passed under the gate, Cassana felt the guard watching her as he returned to his duties beside his companions. Flicking a nervous look over her shoulder however, she was relieved to see that his attentions were now fixed on the torch lit Valian Mile, dropping down into the grip of the city beneath them. Letting out a calming breath she looked back again, finding herself in the entrance courtyard of the high duke's keep. It was a breathtaking sight; the main keep and its towers reached up into the darkening sky before her, watched over by a bright half-moon that gained in strength as it sucked the remaining light from the day. There was a long marble pathway that led from the courtyard to the keep's entrance steps; lined on both sides by burning lanterns and fronted by dozens of sentries. An imposing structure of architectural beauty, Cassana found herself thinking of her father's more humble keep back home and swallowed back wistful emotions. There were also many outbuildings that surrounded the immediate courtyard and as a curious distraction she busied herself to identify them as livery stables, a cold forge, the mess hall and two barracks.

"If you follow us to the chancellor's office my lady,

I will see to it that your presence here is formally announced." Fawn said quietly, as they began to head off along the marble path towards the great keep, their mounts hooves echoing over the respectful silence of the grounds. She caught the look of confusion on her charge's face. "I did not wish to alert the guard to your arrival, as we cannot be sure how far this dark plot reaches and from which side of the vales it has been orchestrated."

Colbin and Kallum shared swift looks of surprise and intrigue as Cassana nodded slowly to herself. If these people, whomever they were, had the resources to infiltrate her father's house, then the same people may have also have taken precautions, should she escape their clutches and make it to the capital. Cassana nodded her accord and offered the captain a weak smile.

Leading their mounts along the path Cassana marvelled at the beautiful lawns on both sides of them. They were immaculately tended and starting to glisten with the first chill of the evening. She would have expected nothing less from the high duke; a man who reportedly had the proclivity towards the perfect. In the centre of each lawn there was a marble fountain, silvery, moon-kissed water spraying majestically into the air from the mouths of two expertly carved dolphins.

As they reached the keep, Fawn guided them around its side towards their right. Here they found themselves in a smaller, darker courtyard with stabling and several outbuildings, lights flickering from their windows to hint at the life within. With swift orders, Fawn passed the reins of her mount to Colbin and directed Kallum to take Cassana's. Whispering her thanks to her steed, Cassana passed him the reins. As she did, their hands touched briefly and Kallum winked roguishly. Drawing back into her rising embarrassment, Cassana stepped away and blushed furiously as she busied herself with retrieving her belongings and her bow.

"Well, good luck then, miss!" Colbin offered with a comforting grin.

"It's been a pleasure, my lady." Kallum added, although his words were tinged with disappointment.

Cassana regained her composure somewhat and straightened herself. "Thank you gentlemen. You have done me a great service and some day I hope I can repay the compliment to you both."

Both men smiled as she curtsied and bowed in final farewell. Excusing themselves they led the horses away towards the stables for some feed and water. Once they were out of earshot, Kallum shared a quiet word with his companion and Colbin laughed.

"I think you have made an impression there, Cassana." Fawn observed, her eyes bright with mischief. When the young woman's face nearly exploded with embarrassment, Fawn eased her discomfort by leading her away towards the doorway of a large building attached to the side of the keep. It's entrance porch was lit by an oil lantern, several moths dancing around the secure light within and Fawn knocked firmly on the dark wood. As they waited, she turned back to Cassana and took her by one hand, squeezing it reassuringly.

"I'll do the initial talking," she stated, caressing the young woman's cold hand. "It'll be fine, you are safe now." Before Cassana could reply, they heard the approach of shuffling footsteps and muttering from within. Turning their focus on the door, they waited in silence and listened in faint amusement to the cantankerous grumbling as a latch was drawn back and the stiff door was hauled slowly open.

A wrinkled, bespectacled old face peered from the shadows of the room beyond and twisted grumpily.

"What time do you call this? I was just going to go and have my supper. A well-deserved supper, I might add!"

Fawn fended off a wide smile. "My apologies Edward, but we arrived late. The traffic was terrible on the great road this afternoon."

"My, my, if it isn't Captain Ardent." the old man said brightly, opening the door fully. "We don't see you very often these days! Come in my dear, come in."

He stepped aside and ushered them both in quickly, complaining about his old bones and the cold air outside. Cassana turned to help him close the heavy door, but the old man huffed and shooed her away. Turning, she caught the amusement on Fawn's face and smiled quickly.

They were in what would have once been a large office, were it not for the heaving shelves and cupboards that ate up most of the space in the room. A large desk in the centre of the clutter was just as messy, parchments, books and numerous other items of importance fighting for space and clamouring for attention. Candles flickered in the fresh draught from holders on the walls and an archway at the rear of the room led away into shadows.

"Please ladies, be seated." Edward said, offering them the two chairs this side of the desk as he closed the door and shuffled by them. As the women both sat down, Cassana wearily studied the old man. He was dressed in heavy blue robes that hung from his thin

111

frame and his sandals scraped over the stone floor as he dragged himself back to his chair across from them.

"I must apologise for the turmoil ladies," he said, offering a defensive hand in gesture around the room. "The chancellor has finally allowed me to take on another aide, my grandson Thomas. But the lad is not the sharpest blade in the sheath and I fear at the moment that he is more of a hindrance, than a help." Edward's soft, almost feminine features broke into a warm smile, robbing his words of any hurt, replacing them with evidence of his pride and love for his grandson. He scratched at his surprisingly thick head of silver hair as he tried to remember what he had probably been about to say.

"I must admit that I thought you would have retired by now," Fawn said, passing the old man the documents from within her satchel. "Finally taking that well-deserved rest!"

"So would have I," he snorted, his thin, liver-spotted hands shaking as he took the papers from her. For a moment he stared at the carnage on his desk, searching for a safe place to lay them and then grinned, putting them on the top of an ever increasing pile of similar parchments.

"So ladies," he said, his green eyes taking them in. "May I offer you some herbal tea? Thomas may not be very good at filing things in alphabetical order, but at least he can brew a fine cup."

Cassana looked at Fawn for guidance and she caught her gaze and nodded. She turned back to answer the old man and saw that the exchange was not lost on him.

"That would be lovely, yes, thank you Edward." she replied, as he reached inside one of the desk's drawers and produced a silver hand bell. "However…"

Edward rang the bell with conviction and then tossed it back in the drawer. As the echoes bounded around the room and off down the corridor beyond, he fixed his eyes upon the captain.

"You were about to tell me the real reason why you are here, my dear?" he surmised, smiling.

Fawn grinned and Cassana counted the heavy beats of her heart, as they thundered in her chest. This was it, the moment that her cards were out in the open for all to see. Any would-be allies and of course, any of her enemies. There was no hiding now from what had happened. There would be no turning back.

"Yes, of course Edward," Fawn said, smiling warmly. "May I present to you Lady Cassana Byron, daughter of Alion Byron, Lord of the North Vales."

The old man was visibly shocked and his eyes flicked in surprise to the young woman sat across from him. At Fawn's words, Cassana suddenly felt that a huge burden had been lifted from her shoulders.

"My lady," Edward fussed. "May I welcome you to the capital. If I am correct, I understand you are to attend the Valian Council on your father's behalf?"

"Yes, sir," she answered. "We were expected yesterday, I believe. But I am afraid to report…that…"

"What Lady Byron is trying to say my friend is that her party was attacked on their journey here." Fawn finished for her, seeing the perplexed look on Edward's face.

"Attacked?"

"Yes sir," Cassana said, taking over again. "We were attacked at dawn, two days before last, in the Moonglade Forest."

"Bandits are–,"

"Not bandits, sir. Reven."

A heavy silence smothered the room as the old man nearly choked on his shock and Cassana sat listening to the fear creeping up on her, coming closer to the fore again with every heartbeat.

"Reven?" Edward said. He was clearly in shock and took several moments to assemble his thoughts and his composure. "This is incredible. Reven this far into the Four Vales. This is terrible!"

"Indeed, old friend." Fawn said, taking control of the proceedings. "Fortunately the lady managed to escape their clutches, although her gallant companions were lost; and she came to Havensdale seeking help to get to the city and report what had happened. I fear some dark plot is manifesting, though I know not what and I thought it prudent to announce the lady's arrival here in the city to someone I know I can trust."

Edward nodded, his features still twisted in disbelief. "Indeed captain. I thank you for your gesture of faith and I will ensure, of course that your good service is recognised."

Fawn shook her head. "The lady's safety is of prime importance to me Edward. I wish nothing more, other than her story is heard by the high duke and that she is protected while the investigation into this matter is carried out."

"But of course, Fawn." Edward said, looking over his shoulder. "Where is that darn boy?" Reaching into the drawer again he shook the bell urgently.

Fawn took the time to catch Cassana's eyes and offer her support. Cassana smiled in return, and gripped her hand under the desk in thanks.

The young lad that hurried into the room via the archway very nearly tripped over his own sandals in his haste and was clothed in similar blue robes to his grandfather. His youthful boyish features were stained with panic and he had a thick black head of hair, similar perhaps to his grandfather's in his youth.

"Sorry grandfather, uh, I mean sir." he said, his green eyes blinking rapidly as he skidded to a halt before the desk. His grandfather sighed.

"Never mind that! Please will you ask the chancellor, if he has not retired for the evening, to attend me at once." Edward snapped. "And if he isn't there, go and find him for me."

"Yes…sir." Thomas said, flicking a blink-filled glance at their guests. Turning he hurried off again, hitching up his robes as he ran.

Edward shook his head and turned back to the women. "It seems I shall have to fetch the tea myself! Ladies, if you would excuse me?"

Both ladies nodded, but it was Fawn who spoke. "Thank you, Edward."

As the old man rose stiffly from his seat, he looked towards Cassana. "Do not fret my dear. Your ordeal is now over. Chancellor Valus will tend to your immediate needs and see that the High Duke is aware of what has transpired." Turning, he shuffled off towards the archway.

"Thank you for not mentioning the woodsman." Cassana whispered, when he was gone. Realising she was still holding Fawn's hand, she gently let go. "I had asked him to escort me to the city, but his reaction was venomous and I sensed that he has a history with this place."

"Your tale is yours alone to tell, my friend," Fawn said. "It is up to you how much or how little you divulge, but I do understand your reluctance to bring him into this."

Cassana sighed in relief. She had not thought of the woodsman for some time now and immediately his weary face came into her mind. Strong, purposeful and confident. It was his weary eyes that held the bitterness of his past and she was not about to betray him by drawing attention to his hand in all of this. Even though she did not know his name still. Whoever he was, she owed him her life. He had saved her from being used as a pawn, or worse and she would never forget him. Something inside of her stirred unexpectedly and she found herself hoping that she would meet him again. Perhaps then, she could prise a name from his guarded, fiery lips.

Fawn kept to her own counsel. She also sensed that there was a storm coming as somebody had taken the trouble to arrange a Reven hunting party this side of the Great Divide to try and capture the young woman. Such lengths only began to hint at what these people were capable of and as they sat in silence, lost within their own thoughts. Fawn, for the first time, began to wonder and worry about what she had gotten herself involved in.

CHAPTER SIX

"What doesn't kill us..."

The four black robed figures dragged their captive in silence along a dark roughly hewn corridor, its featureless stone walls glistening in the group's flickering torchlight. Supported under the arms by two of his nameless captors, Khadazin relaxed in their firm grip and tried to conserve his strength as best his injured body would allow him. His feet and knees scraped across the broken stone floor, stoking up fresh waves of agony as he bowed his head in submission and tried his best to focus his thoughts above his rising fear and prepare himself for what was to come.

"Be strong." Cornelius had told him. No doubt the old man knew where he was being taken and had firsthand experience of what he was about to face. Khadazin was no fool either. He knew that his questioning would probably involve torture at some stage and try as he might, he could not help but succumb to the fresh apprehension rising above his brittle determination; choking off his hunger for revenge and ultimately, his freedom. Keeping his head bowed the stonemason flicked guarded looks around his surroundings, as he tried to take the edge off his fear. The long corridor before him was blocked by the lone captor leading them on and behind him, the torchbearer followed along in silence. Their footfalls echoed loudly as they passed by two dark doors with small barred windows, that faced each other solemnly across their path. Khadazin could detect no sounds from within, and even if there were any occupants inside, they chose to keep to their own incarceration and not involve themselves in the fate of others. In his current predicament, Khadazin wished he had done the same.

The small undignified procession stopped soon after, waiting quietly as the lead figure fumbled at a closed door with a ring of jangling keys. Finally, the door was unlocked and after hauling it open, the hooded doorman watched them through. As Khadazin was dragged beyond into a shorter corridor, he heard the crash and turn of the door being locked behind him. The stonemason steeled his determination and promised himself that should the opportunity present itself, his captors would not get the chance to unlock that door again.

Dragging him on, Khadazin's captors tightened their grips on him as they neared a similarly closed door. Unlike the previous corridor, this one was devoid of any cells and as they stopped in front of the door, the torchbearer stepped by them to haul it open. Fresh torchlight burned at the stonemason's eyes as the torchbearer stepped through the opening and led them into a passageway that swept across the doorway to their left and right. Blinking the blotches from his eyes,

Khadazin could see that several torches lit the passageway on both sides, burning brightly from rusted brackets and, as the stonemason was dragged away to the left, he flicked a swift glance to his right. At the end of the long featureless passage a set of stone steps swept up into the darkness, filling Khadazin with fresh hope.

"Keep your eyes on the floor, scum."
The figure supporting him on his right snarled and punched him fiercely in the face with his gloved, free hand. Khadazin's head snapped back and silver pin-pricks of light dotted his darkening vision as his surroundings blurred on the wave of fresh pain that exploded over him.

"Better go easy on him, he has a long night ahead of him." the torchbearer pointed out, as the stonemason tasted fresh blood on his split lips.

The other hooded figures chuckled amongst themselves knowingly as they dragged the stonemason on, his head lolling drunkenly about his sagging shoulders.

Through his pain, although no worse than the rest of his agony, Khadazin kept up the pretence that he was teetering on the edge of unconsciousness. His head started to pound furiously again as they dragged him towards a closed heavy door at the end of the passage. Passing by several other closed doors Khadazin took in his surroundings through heavy lids and rolling eyes. The door they dragged him towards had a faint orange glow seeping from underneath it and as they stopped before it, Khadazin's bloody mouth twisted grimly in anticipation.

"Here we are then," said the torchbearer, his tone both motherly and mocking. Reaching out with his free hand, he turned the ringed handle and pushed it open. Immediately a blast of hot air blew from the room beyond and Khadazin's ruined nose wrinkled at the sooty fumes borne away on the thick air behind him. Wordlessly, they led the stonemason through the doorway and Khadazin found himself in a large shadowy room, its true size lost in dancing shadows and billowing cobwebs. A large, high-backed chair waited patiently in the centre of the room, facing them ominously and in one darkened corner to the left of the chair, a large brazier burned brightly. A long poker was thrust deep into the heart of its glowing hot black coals, its cool metal hungrily sucking up the heat it found there. A long table lined the wall beside the brazier and Khadazin could see numerous, wicked-looking implements laid out carefully on the darkly stained wood. Turning his head, inadvertently, the stonemason could see two pairs of manacles chained to the wall away to his right and he shuddered as he saw dark stains on the floor beneath them.

"What did I say before?" the figure to his right snarled, as he caught Khadazin looking around. He raised his free hand above his head to punch him again.

"That's enough," the torchbearer snapped, staying his companion's hand.

Amidst the momentary tension, Khadazin stood up in his captors loosening grip and moved deftly away from them. As they stood in collective surprise behind him, the stonemason strode purposely across the floor, slick with a mottled tapestry of brown stains, towards the chair. Turning, he sat down on the warm wood to face them.

"Let's get this over with then, shall we?" he said, grinning devilishly at them.

For a moment his four captors stood in stunned silence, their free hands still reaching into the folds of their dark robes for the weapons concealed there; before the torchbearer threw back his hooded head and roared with laughter.

"You're a cock-sure bastard, I'll grant you that!" he chuckled, his hood shaking from side-to-side in disbelief.

The pugilist snorted as the torchbearer motioned him forward to secure their captive. As he leant in close to secure Khadazin's wrists to the arms of the chair with the straps there, the stonemason could tell that he had been drinking, as he could smell the spirits on his foetid breath. Looking up into the shadows of the cowl, Khadazin could see a pair of dark glittering eyes staring down in hatred at him. Grinning mockingly in return, the stonemason could see his captor tense and watched triumphantly as he stalked angrily away. Khadazin's small triumph would be short lived, he was sure. But he had to take anything he could get at the moment.

Wordlessly, his captors turned and began to file from the chamber. The torchbearer stood in the open doorway for a moment and watched the man strapped to the chair. With a final shake of his concealed head he closed the door behind him. Moments later their retreating footfalls had faded into the distance, lost to an ominous silence.

Alone now and despite the heat of the room, Khadazin's naked body bristled with fresh fear as his eyes were drawn inexorably towards the table and the array of torture implements waiting there. Tongs, prongs, spikes and many other sharp and wicked looking implements waited patiently to be called to work; some of them rusted and all of them used and unclean. Calming his hurried breathing, Khadazin decided to divert his attention elsewhere and began to study his wounds. The nasty wound he had taken to his left forearm during the fight in the alleyway had scabbed over well now and was tight and numb. He still had movement in his left arm, but it felt heavy and weak. It would have to heal a lot more before he could use it confidently again, but in his current predicament he doubted whether or not he would get that chance. The wound across his ribs had fared slightly better and although the pain was still fierce, he could tell that it was shallow and starting to heal well. He would just have to be careful that he didn't exert himself too soon and open it up again.

As he checked his other cuts and bruises his ears picked up the distant sounds of approach. Licking his bloodied lips in apprehension he listened reluctantly as the footfalls became louder. Closer still, the footsteps marched in tandem with the wild beating in his heart and as they stopped outside the door, a large shadow slipped under the door and stretched menacingly out across the floor towards him. Khadazin held his breath and blinked away the bead of sweat that rolled down his forehead and stung his left eye. The door swung open.

Subconsciously Khadazin gripped the arms of the chair for support as a tall thin man in dark brown robes swept confidently into the room. Unmistakably male, because unlike his other captors, this man wore no hood. Instead he wore a black face mask that concealed the ageing, gaunt face above his lips. He had a thick, neatly trimmed, dark beard on his chin and his head was bald. As he stepped nearer, he folded his pale soft hands in the sleeves of his robes and took in Khadazin's appearance with disdainful, glittering eyes of emerald.

"There's hardly any need for us to start, is there?" he said. Khadazin was about to reply when a burly man stepped into the room behind him and moved to stand beside the first man.

This was more the kind of man Khadazin had been expecting. A big, ugly brute. Perfectly suited for the task. He had thick hands, thick arms and a face that appeared just as dense. He too wore a face mask, that only covered his eyes and did nothing to hide his concealable features. He had a scar on his right cheek and the lobe of the nearest ear was missing. Khadazin guessed that other subjects had not taken well to the horrors he had inflicted upon them and the stonemason promised himself that he would also add to the collection. The torturer's upper body was naked and he wore a long leather apron to cover his decency. A leather kilt hid away everything else that the stonemason did not want to see and he wore tattered sandals on his feet.

"I'll start when you ask me to," the burly man wheezed, in answer to the robed man's question.

"Then close the door and let us begin."

Khadazin tensed every muscle in his body as he watched the burly man close the door and then move round to stand behind him. As the robed man stood where he was and looked him up and down again, Khadazin could hear the reaching breath of the man behind him. Removing his hands from their opposite sleeves the robed man stepped forward, his lips twitching into a smile.

"I am told that you will probably want to do this the hard way, but I wanted to find out for myself first," he said. "So which will it be, stonemason?"

"I have an option?"

The man smiled. "Of course! If you tell me what I want to know, you will not suffer any hardships."

"What am I supposed to have done, to warrant such an imprisonment," Khadazin growled. "And by whose authority do you hold me?"

The man chuckled. "Come now, let us not play games shall we? You know full well why you are here. But if you would like me to spell it out for you, I shall indulge you this one time only."

"Indulge me then," Khadazin said, realising he was quickly running out of options.

"Very well," the robed man sighed. "You were hired to work at the high duke's keep and overheard a conversation that you should not have. Is that simple enough for you?"

"I don't know what you are talking about," Khadazin said earnestly. "I did not overhear any conversation."

"It is the hard way then, I see," the man said, somewhat disappointed. "Very well…"

Before Khadazin could say anything else the man's demeanour changed and he stepped in close to strike him heavily across the face. The stonemason's head snapped to the right with the impact, leaving his senses reeling behind him. As his momentum carried him over, the burly man steadied him and the chair, holding them both upright.

"We know you heard the conversation," the robed man hissed in Khadazin's ear. "What we need to know is if you have told anyone else? Tell us that, and you will be released."

Blinking back tears, Khadazin drew himself up in the chair and met the man's eyes. "I am sure you will release me, and that is why I will tell you nothing."

The man backed away, nodding to himself. "Very well, stonemason."

The burly man moved away to the table and began to slowly drift a fat hand across the implements. Khadazin felt the fear eating away at his stomach and shuddered. Should he say something? If he admitted that he had heard the conversation, would that strengthen his chances of survival, or weaken it? His naked body was glistening now with sweat from the heat of the brazier and was cold at the same time from the terror spreading through his body.

The burly man turned back to him and moved to his side. Khadazin's eyes widened with fear as he saw that he carried a long, thin sharp steel needle. Grabbing hold of the stonemasons head, he yanked it back. Leaning close, he ran the needle across his right cheekbone, over his chin and down his neck.

"Who did you tell?" the other man purred seductively, stepping closer.

Khadazin said nothing and trembled in the torturer's grip as he ran the needle back up his glistening neck. Before he could think of anything to say, fire exploded in his right ear as the needle roughly pierced through the upper cartilage. Blood splashed down his neck as he rocked back in his chair and fought against the agony. The burly man pulled the needle from his ear and held it in front of the stonemasons face.

"That's just me saying hello," he chuckled. Letting go of Khadazin's head he moved back to the table.

"Who did you tell?" the robed man asked him again.

"I told no one." Khadazin said, turning his head to

look at him through his tears of pain.

"So you did hear the conversation, then?"

"I never said that!"

"Ah, but you did," the man said. "I asked you who you told and you said no one – surely your answer should have been that you had nothing to tell?"

"You are putting words in my mouth," Khadazin said, glowering at him.

"Am I? It was you who told *no one*, not I."

Khadazin shook his head, feeling more hot blood run down his neck. The burly man was back again before he had even realised. This time he took hold of the stonemason's injured ear and wrenched it heavily. Khadazin cried out in pain as he twisted it furiously. It felt like he was going to pull it off.

"Tell me!" the robed man demanded. "Who else knows about the girl?"

Even through the pain, Khadazin's eyes widened in surprise as he managed to focus on the man, his masked face hovering in front of his.

"Yes, I see in your eyes you know of whom I speak," he continued sweetly. "That must have been a terrible thing for you to bear those few weeks?"

Khadazin said nothing, but his silence said much as the robed man's eyes flicked up to convey a message to the torturer. Khadazin felt the air flow back into his ear as the burly man released it and stepped away from view behind him. The stonemason went to nurse his ear, then remembered that his hands were still strapped tightly in place.

"Surely a secret that ate away at you?" the man went on, relentless in his pursuit for answers. "That poor girl, riding towards her fate and you, powerless to help her. I understand you are not a man to carry problems very well, it must have been such a heavy burden to carry alone? You must have told someone? Who was it?"

"I told no one," Khadazin persisted. "There's nobody in this city that I hate *that* much!"

The robed man licked his lips. "Trust me, if you continue to say nothing – there will be."

"I cannot tell you something, when there is nothing to tell!" Khadazin said, shaking as his anger finally got the better of him. He glared at the man as he stepped away from him and looked towards the torturer.

"And that is what we are here to find out, stonemason."

The man watched as the burly torturer returned. In his newly-gloved right hand he carried the hot poker from the brazier, glowering and hissing with heat. Khadazin tensed as the man stepped round in front of him and wafted it idly in front of his face. The heat blasted the sweat from his face and he could smell the fury in the iron.

Khadazin panted heavily, as his fear escaped him. The poker was held dangerously close to his right eye and he tried to avert his gaze.

"If you will not tell us, Khadazin," the robed man said. "Then perhaps the fire will coax an answer from you."

The torturer moved the poker slowly down towards his injured side and pressed it close…

Cornelius started in fright as a long, guttural scream of agony roared somewhere off in the distant dark. Burying his head in his hands, he shook backwards and forwards as he tried to comfort himself. Although he had expected them to torture the stonemason, he had hoped they would simply question the Redani at first, giving him a few days to gather his strength. Cornelius shuddered. He had only suffered the same fate as the stonemason once before and then out of some sick sense of enjoyment for his captors. The stonemason's information, or lack of it however was invaluable to these people. If it wasn't, he would have already been killed. As long as Khadazin remained alive, they both had a chance to be free of this damnable tomb.

"Be strong, Redani!" he pleaded to the dark, as the scream finally died away. "For both of our sakes."

"He's had enough for today, Borin," the robed man said finally, holding the hem of his robe over his nose to stifle the smell of cooked flesh hanging in the chamber like an accusing spectre. The torturer stepped away from the unconscious man and nodded, although he clearly looked disappointed. Moving back to the brazier he thrust the poker back into the hot coals and it hissed as it hungrily sucked up the heat again.

"Will he talk?" Borin asked amiably.

The robed man was silent for a time, as he studied the stonemason thoughtfully. The large man was slumped to one side in the chair, his body a sheen of sweat and his side still hissing as the skin cooked away slowly.

"Everyone talks," he said finally. "If not to me, then to someone else."

"Why not tell us either way," Borin said. "What does he have to lose?"

"Everything!" the robed man said meaningfully. Turning on his heels, he strode to the door and hauled it open. "We'll have him back here in a few days time. Give him chance to recover a bit and mull over what's going to happen again if he doesn't tell us. I'll send the guards to fetch him. Watch over him and leave him alone. I know you enjoy your work Borin, but there is no further sport to be found here today."

Borin nodded and watched the man head away, his robe still covering his nose and mouth. Shaking his head, he chuckled to himself. Once his companion's footsteps had faded away, he dealt a playful blow to the side of the prisoners head and watched in amusement as he tumbled to the floor, still strapped to the chair. Borin turned away to his tools and decided on which ones he would use on him next. He had never employed his skills on a foreigner before, but it was an experience he could definitely start to enjoy.

CHAPTER SEVEN

Farewells

Fawn listened to Cassana's rapid breathing for a time, before she decided to take her friend's mind off the daunting road that was about to appear before her. Once her presence in the city was known, any enemies working in the high duke's court would come to know, if they didn't already, that their attempted abduction had failed and that the young woman was now under protection of the capital. This in itself should have been enough, but once again Fawn felt that this was only the beginning.

"You should be safe here," Fawn said reassuringly, diverting Cassana's attention as she looked timidly around Edward's office. "I know very little about the chancellor, but I am told he has the ear of the high duke and Edward has worked for him for many years now!"

Cassana turned in her chair to face her and smiled weakly. "Thank you, Fawn. I need all the friends I can get at the moment."

An uncomfortable silence fell between them and Cassana could see the regret in her friends eyes. "What are your plans now, my dear friend?"

"I shall head back to Colbin and Kallum once the chancellor arrives. We shall take our lodgings in the city tonight and then head back to Havensdale in the morning." Fawn answered.

"I know we have not known each other for very long, Fawn," Cassana said shyly. "But I am going to miss you!"

Fawn blushed. "As will I you, my friend," she looked towards the passage for any sight or sound of Edward's return. "And as your friend, I would offer you this advice." She leant close, until her face was close enough to whisper in her friend's ear. "Trust your own instincts before you trust anyone else. Although we have not known each other long, I can tell that you are good judge of character. I fear you will need it in the capital, far from home and with nobody you can trust for counsel."

Cassana pulled back slowly, her face wrinkling with confusion. "But I thought you said I would be safe here?"

"You should be, my lady. But if there are people in the city who are behind all this, they may seek other alternatives now their plan has failed."

Fawn regretted her words, but she felt they had to be said as Cassana was still a young woman. A young woman who would have received a comfortable upbringing, sheltered away from the world by a proud father; she was going to have to grow up quickly if she was to get through this. Fawn didn't doubt the steely determination that she had seen on occasion in her friend's eyes, but there were many different layers of strength she would have to discover and use, if things took a turn for the worse.

Cassana bowed her head, pulling at her clothing as she digested her friend's words. She was about to reply when they heard the distant clink of a tea tray and the shuffling of elderly feet. As they both looked towards the archway, Edward hobbled into view and paused momentarily.

"Am I interrupting anything?" he asked, his eyes glinting in the candle light. When both women quickly shook their heads to indicate that in fact he was, he smiled ruefully and headed over to the desk. After some hasty rearranging, the three of them managed to clear a space on the desk for the tray. Cassana could smell the herbs, boiled to life in the hot water and she gratefully accepted the plain cup that Edward passed her.

"Here my girl, drink this!" he said, withdrawing his thin shaking hand. "It's a mixture of herbs and sugar that I often use to help calm me after a stressful day. I put double the dosage in for you."

Both women chuckled as the old man winked knowingly at them and Cassana gently sipped at the sweet hot drink, breathing in the calming aromas of mint, rosemary and chamomile.

"Hmm, that's better!" Cassana said, relaxing back into her chair with a weary sigh.

"It should also help you get to sleep tonight," Edward said. "Well it helps me, and I have to put up with Thomas' snoring from the next room."

For a while the trio sat in relative silence, sipping at their hot drinks and lost to their own silent counsel. After a while Edward stoked up some general conversation, chatting with relish about the city and the general news from around the Four Vales. It appeared

132

that the high duke's plans to strengthen trade with the Reven people had not met well in some quarters of his marble court. Many of the old hard liners had not forgiven the high duke's father for not finishing off the tribesmen when they had the clans at their mercy. For his son after all these years, to be trying to open up trade routes with them was seen by many as weak leadership. Edward vehemently did not agree. He told the women that he believed the only way to stop another uprising in the future was to trade peacefully with them. It was reported that many of the Reven people were starving because of the civil war raging across the Great Divide. Trading food, grain and other produce for the minerals found in their hills and mountains would help the two nations. Hopefully healing some of the open wounds of distrust that still bled trouble on the borders, from time to time.

"I think it's a brave thing to do," Fawn said. "It is a strong leader who offers the first hand of reconciliation, not a weak one."

"Agreed," Edward said, pleased. "Those fools who meet in the great chamber each season are too scared to voice their concerns openly. I think it is they who are weak, not the high duke. We people of the Four Vales are a soft bunch, really! Had we conquered the Reven once and for all, it would have taken centuries for us to adapt to their harsh mountainous regions and cold barren wastelands. I did not march across the mountains all those years ago to wipe the tribesmen out, I did it, as did my leader, to protect our lands – not to take theirs from them."

"You fought in the Reven War?" Cassana said, eyes alight with admiration.

"I did, my lady," Edward said softly. "Not because I

wanted to mind you, unlike some. But because I had to."

"My father was a young boy back then," Cassana said. "He was squire to my grandfather and can only recall the horror of it all in fragmented recollections these days."

"My grandfather also fought, but he died on the last day of fighting," Fawn said, her eyes distant. "My father was a newly born back then, too young for anything other than the milk from his mother."

They sat quietly in respect for a moment, before Edward spoke again.

"Perhaps, Lady Byron, you are best placed to offer some thoughts on this current topic of debate?"

"I am, sir?" Cassana answered, perplexed as she sipped at her tea.

"Well yes, that's why you are here, isn't it?" Edward said, frowning.

Cassana blinked in realisation. She had not really thought about her real reason for coming to the city, since the attack.

"Well, yes I was, I mean, I am!" she said finally. "My father however did not issue me with any specific instructions, or offer me advice – other than to say that I am his voice in all discussions and that he trusts my judgement above that of all other men."

"A high vote of confidence indeed then," Edward admitted, smiling through sips of his tea. "So, while we await my grandson's pathetic pursuit of the chancellor, let us use this topic to test your judgement." His eyes blazed with youthful mischief.

Cassana looked to Fawn and was relieved to see that she was smiling, as she twisted a lock of her thick, dark hair idly around one of her fingers. Cassana nodded, although somewhat reluctantly.

"Very well," Edward said. "So what are the views of the one person in this room who can speak first-hand about the Reven and their current predicament?"

Cassana chewed her lip. "Well, the people of Highwater live daily with the threat of attack and sleep under the constant shadow of the Reven. Our borders however are carefully watched for those who try to cross the Great Divide and enter the Four Vales. Equally, we guard against those who would cross into the Reven lands to try and mine the precious minerals from land that does not belong to them."

"Evidently by your recent experiences, not close enough." Edward said, raising a calming hand as Cassana's face darkened. "I am testing you girl, like others may do. I however, have nothing to gain and seek only to help your skills flourish."

"Sorry, Edward," Cassana said, dealing him an apologetic smile. "It is true, as you say, that the borders are very hard to monitor. There are many passes and trails through the mountains that cannot be constantly watched and, sadly, because of this, many smugglers operate from inside the Four Vales. However, with Highwater Keep heavily garrisoned, the main pass into our country is blocked; keeping immigrant numbers down and acting as a constant deterrent to any chieftains with aspirations to emulate Reven Skarl."

"A very good defence, I am sure," Edward said. "So I can sleep safely in my bed, knowing that the Lord Byron has my best interests at heart. But what about the Reven people? What is their future? Not as bright as ours, I fear."

Cassana had spoken at length with her father about the Reven over the years and although her father was a great warrior, he was a better leader. It was testament to his abilities of office that the city of Highwater thrived despite its location, and as a man, he held much sympathy for the Reven people. While their women and children starved, the men fought for dominance over their neighbours. Holding on to a long-dead torch of something they would never have, strength and unity. Reven Skarl had managed it, uniting the warring clans together for nearly a year, with promises of a better life for future generations. Inadvertently, he had set the Reven people on a path to war and famine, rather than peace and prosperity. Like all of his kind before him, he had been a man of strength and courage, seeking only to brutally conquer and better those around him. He was a warlord, not a scholar. Had he been the latter, he may have sought peace with the Four Vales, rather than trying to take their lands from them. If he had, their nation could have flourished. Sadly, it has not.

"The Reven are sadly on a road to destruction," Cassana said. "Mistrust, hatred and brutality flow through the veins of the clans. They fear losing what they have to their neighbors', rather than focusing on their starving people. Children often come to the walls of Highwater Keep, running away from their proud mothers to beg for food. They risk much by doing this and yet still they come, so desperate is their need that they must turn to an enemy that their parents blame all their hardships upon."

"And what do the soldiers of the keep do?" Fawn dared to ask. Edward nodded his head, suggesting that he had been tempted to ask the same question.

"Many soldiers throw bread and food to them, although under current law they are not supposed to. But sometimes there are just too many to feed, and for

136

fear of starting a fight below, they are simply ignored. The garrison priests sometimes offer them prayers of protection from the battlements, but most who come do not understand our tongue."

"What happens to them?" Edward asked.

Cassana sighed. "They normally leave when the sun begins to fade, their bellies forcing them to look elsewhere. It is a sad thing to witness, especially when there is little we can do to help, as things stand."

"Some would say that the best thing to do is to put them out of their misery," Edward said sadly. "What would you answer to that, my lady?"

"I would refute that argument," Cassana said swiftly. "I would support the high duke's plans to open up trade – rather than open up their throats."

"Very good," Edward said, putting his empty cup back on the tray. "But that would open you up to further enemies at court. If you wish to put your views so openly on the table, you must also be prepared for the consequences."

"Consequences?" Cassana asked reluctantly.

Edward nodded. "High Duke Stromn has few people on his side with this proposed policy. If you openly join his side in any debates, you will be ostracised by the majority for being weak. My advice, as it will only be debated for now, is to keep your personal views to yourself. Tell only what you see, rather than what you feel. If it is Highwater's wish to support the high duke, you should pass on your thoughts to your father so that when the time comes, he can vote accordingly."

"I agree," Fawn said. "Stay neutral, stay quiet if you can. Remember you told me that you are here to represent your father in his absence, not to change the

137

world."

Edward chuckled suddenly. "With all due respect my lady, most people will not listen to you anyhow. Their heads are too far up their..." he paused, coughing meaningfully. "Umm, too far up their own social ladder!"

Cassana laughed and turned to look at Fawn. She looked back at her and shook her head as she chortled.

"So what other news, Edward?" Fawn asked the old man, as she finished her tea. Edward frowned, as he sifted through matters of little importance.

"Well, as you probably both know, the harvest games will be held a week later this year, as the new arena is still being constructed."

Cassana nodded. Her father had told her about that, following his last visit to the city. Someone had set fire to the old arena the previous year, but was never caught. Every year the city hosted a grand tournament, drawing competitors from all across the Four Vales. Many events were held and all were welcomed and encouraged to compete. From running to wrestling, archery to jousting, all kinds of events were held to find the champion in that particular field. Many knights entered and most events were normally won by someone already on the high duke's chivalric list. But every once in a while a champion rose up from out of the general populace to lift a trophy and receive the adulation of all.

Cassana's own father himself had lifted the prize for the best swordsman when he was only twenty. He had defeated the reigning champion of some seven years in a memorable duel that had lasted many rounds, to lift the coveted silver blade. A rapier of pure silver, its hilt wreathed with platinum and encrusted with diamonds and rubies. Sadly, he had lost the title a year later to an experienced swordsman from Ilithia, but he still recalled that moment with great pride and his name was forever remembered on the city's roll of honours.

"What you didn't probably know is that several local groups have called for the games to be scrapped, as they say that some of the events are fixed."

"Fixed?" Fawn asked. "How do they know that, and who are they?"

Edward snorted. "Well, one of these fools is a local merchant. He had bet heavily on his son getting into the final of the jousting, although in all honesty he never really had a chance of winning it. Unfortunately for him, his son lost in the first round to the eventual winner and his father believes that the draw was rigged."

"Sounds like sour milk to me!" Fawn observed.

"Very sour," Edward replied. "He lost a small fortune, and cannot believe that it was just plain bad luck... or stupidity on his part. His son, no matter how skilled was still only a lowly squire and had no chance of winning. The merchant himself runs a small guild for independents; they come together to help each other in the competitive trade market – jointly investing their money in stock to try and compete with the bigger merchant companies. He naturally has the backing of his guild, as his portion of investment is important to them all."

"But even if they were successful in getting the games cancelled, he would never get his money back, would he?" Cassana surmised.

"Indeed not," Edward answered. "Sadly for him, his pockets are not as deep as the love he has for his son. Once the arena is complete the games will progress regardless, no matter what they say."

"Do you think he was behind the arson, then?" Fawn asked quietly.

Edward nodded, as he lent closer over the table. "Most people believe that to be true, but without proof, any accusations are as weak as the merchant's own case for event fixing."

"Losing is all the more difficult when money is involved," Cassana quoted, but she could not recall where she had heard that from.

"Any other news of note, Edward?" Fawn enquired.

Edward's face darkened. "I suppose I should tell you about some terrible happenings in the poor districts of the city, although it is very distressing and I apologise in advance. There is a killer on the loose at the moment. Five victims in as many weeks, normally ladies of the night, and all of them gutted like fish."

Revulsion showed on both women's faces and Cassana looked at Fawn in horror.

"Do the Watch have any clues?" Fawn dared to ask, not sure if she really wanted to hear any more details.

"Nay lady," Edward shook his head. "Only that they take place late at night and that nobody has yet managed to catch sight of this murderer. As to why this is happening, why this person commits these despicable acts, who can tell. There are many reasons, many causes for such things to happen. But there are no excuses."

"That is awful," Cassana said, shocked. "I know that in cities murders often happen, but a serial killer? That must be very worrying for everyone?"

"Indeed so, my lady," Edward agreed. "The high duke has offered twenty thousand crowns for information that leads to the killer's capture."

140

Fawn whistled. "Let's hope that they don't capture Devlin Hawke that week as well then. Otherwise the high duke's coffers will be very low, indeed."

Edward nodded, but did not smile. "Forgive me, captain, but I get sick of hearing that name. Every despatch I get from the West and North Vales seem to have some mention of that blasted brigand. He's taken this, he's stolen that. He did this to them and stuck two fingers up to that! The man's a blasted nuisance, the sooner he swings from a gallows, the better for my eyesight."

"Some people actually idolise him," Fawn admitted, somewhat begrudgingly.

"Bah!" Edward complained angrily. "Fools, I call them. Championing anything or anyone that sticks the proverbial up to the authorities. Always too busy complaining about everything that doesn't matter, it makes me sick."

"I would have never guessed, Edward!" Fawn said, from behind a bright smile.

Edward laughed, shaking his head as he squinted at the captain in mock anger across the desk. "I guess the only scant consolation for those people who have suffered at his groups hands, is that they only take possessions not lives with them, as they disappear back into the forests they hide in. Unlike some of the other brigands around the region."

"Many say he is actually quite gallant, speaking politely as he robs them." Fawn added, looking at Cassana.

"Hmpf!" Edward scoffed, drawing her attention back. "That's supposed to make them feel better, is it?"

"No," Fawn said, defending herself. "Just reporting what I heard, that's all."

Edward waved a thin hand at all of the despatches piling up on his desk. "No need to tell me that girl, I know that already."

Cassana smiled, letting herself enjoy the prickly banter. She was about to offer that little is known about the highwayman Devlin Hawke beyond his name, when they heard the sounds of urgent approach from the passageway behind Edward's left ear. All attention was now turned to the imminent arrival and a man's voice could be heard, muttering in exasperation.

"This had better be worth it, Thomas!"

As they neared the office, Thomas could be heard mumbling and stammering his assurances that his grandfather had been earnest in his request. Fawn flicked a glance to Edward and could see that he was smiling fondly.

"So, what's so important Edward, that you…"

The man who strode into the room almost came to a halt, as his surprise choked off the rest of his words and Thomas nearly walked into the back of him.

"Forgive me, Edward," the man continued, expertly regaining his composure as his piercing green eyes took in the old man's guests. Edward rose stiffly to acknowledge his presence and the two women felt compelled to do likewise.

Cassana had been around many high officials before, but none of them quite radiated the same air of confidence and assurance that this man did. Dressed in long flowing robes of blue velvet, which judging by the current fashion in the room must have been the symbol of the chancellor's office, his assured middle-aged features creased with a warm smile as he offered both ladies a fluid, courteous bow. With his hair greying at his temples and his features stained by the ravages of office, the man walked towards Edward, silently questioning him with an encouraging rise of his greying eyebrows.

"Chancellor Valus, may I present Captain Ardent of the Havensdale militia," Edward said, motioning to Fawn as she moved round the table to offer him a hand. The chancellor took her offer of greeting by the fingers and kissed the back of her slender hand.

"Greetings, captain," he said, smiling warmly.

"Chancellor Valus," Fawn replied, tilting her head in greeting as she received her hand back.

"May I also take the pleasure in presenting Lady Cassana Byron of Highwater," Edward did not need to gesture to his final guest and Cassana was taken aback by the look of shock that filled the chancellor's face as his eyes darted to find her.

"M-my Lady Byron," he said, somewhat less-assured now. "Welcome to Karick, we had expected you to arrive yesterday!"

He took Cassana's shaking hand and kissed the back of it, as he had with Fawn. His skin was smooth, like many of his brethren in high-office and Cassana found his hand cold and clammy.

"Your Excellency," she said, curtseying formally.

The chancellor was quick to release her hand and he turned to take all three of them in. "May I apologise for my sudden look of confusion ladies, I did not expect to find such distinguished company in my own offices at such an hour." He wrung his hands together as he drew in their full attention with an apologetic smile. "I would have expected you to have arrived and formally announced your party in the capital in the usual manner. My lady?"

Cassana looked to Edward and Fawn for assistance

and thankfully, it was Edward who took hold of the proceedings for her.

"I am sorry to announce sir, that Lady Byron's party were ambushed on their way to the city and her entourage brutally killed."

Any of the weight that Cassana still bore was passed immediately on to the chancellor. His face froze with horror and he looked fearfully towards her.

"Fortunately for us, Lady Byron escaped their clutches and made it safely to Havensdale. Captain Ardent decided that the best course of action was to safely escort Lady Byron to the city so that she could report these terrible recent events."

"A very wise decision indeed," the chancellor said, turning his attention briefly to Fawn. "You have performed a noble service to the Four Vales and I am sure your bravery and generosity will not go unnoticed, my lady!"

Fawn nodded her thanks as the chancellor turned his urgent attentions back on Cassana.

"I am truly sorry for your loss, Lady Byron," he said earnestly. "Where did this all happen? I will see to it personally that their bodies are recovered and shown the honours they deserve?"

Fawn listened intently as Cassana recounted her tale of those terrible events. As she spoke, Fawn watched the chancellor. He was typical of his kind, outwardly very concerned for her welfare, but his posture and demeanour appeared impatient. People in his position always had too much to do and so little time to fit everything in. Adhering to etiquette, he would see to her needs no doubt and then palm her off to the high duke's office as soon as he could. Cassana probably read that too, but she had been around enough officials in her time to play her role in the game. As long as the chancellor saw to her safety, that was all that mattered here.

Everything changed however, when Cassana mentioned that her attackers had been Reven, and that they were trying to capture her, not kill her. Chancellor Valus' face nearly slipped off his chin and he covered his mouth to hide his disgust.

"This is grave news," he said, shaking his head darkly as he listened to his own thoughts. "Grave news indeed!"

Cassana was regaining some of her composure as the chancellor's deserted him and she took hold of the proceedings with a sudden maturity well above her years.

"I am aware chancellor that this news will cast a dark shadow over the meeting, the day after tomorrow," she said, her voice clear and confident. "And I am also aware of the delicate position that the high duke finds himself in, over his proposed policy to start trade with the Reven people. It is not my wish to bring such bad news to the table and undermine the high duke's position, all I wish is for the matter to be investigated and the reason for my attempted abduction to be discovered."

Chancellor Valus was watching her intently now and his green eyes blazed with intensity. "But of course, my lady. That is natural, I would expect nothing less. I can also see that you are indeed your father's daughter and can quickly grasp the intricacies of state. I, of course, will play my part and arrange a meeting with the high duke for tomorrow so that you may tell him first-hand of these terrible circumstances, before you attend the Valian Council the following day. In the meantime I shall ensure that you are given care and attention."

He turned to Thomas, who was looking aghast at all he had heard. As he ordered the boy off to find his housekeeper so that she may come and attend to Lady Byron, Cassana let out a soft breath and met the gazes of the others in the room. Fawn offered her a smile of support and Edward nodded supportively, winking at her.

"Now, my ladies," the chancellor said, turning back, and Cassana barely managed to drop her smile in time. "If you would excuse me, I must attend to matters that arise on the back of this. Rest assured my lady, that I will not divulge any of this until we have spoken later. As you have already indicated, any news of Reven involvement in this matter could seriously undermine everything the high duke wishes to achieve. I will arrange, as I have already indicated, a private meeting for you for tomorrow with the high duke himself. It will be for you and him to decide whether the identity of your attackers remains hidden, not I."

He turned to Fawn and bowed again. "Captain," he said, acknowledging her rank once more. "Rest assured, I will see to it personally that you are rewarded for your involvement in this matter. If there is anything my office can do in the meantime, please speak to Edward." Fawn nodded her thanks, but remained quiet.

Turning back to Cassana, he took both her hands in his and smiled into her eyes.

"Eat, bathe and rest well my lady," he said. "My housekeeper Eleanor will attend to you presently and I will see that your belongings are delivered to your quarters. Leave the matter with me for now, we will get to the bottom of this, I promise you!"

Cassana smiled. "Thank you, Chancellor Valus."

With that, the man released her hands and after nodding to Edward, he turned on his sandalled heels and swept urgently from the room.

After he was out of sight and sound, Edward turned to Cassana and clapped his hands together.

"Very good, young lady," he said. "A terrible case, eloquently and concisely put. The chancellor will no doubt pass it on to the high duke now. But he is a thorough man and will not wash his hands with it. If there is anything further he can do, I am sure he will help you. He is the high duke's man and with your statement about not wishing to undermine him, he is now an ally of yours also."

Cassana blinked. "Do you really think so, Edward?"

"Indeed, my lady," Edward replied. "You have inadvertently picked a wise ally. Trust me, I have worked for him for fifteen years now. Chancellor Valus is a man you need to keep on side. He is a dangerous man to cross swords with, but as an ally, there is no one better in the high duke's court."

Cassana chewed over the information as her heart pounded loudly in her chest. She had not decided yet whether or not to put the information about the Reven out into the open domain. Proceedings were moving far too rapidly now for her young mind to keep up with. Perhaps her head would be clearer after a hot bath and a hearty meal. The high duke was an honourable man, perhaps it would be best to allow him to decide. As long as she had his support to find the real reason behind all this, what did it matter if her attackers became bandits, as far as everyone else was concerned.

"I can see that you have a lot on your mind now, my lady," Fawn observed. "I think it is time for me to be on my way."

Cassana turned to her friend and felt her throat thicken with emotion.

"Ahem," Edward said, tidying up the tea cups. "I'll just take these off, give you time to say your goodbyes in peace. Fawn, as always it is a pleasure, if somewhat a rarity these days."

Fawn helped the man with the tray and gave him a kiss on one cheek. "I'll see you again soon, old friend. In better circumstances next time, hopefully."

"Agreed," he said. "I'll make sure you are not forgotten in all this, be sure of that."

Fawn nodded modestly as he excused himself, and clinked his way out of the room.

"But make sure you come a bit earlier next time," he called back, as he disappeared. "I am not used to these late nights nowadays…"

Fawn smiled and turned back to Cassana, who was crying now. Moving silently to her, she wrapped her in a warm embrace.

"You'll be fine," she said, leaning back in her arms. "You are stronger than you believe. I said it before, I'll say it again, trust in yourself before all others. If you do, you'll get through this."

Cassana's glistening eyes held Fawn's as she sniffed and blinked away her sadness. "I cannot thank you enough for what you have done for me, Fawn."

Fawn smiled, kissing her on the forehead and holding her close again as she felt her trembling. "The only reward that I need is that you see this safely through to the end, Cassana. After the dust has settled, come and see me – you will always be welcome in Havensdale."

Cassana nodded into her shoulder. "I promise, I will. Perhaps you could come and visit Highwater too? I want you to meet my father and after he has heard about all of this, I am sure he will want to meet you as well!"

"I would like that very much, Cassana," Fawn said, pulling back to hold her at arms length. "Right, this is it. No farewells, only a parting of friends."

"Until next time," Cassana said, as they slipped apart.

Fawn backed towards the door, smiling. "I'll send word to your father as promised, if I don't hear from you inside of two weeks, Cassana."

The young woman nodded, fighting back tears again. "Thank you, my friend."

Smiling warmly, Fawn turned, hauled open the door and stepped out into the fresh night air. The last glimpse she got of Cassana, as she turned back to close the door behind her, was of the young woman watching her forlornly.

Outside, the courtyard was quiet now. The stars were in bright attendance in a clear, dark night sky and a dog barked away, somewhere off to her left. Breathing deeply Fawn closed her eyes and allowed the fresh night air to wash over her. As she started towards the stables to look for Colbin and Kallum, who were most probably in the barracks having a drink by now, she finally allowed her tears to fall.

Edward waited quietly in the corridor beyond the archway for a few minutes more, allowing the young woman to regain some of her composure. He had overheard the last few exchanges of their conversation and was pleased that the captain had her charges' best interests at heart. It was rare these days to find somebody willing to do something and not require anything in return. Of course, Edward was certain that once High Duke Karian heard of Lady Byron's terrible misfortune, his office would notify her father immediately. But it didn't hurt to have a guardian watching out for you, just in case the matter was lost in amongst the other piles of politics and bureaucracy stacking up around the capital. Edward's own rising pile of work was testament to that.

"Can I get you anything else Lady Byron, whilst we wait?" Edward coughed politely as he shuffled noisily back into the room.

Cassana was still staring at the closed door and she turned, hastily wiping away the tears from her reddened eyes.

"I am fine, thank you, Edward," she said, forcing a smile. "I might just take a seat again, however, if I may?" She followed Edward's gesturing arm to a seat and took up residence there again.

"I think you have found a good friend, in Captain Ardent," the old man observed, sitting across from her with a weary grunt as he settled his bones. Cassana nodded, but remained silent, as she fiddled and wringed her hands nervously under the desk.

"I knew her father very well, before he married and was moved to Havensdale years ago," Edward continued. "He was, and to my knowledge still is, a loyal servant to the high duke and, as reward for his faithful service, he was given the post as mayor there. Sometimes, it is better to spread your good cards out across your table of power, rather than keep them with you safely under your seat."

Cassana smiled brightly, her plain face lighting up with genuine strength and subtle beauty. "Eloquently put, Edward! I did not have the chance to meet with him, sadly. But in his absence I was privileged to have met his daughter."

"A lovely young lady, reminds me of her mother at the same age." Edward said, wistfully.

"I did not meet her, either." Cassana said.

"Well, I am sure you will at some stage of your adventure," Edward said idly, as he picked at the corner of a parchment tucked deep at the bottom of a tall stack of parchments.

As Cassana was about to say more, they heard the echoing approach of hurried feet again and both turned to witness the arrival of a short, middle-aged woman. She was dressed in a long flowing dark skirt, protected by an apron and wore a pretty blouse with a high, lace-frilled neck and similarly fashioned long sleeves. Her long greying hair was twisted into a bun on the top of her head and her thin, harsh face softened quickly into a smile as she met their welcoming stares.

"Sir, my lady," she greeted them, curtseying. Her green eyes held them both, as she took in Cassana's appearance over her thin, sharp nose.

Edward rose, forcing Cassana to follow him as she remembered that she was now amongst those who adhered to formality and recognised her social class and standing.

"Madam Grey, I am sure that Thomas has already passed on instructions from Chancellor Valus, with regards to our care of duty for Lady Byron, has he not?"

"That he has, Mister Neve," she replied, curtseying again. "I am now at your service, my lady. My staff are already preparing a lovely quiet room and a bath for you in the west wing of the keep. I have just sent Master Thomas on to the kitchens with instructions for the chef to prepare you a lovely supper, also, my lady!"

"Thank you very much, Madam Grey," Cassana said, smiling.

"Excellent!" Edward said, clapping his hands together softly. "My lady, it has been a pleasure." He bowed stiffly.

Cassana smiled. "Thank you so much for all of your help, sir. I hope we may share tea again, before I depart for home?"

"I am sure you will be far too busy to accommodate an old man, my lady," Edward replied, a glint of a smile in his eyes. He turned his attentions to the chancellor's housekeeper. "Madam Grey, I will detain you and Lady Byron no longer. If you would be so kind?"

The housekeeper nodded. "My lady, if you would be so kind as to follow me, I shall escort you to your quarters."

Cassana reached for her belongings, but Edward quickly waved her away from them.

"Leave them, my lady," he said firmly. "I shall have Thomas bring them to you, as soon as he returns from his errand."

Cassana nodded her thanks, as Madam Grey hovered impatiently. "Thank you, sir! Until next time, then?"

Edward smiled and offered her a slight bow, watching as she followed the housekeeper out of the room through the archway. Shuffling over to the heavy door, he locked it with an old iron key from within the pocket of his robes. Turning, he went around his office, snuffing out most of the candles.

As he headed back to his chair and sat down, a swift spasm of pain shot through his old body.

"The only thing that seems to get stiff these days is

my blasted back!" he mumbled to himself ruefully, as he waited uncomfortably for the return of his grandson.

"Judging by the circumstances of your arrival, my lady," Madam Grey said to Cassana, as she led her hurriedly through a network of servants' passages. "I thought it prudent to take you to your quarters via a less public way."

Cassana thanked her and concentrated on keeping up with the woman as she took her swiftly through several more dimly lit corridors and up two flights of carpeted stairs. The rest of their breathless journey was undertaken in silence and Cassana soon became totally lost. As they climbed yet another set of spiralling stairs, Cassana could not help but be impressed by the design behind the high duke's keep. All of the staff could travel swiftly from wing to floor, conducting the daily maintenance of the keep, without interrupting the affairs of those they served. Her father's household back home was far more modest in design and required only a handful of such corridors.

After several minutes climbing the spiral staircase Madam Grey finally stopped at a closed wooden door. An oil lamp burned brightly from a bracketed hanger above the doorway and Cassana could see a wooden sign on the back of the door that read 'West Wing – Floor Three.'

Opening the door, Cassana's guide led her onto a magnificent landing. A lushly soft red carpet swept away from her, enticing them on through the white plastered walls that flanked them on both sides. Deep red velvet drapes were pulled close about a quarter of the way along the corridor on their left and Cassana felt a breath of air from the window beyond as she went by.

Halfway along the landing on their right, a large door was closed and Cassana could also see another draped window further down on the left. At the far end of the corridor, she could barely make out the top of a stairway, that dropped from view to the lower levels of the keep. Three large chandeliers hung from the high ceiling, their candle-flame lights fuelled by oil and as Madam Grey stopped at the doorway, Cassana studied the magnificent oil painting hanging on the wall opposite. The gilded frame was wreathed in golden leaves and the canvas depicted a beautiful landscape scene of a shimmering waterfall, its foaming diamond waters cascading down into a large pool of silver, brought to life by the watchful full moon in a clear, starlit, dark blue night sky. Tall, dark trees protected the pool and the plaque underneath the highly skilled work of art told her that it was a scene of the Silver Falls, in the South Vales.

"Your quarters, my lady," Madam Grey announced drawing back her attention as she was about to try and read the artist's name.

Opening the door, the housekeeper curtseyed, sweeping her left arm in a graceful arc to welcome her inside. As Cassana stepped by, she noticed a plaque on the door that told her she would be spending her time in the Silver Falls suite. The portrait would only be the beginning of Cassana's marvel that night, as Madam Grey showed her around her quarters that she would soon discover encompassed the entire third floor of the west wing. The immediate room was a large and elegantly furnished reception room with beautiful soft chairs and sofas, arranged around an antique low table. Soft natural candlelight cast a serene pallor over the room and Cassana barely had time to take in several other paintings of landscapes and portraits hanging from the subtle blue walls, as Madam Grey led her across the deep green carpeted floor towards a door to their left, ignoring a door that had faced them across the reception room as they entered. The next room was a large bathroom. The walls and floors of the room were made entirely of finely carved and decorated marble. A large walk-in-bath waited enticingly in the centre of the room; its waters steaming invitingly and heavily scented with oils and rose petals. Madam Grey directed Cassana's wide eyes to the soft white robes hanging from hooks on the marble walls to their right.

"When you feel ready my lady, feel free to relax and ease the strains from your weary limbs."

"Indeed I shall, Madam Grey. Thank you!" Cassana said, failing to keep the childlike excitement from conquering her voice. She had never seen quarters like this before, never! Her own quarters back home would have already fitted twice into these two large rooms, and she hadn't even seen her sleeping quarters yet!

As they faced the bath, Madam Grey led them on through an archway to their right. Beyond, Cassana found herself in paradise. A huge bedroom magnificently furnished with an antique dresser, mirrors, paintings and a writing desk. The enormous four poster bed in the centre of the marble room was covered in plump soft pillows and deep blue bed sheets. Four long silk drapes were tied back on each post, ready to protect the sleeper's dignity. To her right Cassana could see a walk-in wardrobe and as she wandered across the marble floor, marvelling at a large fur rug, she ran one excited finger over the leather back of the large sofa that was positioned in front of a low marble breakfast table. A large bookcase lined the wall next to the walk-in wardrobe and Cassana promised to choose herself a suitable read that matched her current mood.

"I will see to it, my lady, that you have suitable attire available to you for your council meetings and the closing function, later this week," Madam Grey promised her.

"That would be wonderful, thank you," Cassana said gratefully. All of her belongings were probably still in her tent, back in Fox Glade.

Madam Grey smiled. "Relax a while, my lady. I will see to it that your supper is brought to you in an hour, allowing you time to bathe and rest. In the meantime, if you require anything, pull the cord next to your bed and I will send someone to attend to you."

Cassana smiled and acknowledged the housekeeper's curtsey as she excused herself, leaving through a door that took her back into the reception room. As Cassana waited for the main door to close, she listened to her heart beat thrumming rapidly with, for once, excitement and pleasure, rather than fear and panic.

Once the door had closed, Cassana moved and sat at the dresser. Merrily, she scanned the array of perfumes, powders and make-up. It was then that she caught herself in the mirror and paused. Her eyes were lined by stress and dark with worry, giving herself a haunted look. Her complexion was also filthy, dusted from her journey and streaked by dry tears. She smiled suddenly, laughing at her appearance. Anyone back home would probably not recognise her now, if she were to walk into the room. She smirked at herself, but her reflection's smile was tinged with apathy and did not share in her amusement. Hide behind your smile if you wish, it accused her, but a terrible thing has happened to you and no amount of merriment or make-up will hide away your demons for you.

Scowling, she picked up an ornate ivory brush with gold teeth and fought against her tangled hair as she brushed the knots free. After a few fruitless attempts, she was forced to give up; deciding that she was in desperate need of a bath. Rising stiffly from the dresser, she kicked off her boots and slowly stripped off her clothes. Checking the healing progress of the bruises and cuts on her lean body, she stretched out her aches and pains for a few moments, before moving eagerly through to the bathroom.

Once Cassana had eventually acclimatised to the heat of the bath and had walked down the last few steps to lay back in the water, she found it to be a heady concoction of calming scents and muscle relaxing sensations. For a long while she seemingly floated away on a carpet of steam, finally allowing herself to relax and clearing her mind of any thoughts for a while. As she drifted sedately in the bath she could feel her weariness start to creep up on her and for a time she gave in to the demands of the day, before coming awake with a start. Sighing, she reluctantly hauled herself out of the bath and dried herself off. Timely indeed, for she heard a brusque knocking on the door to her suite that sent her hurriedly and hungrily to answer it.

CHAPTER EIGHT

Secrets and Lies

Cassana woke with a start, peering dazedly through a curtain of wild hair and heavy eyelids. For a while her senses failed her as she tried to focus on her surroundings. Finally, as she struggled up from a maze of soft sheets, she could tell that she was in her bed in the Silver Falls suite. Groaning, she lay back down as her head began to pound furiously and she covered her eyes with her hands, massaging her temples with each forefinger. A sparse glow from a lamp shed a placid light across the room and when she felt her head would allow her to look again, she could see her half-eaten supper on a silver tray, laying forgotten on her breakfast table.

Of course! Cassana remembered now. She had only just got out of the bath and dried herself off, having drifted off for some time, when Madam Grey knocked on her door. Hurriedly dressing in her soft robes, she had received a light supper from the chancellor's housekeeper and her apologies that her master had not been able to come and see her. Cassana had thanked her and Madam Grey had left her to her supper, with assurances of the chancellor's attendance, early the next morning. After she had gone, Cassana sat in her bedroom, idly sipping at the lovely onion soup and pulling at the soft bread roll. After she had finished the soup, she cut a slice of cheddar from the cheese dish and poured herself a cup of tea from the silver pot. Finally, full and not yet finished, Edward's tea must have started to work itself into her system, as a heavy weariness came upon her. Finishing off her tea, Cassana had retired for the night.

Sitting up gingerly, Cassana felt her stomach knot with pain. Laying on her side, she chewed her lip until the pain had subsided. Finally, after nearly an hour, she was able to get out of bed and wash. After she had nibbled on a bit more of her supper, she sat at the dresser and began to comb her hair and apply her make-up and perfume. When she was done, she found a familiar face looking back at her. She had been away for quite a while now, but as she studied herself a little too closely, she could still detect her weariness and the lines of stress beneath the eye and face make-up. As she applied some colour to her lips, she heard a loud knock at the front door of her suite. Hurriedly applying some Moon Mist perfume to her wrists and neck, she wrapped herself tightly in her robes and raced through to the reception room.

As she unlocked and opened the door, bright mid-morning sunshine dazzled her eyes as the staff had already gone along the landing and pulled back the drapes. Shielding her eyes, she could barely pick out the blotchy shape of Madam Grey.

"Good morning, my lady," she greeted. "I thought it wise to let you sleep in longer this morning, as you did not supper until very late."

"Thank you, Madam Grey," Cassana replied, allowing the housekeeper to enter. As she turned, she could see that she carried a breakfast tray, laden with an enticing array of food. Placing the tray on the reception table, Madam Grey retrieved the supper tray from Cassana's bed chamber.

"Was everything to your liking, my lady?" she enquired, studying the remnants.

"Fine, thank you," Cassana said. "However, I think I must have eaten a bit too late, as I have terrible stomach pains and the stirrings of a furious headache."

Pity crossed Madam Grey's face. "I am sorry to hear that, my lady. I shall fetch you some remedies that will help to calm your ailments."

Cassana smiled with relief. "That would be wonderful, thank you. I fear my journey has taken much from me and I have a busy schedule ahead of me the next five days. I will need to be at my best, if I am to see this through."

Madam Grey curtseyed. "Of course, Lady Byron. Chancellor Valus asked me to inform you that he will attend to you within the hour."

"Thank you," Cassana said. "Would you be so kind, as to ensure that we have tea when he arrives?"

"Of course, my lady. And I shall also bring you some formal wear to choose from, before he arrives." Madam Grey curtseyed once more and left the reception room hurriedly, closing the door behind her.

Cassana took her seat and attended to her breakfast. Despite her knotting stomach, she still managed to get through all of the soft, buttery pastries, jams and bread rolls. To finish, she washed away the sweet, stickiness on her lips, with a large glass of fresh apple juice. After that, Cassana felt much better and a short while later, Madam Grey returned to collect the tray and deliver her some clothes, as promised. Thanking the woman, she saw her to the door and then hurriedly selected the smartest casual dress from the three, hanging the other two elegant dresses in the walk-in wardrobe. The wardrobe was huge and the two dresses, no matter how beautiful and captivating, looked forlorn and lost in there. As Cassana fixed her hair into a neat bun with pins, she studied herself in a long mirror in the wardrobe. Normally, Cassana would have someone to tend to her hair for her, but she was enjoying the control she had away from home and despite the grandeur of her surroundings, she felt that she was free and not being smothered by the affections of a doting father for once. The long emerald green dress she wore was plain and simple, but still beautiful. Unlike the other two dresses, this one had a high neck line, perfect for matters of state and informal meetings. She was not trying to impress, or seduce anyone. If she was, she would have chosen one of the other two dresses, that were very low cut and had more feisty colourings of red and midnight blue.

After adjusting her hair several more times, Cassana was finally happy with her efforts and returned to the reception room to wait for the chancellor. She didn't have to wait too long and snapped to attention when three firm knocks shook her from her thoughts.

"Come in chancellor," she said, showing him in with a smile. There was better light in the room now as Cassana had lit some more lamps and candles. "Please, have a seat, sir!"

161

"Thank you Lady Byron, but I am afraid I cannot stay."

Cassana could see that the chancellor, dressed once again in his formal blue robes of office, was exhausted. His face was pale, more so than normal and his eyes were heavy from lack of sleep. Quickly closing the door behind him he turned to face her once again, his face grave and his eyes haunted.

"My lady," he said falteringly, his usual strong demeanour troubled. "I bring grave news from the high duke. I have told him of your arrival and of the fact that you seek an audience with him, and indeed he was all ready to meet with you this afternoon." He took her hands in his and Cassana could feel his cold hands trembling nervously.

"But a terrible thing has happened, and I do not know if it is connected with your misfortune," he paused, as his eyes sifted through his thoughts for the correct words. "Only this morning, the high duke's office received intelligence that a threat has been made against the high duke, his family and the council."

Cassana gasped. "A threat? What? Not to kill?"

"At this stage, who can tell, my lady. But we cannot afford to take any threats against the high duke's safety lightly."

"Of course not, sir." Cassana's mind was beginning to work overtime and she felt her headache start to return.

"Perhaps the people behind your attempted abduction are also plotting other foul deeds to other members of the Valian Council." the chancellor offered. "But whatever their reasons, the high duke has decided that the council meeting must be cancelled until we can find out who is behind these threats and why."

Cassana felt another burden lift from her. She had been secretly dreading attending the council. This delay would hopefully allow her to recover from her ordeal and gather her strength and wits properly. Perhaps the high duke would even be able to find out who was behind her attempted abduction for her.

"I fully understand, Chancellor Valus. Any threat against the high duke is indeed serious. Hopefully, I might be permitted to stay in the city, until this matter has been resolved?"

"The high duke himself has asked that I look to your security personally while you are here, Lady Byron. He has asked that I station a guard at your door and that we send word to your father about the events transpiring here in the capital."

Cassana nodded, releasing the chancellor's hands. "Thank you sir, I would sleep all the better knowing that I am guarded and that my father is aware of all that has befallen me and his men. If I write a letter this afternoon, might you see that it is delivered as soon as possible?"

"Of course, Lady Byron. I will, also, ensure that I have a guard stationed here within the hour, my lady," he said, some of the worry fading from his eyes. "The high duke's elite guard have already moved his Lordship to a secure location and the other members of the Valian Council are being protected as we speak. It may be a political statement by an anarchist group, or it could be related to your misfortune. I fear the latter, if the truth be told, my lady. The timing of this threat is far too coincidental. There has never been a threat like this before a council meeting, as far as I can recall!"

"Indeed, sir," Cassana said. "I must thank you for all of your help, chancellor. I promise that I will keep out of the way, as I am sure you have much to deal with as things stand."

"Indeed I do, my lady," the chancellor said. Bowing, he turned for the door. "Keep to your quarters my lady, for now. Until we can be sure of your safety, my staff will see to it that you have everything you need and that you are kept up to date with what is happening."

"Thank you Chancellor Valus." Cassana smiled and watched him leave.

For a time she stood watching the closed door, her mind raging with another storm of worry and doubt. The attack on her camp by the Reven must have been an early attempt at stalling the council meeting. But for what? Perhaps I was going to be used as leverage, for these people to force their demands upon the high duke. Maybe they wish to stir up support to force the high duke to cancel his plans to trade with the Reven? Cassana shook her head thoughtfully. She knew the Reven people were far too busy fighting amongst themselves to come up with such a plot, far across the mountains and deep in the land of their enemy. But if it wasn't them, who then?

Moving from the door she crossed to the writing desk in the right-hand corner of the reception room. Sitting at it, she located some paper in a drawer, a quill and ink. Calming her breath she sucked on the tip of the quill, dipped it in the ink and began to write.

By the time Cassana had finished the letter to her father for the third time and was completely happy with it, Madam Grey returned with a fresh pot of tea once again. Drawing Cassana's attention to the guard stationed outside, she also gave her two small jars of herbs.

"The first jar will help to settle your stomach ache, my lady," she instructed her. "Just a small pinch taken twice a day in some water with your meals, at lunch and dinner. The second pot, a small pinch in some tea will help to calm your headaches, whenever you feel them coming on. But hopefully after one dose, you should be fine."

Cassana thanked the housekeeper and poured herself a fresh tea. Opening the second jar, she took a finger pinch of the dried green herb within and stirred it into her tea.

"Excellent, my lady," Madam Grey said.

Cassana smiled and sipped on the fine tea. "Hmm, lovely!" Setting aside the cup, she rose and handed the letter to the housekeeper. "Chancellor Valus said he would ensure that this letter was delivered urgently into the hands of my father in Highwater. Would you see to it my lady, that his instructions are carried out?"

Madam Grey clutched the letter protectively to her breast. "Of course, Lady Byron. I will arrange a courier to be despatched within the day."

Breathing a deep sigh of relief, Cassana thanked her and allowed the busy woman to depart. After she was gone, Cassana went back into her bedroom and found a book to read while she drank her tea.

By mid-afternoon, following a pleasant lunch, Cassana's headache had returned again. Setting aside the book she had been reading by the Valian philosopher Aliandas, she retired to her bedchamber. The herbs she had taken with her lunch had kept her stomach pains largely at bay, but her headache was slowly returning. Filling a goblet of water from a silver pitcher at her bedside, she stirred in a few leaves of the green herb and drank the liquid. She didn't want to rely on it every time she felt the onset of a headache, but perhaps small doses and some rest would see her back to her best. As she stretched out on top of the luxurious bed, she rested her head on her hands.

'That what doesn't kill you, makes you stronger!' Aliandas had said in one of his chapters, where he mused about the journey of life and spoke of the unpredictable road everyone had to travel to find their destiny. Cassana felt that she was certainly journeying through that particular chapter of life at the moment and as she tried to recall more of the book she quickly slipped off into a deep sleep, plagued by a dream of dark brooding clouds, gathering menacingly on a distant horizon...

The man paused on the twisting marble stairwell to catch his breath, his chest reaching for air as his lungs choked from his efforts. Pulling the hood of his dark robes tight about his face with one hand, he held the small lantern before him with the other to guide him on. His shadow sprung to life on the walls, stretching away from sight around the curved staircase and enticed him on a little further. Necessity pulled him on his way after a few moments respite and through controlled breaths, he carried on up the remaining three hundred and forty-eight steps.

By the time the man finally reached the top of the tower, he was utterly exhausted. He had undertaken this arduous journey many times before, but never before with such urgency and haste. Because of this, he spent many moments regaining himself before he could hang the lantern from a gold bracket on the marble wall of the circular chamber. Several large windows in the chamber offered the man brief glimpses of the clear night sky outside and as the light from the lantern spread out away from it, the orange glow came alive in the dark marble floor. Polished far beyond necessity, the lantern light seemingly seeped into the dark marble floor and brought the multitude of silver etchings carved there to life. As the man watched, burning stars glimmered faintly, tracing out the constellations of the sky on the floor before him. The effect was pitiful and ignoring the lure of viewing the sprawling city beneath him, the man moved to a small winch on the wall next to his lantern. Cranking the well-oiled winch a couple of times, he detected the shifting of the roof above him. As the strain required increased with each turn, the man could see a generous portion of the roof slide free, revealing a sparkling curtain of silver lights in the inky night sky. After several more turns, the man released the winch and locked it into place with a latch. Blowing the lantern out, he moved through the fading glow to stand in the centre of the chamber, where a large full moon had been expertly carved and waited patiently with hooded head bowed.

For a time nothing happened and then, as the lantern's light finally died, the constellations in the floor began to flare to life, mapping out the stars in the sky with bright pulsing silver. After several minutes the man opened his eyes wide and stared at the miracle beneath his feet. The marble's effect was exhilarating. It felt as if he walked the heavens, striding his way across the constellations, the dark sky his alone to command. No matter how many times he experienced this sensation, the man was never prepared for the emotions and effect it had upon him.

Closing his eyes, the man drew in a deep breath. Holding it there for a moment before gently letting it escape. Twice more he repeated the process. He waited a moment and then proceeded, picturing in his mind the stars that encompassed the moon beneath his feet. As he focused on them, he felt his feet become one with the marble, sinking deeper into the blackness that pulsed with pinpricks of glittering silver. A brilliant silver light formed in his mind, small at first and then growing larger as it spread from the surrounding constellations, drawn to the platform that was the moon. The moon underneath him began to glow brightly and the man's heart fluttered with the anticipation of an expectant lover. Spreading, the silver light enveloped the man's feet, twisting its way up his legs. With each swirling climb, the man's ecstasy heightened, until he felt he could contain it no longer. Just when he felt that he would have to pull away from the union, the silver light completely covered him, surrounding him in a gentle embrace.

"Carry my wishes forth," the man whispered. "Hear my words, brother!"

Opening his eyes, the man released his imagination and looked about the chamber. The room was utterly dark again, the marble dark and the etchings devoid of life.

"Brother? I call you to me, once more," he said, closing his eyes again. Clearing his mind from all emotion, he waited patiently, feeling the chill of the night claim the chamber for the first time.

Time slipped by calmly and without recognition for the man, until finally his calls were answered.

"What news do you bring to me, my brother?" a voice echoed in his mind suddenly and he felt his emotions return. "I thought our lord's wishes were known to you? Why do you contact me again?"

"I ask forgiveness for disturbing you brother," the man said through his own thoughts. "But events have not followed the road we had planned."

"Our time is short, so save your pathetic attempts at grovelling and get to the point, brother!"

"Forgive me. In short, the girl escaped the Reven. I do not know how she managed it, but she did and they are all dead."

Silence.

"W-with help," the man continued hesitantly. "She managed to reach the city."

"This is grave news indeed, brother," the voice growled, cutting through his mind.

"Had we not agreed that this would be the first move on our table? If you can't even get that right, then perhaps our lord should seek another to carry out his will?"

"No brother, please! I beg of you," the man panicked, falling to his knees. "Hear me, please! All is not lost. She has been inadvertently delivered to us and I have managed to secure her away without the high duke's knowledge."

"Hmm!" came his reply finally, after several moments of distant contemplation. "Fortune, apparently, still favours you brother, it would seem. What are your immediate plans for her? What about the Valian Council? When she does not appear, questions will asked, will they not?"

"Indeed, brother. But I already have the girl secured away in a quiet wing of the keep. She believes that the high duke has had to cancel the meeting because of a threat to his family and that I have sent a letter on her behalf to her father, telling him all that has befallen her. The high duke meanwhile will spend all of his time with the concern of a false threat against him and his family. I have assured him that she is being cared for and protected whilst recovering from an illness. This confusion will buy us, I mean me, valuable time to get her out of the city. Once she is away, we can secure her properly as planned and start putting in place our lord's wishes."

"But what of the girl? What if she becomes suspicious? I do not have to tell you what will happen if this fails!"

"I understand, brother," the man accepted. "The stonemason is already in our hands and is being questioned to find out if he told anyone. Once we are sure, he will be disposed of in the usual way. As for the girl, she will not be a problem. Madam Grey has been slipping her some drugs with her meals, which will render her useless in a few days time, adding further credibility to the information I gave to the high duke. Once she is ready, we will get her out of the city."

"I will send you the Kestrel. You cannot reveal yourself in all of this brother, no matter how much of this is your doing. Her men will be able to move her, without drawing attention to you any more than you may have already done yourself. It will take her a week to arrive, so until then, I do not want to hear any more from you. If I do, I will instruct her to bring you along with the girl..."

The man shuddered. "I understand, brother. I will not fail our lord again."

"There must be no loose ends, none that could tie a thread to you. What of the girl's help? Who else knows about her?"

"The girl's entourage were all killed in the attack, but she somehow and that still puzzles me, managed to get to Havensdale. The captain of the militia and two of her men escorted the girl here. Apart from two members of my staff, who can easily be taken care of, there are only those loyal to our cause. The girl's desire to enter the city, without drawing attention to herself, has, inadvertently, become her own downfall."

"I shall contact our brother in Highwater and tell him to control all of Byron's letters. If word somehow gets through, we had best hope that we already have the girl in chains. Once we have, we have many means at our disposal to find out how she actually managed to escape the Reven."

"And what of the captain?" the man asked. He felt their time coming to an end as each time he heard the voice, it grew fainter and fainter.

"Once our storm breaks out over the Four Vales, we can engineer an attack on her town. By then people will be too busy looking to their own safety to worry about a missing girl. I will instruct the Kestrel to dispatch the girl Cassana, if we cannot guarantee her safe removal. If that happens, then we will have to turn our attentions elsewhere."

The man nodded, calming his fear as he focused on the fading voice. "Agreed, brother. I will wait to hear from the Kestrel. In the meantime I shall ensure that the girl's presence here in the city remains a secret...and I shall get the information we seek from the stonemason."

"Excellent, brother," the voice whispered, pulsing faintly in his mind. "Through incompetence, you may have unwittingly helped our cause. But no loose ends this time... it would not be the first time the Kestrel has had to clean up a mess for you. If you fail us again, I assure you, it will be the last!"

The man felt a huge release as he felt the final break in their contact and he slumped forward onto the cold marble, now glowing with the light of the stars once again. With his left cheek pressed against the floor, he breathed raggedly, misting up the immediate floor around him. There was far too much at stake, beyond that of his own life. If he failed now, then all of his work over the last decade would have been for nothing. Rising slowly, the man smoothed down his crumpled robes. Freeing the winch, he wound the roof back into place and relit the lantern. The man looked behind, casting a final look out across the dark marble sky and shook. If it came down to it, he would kill the girl himself.

Turning, Chancellor Relan Valus left the Moon Tower and headed back down the spiral staircase as quickly as secrecy would allow him.

CHAPTER NINE

Frailty

Khadazin struggled in the dark waters of his unconsciousness, fighting madly against the cold darkness that threatened to pull him down to his death and the urge from his body to give in to its demands. The warmth of a distant light shimmered enticingly above the black surface, its distorted rays offering him some weak strength and faint hope. Clinging on to the light, he struggled through the cold darkness and reached out weakly towards it.

The stonemason broke the surface and gasped as his head bobbed above the dark waters of his unconsciousness and his ears picked up faint, fragmented words.

"Kha...ke up...Khadazin?"

He tried to focus on the familiar voice as his mind began to spin. Fresh pain ignited in his body and as the faint words scattered in the shadows before him, the dark waters of his unconsciousness rose up again to drag him back down into its cold embrace.

Cornelius watched helplessly from his cell as the Redani fought for his life, alone, wounded and naked on the cold floor of his cell. Their captors had dragged him back some time ago now, locking him in his cell with a parting kick to the side of the head and as soon as their torchlight had faded, the old architect had tried to wake him. If he didn't wake him soon, he feared that the stonemason would never come back to him, stealing away any hope that they had left of escape. Cornelius's old eyes had become accustomed to the blackness of his surroundings over the years and as he watched the shadowy thrashing form across from him, he heard the sounds of scuttling feet as the rat returned again.

"Get away from him!" he shouted, hurling a small piece of excrement through the shadows at it. Squealing, the rodent scurried away, its fright overcoming its hunger this time. Since he had first noticed it feeding on the stonemason's injured side, Cornelius had scared it off twice already, but soon he would run out of things to chase it off with and the rat would be able to take his fill on the multitude of open wounds on the stonemason's body again.

"Come on Redani, fight for your life!" he urged the unconscious man. Reaching out suddenly through the bars of his cell Cornelius sucked in a fearful breath and watched helplessly, as the stonemason's body stopped moving.

"Khadazin?" Cornelius dared to ask. The stonemason groaned weakly in response and Cornelius let out a thankful whistle.

"By the storms lad, you gave my old heart a fright!" he said, shaking his head. "Now don't try to move, use all of your strength to fight the pain those bastards inflicted upon you."

Khadazin clung onto the words floating about his head and slowly formed them into a sentence he could understand. The old man's words did little to describe the pain rampant within him, but they did offer him some comfort. He was not alone!

Moving his head slightly, Khadazin rested his left cheek on the cold stone floor and tried to inspect his side. The last thing he could remember was the hot poker, mercifully beyond that there was nothing. With tentative, feeling hands, he could tell that the initial wound was now gone, the burnt flesh around the area blackened and charred. The smell of his own burnt body was insufferable and the pain even worse. Many years ago he had seen a man burn to death in the street across from him. He hadn't known the man well, but the man had gone back into his house that was ablaze to rescue his son, trapped in his room upstairs. The flames had eventually beaten him back and the human torch had stumbled from the inferno to collapse on the street, twitching into stillness before horrified onlookers. By the time anyone had recovered their shock enough to douse him with water and smother him in blankets, it was too late. Khadazin could still taste his own disgust at his lack of help that day as he stood transfixed, watching the man burn to death before him. The smell had stayed with him for many weeks and until today, Khadazin had thought it the worst of all smells. The stench of his own charred flesh, however, was somehow even worse.

Inadvertently, in the long term, should he live long enough, they had actually helped him. The knife wound was cauterised and once the scabs went to work, it would hopefully speed up his recovery. His ear was no longer bleeding and compared to his side, the wound was superficial. The knife wound to his left forearm, received during his fight in the alley, had scabbed over now and he could feel some use returning to his hand. With his eyes slowly adjusting to the differing shadows in his immediate surroundings now, he could tell that he seemed to have acquired several more angry welts and cuts that were not there before; but all of his energies were focused on fighting the pain in his side for now.

"How long was I gone?" Khadazin asked, his head pounding with each word.

"A couple of hours," Cornelius replied, his voice trembling with anger. "That fat bastard really went to work on you, friend."

Khadazin nodded weakly. "I'll have my time with him one day."

Cornelius's wizened face grinned impishly. That was the kind of talk he had hoped to hear from the stonemason. Far too many of his previous cell mates, well actually all of them, had quickly given into the demands of their captors and their stay after that had been very short-lived indeed.

"That's the spirit Khadazin," he said encouragingly. "Your time will come, if you can keep your silence long enough. After the initial probing, they will leave you for a time to let you fight against your own demons. After that they will start back on you again."

"I have nothing to tell them, but as long as they think I do, I have the chance to escape," Khadazin replied softly.

"Ahem," Cornelius coughed. "What about me?"

"And you, of course, my friend," Khadazin said, managing a weak smile. "I swear on my blood that if I can, I will free you, Cornelius."

176

"Good enough for me," the old man said, nodding. "I know, knew quite a few people who I wouldn't trust if they said that to me – but you, you are not like anyone else I have ever met and I believe you Redani. For what it's worth, if by some miracle I manage to escape from here, I will find help and get you out of this cesspit!"

"Thank you, Cornelius."

"In the meantime, I can offer you some help. Here!"

Khadazin looked blindly towards him as the old man picked up an object at his dirty feet and threw it across to him. Something soft struck the bars to his cell and fell outside.

"Bugger it," Cornelius swore. "I can't even piss straight these days, either."

"What is it?" Khadazin asked him.

"It's now a dead rat, I caught it earlier," came his reply. "If you can get to it, tear its head off and drink its blood."

"I do not follow you?" Khadazin said curiously.

"Just trust me; rat's blood is very good for your strength and recovery. It's kept me alive through the weeks when they couldn't be bothered to feed me. Just be careful with the ones that are alive down here, they have been very interested in your blood and I have had to chase them off you a few times already."

Khadazin shook his head and started dragging himself across to the bars of his cell. It was like pulling himself across a bed of hot coals as with each movement, his body burnt with agony and his muscles pulled with the strain. By the time he reached the haven of the cold bars of his cell, his body was covered in a sheen of sweat and he shook uncontrollably. Reaching through the bars, he searched around the floor until he finally grabbed hold of the rat's tail and dragged the dead rodent towards him.

"That's it," Cornelius encouraged him. "Now pull his head off and squeeze out as much blood as you can. Your stomach won't be able to cope with its flesh for now, so toss it where the guards can't see it and we'll catch a few more when they come sniffing around again."

Khadazin felt his stomach turn at the thought and he swallowed back the concerns of his stomach. Turning over, he pulled himself up, fighting unsuccessfully against the sharp stabs of protest from his side. Shaking his head bitterly Khadazin began pulling at the rat's head as he rested his back against the bars of his cell. When the furry head finally came free, he tossed it away into the dark in disgust.

"Tails up!" Cornelius said grinning, as the stonemason put the carcass to his lips.

For the next two days Cassana's life was spent trapped in a nightmarish existence, helpless in a body wracked by a feverish illness. Madam Grey visited her regularly, evidently concerned about the girl's welfare as she helped her to try and get some food and medicine to stay down in her stomach long enough to make a difference. Not much did and soon Madam Grey was forced to bring stronger medicine to feed to her, one that left Cassana bedridden and unable to manage more than a few incoherent sentences at a time. The one time when she did manage to string some coherent words together, she begged Madam Grey to send for a physician who might be able to diagnose what was really wrong with her. The housekeeper told her that she had sent for the high duke's personal physician the day before and that he had promised to come and see her as soon as he could.

After she had gone, Cassana sank back down again into her clean bed sheets and slept. Sleep was about the only thing she could manage now and the weaker she became, the more irrational her mind became. Why hadn't the chancellor come to see her? What was wrong with her? Apart from being exhausted by the time Fawn and her men had delivered her safely to the capital, she had felt fine. Now, however, she could have lost a fight to a week old kitten. Thankfully her headaches had subsided now, only to be replaced by the sensation that she was floating in dark water, treading her way through long lonely hours, punctuated by terrible moments of agony as her stomach heaved and protested at its contents. Sleep, although welcome, was still a fragmented affair. Broken by vomiting and dreams of shadows chasing her through the night. With each night that passed, the dreams warned her of the danger catching up to her. The more she tried to get away from it, the closer it came. The danger breathed down her neck now, whispering its malicious intent. Something was seriously wrong about all of this, Cassana decided. But try as she might, her mind couldn't hold on to a thought long enough to decide what it was! In the end she gave up all hope of a clear answer and clung on to the desire to see her father, Fawn and Edward. None of them came, although they stepped from the shadows of her dreams occasionally to taunt her with glimpses of their faces, before disappearing again to leave her weak, vulnerable and alone. If anyone wanted to abduct her now, they would find their task a lot easier than the Reven had. There would be no mysterious woodsman to save her this time. Bitterly, she cast her thoughts from her mind and settled down to try and get some more rest. If the high duke could overcome his hardships with the threats made against him, then she could beat this illness. However she did not quite feel the same several minutes later when she was sick all over her bed. Too weak to move, Cassana's attempts left her exhausted and moments later she passed out.

For a further three days Cassana was trapped in her bed. Her body was lifeless now and she could barely move without assistance from Madam Grey. The woman spoke to her softly on the third day, as she helped her to take some more medicine, but her words were muffled and slurred. A tender smile touched her face as she left, but as the housekeeper closed the door behind her, Cassana could not detect the same warmth in her eyes. Confused and unsure, Cassana chewed over the seed of doubt growing in the back of her mind. By the time she woke from her next deep sleep, Cassana's drug-soaked mind had forgotten what had been bothering her and once again, she awaited Madam Grey's return with longing. When she did arrive, later that day, Cassana was sure that someone else was with her. As she strained to see the shadowy figure watching her from the doorway, the apparition disappeared from view, leaving Cassana to question if someone had actually been there. Sipping at the water Madam Grey held to her lips, she noticed that she had not brought her any food this evening. Madam Grey read the look in her eyes and told her that they would try her on liquids for a few days, to see if that helped to settle her stomach. With the thought of living through another few days of this pitiful existence, Cassana slumped back into her pillows and wept. When she looked again some moments later, Madam Grey was gone.

The following morning, however, events took a surprising turn. Cassana was already awake and felt her hopes light with curiosity, as the door to her bed chamber opened and a woman entered. It was not Madam Grey. This woman was much younger, several years older than Cassana perhaps, but younger than Fawn. She was dressed in a simple dark skirt and blouse. A white apron covered her clothes and her long, curling, dark hair was tied back into a tail. She carried a tray of food and a glass of what looked to be apple juice. Balancing the tray under one arm, she closed the door behind her and hurried to her bedside. Placing the tray on a bedside table, she leant over her. Cassana looked up at the pretty face that looked down at her with horror, framed by lustrous, chestnut tresses.

"What have they done to you?" she whispered into Cassana's ear. As the bedridden woman frowned in confusion, she held a finger to her lips to stop her talking. Fussing around Cassana's pillows, the woman straightened her bed sheets and reached into her apron. Cassana watched her curiously, confused and yet, the attrition of the last few days momentarily forgotten, as the woman produced a note and held it before her bleary eyes to read.

Cassana focused hard on the words scribbled on the paper before her, until the letters arranged themselves into some semblance of order for her to read.

'You are in grave danger, Lady Byron. Eat only the food, do not drink!'

The woman held Cassana's wild stare until she was sure that the message had sunk home. Once she was satisfied, she hid the note in her apron again and took the glass of juice through to the bathroom. Cassana turned her head, weakly, but could not see the woman again until she returned moments later, with an empty glass. Moving to her side, she proceeded to spoon the hot tasteless soup into her mouth, holding a cloth to her lips to ensure that no further mess was added to the sheets. When she was sure that her patient had taken her fill, the woman wiped Cassana's lips for her and put the half-full bowl of soup back on the tray.

"I must go, my lady," she whispered again. "We have managed to get Madam Grey out of the picture for you and I will do all I can to help you regain some of your strength."

"Who, who a-are you?" Cassana murmured. Her head was beginning to pound with fresh agony.

"I am your friend, lady," she replied, smiling, her hazel eyes bright with honesty. "We do not have much time and you must be ready!"

"Ready? For what?"

"To flee this place, before they come for you." The woman held her down with a firm hand as Cassana struggled in panic. Brushing lank, greasy hair from out of Cassana's eyes, she rose and picked up the tray.

"I will see you later, rest now."

Cassana watched helplessly as the secretive woman left the room. For a time Cassana lay back in her bed, listening to the churning of her stomach as it hungrily devoured the soup. When the expectant heave and knot of pain did not come, Cassana breathed a sigh of relief. Madam Grey was out of the picture. What did that mean? But the note had said to eat only the food, not the drink. Had Madam Grey been giving her something other than medicine? Why would she do that? Was she working towards another end, without the chancellor's knowledge? Or was this new woman the threat? Had she got rid of Madam Grey, so that she could kidnap her for herself?

Sobbing, Cassana turned over and buried her face in the soft pillows. Her fragile head was still drowned in medicine and awash with fresh pain and confusion. Normally, she would have been able to tell who was telling the truth, but this illness had crippled her judgement leaving her weaker and more vulnerable than she could ever recall. Whatever was transpiring here, the woman was right. She needed to regain her strength, and fast. Cassana's first goal was to discover enough strength and balance to be able to get out of bed on her own and reach her travelling boots so that she could get at the dagger in the sheath of her left boot. She would feel a lot safer with that under her pillow. As she looked up and glanced around the bedroom, she searched for her other belongings. She could not see them from the bed. For whatever reason, Edward's grandson may not have delivered them. That secured her second goal. Get to the reception room to see if her sword and bow were there. If she was in danger, she would need to protect herself, before trusting anyone else. Trust your instincts, Fawn had said and how right she had been. Settling down again, Cassana tried to get some sleep to shut out her body's need for a drink.

Sometime later that day as Cassana was still struggling with her need for water, the woman returned with her supper. Once again, she tended to her needs and fed her some of the hot broth with a spoon. When the bowl was finished, she emptied the glass of water on her tray into the bath again. When she returned, she inspected the sorry looking woman in the bed before her and shook her head.

"We do not know what they are giving you, my lady. But whatever it is, you are better off without it!" she whispered to her as she sat on the bed beside her. "The drugs were putting you into a coma, dulling your senses so that they could easily move you somewhere else."

Cassana shook her head, regretting it immediately. "I-I don't understand."

"I am sure you don't," the woman replied. "I must go. Rest well my lady, be watchful and be ready!"

"Why are you helping me?" Cassana managed weakly.

"Because at this moment in time, no one else can!"

The woman rose and collected the tray. "If anyone else comes to see you, act worse than you already are, my lady. They will think the drugs are working and leave you alone, until they are ready to move you."

Cassana nodded submissively and watched her leave. After a while she tried to sit up and then fell back onto the bed. Despite the orders from her mind, the physical demands on her body were still too great at the moment. Cursing, Cassana settled down for the night. She was still very ill and further rest would help to quicken her recovery. For the first time in several days, Cassana slept well that night, her body free from disturbance and her mind devoid of any unsettling dreams.

The following morning Cassana woke feeling tangibly better for the first time. Despite the absence of pain in her stomach, her body quickly reminded her of how weak she was and a wave of light-headedness forced her back down onto her bed as she attempted to rise. Gently, she calmed the frustration rising up inside of her and slowly began to raise herself from the comfort of her pillows. It took a while, but eventually Cassana managed to negotiate herself to the side of the bed, where she swung her feet over the side and sat there for a time, catching her breath. She was in a terrible state, the drugs in her drink and maybe even her food had done their job well and she was still weaker than that week old kitten. She had always wanted a cat when she was growing up, but her father was a traditional Valian man who favoured dogs for their kinship and loyalty. He had raised three hunting hounds when Cassana was growing up and although she had come to love them all, she found them to be needy creatures that clung to their master's side, desperate for praise and constant attention. Cassana was more akin to a cat, being both independent and wilful. Growing up, she had endlessly found ways to frustrate her father. Getting lost in the corridors of their home, playing tricks on her tutors and being rude to the members of their household staff. It had taken a long time for Cassana to find happiness growing up. Her tutors had told her father that she was an intelligent girl who could achieve much if she bothered to listen and could curb her temper long enough to learn. Cassana had overheard her maid Clara one day, talking in hushed tones to a member of the kitchen staff. They were discussing Lord Byron's daughter and commenting on how exasperated he was becoming with his child's wild spirit. They then went on to dissect how Cassana's behaviour may be down to the fact that she had never had a mother's love growing up and that she had grown up amongst the politics and the rough and tumble nature of a male dominated society. That night, her ears still ringing with the pity and disdain of their words, the twelve summers old daughter of the Lord of Highwater had decided that she would change. She would change, not to conform with the requirements of a society who expected better from her, nor for those who held sympathy for the circumstances of her upbringing. No, she changed for the one person she loved above all others and yet seemed determined to do anything and find everything that would annoy him. Her father! The next morning Cassana had attended breakfast on time and, much to the joy on her father's face, she announced to him that she was sorry for her selfish behaviour and that from now on she would do her best to learn all she could from him to be a better person and an even better daughter. Cassana would never forget the relief and joy on her father's face that morning and she spent the next four years learning how to be the daughter of a lord and how to conduct herself properly. In doing so, she would come to meet her one true friend in society, Lysette. She never did get a kitten for her birthday, however, although she dropped enough subtle hints. But she did finally grow to love her father's trio of hounds, especially Wraith - who at twelve years old now, was still a faithful and loving servant to his master.

Cassana felt the early morning chill of her room, as it brought her attentions back to the present. The room was dark, the candle at her bedside having long-since burnt itself out. Bracing herself, Cassana gripped the bedsheets as she slid off the side and touched the floor with her feet. Her legs felt heavy with her lethargy and as she allowed them to take her full weight, she collapsed to the floor in a heap, taking some of the bed linen with her. Snarling, Cassana forced herself up onto her knees and began to crawl across the floor towards her boots. Tears began to slide down her cheeks as she realised how pathetic and hopeless she must look, and by the time she finally reached her destination, she was exhausted yet again. Fumbling for her boot, she gasped as she realised that someone had taken the blade from the sheath and she swore furiously. Sitting on the marble floor, she hurled the boot to one side. No doubt Madam Grey had removed the weapon at some stage and if Cassana could muster the strength to get to the reception room, she would probably find that the rest of her belongings were missing as well. The cold of the marble soon dissipated as Cassana felt her customary anger rise again. How dare Madam Grey do this to her! As soon as she was well enough she would expose her treatment to the high duke and demand that her captors were brought to trial. Cassana knew that it would cause a storm within his court, but the high duke needed to know about the kind of people working in his household, plotting behind his back.

The loss of the bow, given to her by the woodsman was also strangely irritating. Perhaps it was because it was her only connection now to her saviour, or maybe it was because she had felt so comfortable with the weapon. Whatever the reason, she promised that she would try to get it back somehow! First however, she had to get well enough to get away from her incarceration, before Madam Grey's people turned up to take her away. The guard posted outside would certainly pose a problem and she would need her mysterious new benefactor's help if she was to get by him. Her immediate concern, however, was to get back to her bed, before anyone came into the room and found out that she was not as incapacitated as she was supposed to be. Ignoring the nausea in her stomach and the general feeling of disgust she held for herself and her appearance, she turned round and started pulling herself back across the floor towards the sanctuary and comfort of her bed. By the time she managed to pull herself back into bed, she was covered in a sheen of sweat and teetered on the edge of unconsciousness. The drugs in her system clawed at her nerves, tearing at her resolve as they demanded satiating. As Cassana fought against their demands, she curled up into a tight ball and cried through her cravings and her pain. As she sobbed into her pillow, fresh with spittle and tears, she sensed the return of her ally. Looking up through her matted veil of tangled hair, she cleared her vision long enough to see the woman enter the room, carrying her breakfast.

"Good morning, Lady Byron. How are we feeling this morning?" she said brightly with an arch of her eyebrows behind her. Cassana look past her to see a guard peering curiously into the room behind her.

"I am feeling terrible," Cassana sobbed. Playing her part with sincerity.

"I am sorry to hear that my lady, I have your breakfast here and some medicine to help you recover."

Cassana's mind screamed its demands to her as she fought against the desire to snatch the water and the powder from off of the approaching woman's tray. The guard hovered around long enough to see the woman stir the powder into a glass of water, before heading back to his post outside the suite.

"Here we go, my lady," the woman said, loud enough for the guard to hear. "That's it, you'll feel much better once the medicine starts to work again."

188

The front door to the suite closed and the woman's jovial masked slipped from her face.

Moving to the doorway of the bedchamber, she nodded to herself and then took the glass away to dispose of its contents, as she had done so several times before.

"Sorry about that," she whispered when she returned. "He is getting a bit too curious for my liking."

Cassana nodded, accepting the breakfast tray from her eagerly. "I feel quite terrible today, I think my body is rebelling against my attempts to fight off the drugs."

"That is only natural, my lady. If it is any consolation, the worse you feel, the easier it will be for you to play your part in all of this."

"My part in this?" Cassana murmured, more to herself than the woman. "I wish I knew what that was!"

"As do I," the woman said, nodding in agreement. "For the moment my lady, all we must do is concentrate on getting you out of here."

"How do we do that?" Cassana growled. "I can barely move."

"I understand your frustration my lady," came her swift reply. "But you must understand that I risk much in helping you. If I am found out, all of my employer's hard work over the last few years will be for nothing."

"Your employer?"

"I cannot tell you anything at the moment."

"You cannot, or you will not?" Cassana said bitterly.

The woman smiled. "In truth, both! But for now all I can say is that you have nothing to fear from us. You will find out the truth when we have you safely away from here. Until that time comes, however, I must keep up this pretence, lest I raise suspicion with the head chef who has been supplying you with the drugs. He is Madam Grey's man and I must carry out his wishes, lest he entrust this task to someone else."

"At least tell me your name?" Cassana pleaded, desperate for anything. The woman shook her head regrettably.

"I cannot! Not now. If you are questioned at any stage and are forced to reveal my name, my cover here and my life would be over."

Cassana chewed thoughtfully on an apple and savoured the taste that was slowly returning to her palette.

"So be it. I fear I am beginning to understand and will have to play my part in this game. Answer me this one question, however, please? What has happened to my belongings? Edward said that he would have his grandson deliver them to me the morning after my arrival."

The woman looked away momentarily towards the reception room and then when she returned her attention back, her face was dark and her eyes troubled.

"I will be honest with you, Lady Byron," she said softly. "Edward and his grandson have not been seen for several days. Madam Grey said that they were called away on urgent family business, but I fear the worst for them."

Cassana's skin crawled and she began to feel sick and light-headed again. "W-what of Chancellor Valus? I have not heard from him, and he has not come to see me for some days now."

"I can assure you that Chancellor Valus has been very interested in your health, my lady," the woman surrendered. "He has had much to deal with however, following the postponement of the council and with

Madam Grey's disappearance, he has been too busy to see you personally."

Cassana nodded thoughtfully, her mind troubled by doubt and apprehension.

"I really must go, my lady."

The woman hurried from the room before Cassana could delay her any further.

It wasn't until sometime later however when Cassana was drifting off into a sleep, troubled by her concern for Edward and Thomas, that she suddenly sat bolt upright in her bed.

"Fawn!" she said, fear catching in her throat and her heart racing with panic.

The rest of Cassana's day was spent tussling with her anxiety about Fawn's welfare and the mess she had inadvertently steered some innocent people into. If anything had happened to those who had assisted her, Cassana would be devastated and her conscience would never allow her to forgive herself. To divert her attentions away from the problem, the mysterious woman returned to her later that evening to bring her supper and take away the remnants of her breakfast; but she was guarded with what she said and deftly dodged any further questions from her charge. After she had wordlessly tended to Cassana's needs, she excused herself and hurried from the room, leaving Cassana confused by her sudden change of demeanour.

Over her supper, Cassana fretted about what could have happened to bring about this sudden change and her paranoia began to return. Perhaps the woman was becoming worried about her true intentions being revealed, or maybe she was actually working for Madam Grey and trying to lull her into a false sense of security?

Or maybe the head chef, as she had said, was becoming suspicious and she feared that they were being spied on. But with her help, she had aided her recovery and although she was still feeling very ill, Cassana had to admit that she felt a thousand times better than when Madam Grey had been tending to her. Cassana's confusion soon backed away to allow a fresh headache to the fore of her concerns and after finishing her supper, consisting of a hearty stew and fresh bread, she settled back down to try and get some rest. Sleep did not come for a very long time and Cassana looked around the dark room, searching for answers that hid away from her, refusing to offer any comfort to her predicament. Finally however, when her mind was exhausted from the strain of worry and her weary body could not support her any longer, Cassana collapsed into the arms of a deep sleep; haunted by wild imaginings of what had happened to her friends and plagued by their whispering accusations about the trouble she had brought down upon them.

Cassana woke with a start and stared blindly out into the darkness. For a time she lay where she was, questioning if she was, actually, even awake. After a while, she convinced herself that she was indeed awake as she could feel the cold chill of the room biting at her toes. Laying perfectly still, she listened to the silence of the darkness and pulled her bedsheets up protectively around her neck. Something wasn't quite right, but she couldn't place a finger on what it was. In her drug-induced state she had slept soundly for several nights in a row and nothing had managed to rouse her. But now, free of the drug's effects, something had woken her. A noise? Perhaps! She couldn't quite tell. Nervously,

Cassana listened to her dark surroundings, fearful of the demons plaguing her mind and powerless in the grip of her fear. Despite being wrapped heavily in her sheets and clothed in a nightgown, she felt naked and unable to defend herself. She would have felt slightly better if she still had her dagger, even though she doubted she could defend herself in her current condition. After several long minutes that felt like hours, Cassana finally managed to calm her nerves long enough to think rationally. If someone was out there, she would have heard them by now, stumbling about in the dark. But the only thing to be heard was the sound of her ragged breath and the pounding tension of her head.

"Silly!" she said, chiding herself for being so paranoid. Smiling, she turned wearily on her side to try and get back to sleep again.

Something moved suddenly through the darkness towards her and before she could react a hand clamped firmly over her mouth and nose, silencing her scream and roughly choking off her breath.

CHAPTER TEN

Chances

Cassana thrashed in panic as she struggled madly against the hand that covered her mouth and pinched her nostrils together between a rough thumb and forefinger. With any strength she had left now gone, she found that her struggles were futile and as she clawed vainly at the hand across her mouth, she could feel the studs of a leather guard protecting her assailant's forearm.

"If you want to live, Lady Byron, do exactly as I say!" a male voice hissed in her left ear, above her muffled screams and choking pleads for air. The man's other arm wrapped tightly around her waist and Cassana was dragged from her bed onto the cold marble floor below.

"Will you yield, lady?" the man hissed again, as he straddled her stiff body from behind. He could see the woman's bright blue eyes bulge with terror as he pulled her head back for confirmation and she nodded hurriedly as her lungs began to scream for fresh air.

"Very wise!" the man said and Cassana felt the pressure on her nostrils relent. The man sat back off her, dragging her with him into a firm embrace and he allowed her to breathe deeply for several moments.

"I know you are weak, so save your strength and listen to me," it was a statement, not a request and Cassana nodded slightly as she continued to breathe through her flaring nostrils. "I mean you no harm, but if you jeopardise me in any way, I will not hesitate to finish you off for them. Is that understood?"

Cassana's head was dragged back to look up into the darkness. A pair of stern, flint-grey eyes fixed on her meaningfully. Shuddering, Cassana nodded. She had no idea what was happening. Was this man an ally of the woman's? If he was, he had a strange way of going about it. But if he wasn't, then Cassana realised she was in big trouble. Trying to mask her fear, she met the man's eyes boldly and nodded again.

"Good," the man said softly. Whether he detected the defiance or terror in her eyes, he chose to ignore them both and relaxed the hand that gripped her mouth slightly. "I am going to remove my hand. Do not scream for help, or it will be the last thing you do. Understand?"

Cassana nodded angrily and the hand slipped from her mouth. Sucking in a full breath, Cassana felt the man relax his arm about her waist as he shoved her from his embrace. Without a sound the man rose and came to her side again. Kneeling once more, he hauled her to her feet and then had to support her, as he felt her sink to the floor again.

"Hmpf!" he said, his voice laced with frustration. "You are weaker than I was told, but no matter."

"Who are you?" Cassana whispered.

"My name is not important," came his expected reply and Cassana growled. This was becoming predictable, did everyone hate their name, or simply not trust her with it? "But you must believe me when I say that I am here to get you out of this keep and to safety, before it's too late!"

Cassana nodded, leaning reluctantly on him for support. "Are you with the maid? Or are you with Madam Grey?"

The man began to lead her through the darkness and Cassana reluctantly leant on him for support as he expertly negotiated them towards the bathroom. He was a good deal taller than her and through her flimsy nightgown she could feel that his strong body was clothed in leathers and a thick cloak.

"I am *with* neither, but I work for the former!"

Cassana felt herself relax slightly. "How are we going to get out of the keep?"

"The same way I got in."

The man led her into the bathroom and as they moved across the marble, he steered her towards the wall to their right. Cassana's eyes were starting to become accustomed to the dark now and the tall shadow at her side was starting to take shape. She could tell that he wore, as she had suspected, a long cloak and leathers. Shrouded all in black, a deep hood was pulled up over his head and only his piercing eyes were visible as the rest of his face was hidden by a scarf that covered his nose and mouth. For a brief moment Cassana wondered if she had been rescued by the notorious outlaw Devlin Hawke, such was the man's appearance.

He stopped before the blank wall and pressed a section of the tiling. Silently part of the wall swung inwards, revealing a narrow landing and a stone staircase beyond.

"I would never have known this was here," Cassana said and then felt foolish as the man dealt her a disdainful look. "What about the guard outside? Won't he hear us?" Cassana whispered, trying to divert his focus.

"He will if you don't shut up!"

Ignoring the colour burning her pale face, the man dragged her through the secret opening and propped her up against the rough cobwebbed wall. Leaving her to teeter at the top of the steep staircase, the man turned and pulled on a bracketed torch holder fixed on the opposite wall. Silently the secret door closed again and as it slid into place, Cassana could see the fresh oil on the door's hinges. The man produced a tinder and flint from within the depths of his cloak and after a single strike and spark, the torch residing in the holder flared to life. Taking down the spitting torch the man turned, its glow reaching out to cast a bright warmth over their surroundings. Cassana shielded her eyes protectively from the light, having spent several days now in the company of shadows. When she looked again, she blinked the blotches from her mind and studied the man properly for the first time.

He was tall, lean of frame and cloaked in shadows. Dressed entirely in black, from his long hooded cloak, down to his soft, knee-high leather boots. He wore black leather trousers, a dark vest and leather studded guards, that protected both his forearms. Because one of his arms held the torch aloft, Cassana could see the numerous pouches and a long crescent shaped knife, belted at his waist. But above all, Cassana's attention was drawn back to those compelling flint-grey eyes, bright with intensity and steel, glinting in the shadows of the dark hood. Subtle lines creased at the corner of his eyes, hinting that perhaps this man was in his later twenties, or even early thirties. The eyes in question gleamed wickedly and Cassana detected a grin behind the masked face.

"I'll be sure to find time to let you thank me properly, later!" he said roguishly and Cassana looked away in embarrassment, rather than irritation. The light from his sputtering torch cast an orange glow out and over the stone steps, disappearing deep down into the darkness below them. To the right, a narrow tunnel slipped away from their view, leading, Cassana guessed, around the Silver Falls suite to allow people to spy and eavesdrop on the people within. She shuddered when she thought that someone may have overheard the mysterious woman talking to her and quickly banished any images of what may have then happened to her, from her mind.

Turning her attention away, Cassana felt nervous as she looked into the depths below and started to sway. The man pushed by her and she clung onto the wall for dear life.

"I had better go first then," he observed ruefully. Cassana nodded thankfully. She had never had a good head for heights, above or below ground and in her weakened state she didn't trust herself to avoid a rapid descent down the steps. Above ground she felt naked and exposed, below it, she felt trapped and claustrophobic. The man started heading silently down the steps, leaving Cassana to stare wordlessly after him. Tentatively she put a hand on each dusty wall and listened to the blood rushing in her head for a few seconds, before shuffling down the first few steps.

After a few moments she began to feel weak again and she stopped, fixed between two steps.

"I-I don't think that I can make it on my own," she said, reluctantly. For a brief moment she had the desire to collapse and crawl back to her bedchamber, to accept her coming fate. But as the man turned and fixed her with a withering glare, she realised, for better or for worse now that she was this man's prisoner and he would do with her as he pleased. Judging by the venom in his words and the ice in his eyes thus far, Cassana decided that she would try not to antagonise or anger him in the future.

Without a word, he grabbed her around the waist and unceremoniously tossed her over his shoulder. Turning on the step, Cassana found herself mercifully staring up the staircase now and, without another word, the man began striding down into the depths of the high duke's keep.

Minutes slipped roughly into what felt like hours as the man carried Cassana down the steps into the unknown. The motion of his unwavering pace left Cassana feeling sick and at one point of their descent, she pleaded with the man to set her down. He did so without complaint, although his eyes betrayed his impatience and he turned away from her as she brought up her supper and then later on, the bile in her throat. Twice during their flight, they came to several other doorways on small landings, each concealed on the staircase and flanked by torch holders. Once they were out of earshot from them, Cassana's curiosity got the better of her.

"Are there many hidden staircases and passages in the keep?" she dared to ask, as she jostled up and down on his shoulder.

"Many? Fifty at least, I would guess," the man answered. "Most are used for spying on guests and for other nefarious purposes, which is why they are built onto the suites and reception rooms. And also for escape routes, should the keep ever be attacked."

Cassana chewed on her dry lips. "Then where are we heading, sir?"

The man chuckled. "Into the city's sewers, my lady. I always find it quite amusing how most of the aristocracy use the shit to get them out of it."

Cassana disapproved of his language, but was not surprised by it and listened quietly to him as he laughed away at the apparent amusement of his own analogy.

"You will find a much different world than you are used to, down there," he said finally, as he shifted her weight on his shoulder slightly. "The duke may have need of those tunnels one day, but there are those who use them as pathways for their businesses and as means of avoiding detection by the authorities."

"Thieves, you mean?" Cassana pointed out.

"Thieves, racketeers, call them what you must. The sewers attract the flotsam and jetsam of the city, it's a veritable underworld inhabited by brigands, liars, cheats and bastards – all tucked away from the high duke's officers and men. I love it!"

Cassana didn't doubt that for a second. But his description of where they were headed left her feeling more exposed than she already was and her nerves began to chew at her mind; leaving her to wonder if she had been spirited away from the clutches of those who sought to capture her, only to be delivered into the hands of Karick's criminal underworld and used to obtain a ransom from her father.

"What will happen to me, once we get down there,

sir?" Cassana dared to ask.

The man's hooded head turned. "That's not for me to decide, nor care about," he said bluntly. "But you need not fear my employer. In fact I think you will be mildly surprised! And stop calling me sir, you are not at court now princess and I am no sir!"

"That much is clear!" Cassana said, before she could stop herself.

The man threw back his hooded head and chuckled softly. "Feisty, I like it!"

He patted Cassana's backside with the hand of the arm carrying her and risked a loud chuckle as she demanded an immediate apology and fidgeted to try and get off his shoulder.

"You'll get an apology on the day you kiss me," he said, his eyes flashing mischievously.

"You will have to wait a very long time for that then, sir!" Cassana said, flustered and outraged.

The infuriating man held the torch higher as he picked up his pace and hurried on down the steps into the awaiting darkness.

"I'm a patient man, lady," he said, his voice soft for once. "In my line of work, you have to be!"

Thankfully for Cassana, the steep stairway came to an abrupt end, but any relief she felt was short-lived as she found herself unceremoniously dumped on the dusty floor. Coughing, she held a hand over her mouth to ward away the resulting dust cloud and blinked the grit from her eyes. Her captor, if that was what he was, stood before a heavy looking barred door. As he reached out with his free hand to haul it open, he looked back over his shoulder.

"Come on then!" he snapped, eyes narrowing

impatiently.

Without waiting, he hauled the door open and stepped through into the shadows beyond. Cassana watched the glow of his torch fade as he moved from view to his left and she felt a chill blow through the opening as the shadows filled back in behind him. Hugging herself, she rolled onto her knees and growled. Channelling her anger into her legs she managed to rise shakily and stumbled through the opening after him.

Beyond, she found herself in a short tunnel, its rough stone walls draped in decades worth of cobwebs. The man stood several yards away from her, burning a much larger path through the cobwebs than he had made earlier. Cassana guessed that nobody had used this secret way for many years now, perhaps even since they had been built. Beyond him, she could see a closed stone door and when he reached there, he sighed and turned back to check if she was still following him. Cassana headed towards him as fast as she could manage and when she reached his side, his eyes studied her scornfully.

"Beyond this door, we will be in the sewers," he said, irritated. "We will have a half hour journey through them, so if anyone accosts us, stay behind me."

"Is it dangerous down here, then?"

"For you, yes!" he said, turning away and shoving hard on the door. "For me, no!"

A terrible stench hit Cassana as the door shrieked its protests and reluctantly opened. Beckoning sharply for her to follow, he led her out onto a slick narrow walkway that ran by the opening and offered them a chance to avoid the slow moving river of filth that churned its way through the low ceilinged sewers of the capital. Cassana gagged and felt her nausea return as she choked on the natural fumes hanging in the thick, suffocating air above the sewerage like a watchful spectre.

"Not what you're used to, I take it?" the man said, his eyes alight with merriment. He was clearly enjoying this! Cassana shook her head dumbly, her eyes glistening with tears as she used a sleeve of her nightgown to cover her mouth and nose. She was too weak, too upset to rise to the bait and fight back. As he headed off, Cassana followed obediently after him, her eyes focused on the treacherous ground before her as she purposely avoided looking at the contents of the slow moving sewerage. Cassana shuddered as she nervously followed him and hugged herself as she tried to keep warm. No doubt she now looked as bad, if not worse than she already felt. Her flimsy nightclothes did little to warm her ice-cold body or hide away her dignity. She had never felt so vulnerable in her whole life and as the cold overcame her completely, she gave up and submitted to its numbing caress. As she stumbled forlornly through the sewers after the dark figure, she tried to hide her pitiful sobbing from him by crying quietly into her sleeve; but the pathetic look he dealt her told her that his hearing was just as acute as his ability to move quietly about his business. Cassana sniffed and wiped her eyes as she forced down the nausea in her throat. She could not believe what had happened to her these past few weeks. If she was somehow able to take a step back from it all and observe what had befallen her recently, she would have thought it impossible for anyone to have gone through so much turmoil in such a short space of time and still not really know what was happening to them. Cassana slipped and scraped her knuckles on the filthy wall as she threw a hand out to steady herself. *Focus!* She snarled silently, berating herself for not paying attention. One wrong step and she really would be in it...

The man ignored her plight and took his charge through a large network of dripping sewer tunnels, across makeshift footbridges and down several passages of the familiar terrain. He had traversed these paths many times before and knew his way around them as well as he did the streets in the city above. A few minutes after leaving the secret tunnel however he was forced to carry the emotional woman again, as she was clearly still suffering from the effects of the drugs in her system. Overcome by the stench of the sewers and exhausted by her ordeal, she passed out a few moments afterwards, anyhow. From that point on, the remainder of their journey was made in merciful silence and that suited him just fine. He had nothing in common with the woman anyway and had little interest in her welfare, apart from the fact that he had to get her back safely and in one piece to collect his handsome reward. She looked like she had just spent several weeks in an opium tent in the slums of the city, a pale ghost that hung off his shoulder like a sack of grain. He shrugged indifferently and concentrated on the coin he was about to collect. After claiming that he would be able to enjoy his life for a few months, do what ever he liked and to whomever he chose. With that amount of coin he would be able to pay for the best whores in the city, and get the pox cleaned up afterwards. Just a little further now and he could be rid of the girl and out of this mess, before he really got his hands dirty with the whole affair.

When he had initially been offered the job, he had

taken it without question. He was a freelancer whose dark reputation commanded good coin because of the things he was prepared to do to get it. With the old maps he had got as payment off a client some years back now, he was well aware of the secret tunnels that would get him unnoticed into the keep. His employer already had someone on the inside as well and they had fortunately managed to locate where the woman was being held. Simple then perhaps? But extremely risky! It certainly wasn't the usual type of job he accepted and stealing into the high duke's keep at night to spirit someone away from under his nose was a different proposition altogether. Why she needed to be rescued, if that was indeed what he was doing, was of no concern to him. If they ransomed her for more than he was being paid, then good luck to them! All that had mattered to him then and now, was that he completed his mission without any unforeseen hindrances and lived long enough to spend his reward.

As it turned out, the sewer network was deathly quiet that night. Only the bats, rats and insects were abroad and even they decided to stay clear of the dark apparition that stalked the misty hot tunnels with a motionless form thrown over its shoulder.

Finally, when even the man's shoulder was beginning to feel the weight of his burden, he arrived at a dank side tunnel that mercifully left the stench of the sewerage behind and led him up to a featureless stone wall. Cassana jolted from her unconsciousness as she was pitched roughly from his shoulder onto the cobbled floor and she leant weakly against the tunnel wall. Staring dazedly about her surroundings Cassana whimpered as she massaged her temples with the palms of her hands to try and free herself from the grip of a furious headache. The man stood with his back to her and, as she watched him, he slowly knocked four times on what appeared to be a blank stone wall. He paused and then knocked rapidly a further three times, the sound of his solid fist echoing dully.

Although Cassana doubted that anyone would even hear him, she felt her heart begin to pound as her anticipation began to rise. Was she about to find out who had sent this man into the high duke's keep to retrieve her? Would she finally start to find out something about what was going on? And would she then like what she found?

"Not long now, princess!" he said ominously without turning and Cassana swallowed back the large lump of doubt settling in her throat.

The man's definition of 'not long now' proved inaccurate however, as the pair were forced to wait in silence for quite some time. After a few minutes the man began to pace impatiently, repeating his coded knock on the stone wall every few minutes and Cassana was sorely tempted to point out that he had said to her earlier that in his line of work you had to be *patient*! Seeing the thunder in his eyes at one point, however, she decided it was best to concentrate on her own worries for a change and let him rant away to himself in silence. Hugging herself as tight as she could to keep warm, Cassana watched the man out of the corner of one eye. He moved gracefully, with a speed and purpose that suggested to Cassana he was a confident and driven man. There was no doubt that he was skilled. Even in his current frame of mind, he still paced around quietly and his eyes were constantly on guard – taking in everything around him without drawing attention to his interest. Every time his eyes flicked past where Cassana was huddling, she could feel his gaze linger long enough on her to take in her long bare legs and any other part of her body that offered him some interest. Unnerved by this attention, Cassana decided to engage him.

"Will you tell me your name now, please, sir?"

He looked back to her again, his eyes holding hers. "Why are you so keen to know my name?" He stopped pacing and faced her, holding the dying torch towards her.

"Because you have rescued me, and I would know the name of my saviour," Cassana said softly, a little intimidated by the dark look he gave her.

"And what makes you think that I have *rescued* you, princess?"

Cassana felt a cold fear spread through her as those piercing eyes flashed meaningfully at her. Before she could find courage to offer a reply, the wall behind him began to grind as it shifted slowly to one side. Turning, he faced the shadows beyond and he clenched his free hand into a fist, then relaxed it again.

"Sorry about that, I was having a piss," a gruff voice said from the shadows beyond.

"More like taking it!" the man said without humour, turning back to her. Moving to Cassana's side, he grabbed her by one arm and helped her up. A short man stepped from the opening to help and then thought better of it. He was a bald, thickset man, dressed in dark brown leather trousers, a tattered cotton shirt with short sleeves and soft leather shoes. His thick hairy arms were covered in tattoos of various naked female forms and as Cassana was pulled up into the torchlight, she could see that one of the women was doing something quite repulsive with an animal. The man's podgy face was lost in a thick red beard and his small nose wrinkled as he fixed his one good beady eye on her as she tried not to be sick.

"The boss is going to be impressed with you, mate!" he stated, obviously impressed. His eye wandered over Cassana's body hungrily and she felt sick again.

Fortunately Cassana was pulled through the opening before she could retort, as her escort ignored the man and pushed roughly passed him.

"Where is your master?" the man asked, as Cassana found herself in a small entrance chamber at the foot of a very steep set of stone stairs, lit by dim torchlight at the summit.

The short man had followed them back inside by now and he pulled hard on a lever, that slowly drew the wall back across into position again. Cassana could now see that the door was actually made from a composite of outer stone and thick wood at the rear.

"He is otherwise engaged, but instructed me, should you return," the short man said, inadvertently pausing long enough to draw attention to fact that he thought his reply might have sounded offensive. "Ahem, he asked me to see to the lady's needs until his return."

"Fine," the tall man said, starting up the stairs quickly. Cassana followed him, feeling uncomfortable as the bald man followed behind them. She could hear him panting heavily as they climbed and could feel his eye on her at every step of the way. Cassana found the ascent difficult and she nearly fell at one point. But she was determined to make it to the top and with her escort's help, she reached the torch-lit landing at the top of the stairs without having to stop for breath. A feat in its own right and one she clung onto dearly. She had not had much to feel good about recently and this small triumph offered her some hope for the future. Tossing down his dying torch, the hooded man dragged her towards a closed wooden door and hauled it open. They had put some distance between themselves and the short bald man and it appeared to Cassana that he wasn't prepared to wait any further for him that night. They moved through the open door into a plain room, inhabited by a worm-riddled wooden table and four accompanying chairs. A lantern shed strong light across the room from the table and a half-eaten supper lay forgotten on a steel plate. An open door behind the table led into a carpeted corridor beyond.

"Have a seat," the man said, leading Cassana by the arm to the table. Kicking a chair free for her, he let go of her arm and watched as she sank gratefully onto it. "If you are hungry, help yourself." he said, indicating to the half-eaten supper across from her. Despite the ravenous appetite developing inside of her, Cassana fixed a suspicious look on the food, consisting of cold peas, boiled potatoes and a half-chewed meat pie and shook her head regrettably.

"I am not hungry, thank you," she lied. "But if you would find me a blanket to keep warm please, I would really appreciate it?"

His flint-grey eyes flashed with something, as he studied her silently for a time, before he nodded slowly and turned away from her. Moving to the corridor, he stepped from view. Shuddering, Cassana lay her arms on the table and rested her head on them. Her exertions had left her utterly exhausted and for the briefest of moments she tried to imagine that she was back at The Arms of the Lady in Havensdale.

Unfortunately for Cassana though, that lovely thought soon scattered as the short bald man huffed and puffed his way into the room and shuffled over to her side, not Joseph Moore's daughter, Scarlet.

"Can I get you something, miss?" he gasped, sweating profusely. As she looked up at him with her weary eyes, he began to fidget uncomfortably.

"No, thank you," she said.

"I'll leave you to gather your breath then, miss," he said, shifting from foot to foot, as if he stood on hot coals. "I'll send one of the girls to show you to a room, so that you can rest while I send word to the boss that you are here!"

"That would be kind...Mr?"

The short man chuckled. "No Mr here, Lady Byron. Just call me Cullen, that's what everyone else calls me...well those who like me, anyway!"

"Thank you, Cullen," Cassana said, warming him further with a false smile. "May I ask who your employer is?"

Cullen looked over his shoulder, then turned his good eye back towards her. As he was about to speak, the hooded man swept back into the room carrying a woollen blanket in one hand. Cullen jumped in fright, and after excusing himself, he hurried from the room without another word. The man watched him leave, his eyes narrowing as he slipped by him and then wandered over to her.

"Here, take this," he said and tossed it onto the table beside her. "You look frozen!"

Cassana thanked him and wrapped the blanket about her shoulders. *Shame you hadn't realised that earlier*, she thought to herself.

He stood silently, watching her again for a time,

210

before turning to leave.

"Wait!" Cassana called after him, and to her surprise he stopped obediently. "Where are you going?"

"Missing me already?" he said, rich amusement in his voice as he turned back to face her again.

Cassana felt the colour return to her cheeks again. "No, I- I just wanted to know what was going to happen to me now, that is all?"

He folded his hands across his chest and his hooded head tilted thoughtfully as he considered his answer.

"I would tell you if I knew, princess," he said. "But I don't! All I can say is that you are safe, for now. Beyond that," he shrugged. "I know as much, or as little, as you do."

"Wait!" Cassana said again, as he turned away. He growled in frustration and his shoulders dropped as he turned back again.

"What do you want from me now, woman?" he snapped angrily.

"Will you never tell me your name, sir?" Cassana asked.

He stopped, his eyes holding hers. "My name is Arillion!" Turning on his heels he stalked silently from the room, leaving Cassana alone and offering her the chance to flee if she wanted it.

"Arillion," she said, repeating his name. It suited him, somehow. Overcome by weariness, Cassana yawned and rested her head on her arms, relieved that she had finally got someone to divulge something to her.

A young girl came into the room as promised, some minutes later only to find that Cassana was already fast asleep. Unsure of what to do for a few moments, she hesitated before picking up the blanket that had fallen to the floor, draping it carefully over the sleeping woman's shoulders.

Cassana woke some time later with a terrible cramp in her neck and stiffness in her back and shoulders that left her unable to move. Her arms were also numb and as she raised her head up to let the blood flow back into them, she heard somebody talking.

"Why didn't you just wake her girl?" It sounded like Cullen, and he wasn't very happy. "Well?"

"I'm sorry," came a meek, terrified squeak of a reply. "She looked so peaceful, I didn't want to..."
There followed a slap, that left Cassana wincing in sympathy and her cheeks burning angrily.

"You are not here to think, just do as you're told," Cullen raged on. "Go and wake her and get her something decent to wear. *I'll* have to go and explain why she is not ready to meet the boss."

"Yes, sir." Cassana could hear the hasty sounds of heavy retreating footsteps as Cullen headed away and she wasn't at all sorry about that. The man was obviously a bully and enjoyed taking out his own shortcomings on others weaker than himself. No wonder Arillion seemed to terrify him.

A waif of a young girl scuttled into the room and drew up short as she saw that Cassana was already awake. She was stick thin, with short blonde hair that had not seen the attention of a brush for many days. She was dressed in loose-fitting pantaloons and a filthy blouse that was smeared with grime, much like her pale face which was now coloured by a smarting slap on one cheek. Her dull blue eyes flitted furtively about the room as she tried to avoid revealing the shame evident in them and she rubbed her bare forearms with the opposite hand as she struggled to speak. If Cassana hadn't heard her out in the corridor, she would have thought her a boy.

"It is okay," Cassana said with a smile as she tried to coax the girl, who was no more than twelve winters old, to speak. "I will not hurt you."

The girl failed at a smile, but some light returned to her haunted eyes. She moved forward warily and stopped at the corner of the table.

"The boss will want to see you soon," she said softly. "First though, I have to show you a room and give you clothes."

Cassana smiled and nodded encouragingly. "Thank you, please, lead on." She rose stiffly, keeping the blanket tight about her shoulders as the girl spun on the balls of her bare feet and headed towards the open doorway. Cassana followed gingerly after her, allowing her anger at the girl's treatment to keep her warm. What an earth was a girl of this age doing down here in the sewers, surrounded by thieves and brigands? The girl was probably a street urchin and Cassana had not lived that sheltered a life to know that this kind of thing happened in the world outside of her luxurious lifestyle. Back home, her father had tried for many years to deal with the problem of poverty in the poorer areas of the city; but there were still those elements that preyed on the weak and vulnerable, exploiting them for their own needs and dark purposes.

The girl led her along the same carpeted corridor that Cullen and Arillion had vanished down earlier, past several closed wooden doors and turned left before a short flight of stairs that rose to a closed door. At the end of another corridor, she stopped at a door and pushed it open. Stepping aside, she nodded for Cassana to enter. Cassana smiled her thanks and entered, finding herself in a small bare room consisting of only a rickety looking bed and fragile side table.

"That should keep you a bit warmer," the girl stated, motioning to a dark bath robe that lay on the bed. Cassana moved to put it on and realised that the wool had once been white. Swallowing back her pride she gave into the cold and put it on, leaving the blanket on the bed, whose sheets looked like they hadn't been changed for quite some time.

Not quite the clothes she had in mind, but it was a start.

"Thank you," Cassana said, trying to hide the disgust on her face. "You are very young. How long have you lived here?"

The girl's eyes narrowed as her face wrinkled with distrust. "Ever since I can remember, though that's my business and not yours."

The girl turned abruptly, leaving Cassana to stare wordlessly after her as she left the room. Swallowing back her shock Cassana followed the girl, trying to banish the image of an unruly girl who had once terrorised her father, from her mind. With her cheeks burning with guilt, Cassana followed the girl back outside and up the staircase, moments after.

The door at the top of the short flight of steps opened out onto a landing, covered by a surprisingly soft and clean carpet of emerald. Ignoring the closed door before them the girl turned right and led Cassana towards another closed door at the end of a corridor, flanked by exquisite oil paintings of landscapes and battle scenes. Cullen waited impatiently before the door and his face reddened further as he saw that the girl had

214

not found their guest suitable attire. Sensing his fury, the young girl slowed as they approached and Cassana stepped by her to greet the repulsive little man with a reluctantly warm smile. She had met many people over the years who she despised, at the various social functions she had been forced to attend, in Highwater, and she was well trained by her friend Lysette on how to mask it.

"Ah, Cullen," Cassana smiled, tasting her own disgust. "My thanks, this is much better." She plucked at the robe to indicate the source of her apparent delight and regretted it immediately as the wool felt sticky.

The short man failed to hide his disgust and although he didn't believe a word she had said, he thankfully played along with her little game.

"Excellent," he said, waving the girl away. She needed no excuses to be away from Cullen's wrath and when Cassana turned to thank her, the girl was already at the top of the stairs. Smiling guardedly, Cassana turned back to Cullen. She had delayed a beating for the girl, but only for now, she guessed sadly. Cullen knocked on the door behind him and a voice answered from within, calling for him to enter.

"Follow me," Cullen said, opening the door and stepping inside. With her heart pounding, Cassana obeyed and followed him into the room beyond. Cullen waited only until she had entered the room and then quickly left without a word, closing the door quietly behind him.

Swallowing, Cassana looked about the dimly lit room and felt her nerves dance across her worried face. She was in a fabulously furnished room that reminded her immediately of her father's study back home. From the thick soft carpet underfoot, to the large oak desk and numerous heavily laden bookshelves, everything about this room reminded her of home and Cassana nearly collapsed under the weight of her desire to see Highwater again. Two empty leather chairs faced the large antique desk and from the other side, a man relaxed in a high-backed chair and watched her intently. A huge painting of a wolf howling from a hilltop with a large full moon rising into the night sky above it, hung from the wall behind the man and as he rose fluidly from his chair, Cassana was overcome with the feeling that she was in his den and at his mercy.

"Lady Byron, please let me say how relieved I am that you are safe and sound!" the man moved forward and took her left hand in his right hand, its fingers adorned with rings of gold and silver. Bowing low in respect, he kissed her trembling hand and smiled up at her. Cassana started with fright and recoiled, her gold bangle jumping off her wrist and sliding up her bare forearm. Dressed in long flowing robes of ruby, this tall middle-aged man was handsome and immediately captivating. Framed by a head of thick raven-black hair that was groomed to perfection, his face was clean-shaven and free from the expected ravages of time. His small nose was upturned and it wrinkled as he sensed her distress.

"Lady Byron, is something wrong?" his dark oval-shaped eyes flashed with genuine worry.

"Forgive me sir," Cassana stammered, as she looked away nervously.

Cassana felt her composure desert her as she looked down her arm into the man's eyes. His Reven heritage was obvious and she couldn't look at him directly. Was he behind her attempted abduction? Although he undoubtedly had Reven blood, he also had the softer features of their Valian neighbours and Cassana's mind scattered to the four winds on several confused trails of thought.

"I must apologise for the necessity and the circumstances of your arrival, Lady Byron. I trust that you were not harmed?" the man asked her, straightening slowly and releasing her hand. His voice was clear of any accent and hinted that he had been well educated.

Cassana clutched her hand to her chest and avoided his gaze. "I-I must confess that I was terrified at being manhandled from my bed in the middle of the night."

"Well perhaps you would like me to escort you back to your quarters in the keep then, your Ladyship?"

Cassana gasped in fright and jumped as Arillion stepped from the shadows of the room, behind her and away to the right. She looked aghast at him and could see his eyes flash mischievously towards her from the depths of his hood. He strode silently by to stand beside the robed man and turned to face her. Although his features were still hidden away by his mask and the shadows of his hood, Cassana could sense the enjoyment emanating from him.

"Enough Arillion," the robed man snapped, turning back. "I must apologise my lady for any heavy handedness on our part. But the necessity to extract you had to take precedence over your immediate welfare and the chance that you might scream. Please, you must be exhausted? Take a seat!"

Cassana nodded dumbly and followed his gesturing arm to sit obediently in the left leather chair. The robed man moved back hurriedly to take his seat behind the desk and Arillion wandered to the vacant chair, collapsing into it with an over-exaggerated sigh.

"Introductions!" the man announced, folding his hands on the desk before him. "My name is Savinn Kassaar. I am a respected merchant in the capital and for now at least, I am your friend."

Cassana stared blankly at him. Was he seriously expecting her to believe that he was a businessman and not some vicious crime lord that controlled the city's underworld? Or perhaps he revealed to her that in Karick, they were both one and the same.

He saw the look in her eyes and smiled boyishly. "I see that you do not believe me, Lady Byron. I can allow you that, at the very least. But in business these days let me tell you that to control the streets above, one is now forced to *manage* the situation below, also!"

Cassana met his eyes for the first time and read only the truth there. "Please excuse me sir, if I appear suspicious."

Savinn ignored Arillion's derisive snort. "I fully understand, my lady. Let me alleviate some of your confusion."

Finally! Cassana thought, her heart racing in anticipation.

"Nearly two weeks ago now, I received a letter from an old friend of mine," Savinn said, spreading his hands wide on the table. "It was hurriedly scrawled and the words were, I believe, written in haste and chased by fear."

Cassana's curiosity was overcoming her and she sat forward, leaning on the desk to stop herself falling off her seat.

"The letter said that my friend had been working at the high duke's keep, which I already knew as I had persuaded an official there to give him the job," Savinn continued, his face twisting ruefully. "He had overheard a conversation between two unnamed men in the high duke's gardens and was beside himself with worry."

"What did he hear?" Arillion asked, stealing the same question from Cassana's lips. She sent him an irritated look, but his hooded headed was fixed firmly on the merchant across from him now.

Savinn's oval eyes flicked briefly to him, before snapping back apologetically to Cassana. "He said that an attempt was going to be made on a woman of some importance. She was being coerced into a trap so that they might capture her and use her as leverage in a dark game they were playing."

Cassana felt her remaining strength drain away from her and she sank back into her chair and began to shake. That was it then. The confirmation she had been waiting for. There was a dark plot manifesting in the shadows of the high duke's court and she was to be the pawn that would set their plans in motion. If they had managed to capture her, they could have indeed influenced her father to bend to their demands, whatever they may be. The woodsman had been right with his summation, which also meant there was most certainly a spy in her father's camp. But who? Cassana clenched her fists angrily.

"Did this letter say anything else?" Arillion probed.

Savinn shook his head, lowering his eyes regretfully. "It said only that he believed his life was in danger, as the men probably knew that he had unwittingly overheard their conversation. He also said that he had left the letter with the proprietor of the Mason's Inn, here in the city, with instructions that if he did not attend his establishment for more than a week, that he was to deliver this letter to me... as he believed he would have been killed."

Cassana could hear the sorrow in the merchant's voice and fought back her own emotions.

"I am sorry for your friend, Savinn. Who was he?" she whispered sympathetically and he looked up at her, forcing a smile.

"His name was Khadazin Sahr. A simple man of foreign heritage, like me!" Savinn said, his lips parted by an ironic smile. "Years ago he saved my life and from that moment on I vowed that I would repay him properly for the life he had granted me. I did all I could to get work for the Redani over the years, working in a city full of bigots, but I swore to myself that one day I would truly repay the debt to my saviour... and my friend!"

A Redani? Cassana's eyes brimmed with tears. "I did not know him, sir."

Savinn laughed, his eyes glistening in the candle light. "Nor he you, lady! He did not even know your name; so in that you now have the advantage over him. The only thing he knew was that he was devastated he could not find a way to help you. It tore him apart and even though, and justifiably so it seems, he feared he would be killed – he asked me in his letter to use all of my resources to see if I could help you in anyway. Or at the very least find out what had happened to you."

Cassana struggled with her guilt and began to cry.

"Please, Lady Byron," Savinn pleaded. "Do not cry. Khadazin at least succeeded with his final wish. I had my people listen to the stirrings of the street for any sign of you and because of this, I became aware very quickly that you had survived the ambush and had made it safely to the city. From there, I used my resources to locate where you were staying and then discovered that, in fact, you were being held."

Cassana nodded. "So all that has happened to me, was because of Madam Grey?"

Savinn quickly shook his head.

"Alas, I fear it is not quite so simple, my lady. It is true that she was drugging you, but as to why and for whom, we are not so certain. Khadazin finished his letter by saying that he would tell me everything, if we ever met again. If we did not, then he could depart from this life knowing that he had at least spared his one true friend from all the danger he had put himself in."

Cassana's head ached badly now as she tried to grasp on to the complexities of it all. "What of Chancellor Valus then? Is he involved?"

"If he is," Arillion interjected, "then the Redani's reluctance to name who he overheard plotting has ruined any chance you had of exposing the people behind all of this."

"Unfortunately, I agree," Savinn said gloomily. "I have been aware for some years now that there are those within the Four Vales who are not happy with the direction the high duke is taking us. But they guard themselves well and blind my attempts to find out more with false intelligence and red-herrings."

"Whoever they are?" Cassana pondered thoughtfully. "I cannot thank you enough for orchestrating my rescue, Savinn and I would be grateful for anything else you can tell me?" Savinn drummed his fingers thoughtfully on his desk, before continuing.

"There will be more time for us to speak Lady Byron, once you have rested, bathed and we have finally managed to offer you some adequate clothing," he said sardonically. "For now, all I will ask of you is that you remain here for a few days while my spies continue to monitor the situation and await to see how certain people react when they find out that you have disappeared."

"If you think it best, sir, then of course," Cassana answered. Did she really have a choice?

Savinn nodded. "I do lady and if you would forgive my impertinence, you look exhausted. You have endured much recently and you will need several days to recover your strength, so that you are strong enough to flee the city."

Cassana couldn't have put it better herself and she nodded her thanks. It appeared that Savinn's concerns for her might stretch beyond his sense of duty to his friend and she suspected that she would need his assistance in the coming days.

"In truth, Lady Byron, we have little else to work with at the moment," Savinn admitted. "Madam Grey took her own life before she could even be questioned about the whole affair..."

"Dead?" Cassana gasped and then blushed as the merchant-thief looked quizzically at her. She could read the confusion in his dark eyes. Why are you concerned for her? They asked. Have you forgotten about what she was doing to you? Cassana struggled with her own confusion and embarrassment, remaining silent. She shouldn't feel anything for the woman, but for some strange reason, she did. Fortunately for Cassana, Arillion's snort and sudden movement helped to divert her attention and the direction of their conversation.

"Time for me to be on my way," he announced, yawning. Rising from his chair, he stretched out his left hand towards his employer.

"My thanks, Arillion," Savinn said, rising from his

seat as they shook hands. "I will have need of you again soon, I am sure."

"When you do, you know where to find me," Arillion said. Releasing his hand he turned and strode to the door, without looking at Cassana.

"Thank you, Arillion." Cassana said, her voice even and soft. As he twisted the handle and pulled open the door, he paused in the open doorway and turned.

"The thanks are all mine, Lady Byron," he said, his eyes flashing merrily. With a mocking bow, he turned again and was gone, closing the door silently behind him.

"Do not trouble yourself with thanks for him, my lady," Savinn said, as she turned back to face him. "Be assured that he has been well compensated for his time and cares nothing for your plight!"

For some reason Cassana felt part of her heart sink and she sighed. She had suspected that Arillion was a mercenary of some kind and although the man infuriated her, he still had a certain aura about him. One that she had also sensed in the woodsman; although put together for a comparison, they would appear on opposite sides of a coin.

Savinn regarded her silently for a time as he read the curious disappointment in the young woman's eyes. Propping his elbows on the desk, he touched his fingertips together.

"Following Madam Grey's departure and with one of my own in her place, I spent my time trying to find out what has happened to Edward Neve." Savinn saw the concern flash in Cassana's eyes and she sat forward in her chair again.

"He was very kind to me, sir," she said worriedly. "Did you find him?"

Savinn shook his head regrettably. "I am afraid not. He has simply vanished, along with his grandson, Thomas."

"The woman who helped me to recover told me that they had gone away on family business," Cassana said hopefully, but even her own words sounded hollow.

"I fear that was simply a tale spun to tidy up any loose ends," Savinn said. "Those behind your attempted abduction are obviously trying to cover up their tracks and remove anyone you may have confided in."

Cassana began to shake. She had suspected this already, of course. But she had hoped that the merchant would be able to tell her something to the contrary.

"What of the woman who helped me?" Cassana asked. "What is her name? Will she be safe?"

"Dia is one of my best," Savinn revealed. "She can take care of herself and has been employed at the keep for many years now. She will report back to me in a few days time if she is able to, and let me know what is happening in the wake of your departure."

"I have met so many brave people on my journey to the city," Cassana said humbly. "I hope she will be okay? I could not bear it if yet another person lost their life because of me! I still do not understand why so many people have helped me? I feel so useless that I cannot even look after myself!"

Savinn reached out a comforting hand towards her and smiled. "People will have helped you for many reasons, lady. Some through kindness, others because they felt that it was the right thing to do. I, myself, have done so because I felt it was indeed *the right thing to do*. Try to console yourself Cassana with the fact that because of their sacrifice, you now have the chance to control the situation yourself."

Cassana nodded meekly, and wiped her tears away with back of her right hand. "Thank you, Savinn. I know you speak the truth, but it is a heavy burden I bear and one that I fear will take me a long time to come to terms with."

"I understand, Lady Byron and I am only sorry that I cannot do anything more to help you with that," Savinn said. "But in all other aspects of your current predicament, I am certain I can help you."

"How so, sir?"

Savinn's face darkened. "I have been advised that Madam Grey was to dispatch a letter on your behalf to your father, am I correct?" Savinn waited for Cassana's nod of confirmation, before continuing. "Well, you can be assured that the letter would have never been sent and that your father is still unaware of what has befallen you. The best thing for you to do now, is to flee the city and get back safely to your father so that you can tell him what has happened, yourself."

Cassana nodded in agreement, though her face betrayed her concern. "That certainly is my desire, naturally. But I am unsure of how to proceed from here."

Drawing in a deep breath to steady her nerves, Cassana decided to lay her cards on the table and proceeded to tell Savinn all that had happened to her, since she was attacked in the Moonglade Forest. From her flight through the forest, to her journey to the city, she left nothing out, except, yet again, for the presence of the woodsman in her tale. Something in the way he had spoke about the capital still stopped her, staying her tongue so that he remained a mystery to all and even now, to her. If he didn't want to return to Karick, then she would respect his wishes and keep him out of it. She owed him that much, at the very least! Throughout her tale, Savinn listened silently, his handsome face a mask of emotionless serenity. He did not even flinch when Cassana mentioned that her attackers were Reven and Cassana suspected that he already knew this fact. When she was finished with her account, she sank back into the comfort of her chair, panting wearily.

"A truly remarkable journey," Savinn said, puffing up his cheeks and blowing out an incredulous breath. "I can see, however, that you are on the brink of collapse and I will not keep you any longer this night, other than to say that I will help you return to your father. Leave the arrangements with me, lady. I will organise everything for you. All that I require from you now, is that you rest and regain your strength. The road home will be a dangerous one, as your enemies will undoubtedly expect you to try and return to your father."

"I suspected as much," Cassana said, her shoulders starting to feel the weight of pressure returning to them again.

"Getting you out of the city will not pose a problem," Savinn stated, smiling. "There are many safe routes out of the city through the sewers and they will not be able to watch them all. It is on the open road however, where the problems arise. They will be watching every major route out of the city to Highwater, so you will probably need to travel across country."

Cassana's face paled further at the prospect. "I had thought to travel to Havensdale. I have friends there, they might be able to help me home?"

Savinn was already shaking his head. "Havensdale is *exactly* where they will be expecting you to head to. If Edward was tortured, they will know you have allies there. You must stay well away from there and keep to the wilds. In doing so, you may even protect Captain Ardent and her men."

The recurring thought of bringing harm to Fawn proved too much for Cassana yet again and she broke down, sobbing uncontrollably. Rising from his chair, Savinn moved to her side, laying a comforting hand on her right shoulder. Although she had a strength about her, Savinn could tell that she was still shackled by the chains of youth and hampered by the enormity of the burden she carried.

"Come with me, my lady," he ordered, his soft voice touched by pity. Helping her up he told her that he would take her to some quarters befitting of the comfort she deserved and Cassana nodded gratefully. Guiding the emotional woman from the room Savinn led her carefully along the carpeted corridor, urging her on with comforting words and kind assurances. Despite all the resources and wealth at his disposal, Savinn had not been able to save his friend. But for now, at least, he was in a position to help Cassana save hers...

CHAPTER ELEVEN

Confession

The masked man watched impassively as Borin slammed a large fist into the Redani's face again. The sound of the impact and the snapping of their captive's nose echoed about the torture chamber and was quickly swallowed up by the intense roaring heat from the brazier. The force of the blow sent the Redani backwards onto the filthy floor, still strapped helplessly to the chair and as Borin looked back towards him for guidance, the masked man nodded for him to continue with his work.

"Why prolong this pain?" the man said seductively, as Borin hauled the prisoner back upright and checked to make sure he was still conscious and alive. "Tell us the truth and we will release you from this suffering."

Khadazin spat blood from his mouth and snorted it disdainfully from his ruined nose as he glared at the bald-headed, masked man. The man was still dressed in the same brown robes he had been wearing the first time Khadazin had been tortured and his emotionless eyes rebuffed the stonemason's hatred with a conciliatory smile.

"Such anger, Redani," he continued, shaking his head sadly. "Why fight against it, when all you have to do is impart the truth to us? Believe it or not, I do not enjoy seeing people suffer needlessly and all of this can be over, if you tell me what I need to know!"

Khadazin laughed and shook his head. "And your people have the gall to call me a savage!" He flicked his bleary eyes towards the huge man who obviously relished the pain he inflicted upon people, as he wandered along the long table deciding on what implement to use on him next. Borin was wearing his long leather apron and kilt again and he had left the poker in the brazier as a grim reminder to the stonemason. Khadazin lolled in his chair, his naked body glistening like wet obsidian as he carried on with his ruse, which was sadly becoming all the more easy with each heavy blow from the torturer.

For three days now, as far as Cornelius could tell, Khadazin had slept as much as he could as he sought to regain the strength that would hopefully see him through his next, inevitable round of torture. During that time the two prisoners had received no food, or visits from their captors and for the past two days the stonemason had been sampling the fleshy *delights* of his rodent visitors; as well as their blood. At first the raw flesh was sickening to him and after having been starved of food for many days now, the stonemason had immediately brought the meagre contents of his stomach back up again. But as the dark hours passed away, he had slowly started to keep the raw meat down and after several meals, despite his disgust at the level of depravity he had now sunken to, Khadazin had to admit to the old man that he was starting to feel physically stronger again. There was nothing wrong with his mind of course, such was his desire for freedom and revenge. But for him to succeed at that, he would first need to be strong enough to fight back when the opportunity presented itself. Khadazin was sure it would eventually, but until that time he would have to fake how badly injured he was, lest they torture him to a point where he wouldn't be capable of fighting them. The four robed figures had finally come to fetch him and as he was dragged away, Khadazin had listened to the torchbearer taunting Cornelius again. Still full of determination, pride and hope after all of his years of incarceration, the old man had ignored him, however, turning his back on them all in a show of silent defiance. Khadazin had grinned secretly to himself...

The man stepped closer to the stonemason, folding his hands in his robes as he approached. From behind the mask, his eyes betrayed his impatience for the first time.

"You are a fool, Khadazin Sahr," he pointed out to him, leaning close enough for the stonemason to feel his light breath upon his ear. "You are misguided if you think that by keeping silent, you will protect your friends. I can assure you that it will not! You only delay the inevitable and prolong your pain."

Khadazin turned his head feebly away and the man chuckled. "Take a good look at yourself? The wounds you received from your fight in the alley have already doomed you, and our friend here," he paused and reached behind the stonemason's shoulders to point meaningfully at his companion. "He has not even started to hurt you yet! You must believe me Redani when I say that the pain you have suffered is only the beginning of the unimaginable horrors that will befall you if you do not tell me the truth."

Khadazin focused on the heat of the chamber, hoping that it would stem the cold fear creeping up his spine. He had to be careful not to overplay his stance. If he did, they might decide to start removing parts of his anatomy; Cornelius had told him that they didn't usually start doing that until the fourth round of torture, but as the stonemason turned his head back to meet the robed man's gaze, he felt that he might not get that far.

"I cannot tell you anything more," Khadazin said, shaking as he bowed his head in submission. "Please, you must listen to me! I have nothing more to tell you."

The man withdrew from him and let out a long, disappointed sigh. "I am saddened by that, my friend," he said in earnest. "But we still have plenty of time at our disposal to find that out for ourselves."

He moved back to his position before the door and ordered Borin back to his work with a subtle nod. Grinning, the big man turned and Khadazin's eyes widened in fear when he saw the large pair of rusty pliers in his left hand.

"It's time to stop messing about, Redani," the masked man said, as the flickering shadow of the brutish torturer fell menacingly across him again.

Borin stepped away from the unconscious man and turned slowly, his pock-marked face stained by disappointment. His companion watched him from the shadows of the closed doorway and continued to say nothing as the torturer relaxed his grip on the pliers in his left hand and let the bloodied tooth drop to the floor. Borin shrugged his indifference as he moved back to the table and returned the pliers. After losing all of the fingernails on his right hand, the third tooth had finally proven to be too much for the Redani and he had passed out with a pathetic whimper. Although Borin was actually quite impressed with the dark-skinned foreigner's stamina, he kept his thoughts to himself. He had tortured many people over the years and some had survived a lot worse, but there was something different about this one. He could sense that it was going to take quite a lot more and a lot worse, to break him. Borin grinned, feeling the arousal stirring in his blood. By the storms he was going to enjoy this!

The two prisoners that had been brought in recently by the *hoods* had not offered much in the way of sport for a man of his talents. The abusive old man had died from a heart attack before he could even touch him and the young one had squealed the moment he had waved the hot poker in front of his face. Disappointed, Borin hadn't even bothered to listen as the terrified prisoner spilled his guts out to his interrogator and had only paid attention again when he was informed that they no longer needed the boy. With his enthusiasm now waning, Borin had quickly burnt out both of the boy's eyes, before dragging a bone saw across the lad's throat.

"So what do you think?" the masked man asked, garnering the larger man's attention.

Borin wiped his bloodied hands on his apron, looking absently at the unconscious stonemason as he decided on his response.

"He's not going to tell you anything at the moment."

"Because?"

"For one, he's a stubborn bastard!" Borin said, his gruff voice tinged with respect.

"And two?"

"He's damaged goods," the torturer continued, disappointed. "There's no doubting his strength though! Anyone who can take on four assassins and survive is going to take some serious pain before they break. But he probably won't survive that long."

The masked man cursed and turned away bitterly as if to leave and then paused, turning back again.

"He has to survive Borin, well at least long enough for us to be certain. I can't report back and say that we think he's telling the truth! There is far too much at stake for any more uncertainty."

Borin shrugged indifferently and looked towards the Redani. "If he hasn't confessed to you by the time I have finished with him tomorrow, then he never will!"

"Damn it," the other man said, letting out a deep sigh as he paced about the chamber. "Our other attempt seems to have failed thus far as well, so if he doesn't talk after tomorrow, you have my permission to take both his hands and tongue."

Borin grinned. "That should do the trick, he won't be able to tell anyone then."

The masked man moved to stand before the naked Redani and lifted up the man's bowed head by his broad, bearded chin to study his ruined blood-streaked face. His face was badly swollen now and his nose and lips were spilt and broken from the impacts of Borin's huge fists.

"If you hold any belief for a higher power Redani," he said softly, "then I suggest that you pray to them this night." Letting go of the man's head, he turned and made for the door.

"I shall send the guards to return him to his cell," he said without looking back, as he flung open the door. Borin grunted an acknowledgement as the man slammed the door behind him and his footfalls headed swiftly away. Looking at the Redani again he shook his head and started sharpening his tools in readiness for the coming work.

Khadazin listened intently to their exchange and any triumph he may have felt he held over the masked man soon scattered when he heard what they had in store for him. It had been easy to feign his unconsciousness, as the man he now knew as Borin took his third lower tooth. The pain in his face and body was incredible and it had taken all of his remaining strength to stay conscious as the man took his fingernails, and then moved on to his teeth. But it had been worth it, if only for the fact that he now knew the masked man was bluffing. He had said to him that they had plenty of time at their disposal. But from what he had just heard, it sounded like that was furthest from the truth. But why were they suddenly so desperate to find out who he had told, if anyone? Had something happened? Had their plans failed, or perhaps even succeeded? Or were they just under pressure from the chancellor and his *brothers* to tie up any loose ends? Whatever the reasoning behind this sudden change of pace, Khadazin was no longer in any doubt that he would have to escape before they came for him tomorrow. The stonemason slowly tested the straps that bound his wrists to the chair as he watched the broad back of the torturer through the swollen lids of his bloodshot eyes. He wasn't surprised to find that the straps were tight and he couldn't free himself that easily. If he was going to escape he would have to take the first opportunity that presented itself to him now and whether he lived or died, he was going to have to at least try something.

Despite the masked man's curious advice before he left, Khadazin had never been a religious man and he would have to trust in his own abilities to keep him alive. He had seen many terrible things happen over the years to suggest to him that there wasn't a higher power in the heavens. If there was, then why did they always seem to allow such horrors to go unpunished in the world below them? Where was their celestial justice when a man shamefully raped a woman, or why did the farmer's crops fail, leaving him destitute and broken. Before he had left his homeland Khadazin had witnessed the effects of a terrible drought that had left swathes of the eastern Redani territories plagued by starvation and disease. He had been too young at the time to really understand the full extent of what was happening, but even then he could not understand why the people cried to the heavens, demanding salvation and forgiveness for bringing the wrath of the gods down upon them. Many of the Redani territories worshipped the goddess of the sun, Sharamin. She was supposedly the bringer of life and prosperity; a kind deity who was loved unquestionably by her people. Khadazin had never felt that their love had been reciprocated and his father, a man of little faith himself, had taken him away from a homeland ravaged by famine and starvation, and on the cusp of a terrible civil war.

It was noticeably different in the Four Vales however, as the majority of the Valian people held faith only in their ruler, the high duke. Any talk of a higher power was viewed with open scepticism; a grand tale spun by wistful bards and romantic storytellers. There were some Valian people though, who held faith in a deity known as the Lady of the Vales, and equally a number who often offered up curses to one known as The Father of Storms. The former was believed to watch over the Valian lands during the day, protecting its people and bringing them continued peace and prosperity. The latter was seen as the bringer of trouble, a mischievous entity that brought only darkness and chaos. Because of this, many of their followers believed them to be estranged siblings, one light and one dark; one night and one day. They saw them as opposite sides of a celestial coin, chasing each other across the sky in an eternal attempt to try and settle their mortal differences.

In a surprise departure from the law-entrenched beliefs of his father, the high duke had decided to publicly acknowledge the people who had chosen to follow these deities, after he had chaired his first Valian Council meeting, some twenty years ago now. He had also gone on to say that whilst there was no recognised religion in the Four Vales, he would not stop their followers erecting shrines and temples as long as they continued to respect his authority and abide by the law of the land, not the heavens. It was a shrewd move. In one speech and hastily written law the high duke had legally allowed these new faiths to prosper, whilst retaining his absolute control over their growing numbers, without alienating them. In time a recognised monastic order was also established by a group of men who worshipped the Lady of the Vales. With their own funds and donations from their supporters, the brothers bought some land in the South Vales and built a humble monastery called the Hermitage Retreat, high in the chalky hills that looked out across the waters of the Low Sea. Seeking only peaceful self-enlightenment through contemplation, they hid themselves away from the lure and temptations of sin, spending their time studying ancient Valian texts and learning how to live off the land around them. Farming their surrounding lands the brothers planted vast orchards and used the warmer temperate climate in the South Vales to grow grapes in the chalky soil that had perfect drainage for their roots. They then spent the next decade perfecting their vine growing and wine fermenting skills, eventually going on to produce the widely distributed red wine, Valian Dark. Several years later, the high duke also commissioned the brothers to legally distil the Burning Leaf brandy; allowing a controlled production and low cost distribution of the spirit in an effort to undermine the rampant illegal trade of the drink. For years the Valian navy had struggled to break the numerous smuggling rackets that operated out of Freeman's Cove to the north of the city port of Ilithia and the hundreds of other secluded beaches around the Four Vales. Increased trade with the Far Continent also meant that the Valian navy's time had been spent chasing and engaging the pirate ships that harangued and attacked the merchant ships seeking trade across the dangerous Far Sea. Because of this, the enterprising smugglers had started to appear, trading in Redani goods that the authorities had deemed illegal and yet the people had not. Demand was everything and if you could get it, the rewards usually far outweighed the punishments for getting caught. By legalising and controlling the brandy's distribution however, the high duke had quickly poured cold water onto the illegal trade of the fiery, addictive spirit. Most of the money the Hermitage Retreat received for the production of the spirit was also reportedly given back to the temples in the cities around the Four Vales, in an effort to help the poor and needy. So the high duke's decision had proven to be a very popular one, indeed!

"Alone, at last!"

It took all of Khadazin's resolve to stop himself reacting as the huge man spoke, his voice full of foreboding. Closing his eyes in time, the stonemason could hear the torturer turn from the long table and he could feel the man's eyes burn through him.

"You can open your eyes now, Redani," he said, breathing heavily in the airless chamber. "It may be easy to fool the fool, but I have seen many people try to fake unconsciousness over the years, and most better at it than you are!"

Khadazin panicked, trying to stem the fear rising quickly to the surface of his ruse.

"Our erstwhile friend was far too worried about the wider world to realise that you were still awake," Borin continued, coming close enough now for Khadazin to detect his shadow through his closed eyelids. "I just had to wait for him to go, before we could continue our...little chat!"

Khadazin started involuntarily as the man cracked the knuckles of one hand beside his right ear and chuckled. Opening his eyes reluctantly, the stonemason met the man's gaze and read his dark intentions there.

"You are not to harm me further, you have your orders, Borin!" Khadazin said vainly, as the man laughed down at him.

"I lied to him about your condition, so that we could become better acquainted. You are about to discover that I don't give a damn about his little problem," Borin answered, leaning close enough to touch noses with his prisoner. "Whatever my reasons are, we now have a little time to pass. So let's not waste it, shall we?"

Borin grabbed his prisoner roughly by the chin and studied his strong features for a time. He quickly saw the hatred burning in Khadazin's dark defiant eyes and smiled at him.

"You hate me, don't you?" he asked, pre-empting his response.

Khadazin shook his head as best he could in the man's grip. "I don't hate you, Borin," he said. "I pity you!"

Growling, Borin disdainfully shoved the Redani's face to one side and leant back warily as the stonemason tensed and looked round at him again. Straightening his huge frame, Borin stuck a large hand deep inside the front pocket of his leather apron. Raising a painfully stiff eyebrow, Khadazin held his malevolent stare for a moment and then grinned at him.

"Sorry, I am not that way inclined, my friend," he said, flashing the torturer a bloody grin.

Borin laughed. "I like you Redani, I really do!" he said, removing his hand. "But I am a craftsman and much like yourself, I always strive for perfection."

Khadazin's grin slipped from his face as he saw the salt spilling through the man's clenched fist.

"I won't lie to you, my black friend," Borin hissed, grabbing the stonemason by the throat. "This is really going to hurt."

The three guards dropped the still form of the Redani onto the floor of his cell and locked the barred door behind him as they left. Muttering amongst themselves, they departed through the heavy door, closing out their light behind them as they left. Any hope Cornelius had felt when only the three guards had returned the Redani this time, was quickly extinguished when he saw the stonemason's condition. One of the guards had muttered something about him being 'finished' and the torchbearer had replied that if he survived the night, he would not see the next one. They had ignored him this time as they left and Cornelius felt a huge hole open up in the pit of his stomach. His own selfish desire for survival may have cost both of them their lives.

"Khadazin?" he whispered urgently, his voice still wary of their retreating hosts. "Oh my friend, what have they done to you?"

The stonemason's body was awash with blood from the dozen of cuts that scarified his motionless frame and there was a white powder evident over each wound. Salt!

"Bastards!" Cornelius spat angrily as he reached vainly out to the Redani through the bars of his cell to try and comfort him. Fortunately the old man could just about tell that he was still alive from his vantage point, as he could see his broad chest quickly rising and falling in tandem with his heart's demand for air.

"I am so sorry," he whispered, resting his head against the bars of his confines.

"For what?" Khadazin said weakly, stirring slightly.

Cornelius banged his head as he jumped in fright and let out a deep sigh of relief.

"You are alive, Redani!" he grinned, jumping madly for joy.

"It doesn't feel like it."

"Doesn't look like it either," Cornelius said bitterly. His neighbour was in a terrible state and he could see that he had missing teeth and was badly beaten as well, when the stonemason rolled over and grimaced with the effort.

"Rest, man," Cornelius ordered. "You are in no condition to be moving about."

Khadazin stared through the shadows at the old man and saw the genuine concern in the wizened face that looked across at him. "We don't have the time, my friend."

"We don't?"

Khadazin sat up, crying out in pain as his wounds stretched and the salt tasted his blood again. "If I don't confess tomorrow, I will lose my hands and my tongue."

Cornelius nearly coughed out his own tongue. "They are just trying to force your hand, Khadazin. You must be..." he trailed off as he saw the dark head shaking.

"I feigned unconsciousness and overheard my interrogator saying that he is out of time. Either way, tomorrow I will be silenced forever."

Cornelius felt the rest of his strength seep from his body in a torrent of despair and he collapsed to the floor, shaking his head and bemoaning his foolishness. There was no more time for them, it was now or never. If he ever wanted to see the blue Valian skies again he would have to place all of his remaining faith in this dark-skinned foreigner and stop trying to hedge his bets.

"Perhaps not!" Cornelius said quietly.

Khadazin detected an alien tone in his friend's voice and he frowned. "What do you mean?"

Cornelius fidgeted and looked about the shadows, avoiding the stonemason's quizzical look.

"Well, ahem, I am afraid I haven't been totally

honest with you Redani." When the stonemason didn't reply, he cleared his throat and continued. "Before they brought you to me, our hosts came to me with a proposal."

"Go on," Khadazin said, his eyes glinting dangerously.

Cornelius's ashen face twisted worriedly and he chewed his lip nervously. "Before I tell you Redani, you have to understand that I have been down here for many, many years and I have seen many people come and go during that time. I believed that I would never see my family again and I was bereft of all hope. When they offered me their proposal, I couldn't resist the chance for freedom."

Khadazin nodded. "Tell me, my friend."

Cornelius took a final breath and let it out again before continuing. "They said that if I could befriend you and find out who you had told, they would finally free me from my imprisonment."

Khadazin squinted, studying the old man as best he could in the dark. Was this a last desperate attempt from his captors to find out what he knew, or had the old man been playing him all this time. Helping him to recover so that he could trust him enough to impart with the one thing that had kept him alive, thus far. Uncertainty. Cornelius returned his scrutiny with downcast eyes as he awaited the justified wrath from his neighbour. If possible, he suddenly looked older than he already was. A skeleton ready to crumble to dust.

"How were you to tell them?" Khadazin asked, his calm voice cutting through the dark curtain of tension between them.

"The guard who taunts me all the time, when they come for you," Cornelius replied hastily, eager to confess now. "He would stay back to supposedly beat me, when I finally replied to his abuse. That would be the signal that I had some information for him."

"Cunning," the stonemason admitted, nodding his head slightly.

"I am sorry, Khadazin." Cornelius's eyes glistened with guilty tears.

"Do not be sorry, my friend," Khadazin said. "I do not blame you, Cornelius. If I had been here as long as you have, I am certain that I would have done the same."

The old man broke down, his fragile frame almost snapping with each loud sob.

"Please, do not cry," Khadazin pleaded. "I have not met many people since coming to your shores that I can honestly say I have liked, trusted, or been inspired by. But you are one of those people Cornelius, your courage inspires me!"

"I have courage?" the old man asked, sniffing. "How can you say that after what I have done? I am a coward!"

Khadazin shook his head. "You are not. If you were, you would have taken your life long ago. Instead you have suffered all these years, clinging on to the faintest of hopes that one day you would be free. That is called courage where I come from!"

Cornelius blinked back his tears and studied the Redani in amazement. "I do not know what to say to that, my friend! I am humbled, shamed by your humility, truly I am. I have met many people in my lifetime, but I can honestly say that I have never met, and will probably never have the privilege to meet again, a man like you."

Khadazin bowed his head respectfully. "That is very

gracious of you, my friend."

Cornelius reached out through the bars again, his face lighting up and threatening to set fire to his parched wrinkles. "Well then, seeing as we are a couple again, how about we get out of this cesspit, once and for all?"

Khadazin sat up curiously, wincing as fresh pain tore at his body and salt-powdered face. "How?"

Cornelius grinned a broad toothless grin. "I don't know about you, but I am pissed off with rats for supper. How about we get out of here and go and find a cow to eat?"

"How?" Khadazin said again, grinning as he tried to rein in his eager curiosity.

"With this," Cornelius said. Turning, he scuttled back into the depths of his cell. Moments later, after much cussing and cursing, he was back and he held something in his hands.

"I was a fool to think they would free me," Cornelius admitted. "They probably would have, but not the way I would have wanted. I didn't tell you about it before, because I was waiting to see how things would turn out!"

The old man opened his hands to reveal a small, jagged piece of what looked to be flint. It was nearly twice the size of an arrowhead in length and the old man held it in his hands like he had just found an ancient treasure. Khadazin felt the stirrings of hope rekindle again and he crawled closer to the door of his cell.

"I have been working this out for a year now," Cornelius said proudly. "Chipping away at the back wall with rat bones. At first I thought to dig a tunnel, but then I thought, why not sharpen it. I might even take one of those bastards with me, before my time was up!"

Khadazin reached the bars of his cell, panting heavily. The ancient Redani's had used flint for their weapons, before discovering steel. When sharp, it could cut through most armour, if you had the strength in your arm.

"It's not much use to a streak of piss like me," Cornelius exclaimed. "But with your strength, it could make a useful weapon."

"Most definitely," Khadazin beamed in agreement, his heart pounding with renewed excitement. This was their chance! If he could hide the flint somehow, he could surprise his captors and turn the odds in his favour before they realised what was happening. "Any thoughts on how we can get out of here?"

Cornelius grinned and spat in the dust. "I've waited a long time to hear someone say that and as a matter of fact, yes, I bloody well do!"

The man slumped low in his chair, listening to the sound of the heavy rain drumming out a rapid tune on the slate roof above him. It was often the case in the summer, when the pressure of the day's heat became too much and the clouds could not hold on to their contents any longer. They underlined this fact with a distant growl of thunder, that jerked the man from his morose thoughts and sent him reaching for the glass on the large desk before him.

How many was it now? He asked himself silently, picking up the half-filled glass with a shaking hand. The dark bottle next to the low-burning candle on the desk was nearly empty again and he would soon have to call the girl back to fetch him another one. Sighing deeply the man drained the glass, grimacing as the amber liquid burnt his throat and momentarily chased away his thoughts. Apart from the candle, the large study was lost in shadows and as the man stared into the past, they seemed to close in around him. Shaking his head free of any more surfacing questions, he discarded the glass and reached for the bottle, instead.

Behind him the long pair of red velvet curtains twitched as a draft stole through the two wood-framed glass doors that led him out into the gardens of his modest estate. Numb to the elements from the alcohol now, he failed to see one of the curtains part and did not notice the slim shadow that slipped quietly into the study behind him. As he took another pull on the bottle, he noticed the candle flame twitch and felt a cold fear blow on his neck.

"I take it you are celebrating?" A rich feminine voice enquired.

The man leapt from his seat in fright, dropping the bottle on the carpeted floor. It bounced quietly away, weeping its remaining contents out underneath the man's chair.

"Or perhaps not!" the female voice observed sarcastically.

Catching his breath the man placed both his palms on the desk to steady himself and his nerves as the shadow moved round the desk into the candlelight and sat in the chair across from him.

"Forgive me, I was not expecting you tonight!" the man stated, smoothing down his robes and sitting back in his chair to rest his listless legs.

"So it seems." The figure across from him was wrapped in a drenched, dark cloak and hood that concealed the features of the female within. She leant forward to clasp a glistening pair of thin, pale hands on the desk before her.

"It is my job to come and go unannounced, as you well know. But what I do not know, however, is why you are trembling like a startled deer?"

Chancellor Relan Valus stared expectantly as the woman reached up and slowly lowered her hood. The candle's light revealed a pale and yet striking face that many would have considered beautiful, were it not for the old ragged scar that ran down her right cheek and jumped onto the soft neck below. The woman was in her thirties and her long wet, mousy hair was tied into rows of tight braids across her head. Aware of this scrutiny, she stared disdainfully through a pair of bright eyes of the deepest emerald and down a long, thin sloping nose at him. Silver studs glinted from each ear and her full lips curled into a knowing smile as he looked away from her in embarrassment. She enjoyed these games with the chancellor. He was attracted to her, that was obvious enough when they had met before; but equally her reputation terrified him. He was renowned for his love of the younger woman, especially those he could not have and he had, on occasion been known to take what he wanted whether it was on offer or not. She despised him, but loved to torment him. Unattractive as he was, she would rather slit her throat than offer him a sample of her delights.

"If you have finished dreaming about what you cannot have," she snarled, "perhaps you can start by telling me what we do have and where I can find her?"

The chancellor fidgeted and his face paled significantly. "I-I, there has been some unforeseen developments recently, Kestrel!"

The woman glared at him. "What do you mean, *developments*?" She rose from her seat.

Chancellor Valus rubbed his chin nervously and his green eyes flicked about the room. "As I informed our brother, despite the failure of the Reven mercenaries, the girl was inadvertently delivered into our hands."

"Very fortunate, indeed," the woman pointed out, leaning on the desk.

"Yes, well I am afraid she is no longer here," the chancellor said, bristling as he saw the woman start to speak. "Don't ask me how and don't interrupt me again until I have finished my account."

The Kestrel shrugged non-committally and sat back in her chair, placing her muddy feet on the desk as she folded her arms across her chest. The chancellor followed her bare, wet slender legs up from the tops of her booted feet, lingering over her knees and the enticing shadows offered by her short dark skirt, before moving up her slender and darkly clothed body to meet her steely gaze.

"Proceed," she said, seeing the fear and hunger battling in his eyes.

The chancellor licked his lips and swallowed in a deep breath, before proceeding. "For nearly a week now, we had been able to hide her away in a remote wing of the high duke's keep, drugging her slowly so that she could be moved when you arrived without raising any suspicion. To mask her arrival in the city, I orchestrated false intelligence about an attempt on the high duke and his family, which in turn forced the postponement of the Valian Council, whilst investigations were made."

"Impressive," the Kestrel admitted. "But?" she prompted.

"Four days ago Madam Grey disappeared," the chancellor continued, his voice even and measured.

"My sources have not been able to trace her and even now I do not know what has befallen her."

The Kestrel frowned. Madam Grey had served the chancellor loyally for many years and would not have abandoned her master in his hour of need. Chancellor Valus read the understanding in her eyes and nodded his silent accord. Madam Grey was most certainly dead and no longer their concern.

"In her place I sent an innocent member of staff with her drugged drink and food. As far as she was concerned, Lady Byron was ill and under my protection and care while the high duke's men continued their pursuit of these mysterious assassins!"

"You can vouch for this person?" the Kestrel enquired, unconvinced.

Relan Valus nodded. "I can. She has been at the keep for many years now and worked under Madam Grey for the last four. She came to me, only yesterday with the terrible news."

The Kestrel shook her head impatiently. "Stop stalling and get to the point."

"Very well," the chancellor said angrily. "The maid took Lady Byron her breakfast, as normal, only to find that the guard was not on duty outside her quarters. Upon entering the suite, she found the guard in the reception room within. He had been killed, his throat cut deeply several times."

The Kestrel kicked her feet off the desk, finally interested in the chancellor's account.

"Curious. Surely Lady Byron was incapable of this?"

"She was incapacitated and confined to her bed," the chancellor confirmed. "She had to have had outside help. Whoever it was entered unnoticed into the high keep, killed the guard before dragging his body inside and then got out again without being noticed."

"I'm intrigued! Who else knew about the girl's presence here?"

"Only the maid, my aide Edward and his grandson. The captain of the Havensdale militia who escorted her to the city and those already loyal to our cause."

The Kestrel frowned. That was far too many names already. "And just how many of these loose ends am I going to have to tie up for you *again*, chancellor?" she asked bitterly.

"None," the chancellor replied indignantly. "The old man and his grandson knew too much, so I had them taken care of."

"So much for loyalty," the woman sneered, ignoring the look he dealt her.

"The maid is unaware of what is going on and will prove invaluable, if I am to keep the suspicion from my door. As for the captain, she will not prove a problem, once our plans come to fruition."

The Kestrel rose again and wrapped her cloak tightly about her slender frame.

"And just how are we going to do that, when the girl is no longer in our care, chancellor?" she demanded, her face flushing angrily. "Without her, we have nothing. And the fact she is still alive *and* has had help, suggests that someone is also aware of our brotherhood, or at least our plans."

"Impossible," the chancellor said, indignantly. "We have protected ourselves well, these last few years."

The woman moved quietly around the desk to stand before him. The chancellor looked up reluctantly into the serene face and swallowed. Before he could react, her left hand snaked out and struck him across the face.

"You imbecile," she hissed dangerously, standing over him. "First you expose our plans to a commoner, then your men fail to capture the girl. And then, even when fortune has offered you another roll of the die, you still manage to mess things up!"

The chancellor licked his bloodied lip, recoiling subconsciously as the woman raged on at him.

"Do not think that just because you are in a position of great importance to our cause, that I have not been given the instruction to kill you if you start to become a liability to us, Relan," she said, smiling gleefully. "However, it seems that I have more work before me, than I had anticipated. So humour me chancellor, while you still have my ear. Where should I look next?"

Relan frowned. "I would be the first to admit that my luck has ran out, but I would ask you to stay your hand whilst my sources try to discover who helped the girl?" When the woman failed to respond, the chancellor scratched his sweating forehead and continued. "While they look into the matter, I shall tidy up the political problems that will arise from her disappearance. I can point the finger of suspicion at Madam Grey and perhaps implicate her as a suspected member of the group behind the threat against the high duke and his family. The high duke was already aware of the attack on the girl by the Reven, so it will appear that these two events are linked!"

"Go on," the Kestrel said.

"I will also advise the high duke that a letter was supposedly sent to Lady Byron's father, though I now suspect that it would have never arrived. Another letter will be most certainly sent, but as you know, our brother in Highwater is monitoring all mail that comes to her father's office. So once again, it will never arrive."

"How long will that buy us?"

"A week, at the very least." The chancellor wiped his face with the sleeve of his robe as the woman backed away slightly and perched on the corner of the desk. She crossed her legs and chewed her top lip thoughtfully.

"The girl will no doubt try to get home and tell her father the truth at some point," she said. "I will send word out and have all the roads into Highwater watched. It will cost us greatly, but compared to having the girl expose what has been going on, it is a price worth paying."

"Do we recapture her, or kill her?" the chancellor asked.

The Kestrel shrugged. "That is for the brotherhood to decide. If I had the final decision, I would have her killed. She has been nothing but trouble and with her dead, we can look elsewhere, whilst still keeping our plans a secret."

"A good idea," the chancellor agreed, pleased that she was thinking about things, other than his demise now. "I shall pass on your views to the brotherhood when I update them on the situation and they will also need to know that there are those who would apparently thwart us now."

The Kestrel didn't appear to hear him, as her eyes looked away into the shadows as she thought of other things.

"Kestrel?" he asked softly.

She looked back at him, blinking rapidly. "Have your men got anything from the Redani yet?" she asked.

"Nothing," he replied. "I have instructed them to get on with it, one way or another!"

The Kestrel rose hurriedly. "I sense that he may be the key to all of this, chancellor!"

"I am still not convinced that he heard anything of real importance," the chancellor said. "And even if he did, the man is a foreigner, with very few friends. Nobody would believe him and he has no proof, other than his word, which I am told does not count for much in the city where it matters!"

The Kestrel moved to the curtains. As she turned back, she pulled the hood of her sodden cloak back up over her head. "I disagree. He must have told somebody. Why else would someone go to the trouble to rescue the girl? Protect your cover, chancellor. In the meantime I shall head out to the croft. By tomorrow night, every mercenary and bounty hunter north of this city will be on the lookout for the girl. Ten thousand crowns should do the trick!"

"And then?" the chancellor asked, as the Kestrel prepared to leave.

"I will pay a visit to the Redani," she said, her eyes flashing darkly. "Once he has told me everything I need to know, I will hunt down those standing in our way and kill them all!"

Before the chancellor could reply the woman was gone, leaving him to stare at the curtains as they moved ominously in the rising breeze.

After a time he bent down to retrieve the empty bottle of Burning Leaf brandy and placed it back on the desk. His heart pounded rapidly, joining in with the thrumming of the rain. He could smell the freshness of the cooling night outside and rose to stand in the open doorway for a while, looking out thoughtfully across his estate. The rain obscured his view, falling down in thick diagonal sheets, tossed about occasionally by the wind in swirling arcs of misty spray.

As he closed the door and pulled the curtains tight, he took in a long, deep breath. He had much to do and many loose ends to tie up if he was going to survive through this latest setback. And yet again, it appeared as if it would be the Kestrel that allowed him to do so. The only problem this time, however, was that she was the one in charge of the proceedings, not him. Despite any histrionics, that was something he was just going to have to deal with. He knew what she was capable of and was well aware of the relentless determination and ruthlessness she possessed, when faced with a problem. If anyone could sort this mess out without compromising his position, the Kestrel could. The only thing was, she knew that as well!

Despite everything he had put in place over the last few years and every low and underhand thing he had done to get there, he had never felt saddened about any of his actions before, until now. Turning from the curtains, he went back to his chair and slumped onto it again. Closing his eyes, he massaged his temples gently and let out another deep breath that drifted mournfully about the room and then faded away into a sigh. For years now he had sanctioned actions that were unpalatable to him; it was necessary if the brotherhood could ever achieve their goals and he had slept well afterwards, knowing that his actions had brought them ever closer to that day. But ever since he had ordered his men to take Edward away, the chancellor had not been able to sleep as his conscience chastised him constantly for his betrayal. Edward had worked for the previous high duke, before his death and Relan had pursued him for several years in vain, before finally offering him enough money to come and work for him. It was a clever move, as Edward was highly respected in the capital and it was a very large feather in the new chancellor's cap when he announced that Edward was to be his chief of staff. The old man had worked tirelessly and faithfully for him for years, completely unaware of what was happening in the shadows around him. It was the very reason the chancellor had hired him. Edward was the perfect foil, such was his integrity, for any fingers of suspicion that may have pointed in his office's direction over the years and to repay him for his redoubtable service, the chancellor gave the order to have him dragged away in the middle of the night, to be tortured and then most likely killed.

Relan picked up his empty glass and turned it in his hand, staring solemnly at the final droplets of brandy that raced gleefully around the bottom of the glass. The events of the last few weeks had been a bit like that. Just when he thought everything was going as planned, he would find himself back at the start again. A vicious circle that seemed to demand more lives as payment, with every complicated turn of events.

How many more people are you prepared to sacrifice, in order to achieve the ambitions of others? His conscience asked him.

Snarling he rose and hurled the glass at the wall across from him. Spinning into the shadows, the glass bounced off the wall and disappeared from view. He couldn't even do that right!

"I will sacrifice as many of you as it takes," he promised himself, smashing aside the wall of doubt that had been building up around him. Kicking the chair away from him, he headed for the doorway and dragged it open. The lamplight from the elegant hallway beyond blinded him momentarily, before he regained his senses and his fraying composure. Straightening his robes, he closed the door behind him and with his crisis of doubt seemingly now over, he unclenched his fists and went in search of his bed and the young wife that was waiting for him.

CHAPTER TWELVE

Preparations

The Kestrel stared out at the heavy rain and shivered disconsolately. Ever since it had started last night, the storm had not abated and instead had raged on furiously, showering the lands with its wrath and beating out its anger upon all beneath with bellowing roars of thunder and sparking flashes of lightning. The grounds of the crofter's cottage were flooded now and as she leant against a post on the wooden porch, she closed her eyes momentarily and breathed in the freshness of the storm. Opening her eyes she remained where she was and watched the slow subtle change in the bleak greyness overhead that signalled the coming of dawn.

Since leaving the chancellor to wallow in his self-pity, she and her men had left the capital and made their way south a short way along the Old South Road, before heading east into The Whispering Woods. Ever since the graveyards had become full in the city several years ago now, the authorities had cleared acres of the woods to create a new cemetery there. Daily funeral processions could be seen leaving the city through the south gates as they solemnly made their way into the woods to give their loved ones back to the land that had given them life. Once known as the Old Bandit Woods, the high duke had re-named them, as he felt that the new name would be more befitting. The Kestrel wondered what they would do once this cemetery was full and stared in wonderment as a jagged spear of lightning split the skies across the clearing to the east and briefly lit up the gloom of the trees beyond. She had seen and done many things over the years that had left any joy in her life fleeting and tasteless. But the one thing that still managed to amaze her was the uncontrolled power of nature. It was the only thing the hierarchy who ruled the Four Vales could not control, a powerful thing of untamed beauty and as she stared through the rain, the skies rumbled in agreement with her.

A distant creak on the floorboards inside the cottage announced someone's approach and she did not look back as one of her men stepped from within to stand beside her.

"He's still adamant that he won't send them off until this storm has died down," the man said, his breath clouding as he spoke. Folding his arms across his chest he jumped up and down to keep warm.

"I don't blame him," the Kestrel said softly, flicking him a side-long glance. "Our messages have to get to as many of our people as possible. We can't risk losing the girl because a few of the birds got lost in the storm."

The man shrugged. It wasn't his job to question her, but his blue eyes narrowed slightly as he thought they were wasting time. He was of medium height, slim and clothed in soaked travelling clothes. His knee high boots squelched with each jump he took to keep warm and a drenched, brown cloak hung heavily from his shoulders.

"He has the message, lady" he stated, rubbing his bearded chin. "Do we head for the hold now?"

The Kestrel looked round at him and shook her head. She could tell that he was eager to be off, in truth, so was she. There was an urgency building now because of the chancellor's continuing incompetence and any delays could prove costly. But there was no use risking themselves in this storm, they would have to wait it out patiently before continuing.

"We wait here Tobin," she said, conveying her disappointment to him with a sigh. "At least until the storm passes through!"

Tobin nodded glumly and looked up into the bleak skies. "Could be a while though, and the lads are getting restless."

"That's their problem, not mine," came a snarling reply. "If anyone has anything to say, tell them to come and see me."

Tobin grinned and looked away, running a gloved hand through his wet, shoulder-length dark hair. Like anyone was going to do that! His lads might be a cantankerous bunch, but they weren't stupid. The Kestrel was a ruthless bitch and did not like insubordination. Whether you agreed with her decisions or not, it was best to bite your tongue and get on with it, otherwise she had the tendency to remove it for you.

Together they watched as lightning flashed over the trees across from them and then listened to the boom of thunder several seconds later.

"It's close," Tobin observed.

The Kestrel agreed. "Get some rest," she ordered him. "We will be here for another hour or two yet."

Tobin nodded and stepped away from her. As he moved back inside the cottage to tell the good news to his lads, he glanced back as he closed the door behind him. She was still leaning against the post, a dark sentinel watching, almost welcoming the coming storm. He had worked for her many times before and as far as he could tell, she hardly ever slept. He shook his head and closed the door to hide his grin. The only time he had seen her in bed was not to sleep. Licking his lips in remembrance, he headed for the kitchen.

Alone again now, the Kestrel closed her eyes once more and listened to the rain beating down on the roof of the porch. Tobin was a loyal companion. He had worked for her many times before in recent years and had proved his worth on more than one occasion. The other three members of his team were equally dependable when it mattered, but had the tendency to complain like a trio of old housewives. Not to her face, of course. There weren't many people who did these days. But it was there, nonetheless and once this was all over, she would split the trio up. The most important thing for her to focus on at the moment, however, was getting the truth from the Redani. She was sure, especially now that the girl was gone, that he had told someone what he had heard that day in the gardens of the high duke's keep. The chancellor had fretted for weeks now that the stonemason may or may not have heard something, but could not be sure either way. When the Kestrel had heard what was going on, she had been furious. The fool had sent his men to watch the man, surveying him to see if he spoke to anyone. What an idiot! He should have had him killed that night. It would have negated any uncertainty and they would not be in this mess they are now. No matter! She would get the information from the stonemason and then return to the chancellor with the good news. From there, she would ensure that whoever the Redani had told, was also silenced. Well, once she had extracted the whereabouts of the girl from them, of course.

She hawked and spat out into the rain, as she thought of the chancellor again. It was nearly twelve years ago now, since she had first saved his skin. Admittedly, it had been a lot easier back then than it would be now and the stakes were a lot higher for all of them this time.

If she could find out who stole the girl from the keep and have her men recover her, she could return to her superiors with assurances that their plans could now proceed unhindered. If she couldn't, then they would have to set things in motion immediately. If that happened, then she could at least comfort herself that in six or seven months time the brotherhood would probably no longer need him and she could finally rid herself of the chancellor, once and for all.

Cassana yawned and stretched out in the hot bath, before sliding under the soapy water to rinse out her hair. Surfacing again, she wiped the hair and suds from her eyes and settled back down again for another few minutes of blissful relaxation. Despite the events of the past few weeks and the terrible guilt she was still carrying, Cassana had to admit to herself that, thanks to the unexpectedly grand hospitality of Savinn Kassaar, she was feeling a great deal better. Physically, at least.

Since her arrival, Cassana had not seen the merchant-thief again. But his presence was still clearly evident in the care she had received. True to his word, he had re-located her to quarters of such magnificence, that Cassana had to pinch herself each morning, to remind herself that she was still down in the sewers under the city. For three days now she had been allowed to recuperate in peace, disturbed only for meals and the delivery of fresh clothes and hot water, when she desired a bath. It had taken several baths before she felt that the filth and grime of her recent ordeal had finally been washed from her body and hair. The marks of her ordeal were still with her however, grim reminders in the form of numerous cuts and bruises on her body and despite feeling considerably better, her muscles still ached terribly and her stomach often reminded her that she was not free from the effects of the drugs she had been recently given.

A light knock on the door to her quarters stirred her from her thoughts and she lurched up, sending soapy water up over the sides of the marble bath to splash on the stone floor beneath.

"One moment, please," she called out, clambering from the bath and hurrying through the chilly room to fetch the *clean* robe from her nearby bed. Wrapping herself in the soft woollen garment she ran a hand through her long hair and moved to unlock the door.

Ellie, the young girl who Cullen took great delight in beating was waiting patiently in the corridor beyond and Cassana was pleased to see that the bruise on her cheek from the brute's slap, was starting to fade.

"Good morning again," Cassana greeted brightly, offering her a dazzling smile.

"Hello," Ellie replied, offering her a shy one in return.

Cassana had dealt solely with the young girl these

past few days, the street waif bringing her meals and clothes to her each day. Initially, any attempts at conversation with the girl were met by suspicious glares and truculent responses. But after the first day of her servitude, Cassana had managed to get a name from her and since then, the girl had warmed to her.

The only time Cassana had seen anyone else was when she asked for a bath. It was on those occasions, unfortunately, that she had the pleasure of Cullen's company. The squat man would wordlessly deliver the pails of water for her bath, and then leave again with a curt nod. Although perplexed by his sudden change, Cassana was relieved. She had no desire to engage the man further than she already had and could see the same relief in Ellie's eyes as the bully went about his business. Perhaps Arillion had said something to him? Scattering any rising thoughts of the man from her mind, she stepped aside to allow the girl in.

"I can't stay, miss," she announced, remaining where she was. "Begging your pardon, but the boss would like to see you as soon as you can, err, see him!"

Cassana smiled. "Of course, please could you tell him that I will come and see him as soon as I have dressed."

"Right then, bye," Ellie said and she hurried off again, before Cassana could reply.

Smiling, Cassana closed and locked the door again, before hurrying to get dressed.

Cassana knocked on the door of Savinn's study and waited nervously in the corridor for him to answer. She had taken longer than she had expected to get ready, such was her prerogative and she wouldn't have been surprised if he had got more important matters to attend to. Yet again she adjusted her lustrous locks and gave up without the assistance of a mirror. She was dressed in a long skirt of the deepest blue, low-heeled matching shoes and wore a lovely blouse of the finest silk that she had buttoned all the way up to her throat. She had also wrapped a green sash about her waist and the only jewellery she possessed and wore at the moment, were her two golden bangles and the silver ring on her left index finger. The rest of her original belongings were probably still in her trunk, back in the Moonglade Forest. Fortunately for her, however, Ellie had brought her some make-up and Cassana had spent far too much time adding some colour back to her pale complexion.

"Enter!" A voice commanded and Cassana obeyed, her heart beginning to race again.

"Good morning, Lady Byron," Savinn greeted her, smiling broadly as he rose from his desk and stepped round to receive her. He was dressed to perfection, yet again and Cassana smiled as she offered him her hand. As Savinn stooped to take and kiss her hand, she felt her heart flutter in fear as he rose again and she met his narrow eyes. She quickly lost herself in his handsome face this time, however, all the more so now that her head was clear and her body was free from exhaustion.

"If you would permit my lady, may I say that you are looking fabulous," he said smiling, still holding onto her hand.

"And that sir, is, in no small part, because of you," she replied, stepping in close to kiss him on one cheek. She could smell a pleasing scent upon him and as she stepped away, she could see his eyes light up. He gently released her hand with a flourishing bow, accompanied by yet another charming smile.

264

"I cannot thank you enough, sir, for what you have done for me," she said, following his gesturing arm, as he offered her a seat again.

"Please, lady," Savinn said, holding his hands up for her to stop, as they sat at the desk across from each other. "I will hear no more thanks from you. I have accepted your gratitude graciously already, and, as I have now played my part in all of this, it is time for you to play yours."

"Sir?" Cassana prompted, unsure of what he meant.

Savinn smiled. "As I already eluded to you when you arrived, I am prepared to assist you further by helping you leave the city and get back home. I still intend to honour that, naturally!" he paused long enough for Cassana to smile her thanks, before continuing. "However, before we speak of that, I feel I should bring you up to speed with the events of the last few days."

Cassana nodded, and licked her lips nervously as she fiddled subconsciously with the lobe of her left ear. "Have you had news, sir?"

Savinn nodded, leaning forward on the desk. "The capital is in a state of shock at the moment, as you can imagine. Word has got out about the reasons behind the cancellation of the Valian Council and that its members have gone into hiding whilst the threats are investigated. Which still makes me wonder why you were never better protected! Anyhow, we should be thankful that the high duke and his family are still under armed guard at a secret location and will remain there until this threat against them has been corroborated or dismissed."

"And what of the chancellor, sir?" Cassana asked hesitantly.

"I received word only yesterday from my sources that the chancellor was left devastated by your disappearance. He has returned to his estate in the west of the city and remains there under armed guard, as he believes that his life is also in danger."

"A wise precaution," Cassana admitted. "Who knows what Madam Grey and her cohorts have been planning?"

"Exactly so, my lady," Savinn agreed. "We do not know either, sadly. But what we do know, however, is that the chancellor had, as I believe you were already aware, told the high duke about your attack on the way here. Dia tells me that he is going to arrange another letter to be sent to your father, as he suspects that the initial letter was never sent."

Cassana nodded her agreement. "I would concur, most definitely. I gave my letter to Madam Grey and we both know now that her intentions towards me were far from honourable!"

"Indeed we do," Savinn sighed, clasping his hands together. "So I am afraid that this is all I can tell you at the moment, Lady Byron. The chancellor will meet in person with the high duke tomorrow, so he will be made aware of your plight and will no doubt take matters of your disappearance into his own hands."

Cassana grimaced, as she chewed over her prospects. "Could I not wait until the high duke returns to the keep and then report to him directly?"

Savinn stroked his chin thoughtfully for a moment and then shook his head. "I would advise against that, Lady Byron. We still do not know the reason behind your attempted capture and resulting imprisonment by Madam Grey. Because of this, we cannot be sure how deep this cancer runs in the high duke's keep and you might only place yourself in further danger. No, lady! My counsel would be for you to return home to your father. Root out the spy in his camp and find out what they know. From there, you will be able to conduct your investigations from a position of strength and relative safety."

Cassana listened as her conflicting thoughts argued for a time and then met the merchant's eyes, as he searched her face for a hint of her decision. When she did finally answer, her voice was shackled by her nerves again and strangled by the weight of her decision.

"I will return home, if you will help me still, sir?"

Savinn clapped his hands together gratefully. "A wise choice, Lady Byron. The capital is a dangerous place at the moment. Uncertainty and distrust chase through the shadows in the high duke's court and with your father at your side, I believe that you will have a much better chance of getting to the bottom of all of this."

Cassana breathed a deep sigh of relief. "I must admit, sir, that I yearn to return home to see him."

"Naturally so, lady," Savinn said, smiling. "He would no doubt be expecting your return home soon as well. If you delay any further, he will become worried. The last thing we need is for him to journey to the capital to look for you, possibly putting his own life in danger."

Cassana gasped, covering her mouth with a shaking hand. She had not even thought about that. If she did not return home, it was the kind of thing a worried father would think of and most certainly what her father *would* do.

"I apologise, lady," Savinn said, his handsome face a mask of concern. "I did not mean to alarm you, I only sought to point out some of the many possibilities that might arise from your absence."

"No, you were right to, Savinn." Cassana answered, her eyes steeling. "I now know what I must do and should not delay and impose on your hospitality any further."

Savinn nodded, smiling encouragingly. "Well before we make final arrangements, perhaps I can offer some gifts, to help you on your way?"

He pushed his chair back and bent low from view under his desk. When he straightened up again, Cassana was watching him quizzically and he smiled back at her.

"Compliments of Dia," he announced, presenting her with a sturdy dark bow and a quiver of black-feathered arrows. Cassana inadvertently snatched the bow from him and clutched it to her breast, as she felt her heart begin to race. As Savinn smiled and bent below the desk again, she blinked away the tears that were brimming in her eyes. Savinn then proceeded to return all of the belongings she had arrived in the city with, apart from the dagger that had been stolen from her boot. Cassana received them all gratefully and after she had taken a mental inventory of them all, she glanced up at the merchant and smiled.

"I do not know what to say," she said softly, fighting off fresh tears. "Please pass on my thanks to Dia, she has no idea how much this means to me!"

"I think I do, my lady," Savinn observed, reaching out to clasp her hand. "I shall convey your gratitude to her, when I next see her."

Laying her bow down on the table next to her other belongings, Cassana smiled and squeezed his hand. "Thank you, Savinn."

"Now then," Savinn said, clapping his hands

together merrily. "Let us proceed with our plans, shall we?" Before Cassana could answer, Savinn rose and called out.

"Come in," he commanded, looking over her head towards the door. Inexorably Cassana looked round and as she did, the door opened and someone stepped obediently into the room.

"Allow me to introduce you to your escort, my lady," Savinn announced, his voice laced with amusement.

"Hello princess." Arillion greeted her, his eyes flashing from within the shadows of his hood as he bowed mockingly.

Cassana groaned, burying her head in her hands.

"Now there's a welcome to freeze your heart," Arillion chuckled, moving quietly over to the vacant seat at the desk.

Cassana looked imploringly at Savinn, who was watching their exchange with a wolfish grin on his face and then looked back at the man standing beside her with his arms stretched wide.

"What's this? No hug, no kiss?" Arillion said, his eyes glittering like a cat.

"You have still not apologised to me yet!" Cassana pointed out, blushing as their eyes met. Coughing politely Cassana averted her gaze and focused on the wolf painting behind Savinn's head.

"So I haven't," Arillion agreed, as he sat down and turned his attentions to the man across from him who was watching them both quietly now.

"Are you sure that this man is the best person to escort me, sir?" Cassana asked, when it appeared that Arillion was not about to apologise to her. Which in itself was a relief as she had no desire whatsoever to have to meet her side of the bargain. Although she had to admit that part of her youthful curiosity still yearned to see the face behind the mask.

Savinn rested his hands in his lap and smiled. "Probably not, my lady," he conceded. "But I have no other men at my disposal who would be able protect you as well as Arillion can."

Cassana's worried face told him that she completely disagreed, while Arillion nodded his head.

"Who else will be accompanying me, Savinn?" she asked, aware that the man at her side was now watching her again. She could sense those eyes taking in her appearance with fresh relish and she felt uncomfortable.

Savinn's apologetic expression revealed his reply before he could speak and Cassana's eyes widened with realisation. "Surely not?" she pleaded.

"I can understand your concerns, Lady Byron," Savinn agreed. "But as you will be travelling cross-country, a small party will hopefully be able to go about their business undetected, unlike a large group of travellers."

Cassana looked from one man to the other, finally resting her attention on Arillion. The thought of spending a few weeks alone with him left her emotions reeling. He was brash, immodest, lecherous and infuriating. But despite all of that, she sensed that he would be able to protect her, if circumstances dictated it. She blinked free of her thoughts, as he winked at her.

"Very well, sir," she sighed, looking at Savinn again. "I trust your judgement implicitly. I shall bow to your better judgement and would hear more of our journey."

"Excellent, my lady," Savinn said, clearly relieved. "Before I hand matters over to your guide, please allow me to complete my part in this."

Cassana nodded, flicking a swift glance at Arillion. Was it her imagination, or did she sense his anger at being labelled a *guide*? Smiling, she turned her attention back to her host.

"I have arranged supplies for you both, water, food and all other necessities for such a journey," Savinn began, pausing again to accept Cassana's nod of thanks.

"From here, Arillion will guide you through the sewers to a remote storm drain a mile east of the city. The authorities dug a number of extra cesspools outside the capital some years ago, to help alleviate the pressure on the sewer network during heavy rainfall!"

"Should be nice and ripe at this time of the year then," Arillion chuckled, ignoring the look Savinn dealt him.

Savinn offered Cassana an apologetic look before continuing. "From there, your journey will take you a couple of miles east to a place known as Briar Copse. Cullen will meet you there with a pair of horses."

"Will he be joining us, sir?" Cassana enquired. That would really pile the misery onto her.

"It's just you and *me*, princess," Arillion interjected.

Savinn stiffened, then nodded. "Cullen will return here immediately, my lady. From there on, Arillion will decide your path. Nobody else will know your route, myself included, hopefully ensuring that the remainder of your journey home is made in secrecy."

Cassana chewed over what she had heard and then smiled brightly. "Thank you Savinn. Once again I am in your debt, sir!"

Savinn shook his head. "As I have said before, you owe me nothing, lady. I did this in honour of my friend's memory, it is he you should thank."

"And I shall, sir," Cassana said, rising dramatically. "By returning home and exposing the traitors behind all of this. It will be my tribute to him, for the sacrifice that he made for a complete stranger."

Savinn rose, smiling faintly as he stepped around the desk to embrace her.

"Safe journey, Lady Byron," he said, holding her at arms length. "Know that I shall continue my own investigations into my friend's disappearance, and should I ever discover any information that I deem useful to your cause, I shall send word to you immediately."

Cassana thanked him with another hug and a kiss to one cheek. Arillion rose and looked away, feigning disinterest.

"There is one thing that I would ask of you, however, my lady," Savinn said as he released her.

"Name it, sir," she replied.

"I do not want you to reveal my part in all of this," he stated, his eyes narrowing. "I am, as you are now clearly aware, a business man who operates on, ahem, shall we say many different levels."

Cassana nodded, fairly certain of which direction the conversation was about to go.

"I understand Savinn," she pre-empted. "You have too much at stake to reveal yourself."

"Not only that, lady," Savinn said. "I have far too many enemies above and even some below the city. Those above ground are unaware of my darker side, and would jump at the chance to expose and imprison me. Add into that my mixed heritage and well, I would probably end up being framed for the initial attack on you!"

"I will not tell a soul about what you have done for

me, sir," she promised him.

"Thank you, Lady Byron," Savinn said, bowing low. "I do not want you to find out what would happen if you did."

Cassana swallowed, curtsying in return. Savinn's eyes flashed meaningfully at her as he straightened and for the first time she saw the wolf lurking behind his smile.

"I understand sir," she stammered. Composing herself, she looked to Arillion. "When do we leave, sir?"

"In one hour, my lady," Arillion said formally. "By the time we reach the storm drain it will be late afternoon and any of the surrounding farmlands should be quiet by then."

"Return to your quarters, Lady Byron," Savinn added. "I will have the girl deliver your travelling clothes and supplies. Arillion will come for you, when it is time."

Cassana smiled, receiving her belongings from the merchant-thief. As he passed the bow to her, he paused and then handed it over.

"Good luck my lady," he said. "We shall not meet again."

Cassana nodded. "I understand sir," she said, stepping away. "Gentlemen!"

Turning, she headed for the door. She could feel their eyes upon her as she walked and her legs felt weak from their scrutiny. Turning the handle, she opened the door and slipped from the wolf's den without looking back.

Moments after she was gone, Savinn rounded angrily on the cloaked figure.

"Do not interrupt me again when I am talking,

assassin," he snarled. "And I warn you, I do not ever want to hear that you have mistreated the girl on her way home. I am sick of the lack of respect you show to her!"

Arillion turned from watching the door. "Respect will cost you extra, *master!*" he said, stepping in close. "Do not even try to suggest that I would harm her."

Savinn met the finger pointing at him with a sly smile. "Just checking, Arillion. I know you prefer to pay for your pleasure. I am just reminding you that this is business, that is all. What you choose to do with the money once she is safely home, is your own affair. But whilst you are earning my coin, assassin, you will abide by my wishes."

Arillion relaxed, lowering his finger. "Yes, *master!*" he said, bowing slightly.

"Good," Savinn said, ignoring the sarcasm in the man's voice. "Now that is out of the way, perhaps we can talk rationally?"

Arillion nodded and they both returned to their seats. "What do you wish to know?"

"I want to know what you think about all of this?" Savinn wondered amiably.

"In all honesty, I don't really care," Arillion replied, shrugging. "I do the job, I get paid. Quite frankly, I wish it would go on a bit longer, I am making a fortune out of this!"

"Out of me," Savinn reminded him, scowling.

"That was your choice, not mine," Arillion retorted. "Your fingers are firmly stuck in this pie now. Where as I, however, can come and go as I please. I am quite willing to get my hands dirty, as you know. But what I am not prepared to do is get myself involved in the political mess that is blighting the capital at the moment."

Savinn regarded the cloaked figure across from him and nodded. "And that is why you are perfect for this task, Arillion."

Arillion chuckled, applauding slowly. "Well orchestrated. I know my place and I promise you, that the girl will get home safely. From then on, you are free to cause as much trouble for the brotherhood, as you like."

"You know of them?" Savinn asked, surprised.

"Of course!" Arillion replied. "Why else did you *really* help the girl? It was a blessing that your friend sent you that letter, and despite any guilt you may hold for his death, you are using the girl to hopefully find out more about them."

Savinn shook his head ruefully. "I can see why you are good at what you do, Arillion."

Arillion cocked his head in acceptance. "Unlike the high duke, I don't wander about with my head up my arse. Perhaps now, he will finally come up for air and take note!"

Savinn chuckled heartily. "I doubt it. For years now the hard-liners have rebelled against his authority. His desire for prosperity, however noble and correct, has upset a lot of people in the Four Vales. This so-called *Brotherhood* is clear evidence of that."

"Agreed!" Arillion said, drumming the fingers of his left hand on the desk. "And here we are, back again at the crux of the matter. The girl is the key! They have showed their first hand and it has not been a strong one. If you can find out what they plan, you can reinforce the high duke's authority by exposing them."

"Very perceptive, Arillion," Savinn said. "I am, as you are probably already aware, a stalwart supporter of

275

the high duke. I have prospered and become a very powerful businessman under his rule, I would hate for anything to jeopardise that!"

Arillion studied the man silently. Savinn was not boasting. Over the last few years, since the Redani had saved his life, the merchant had prospered with nobody else to oppose him. He had built up a vast empire, a profitable network of trade routes across the country and beyond. He had achieved all of this through a mix of bribery, fear and an excellent head for business. His fleet of merchant ships traded in legal low-profit goods, whilst smuggling in illegal goods at the same time. Most of the opium dens around the cities of the Four Vales were supplied from goods smuggled in by Savinn Kassaar. Several years ago, he had even been approached to become a member of the Valian Council, such was his prominence. But when the vote to appoint him was put before the council members, it was easily defeated. Even then, it was clear that there were those who would rather die than have one of mixed-race in a position of power. And judging by the merchant-thief's determination, it was something he waited patiently to repay them for.

"I feel a storm coming," Arillion said prophetically. "Not the one breaking overhead as we speak, but a darker, more sinister one."

Savinn nodded his agreement. "I too have sensed it. The threat made against the high duke and the other members of the council was clear evidence of that!"

Arillion stretched and smothered the yawn breaking behind his mask. His head was beginning to hurt. All this talk about things that didn't concern him at the moment was becoming tiresome.

"Well, I am sure we will be around to make a

fortune when it does," he said, rising and stretching. "Until then, I will focus on the job at hand, Savinn."

The merchant rose and they shared a firm handshake.

"I know you will, Arillion. Just be careful, she is precious in all of this, I feel!"

Arillion released his hand and nodded. Turning, he made for the door, stopping only when Savinn halted him with a message of good luck.

"You'll need that in the coming months, more than I will," he answered, leaving before the merchant could reply.

Arillion headed down the hallway beyond, smiling to himself as he left Savinn's room behind him. He had spent the last few days in the company of several whores in the rich district of the city. No lower class offerings this time for him! He had already secured the majority of his money for rescuing the Byron girl with the money broker, Kaylin Baric. The reputable broker would invest his money in small business enterprises, where hopefully he would make enough money to cover his own costs and allow Arillion an acceptable return on his investment. But the rest of his money had been spent on the delectable company of the ladies who worked in the Moon Gardens, a high-class establishment, frequented by the rich and unfaithful, just off the Valian Mile. Arillion grinned away as he lost himself within those memories. He had hired three girls for two full nights and they had really enjoyed each other's company. There were also plenty of girls for him to choose from as, apparently, yet another prostitute had been murdered and many of them were keen to work in a safe environment. With a dry roof over their heads they could relax and hopefully offer a better service to their customers. The Moon Gardens was the cleanest brothel in the region, so much in fact, that Arillion had bought the precautionary medicine from the front desk, when he left there yesterday morning. He sighed and smiled again, feeling himself rise to the memory. The girls had certainly earned their money this time and he had paid extra to watch them, when he felt the need to get his strength and enthusiasm back. Grinning, he licked his lips hungrily and headed for the kitchens. His throat was dry and he would need to clear his head from the after-effects of the opium, before he headed out into the wilds.

As he went about his business, Arillion was painfully certain that the girl would give him some headaches of his own and he shook his head. Once this was all over, he was going to get back to some proper work. In the coming months there would be no end of throats that needed slitting. He was going to be a very, very busy man.

CHAPTER THIRTEEN

Homeward Bound

Cassana paused wearily, slightly adjusting the straps of her pack as they had already begun to dig into her slim shoulders. Sighing, she looked ahead to the tall figure that strode purposefully through the shadows away from her, the light from his blazing torch scattering the darkness aside as he passed. Cassana grimaced. Arillion had set a furious pace after they had left the sanctuary of Savinn's hideout and part of her still wished that she was back there. The sewers were even worse than she could remember, if that was even possible and the stench, now that she was feeling better, was a hundred times worse. To compound her misery, Arillion had taken great delight in the fact that it had been raining heavily through the night and the slick pathways were now ankle deep in all manner of unpleasant things.

Cassana took in a deep breath through her mouth and looked down at her sodden boots, trying not to gag as she saw what she was standing in. She now wore harder boots, more fitting for the initial trek ahead of her and they rose just below her knee. Somewhat ironically she was dressed in brown leather trousers, tied up by laces at the front and wore a black leather waistcoat over her recently laundered silk blouse. The Reven sword, given to her by the woodsman was now belted and hung from it's sheath off her right hip and her quiver of arrows hung from the shoulder above. Underneath the dark green hooded cloak that swept down her back to meet her calves, she carried her pack, full with her other belongings and rations, kindly supplied by Savinn. Her bedroll was strapped to the bottom of the pack and to complete the burden she carried her bow, feeling all the more safe with it close at hand.

Water dripped rapidly from the low ceiling above, spattering on the hood pulled up over her head to protect her hair as she moved off in pursuit of her guide, who was already beginning to leave her behind again.

"Please," she called out, her voice echoing about the sewers. "Slow down, I can't keep up!"

Arillion turned abruptly, whipping a finger to his masked mouth to tell her to be quiet. Stalking back to her, he grabbed her under the right armpit and marched her on in silence. Cassana scowled bitterly. She knew that this journey was going to be a test of her patience and character, but she hadn't expected him to rile her this early on.

"You are hurting me," she hissed, as his fingers dug into her.

"It's going to be a rough journey, princess," he replied, flicking her a disdainful look. "So you had better toughen up and quick!"

"You could have at least offered to carry my pack,

sir!" she pointed out. He carried little visible belongings himself and she was beginning to suspect that she had enough rations for the both of them. The first thing she would do when they stopped for a rest, was to rectify that little problem.

"Could I?" Arillion asked. "And why should I have done that? I am your *guide* after all, not your porter!"

Cassana felt her cheeks burn with anger. "Because you are stronger than me, sir and I am still feeling weak from my ordeal."

For his answer Arillion shook his hooded head, chuckling as he guided her through a thin sheet of filthy water that cascaded down from a large crack in the ceiling and flooded their path onwards. Cassana ducked her head to protect her face as they passed through it and shivered as the freezing cold water still managed to find her skin.

"Not long to go now, princess," Arillion said, changing the course of the conversation as his torch hissed and sputtered angrily. "We'll soon be out in the fresh air and away from all this sh...err, mess!"

Despite the fact she was clearly annoyed with him, she still managed a secretive smile and decided to remain quiet. If she fell out with him after only an hour since their departure, it was going to be a very long journey indeed. No! Better for her to bite her tongue and if possible, ignore his barbed words for now. Cassana winced inwardly. That was going to be as tough a test as carrying her heavy pack all the way home to Highwater! The sooner they met up with Cullen and received the horses from him, the better she would feel.

For the next few hours Arillion led her in merciful silence through the dark, twisting and sometimes treacherously narrow tunnels of the flooding sewers. Three times he had to stop to strike life into fresh torches and each time he threw the used brand into the channel of filth. By the time Cassana began to detect a shift in the density of the shadows ahead, she was utterly exhausted and thoroughly miserable. Every muscle in her body and even some she had never been aware of ached agonizingly, from the fires of cramp and the scorn of fatigue.

"Is it me, or is it becoming lighter?" she asked hopefully and he briefly turned his hooded head to her, nodding his confirmation.

Cassana breathed an audible sigh of relief. She couldn't wait to be free of this disgusting place and longed to taste the fresh air again. Judging by the natural gasses hanging in the suffocating air down here, it would take a long time before she was able to rid herself of the smells and memories of her recent ordeal. But the tangible hope of seeing the skies again spurred her on and for a while at least, her rising enthusiasm helped her to keep pace with her escort.

Sometime later, although Cassana was not sure when because she was having to focus all her attention on keeping her footing and fighting against the desire to refuse to go any further; Arillion took her away from the main passages of the sewers and along a narrow, claustrophobic tunnel that stretched away from her towards the heart- warming sight of daylight.

With her spirits lifting by the step, Cassana shuffled through the shin-deep filth and followed Arillion eagerly. Soon, they arrived at a rusting grate that barred their way to the outside. The light burned Cassana's bleary eyes and forced her to protect her sight with her grimy, free hand.

Arillion doused his dying torch in the running stream of sewerage beneath him and strode forward to the grate.

"Stay back," he warned her and reaching down low he grabbed the grate at the bottom and hauled it up effortlessly. "Hurry up," he hissed, his voice betraying its weight and Cassana obediently slid past him.

"Ah!" Cassana said in ecstasy as she shielded her eyes. She drew in the deepest of breaths and let it out again reluctantly as she stared about her surroundings.

She stood on a narrow, cobbled ledge looking out at the deep cesspool that was half-full from the sewerage that spilled continuously past her into the disgusting gathering several feet below. The pool was surrounded by the rising slopes of a grassy man-made bowl and behind her, the grate and tunnel that led back into the sewers was dug into the side of an oblique hillock. Overhead, brooding clouds cast their doubts on the last few hours of the day and a gentle drizzle fell silently, cleansing the air and almost diluting the stench from her surroundings and clothing. Almost…

Arillion stepped out to join her allowing the iron grate to crash down behind him, forcing Cassana to jump. She looked at him accusingly as he ignored her and occupied himself by studying their surroundings intently.

Without a word, he pushed by her gently and made his way up some steps that had been cut into the earth, away to their left. Cassana watched him as he quickly reached the top of the incline and looked about warily. After a time, he looked back down and motioned for her to join him. Swallowing, Cassana eyed the slick muddy steps and gingerly made her way up them to join the tall figure that waited for her, his long dark cloak snapping impatiently in a stiff breeze.

"Finally," he observed, although for a change his words lacked any real venom. "Welcome back to civilization, Lady Byron."

Cassana followed his sweeping arm, as he gestured gallantly about their murky surroundings and moved them away from the top of the steps. Grassy plains swept away from them in all directions, their long grasses swaying in a breeze that swept furiously from the east and rampaged over nearby farmlands, westwards towards the distant shadow that was the city of Karick. Cassana swallowed hard and felt suddenly naked in the capital's presence and her mind flared to life with memories of her stay there. Averting her gaze, she looked hurriedly to the north and then to the east. To the north, she could see many more farmlands and could just about make out the line of trees that flanked the Great North Road that had taken her into the city, many days ago now. Sweeping her eyes eastwards she could see a couple of nearby farmsteads, their boundaries defined by rickety fencing and their fields bursting with crops of golden wheat. An orchard on the southernmost fringes of the nearest farm was full of apple trees and beyond that she could see the dark shadows of a distant wood. Framing them on the murky horizon, far away towards the north-east, she could also see the rising slopes of the Crescent Hills, their summits battered by a furious rainstorm, highlighted occasionally by flashes of dancing lightning. It was one of the most beautiful sights she had ever seen!

She closed her eyes, marvelling as the cold wind caressed her face and blew the weariness from her body with calming assurances for the future. It was now time for her to look to that future. The events of the last few weeks were behind her now and she had to focus on the journey ahead. There was no point dwelling on what had happened to her. It was done and nothing could change that now. She had to step forward and take control of her fate, shaking free the dust of any doubts she still had, fashioning any information she had into a credible case against those behind all that had befallen her. Well, once she found out who they were!

"Looks like another storm might be heading our way," Arillion complained, wrapping his cloak tightly about him as the howling wind took Cassana's hood off her head. "We had best make haste."

Cassana hurriedly re-adjusted the weight of the pack on her shoulders and then fell hurriedly in behind him as he led her around the rim of the cesspool and took her through the long grasses towards the east. Above her, she could see several crows and she strained her neck to follow their flight as they swept over them towards their roosts, a tall cluster of oaks on the borders of a small farm towards the west. With a spring building in her faltering step and her wild hair whipping about her wet face like angry snakes, Cassana followed Arillion as he made his way towards the orchards, his eyes watching the distant farmhouses for signs of life.

"What are you doing?" Cassana hissed, mindful of Savinn's cautionary words as Arillion leapt effortlessly over the fencing and made his way to the nearest apple tree. Even though no life stirred from within the farmhouse Cassana was sure she could see the glow of light coming from underneath the door of a nearby barn. Ignoring her, Arillion reached up and picked a rosy red apple from the lowest branch of the apple tree and then, with a mischievous glint in his eyes, he turned and tossed it back in her direction.

"Keep a lookout and stop moaning," he hissed, as he turned back and started filling the small sack he had produced from underneath his cloak.

With her eyes wide with fear and her senses prickling with danger, she watched the barn and farmhouse, expecting to be discovered at any moment. For what seemed like minutes, but was probably only a dozen or so seconds, she waited expectantly to hear an angry cry of discovery and was relieved when Arillion leapt back over the fence, the sack bulging with apples.

"We are supposed to be travelling in secrecy," Cassana admonished him.

Arillion winked and headed off around the orchard to the south. Feeling exposed on her own, Cassana rushed after him and breathed a sigh of relief as the farmhouse and barn finally disappeared from view behind the rows of bountiful apple trees. The scents of the orchard's sweet smelling crops were borne on the stiff breeze and Cassana hoped that their intoxicating aroma would nullify the stench of the sewers upon her. All around the chatter of wildlife broke the silence of the grim day as the birds cried their farewells, perhaps singing in hope for a better one the next dawn. She paused momentarily to watch several small birds as they flitted and chased each other through the branches of an apple tree. Life! It was in stark contrast to her existence over the last few weeks and it filled her leaking hopes with fresh determination.

"Stick that in your mouth and put your jaw to good use," Arillion said, passing her an apple as he eyed some rabbits chasing each other in the orchard.

Cassana stared at it reluctantly for a moment, before giving into her temptation. As she took a bite out of the apple, Arillion chuckled.

"Spend a few more hours with me lady and you'll be ready to join up with Devlin Hawke," he said, his mask twisting from his concealed grin.

Cassana scowled at him in disgust and looked away as she secretively delighted in the taste of the delicious apple and took another guilty bite from it.

"Come on, princess," Arillion commanded, striding off, his arms spread at his sides as he allowed the palms of his hands to brush over the tops of the long grasses. "Let's get out of this rain and around a warm fire."

Cassana hurried to catch him up, agreeing with him for once.

Arillion and Cassana finally reached Briar Copse later that evening, under the cover of a misty darkness. The tangled shadowy depths of the woods welcomed them into their arms with reaching thorny bushes that grasped at their cloaks and scratched at bared skin.

"You take me to the nicest of places," Cassana observed sarcastically, as she gently freed the tails of her cloak off a reluctant bramble bush.

Arillion looked back at her and helped her free her cloak. "Well done, lass!" he said. "Don't want to leave any fibres behind to tell anyone we have come this way."

Cassana allowed him to proceed and looked about the woods. The tall grasses were home to a maze of nettles and weeds, absent from any wild flowers that could have commanded her attention and the tall gnarled trees that huddled in tightly about them, reached up into the black night with pleading branches, begging to be free of the twisting and choking undergrowth. It was a grim place, fitting for a grim day.

They both looked to the north as they heard the faint curse of thunder and their eyes met briefly.

"I think we may be lucky after all and keep dry tonight," Arillion observed, as he finally freed her cloak from the reluctant brambles and returned it to her. In the poor light he was just able to make out the curves of her leather-clad backside underneath her bedroll and resisted the urge to give it a playful slap. He certainly approved of her new outfit.

"Do you know these woods well?" she asked him, diverting his thoughts. He started guiding her through the dark, drawing her attention to obstacles and dangers on the uneven ground before them.

"Not really, my lady," he finally admitted quietly. "I know that a glade, frequented by travellers is in the centre of the woods, but that is all! Cullen will meet us there."

They carried on in wary silence from there, both listening for the warning sounds of danger and their concerns edged by the unnatural silence of their surroundings. Arillion led the way, his hooded head searching the shadows as he negotiated a safe path through the woods for them. Overhead, the thick twisting canopy of the tall trees sheltered them from the steady rain and the misty night urged them on into the silent unknown.

It wasn't long, however, before even Cassana's untrained eyes began to adapt to their dark and unfamiliar surroundings. Subtle depths of shadows began to take shape all about them and her footing started to become more assured. Even the local wildlife began to accept the strangers' presence in their domain and Briar Copse was soon alive again with the incessant chatter of crickets and the distant grunt of warning from a nearby badger. The misty air was hunted by bats, deftly sweeping through the dark in graceful twisting arcs as they dined on a supper of flies and moths. As Cassana followed one such bat as it swept into view, dodged around her and disappeared again back into the night, Arillion stopped suddenly. Looking back for her, he pointed abruptly through the trees away to their left. Following his sleeveless arm which was still adorned by a studded, leather guard, she could see the faint distant glow of a fire, burning like a welcome beacon through the mist and the dark.

"F-finally, some warmth," Cassana whispered, shivering. She was suddenly aware of how cold and wet through she was and hugged herself comfortingly.

"Hopefully that fire is Cullen's," Arillion replied, his breath clouding before them. "If it is, I'll let you snuggle up close to me tonight, if you like, princess?"

"I think not!" Cassana hissed in disgust, glaring at him. "I would rather freeze!"

Arillion's eyes sparkled with an answer of his own as he motioned for her to follow him and as he moved silently away, she fell in behind him again, her eyes boring into his back.

It took them a long, cautious while, but once they were close enough to pick out the camp-fire through the silent trees and could hear the crack and spit of its hungry flames, Arillion held up a hand for them to stop. Crouching low, he pulled Cassana down beside him.

"Wait here, while I see who's home," he ordered her and rising, he slipped towards the glade ahead.

Cassana could feel the heat on her ear from his hot breath and she fought down the strange tingling sensation that moved down her neck and cramped her stomach. As she watched the dark shadow creeping towards the fire ahead, she put it down to apprehension and fear. If it wasn't Cullen, then they could be in serious danger. To calm her nerves, she gripped her bow tightly, prepared for the worst and, hopefully, ready for anything! Visions of the battle at the stream in the Moonglade Forest sprang into her mind and she let out an involuntary shudder. She had never really had time to reflect on what had happened in those few bloody moments, perhaps because she had never wanted too! But now, with the fresh possibility of danger and the chance that she may have to kill... Cassana shuddered. To kill someone again, in order to save her own life; she was not surprised that her emotions and guilt of that day had risen to the fore. Cassana shook her head defensively. The woodsman had called upon her to help him that day and, reluctantly, if needed, she would do the same for her new protector. As she continued to watch Arillion creep near the fringes of the glade, her mind continued to reason with her that if she hadn't fought back against the Reven that day, she would probably be dead by now.

Arillion rose suddenly and turned. Blindly, he waved for her to join him and stepped into the light of the glade beyond. As Cassana hurried over to join him, she could feel the night closing in on her and she quickly reached there, chased by a fear that the trees would reach out and steal her away into the night. As she neared the perimeter of the glade, she could hear voices and even managed a thankful sigh as she heard the gruff voice of Cullen.

Arillion was standing before a roaring camp fire, his

hands held out towards its flames as he sought to dry out. His shadow sprung to life on the mist and darkness surrounding the glade and he was looking to his right at Cullen, who sat on an old tree stump and was drawing ponderously on a pipe. Both men stopped what they were doing as Cassana ducked under a low-hanging branch and moved into the glade to join them.

"Welcome, Lady Byron," Cullen said, rising up to meet her. His one good eye blazed merrily as he instinctively shuffled over to greet her.

"Thank you, Cullen," Cassana replied, managing a faint smile.

With her free hand, Cassana tugged her sodden hood from her head and moved towards the light of the fire. Tethered to a tree, in the shadows, across from the fire, Cassana could see three horses, standing solemnly in the cold and huddling together for comfort. There saddles were looped over branches on a neighbouring tree and Cassana could see that they had been recently fed, watered and groomed; each had a blanket over their backs, to keep them warm for the night. She looked at Cullen briefly, confused how a man such as he could take care of these animals better than he could a teenage girl.

"Not the best weather to be setting out in," Cullen observed, as he returned to his seat and drew on his pipe. Tendrils of smoke twisted up into the dark night sky and the tobacco glowered fiercely as he closed his eye, relaxing.

"No, it is not," Arillion agreed.

Cassana moaned wearily and shrugged the pack from her back. Her entire body burned with fatigue and her back stiffened painfully in protest as she made a point of dumping the pack on the ground to show how heavy it was. Arillion did not react until she joined him in front of the fire.

"So what's for supper then, princess?" he asked.

Cassana rounded angrily on him, before she could stop herself. "What? After allowing me to carry that pack all this way, you now have the audacity to expect me to cook for you as well...sir?"

Arillion nodded. "Well, of course! You are a woman, after all." Cullen chuckled.

Cassana was speechless and her attempted reply was lost amongst her incredulous splutters of rage and screams of disbelief. As she strode away from him, waving her arms about to try and catch hold of her frustration, Arillion's eyes followed her, alight with mirth. The Byron girl started untying her bedroll and began muttering away to herself as she laid it out on the ground. Cullen grinned to himself as he rose and moved over to join Arillion, who stood with his back to the fire and continued to watch the girl as she huffed and puffed away.

"As it seems you two are getting on famously, I'll take my leave now I think and return to the boss," Cullen said, drawing Arillion's focus to him.

"Good idea," Arillion responded, a little too enthusiastically.

Cullen looked at Cassana and then back again. "Good luck, Arillion." he said, offering him a bold hand.

Arillion looked down at the hand and then his eyes flicked up again. "I won't need it, but thanks all the same." He shook the sweaty hand briefly and released it back, disdainfully, to the repulsive man.

"Right, er, well then," Cullen said, averting his gaze. "I had best be on my way then, Lady Byron."

Cassana composed herself and rose. Turning, she came over to Cullen, her face full of barely controlled frustration. "Thank you Cullen." She shook his hand and smiled in earnest as he fidgeted under her gaze again.

"I'll tell the boss that you made it safely this far," Cullen reported. "The boss has given you two of his thoroughbreds for the journey, the black and brown, and enough feed and water for them to get you home safely, miss."

Cassana asked Cullen to pass on her gratitude to his master and looked to the horses. She could easily pick them out. Both of them magnificent specimens, worthy of the high duke's stables no less. It appeared to Cassana that Savinn's influences were far reaching and his pockets deep indeed, if he was able to purchase such fine creatures. As Cullen moved over to them and began saddling his own mount, she could see that he had been given a stout, powerful looking grey; a perfect complement to the rider he would bear.

Arillion moved to help Cullen saddle his mount, leaving Cassana to bubble away. Perhaps he shouldn't have wound her up after such a hard trek for her, but he couldn't help himself. There was just something about her that encouraged him to annoy her at every opportunity and he had to admit that he got great enjoyment from doing so. Savinn had tried to bully him about the way he treated the girl, but he couldn't give a damn what he thought. Of course he wouldn't mistreat her, not in the way the merchant had insinuated he might. It didn't mean that he couldn't have a little fun with her at her own expense along the way though. As he helped Cullen he wondered what had given Savinn the idea that he was capable of mistreating her?

Arillion's reputation for ruthlessness was not in question here and he prided himself on that fact too! But he had never forced himself upon a woman before and he certainly wasn't about to start on the daughter of the Lord of Highwater. So why the insinuation? Arillion felt his anger rise the more he thought about it. Normally he didn't care what people thought about him. He was getting paid a small fortune for this task too, so why should he care what the mixed thought, as long as his coin was still good? Arillion put his anger on that matter to the back of his mind for now. He had to focus on getting the girl home safely and he did not need any unnecessary distractions. Perhaps Savinn Kassaar had inadvertently questioned his honour, but that hurt him more than the sharpest blade ever could. To draw a line under the matter, he would have questions of his own for Savinn when he returned to collect his reward. But for now, they would just have to wait.

Untying his mount's reins Cullen thanked Arillion for his assistance and despite his appearance, the squat man climbed deftly into the saddle. Turning his horse to face the fire, he patted its neck.

"Safe journey to you both," he said.

Cassana thanked him and watched as the man guided his mount away into the darkness of the trees. He was soon lost from sight and she stood watching the shadows for a time before turning back to her bedroll. Taking off her cloak, she hung it from a nearby tree.

"The rain has stopped now," Arillion observed, looking up into the dark, overcast night sky. "You should bring your bedroll closer to the fire, my lady. It will be a cold, damp night."

Cassana wasn't sure if that was his way of apologising and she decided even if it wasn't, it was better than another argument. She nodded to him and brought her belongings closer to the warmth of the fire. As she busied herself, Arillion moved off wordlessly into the woods. A stiff whining breeze still gripped the region and the upper boughs of their shadowy sentinels bent and swayed with each furious passing.

By the time Arillion returned, carrying a bundle of fresh wood for the fire, Cassana had repositioned her bedroll for the third time and had prepared supper for them both.

"Cold meat and potatoes, I am afraid," she said, a little embarrassed at her efforts. Arillion dropped the wood on the ground and tossed some of them onto the fire. The flames of the fire spat hungrily, sending glowing embers of ash up into the night.

"Sounds good to me, my lady," Arillion replied, masking his disappointment. She really needed to get out more. Moving to the saddles, he retrieved his bedroll and then returned, laying it out before the fire, across from Cassana. Perhaps he should have suggested Cassana's bedroll was tied to her mount, when he had chosen his mount earlier that day. Grinning, he moved round the fire and accepted the plate with a gracious nod.

Cassana felt her heart pound in unexpected anticipation as Arillion moved back to his bedroll. Any anger she had drained from her as she focused on him through the flames, surreptitiously trying to watch his every move. At first she had been prepared to go without food for the night, just to spite him. He was irksome beyond belief and every word that came from his mouth seemed to infuriate her. While she had stewed over his shortcomings she had smiled to herself. If she prepared supper for them and it was so bad, he would have to do it himself in the future, if he didn't want to starve! As she had busied herself with her plans, she suddenly thought of something else. If Arillion wanted to eat, he would have to take the scarf from over his mouth to do so, as well!

Arillion placed his supper on the ground and then straightened. Lowering his hood, he deliberately took his cloak off and dropped it slowly beside his bedroll. Cassana sucked in a breath. He was tall, as she already knew and she could now see the strong body beneath the shadows. His torso was covered in a vest of dark leather, but his broad shoulders and arms were bare, but for the studded guards on each forearm. As he turned to drop his cloak on the ground, she could see the two sheaths strapped to his lower back, angled so that he could quickly pull the short, twin blades free for combat. She had never seen him without his cloak on before and had not even known they were there. Arillion still wore his black leather trousers and knee-high boots and she could see the numerous pouches hanging off the belt at his waist. The curious crescent-shaped knife was still there too.

All this was forgotten, however, as Cassana studied Arillion's face. He had long unkempt brown hair that fell just above his shoulders and he had tucked any unruly strands away behind his ears. He turned as he felt Cassana's eyes upon him and his flint-grey eyes smiled at her from beneath his serious, arching eyebrows. Reaching up with his right hand he pulled the dark scarf down underneath his chin. Cassana blinked free from her stare and let out her breath.

Arillion was ruggedly handsome and although she had somehow expected it, part of her wished that he wasn't. A straight nose ran between his eyes from brow to tip and his broad jaw line was covered with a week-long growth of stubble. On many occasions the glimmer in his eyes had suggested his mirth and Cassana could now see the accompanying grin, dancing across his face.

"So was it worth the wait, princess?"

Cassana looked away from Arillion and down at her food in embarrassment, as he grinned roguishly at her. Why did he have to be so handsome? She asked herself, groaning silently. Why couldn't he have a big wart on his cheek or look like Cullen and have to wear the mask for a reason.

"Speechless," Arillion observed. "I can understand that, it wouldn't be the first time!" Arillion went on, nodding to himself in satisfaction.

Cassana did not look up as Arillion began to hum and he let out an exaggerated sigh as he sat down on his bedroll. Was it her, or was the fire getting really hot? Perhaps she should move her bedroll back a bit?

"Hmm. Looks delicious!" Arillion said as he picked up a boiled potato and popped it into his mouth.

Cassana continued to ignore him and she did not look up from her food again until her cheeks had lost their colour and her plate was empty. When she did, Arillion was lying back on his bedroll and appeared to be sleeping. Sighing, Cassana put her plate to one side and looked about her surroundings.

The wind had abated now, dropping its roar to a gentle protest and helping to bring some calm to the blustery night. Drawing her knees up to her chest, Cassana rested her chin on them and closed her eyes, finally relaxing. The warmth of the fire had dried her hair and clothes out by now and her aching muscles had even managed to forego their complaints for a little while. As she listened to the calm of the night and the songs of the insects, an owl hooted somewhere off through the trees to her left. It hooted again, its cry perhaps proclaiming its territory to a rival, encroaching upon its domain. Cassana smiled to herself. She was fascinated by birds, especially birds of prey. From her balcony window on her father's estate back home, she had watched a pair of Valian eagles for the last three years now; marvelling at their loyalty to each other and the freedom they had as they glided imperiously about *their* skies, calling out to each other. Cassana cocked her head to one side as the owl cried out again, further away now and she sighed wistfully and smiled. How she would love to be free from all of this! When she opened her eyes again, Arillion was sat up and watching her intently.

"What are you looking at, sir?" She asked, feeling more than a little uncomfortable. His eyes were alight with the flames of the fire.

"Why I'm looking at you, princess!" Arillion grinned.

"Well do not, please." Cassana ordered him, the heat of the fire adding to her embarrassment. "I do not like it!"

Arillion mimicked how Cassana was sitting and he rubbed an itch from his chin on his knees. "Well I sure do," he said, his voice absent from mockery.

Cassana looked away, her heart pounding rapidly. She was frightened, unsure and drastically out of her depth. Back at her father's court possible suitors would flatter her with rehearsed words of nauseous flattery and boastful promises of riches beyond her wildest dreams. Here, with Arillion, life was a lot more uncertain and spontaneous. She didn't know how to react. She didn't even like the man...did she?

"Please do not stare at me, sir?" she implored, avoiding him. "It unnerves me."

"Fair enough, princess." Arillion replied, the irksome edge back in his voice.

Cassana could hear him rise and she resisted the urge to look at him. He moved away to sit on Cullen's tree stump.

"I'll take the watch tonight, lady," he announced. "You get some rest, we have a long ride ahead of us tomorrow."

Cassana looked briefly at him. He was watching her from the corner of one eye as he absently chewed his nails on one hand.

"Thank you, sir," she said, climbing obediently into her bedroll. She turned over, offering her back to him and rested her head on her left wrist as she stared out into the darkness. Just as her heart rate began to even out and her body's demand for sleep was beginning to win her over, Arillion spoke again, his voice nothing more than a gentle whisper.

"You should smile more often, princess!"

CHAPTER FOURTEEN

Time to say Goodbye

The distant crash of a door being slammed jerked the two men from their thoughts and its reverberating echo sounded like thunder as they stared at each other through the darkness, trying to pick out the other's expression. Khadazin could just about make out the old man's eyes; they were wide and fearful and he expected that his own eyes looked the same. Drawing in a deep breath the stonemason held it there, daring himself to let it go as he knew it could be his last. His skin was also alert to these feelings and his heart began to beat wildly as he finally let his breath escape.

"Won't be long now then," Cornelius observed quietly, pausing for more words, then deciding not to speak.

Khadazin nodded back, lost within his own thoughts and then grinned nervously when he realised the old man probably couldn't see him.

"Yes, my friend. It's now or never for us!"

Cornelius shuffled forward to the bars of his cell.

"Never was the only hope I had before you came, so it will have to be now, my friend," he croaked, his courage brittle and his throat choked by nerves.

They had spent many hours formulating a plan to escape, worrying about how it would play out and dissecting what would happen to them if it didn't. In the end, when Khadazin was drifting off into a much needed sleep, they decided that there was no other option left, but to try. No amount of fretting on possible outcomes would change their destiny now. Live or die, it was painfully that simple!

"Whatever happens my friend, we can at least say that we tried," Khadazin whispered, as they heard another door open, closer still. He looked towards the door at the top of the steps and swallowed.

"Agreed, lad," Cornelius murmured. "Best get ready to spit in their eyes then!"

Khadazin nodded. He cast one last, lingering look at the old man and smiled fondly at him. Cornelius's wizened face grinned back madly and then withdrew into the shadows of his cell. The stonemason led on the ground and positioned himself face down, with his right arm under his chin, the other arm spread out on the cold stone floor. As he began to detect the sounds of distant approach, he repositioned the flint in the palm of the hand he hid under him and decided that it was best to let fate decide. If they noticed it, they died. But if they didn't...

The footsteps were approaching now, gaining stark precedence over his thoughts and he closed his eyes, focusing on their sound. Closer they came and with it, the faint glow of a torch again that outlined the door to their prison chamber. As the faint glow brightened, Khadazin could hear muffled voices and a chuckled response. Finally, their captors reached the door and fell silent; keys fumbled in the lock and then the door swung inwards. Torchlight spilled gleefully into the room and blinded Cornelius as he looked nervously towards them. Both prisoners subconsciously held their breath as the hooded figures moved wordlessly into the chamber.

Three of them! Cornelius barely managed to stop himself cheering aloud. They had fretted long into the early hours that if the fourth member of their group was back, it would make things very difficult for them indeed. Judging by his absence however, they must have decided that the stonemason's threat was diminishing with each round of torture he endured and that the extra man was not really needed any more. If what Khadazin had overheard was true, then this would only be a one way journey anyhow.

"Still alive, old man?" the torchbearer said again, as they ghosted down the steps and moved to stand between the two cells.

Cornelius watched him disdainfully as he turned away chuckling and shone the torch towards Khadazin's cell to assist the hooded figure fumbling to find the lock. The old man craned his neck to see what was happening and then heard the click as the man finally unlocked the cell. With a groan of protest the barred door swung open and the three hooded figures made to enter the cell.

"I'll outlive you!" Cornelius said, his ancient voice cutting through the silence. All three of them stiffened in surprise and turned at his voice.

"What did you say old man?" the torchbearer asked, failing to hide the astonishment in his voice. He moved to stand before the old man's cell and held the torch before him, as if suggesting that the flames would help him to hear better.

"I said," Cornelius growled, nodding meaningfully. "That I'll outlive you!"

"I doubt that," the man chuckled in response as he turned to his companions. "Get the Redani and take him on, I need a little chat with grandfather here and then I'll catch you up."

Nodding in unison the two men moved into the cell and positioned themselves on either side of the unconscious stonemason.

"He's as heavy as a sack of stones." One of them complained as they picked him up under each armpit.

"And as dead to the world," the other one observed. Grunting in unison they dragged the Redani from his cell and moved slowly towards the steps.

"Don't take too long then," one of them wheezed as they passed. Struggling up the stairs they muttered amongst themselves about their absent comrade.

"Alone again," the torchbearer said merrily, turning his attentions back to Cornelius, once they had left the chamber.

Cornelius nodded, grinning as he beckoned the man closer to him.

Khadazin's heart thundered with nervous anticipation as his two captors dragged him along the dark corridor. He did not feel the pain of the skin lifting from his knees as he still couldn't quite believe that the first part of their plan had actually worked and that it was now time for him to fulfil his side of the bargain. After several yards Khadazin began to relax his body, allowing his captors to bear his full weight. At first nothing happened, but then, after another few yards, he began to feel the man on his right struggle to keep a hold on him. Wordlessly the man struggled on bravely for another few steps before giving into his weaknesses.

"Hang on, I need a better grip," he grumbled, forcing his companion to stop with him. Ignoring his comrade's colourful reflection on his shortcomings, they went to drop the stonemason on the ground.

As they let go of him, the stonemason was suddenly alive and very alert. Standing up from within their relaxing grip before they could respond, the stonemason was upon the man to his right, ramming the flint up into the darkness of the hood. He felt it bite home and pushed the jagged stone deep into the soft flesh underneath the man's chin. As the man gargled and staggered back Khadazin turned and tussled with the second man. Grabbing his astonished host by the robes the stonemason forced him back against the wall and as they slammed up against it, Khadazin heard the man's breath blast from his lungs in frightened agony.

"Help us!" the man shouted, panicking. Khadazin snarled and punched him in the stomach.

Despite Khadazin's advantage in size, he was soon aware of just how weak he was as the man regained his footing and senses. The blow to his stomach had been ineffective and the robed figure fought back now, forcing him across the narrow corridor. They slammed heavily against the adjacent wall this time, both stumbling over the twitching and forgotten form beneath them.

Panicking, Khadazin gambled. As the man tried to pin him against the wall, he felt him relax one of his grips as he fumbled for a weapon concealed beneath his robes. Parody of strength restored, Khadazin kneed the man between the legs and as his captor bent away from him in obvious pain, he elbowed him on the top of his head. Pain shot up the stonemason's arm as he connected with his skull and the man grunted, dropping to his knees. As the man swayed dazedly before him, Khadazin kicked at the face that was hidden beneath the shadows of the lolling hood. The man offered a meagre groan in response to his snapping nose as he fell backwards and was still. Flicking a glance to his left, Khadazin could see the dancing flames of torchlight as the last man hurried up the steps and appeared in the doorway, a short sword flashing in his free hand. Screaming angrily at the sight that greeted him, the torchbearer raced down the corridor towards him.

Leaping upon the fallen man across from him, Khadazin fumbled desperately through his robes and his blind hands touched the hilt of a blade. As the torchbearer reached him, his sword raised to strike, Khadazin pulled free the concealed blade and parried the attack as he rose. The hooded figure cursed as Khadazin forced him back with a vicious slash towards his head and their shadows leapt angrily about them as they faced each other across the two still bodies between them.

"I think you may have lost that bet," Khadazin stated, his eyes glittering as he found his breath and reined in the fury that might force him into a rash decision.

"You think you can escape from here, Redani?" the man hissed back at him, tensing to strike.

Khadazin leapt forward and drove the blade deep into the man's chest, before he could react. His momentum carried them both back down the corridor and slipping, Khadazin let go of his blade as the man screamed in agony and fell backwards, dropping his blade and torch.

The twitching man lay on his back and clutching vainly at his wound he sobbed pitifully as he felt blood wash over his fingers. The blade was buried deep and he groaned as he fought to cling onto the last light fading in his eyes. A dark shadow loomed over him and he began to moan pleadingly.

"I shall certainly try," Khadazin panted heavily in response as he raised the man's fallen sword above his own head.

Cornelius clung on to the bars of his cell, his thin frame snapping in sympathy with every cry of pain and echo of commotion coming from the corridor beyond his world. He had managed to stall the man with a slow tale of how brilliantly he had managed to coerce the Redani into confessing the truth about who he had told. As the torch-bearer's impatience had got the better of him and he demanded a swift name from his prisoner, they had both heard the cry for help coming from the corridor. Swearing darkly, the man had bounded away and drew a sword from underneath his robes as he raced up the steps.

Alone again now Cornelius listened intently to the muffled shouts and sound of combat rising and falling. His head thundered with worry about the outcome and he jumped in fright as he heard a final pleading cry rise up and then cut off abruptly. All went silent and the old man held his breath, listening to the dripping water of the chamber and the wild pounding of his heart.

For many moments all was quiet. Cornelius pulled nervously at his wispy beard and struggled to see anything in the corridor beyond. The distant static glow from the torchlight suggested that it had fallen to the ground, but still burned. Should he call out? His excitement was palpable. There were no shouts from their wounded captors, no urgent calls for assistance. Had Khadazin managed to kill them all? If he called out to him and one of his captors was still alive, it would reveal where his allegiances lay.

"Just my luck," he muttered to himself. "The Redani kills them and leaves without me!"

Cornelius shoulders sank and he collapsed to the floor of his cell. He couldn't blame him. After all, hadn't he initially planned to use the Redani to ensure his own freedom? So why shouldn't he do the same to him? It was the natural order of things, wasn't it? Despite this, the thought of being left to rot when others were free forced a bitter taste up into his throat. He had been so close, so close!

The old man was so focused on his fate that he did not see the torchlight begin to approach, neither did he see the tall hooded figure dressed in ill-fitting robes move wearily into the chamber.

"Cornelius?" Khadazin enquired, stumbling down the last step.

The old man's head nearly jerked off his bony shoulders as he leapt up and began dancing madly about his cell, cheering and cackling madly.

"You did it, Redani, you did it!"

Khadazin grinned and moved to the old man's cell. It took a long time and a lot of effort he could not really afford, but he finally managed to find the right key from the jailer's set and force it into the rusted lock.

"They haven't opened up that door for six years," Cornelius stated, as the stonemason grimaced and tried to turn the key. The old man jumped up and down like an excited child waiting for a gift and he let out a gleeful roar as the rusted lock gave in and clicked. Yanking the door open, Khadazin tossed the old man a black robe as he stepped tentatively out of the place that had been his home for the last twenty years.

"I can't believe it worked!" Cornelius said, shaking his head in astonishment. Putting down the torch, Khadazin helped him into his robes. They were far too big for the old man, but it was the best he could offer him for now.

"Clothes!" Cornelius observed. "I never thought to wear them again."

The stonemason nodded his agreement, pleased to have some warmth on his naked and scarred body, at last. His was still very weak. The fight had taken nearly all of his strength from him and despite the fact that the wound in his left forearm had healed enough now to offer some grip to his hand, he was still not strong enough to be confident of escape.

"Here, take this," Khadazin said, passing the old man one of the short blades from their captors. Taking the set of keys from the lock, he slipped them inside the pocket of his robe and passed Cornelius the torch.

Cornelius looked ridiculous and they looked at each other for a moment, before laughing. He looked like a ghoulish scarecrow, wild and frightful and he held the sword in one hand and the torch in the other, as if not sure what to do with them.

"You had best lead the way, my friend," he chuckled, looking from hand to hand, "I am more likely to do damage to myself, than anyone else."

Khadazin nodded, his dark eyes glittering from beneath his hood. "Follow me, my friend. It's time for us to say goodbye to Borin!"

Cornelius growled. He had dreamt of the day he

could get some recompense for all of the pain the torturer had inflicted upon him over the last few years. He had never thought he would get that chance until now and as he felt his dark expectations rise, he followed the stonemason eagerly from the chamber. As Cornelius gingerly reached the top of the steps, he turned and looked back at his cell. The torchlight spread out pityingly across the squalid conditions he had called home and he felt tears of shame well up inside of him.

Shaking his head, the old man turned away and fell in behind the Redani as he led him through the carnage in the corridor beyond. All three of his captors were dead. One had the flint rammed under his chin; Cornelius felt some pride at that one, and the other two were both dead from deep cuts to their throat.

"I told you that I'd live longer," Cornelius spat at the corpses, nearly slipping on the blood-slicked stone. "Nice work, Redani!"

Khadazin ignored him and led them on. He could understand the old man's glee at their deaths, but to the stonemason it was sadly something that just needed to be done. He could not think about them at all. Who they were, why they chose their path. Or even if they had families and children of their own. He had to think beyond his conflicting emotions. He did not start all of this! He had not asked to overhear the conversation in the gardens and he had certainly not deserved what had befallen him since. As they left the bodies behind, Khadazin clenched his fists and gritted his teeth. He had to focus. Put aside his emotions and channel his anger into escaping. If he succeeded in that, well, then he could think about what to do next. He wanted to repay the chancellor for what he had done, it was all he had thought about when he was being tortured. Perhaps one day they would *talk* again, perhaps!

Borin finished sharpening the bone saw on a whetstone and tested its teeth. Satisfied that it was ready for the task at hand, he turned his attentions to the other rusty implements on the long table. The interrogator would join him in the chamber shortly, giving him a chance to work on the Redani for a while. When he did arrive, Borin hoped that the stonemason would finally be willing to talk to him, as he was looking forward to the prospect of many years of recreational torture on the huge, dark-skinned foreigner. Picking up a thumbscrew he wiped his sweating brow and cast an accusing look at the brazier. The sooty chamber was suffocating today, even for him and pulling on his glove, he pulled free the poker and marvelled at the ferocity of the red hot iron. Grinning, he slammed it back into the heart of the glowing coals.

As he turned, the door to the chamber opened and two robed figures entered the room. Before his mind caught up with his eyes and he could react, they were upon him like wild demons, blades hacking madly at his body as he staggered back in bloodied shock and reached out for the nearest item on the table. As his large hand snaked around the handle of a thin blade, the smaller of his attackers chopped furiously at his hand.

Roaring with pain Borin clutched the bloody, fingerless stump to his chest and tried to back away from the madmen.

"My turn," Khadazin snarled. Stepping in close he slammed the pommel of his sword into the wounded man's temple, watching dispassionately as the huge

310

torturer collapsed to the ground without a sound and cracked his head on the floor.

Cornelius panted and laughed nervously as the stonemason moved to the door and closed it again. When the Redani turned back, he looked at the old man and nodded towards the huge, still form of their torturer.

"Make it quick," he said.

Khadazin opened the door and stared down the long torch-lit corridor that would hopefully take them to freedom. All was quiet and it appeared that their efforts to escape had so far gone unnoticed. Sighing thankfully, he flicked a glance to his left as Cornelius stepped up alongside him. After sharing a brief look that conveyed their shame they left the torture chamber, closing their guilt and the terrible memories of what they had endured in there, behind the solid door.

As they moved down the corridor, Khadazin heard a voice from the top of the stone stairs up ahead and he dragged Cornelius back into the protection of the corridor that would have taken them back to their cells. With his heart pounding rapidly now, Khadazin wiped the back of a bloodied hand across his sweating brow and listened to the sound of soft, approaching footfalls. Cornelius had discarded their torch by now for the comfort of the hot poker and he huddled behind the stonemason for protection. It sounded like only one person approached and that meant that unless he or she was going mad, somebody else was upstairs. Battling back any surfacing doubts the stonemason tensed and waited for the approaching figure to come alongside him. He had to make this as quick and silent as possible.

A shadow fell across the open doorway and Khadazin held his breath before leaping out to attack the newcomer. It was the interrogator and the man jumped with fright, yelling in fear as a dark shape leapt out in front of him and dragged him back into the shadowy doorway. He was thrown roughly to the ground and a heavy form knelt down on top of him, pressing a blood-red sword to his throat.

"P-please, don't kill me," the man shuddered, his bowels loosening.

Cornelius's nose wrinkled. "Was that me?"

Khadazin pressed the steel blade down across the man's throat. He was not so calm and serene now, his eyes wide and bursting with unconstrained terror.

"Who are you?" Khadazin demanded, watching as fresh terror scattered the fear from the man's eyes. "What is the brotherhood?"

The man closed his eyes. "I will tell you nothing, Redani!" His trembling body relaxed slightly, although Khadazin could still feel the man's chest pounding out a different message beneath him.

"Nope," Cornelius said, checking himself. "Definitely not me!"

Khadazin shook his head. "Tell me who they are and I'll let you live."

The man laughed hysterically. "You will have to kill me. I would rather die by your sword, than give up my brethren."

"So be it!" Khadazin drew the blade across the man's throat and stood up as he gargled and twitched beneath him.

Turning, Khadazin nearly impaled himself on the poker. "Give me that before you do some damage," he said, snatching it from the frail old man's grasp.

312

Cornelius grinned at him and cast a withering look at the dying man as Khadazin motioned for him to follow and led them out into the corridor. If he could have been sure of their imminent safety, he would have questioned the man at length. Although even then, Khadazin doubted that he would have had the stomach to travel the road needed to extract the information from his lips.

As they moved urgently down the corridor, a robed figure appeared on the stone stairs and Khadazin baulked as he saw him level a loaded crossbow at him. Crying out a warning, the stonemason charged down the corridor towards him. The crossbow jerked as the man released the bolt and jilting, Khadazin leant to one side as he felt the quarrel crease the side of his cheek. Snarling he threw the poker he carried in his left hand at the man, who dropped the crossbow and ripped a sword from within his robes. The poker hissed in excitement as it spun through the air, but the man jumped down the last few steps, dodging it easily. They came together and Khadazin barely dodged the man's disemboweling thrust, before opening up a wound on his opponent's right shoulder. Grimacing, the man parried Khadazin's clumsy lunge towards his throat and sent a riposte back that tore through the Redani's robes and opened up a shallow wound on his left thigh.

Snarling Khadazin gripped the short blade in both hands and circled his opponent. As the man attacked him again with a high cut towards his face, he bludgeoned the blade from the man's hands, before burying the blade deep in his throat. Yanking his sword free, Khadazin stepped away from the geyser of spurting crimson that showered the wall behind the falling man and looked up the stairs. The stone steps led steeply up into the shadows and all was thankfully silent.

"Quickly, Cornelius," he called, turning. "We are nearly..."

Khadazin's words died on his lips as he saw the bundle of robes on the dusty floor, the sword discarded beside him.

"NO!" Khadazin cried, his pain forgotten as he rushed to the old man's side and cradled him gently in his arms.

The old man fought for breath, coughing up words laced in blood. "Damn it!" he heaved, fighting for breath as he bucked and shuddered in the Redani's arms.

Khadazin wept. The fragile old man was shaking uncontrollably and as he caressed his leathery face and whispered comfortingly to him, he could see the quarrel sticking out of his body, just beneath his left ribcage. Blood washed over his hands as he tentatively touched at it and Cornelius swatted his hand away.

"Leave it," he hissed, blood sputtering through his gritted teeth. "It's too deep."

Khadazin's heart raced as the old man struggled and went taught in his arms. "Stay with me, Cornelius!" he pleaded. He looked towards the stairs and rising up, he carried the old man towards them.

Cornelius groaned dully and his head sagged against the stonemason's shoulder. Khadazin blinked the tears from his eyes, tasting them on his split lips. The old man was stick thin and light in arms and as he reached the bottom of the stairs, his hands could feel the blood seeping through the back of his robes and his fingers brushed over the point of the quarrel, protruding from his back. Cornelius was so thin and Khadazin guessed that if he had been any closer, the projectile would have probably passed through his frail body.

"L-leave me," Cornelius whispered faintly, his breath ragged.

"I will not," Khadazin said stoically, as he felt his skin crawl with the fear eating away at him. "I am going to get you out of here, my friend."

With that, the stonemason strode up the stairs as quick as his injured thigh would allow him. He could feel the wound open and pull with each step and blood ran down his leg, leaving a trail behind him. Gritting his teeth he carried on into the unknown, his weapon forgotten in the corridor beneath them.

By the time he reached the top, his heart was racing wildly and his breath was hard to find. In his arms the old man coughed and wheezed as his lungs rattled away, keeping him alive.

Khadazin scowled, looking about the small, empty room. A candle burned low on a holder in the centre of a worm-infested table, shedding a pathetic light upon the scene and the four vacant chairs positioned around it. One of them was tipped on the floor, suggesting a hasty departure and Khadazin could see several steaming plates of half-eaten food and mugs of ale, laying unfinished on the table. Behind the table an open door offered a dim glimpse of the short, shadowy corridor beyond and a similar door to his left opened up into a large room with several beds and accompanying wooden chests. Ignoring the barracks, Khadazin stumbled along the corridor, his mind beginning to take a firm hand on his desperation and emotions. There were five beds in that other room...

At the end of the corridor, Khadazin stepped through an archway into a torch-lit chamber. To his left and right, solid looking doors stood closed in the ancient stonework walls, but before him a set of crumbling steps curled away up from view into a spiralling staircase of cobwebs and shadows.

Without hesitating Khadazin moved to the steps and began following them up into the shadows. Soon, faint fingers of light peered around the corner before him, beckoning him on into the unknown. The walls were cracked and alive with tendrils of twisting roots and weeds. Khadazin's mind raced. Where had they taken him?

Passing by the torch burning from a bracket on the curving staircase wall, the stonemason felt his hopes lift as he saw the flames sway rhythmically to the call of a faint breeze. He sucked in the breeze through his ruined nose and his stern, ashen face softened as his lungs filled with fresh air.

"We are nearly free, Cornelius," he soothed the still frame, groaning weakly in his arms. The old man's eyes flickered open momentarily and he managed a faint grin. "B-better hurry..."

Growling, Khadazin muttered a curse and quickened his faltering step. Up the spiral staircase he took them, teased by the fresh air that skipped down to them and enticed them on their way. By the time the shadows began to lessen and the glow of light claimed dominance, Khadazin was exhausted and the form in his arms was still.

"Hang on," Khadazin pleaded with old man.

It didn't take long, but Khadazin could see the light of day above them, burning a path through the shadows and scattering them away to the cracks in the walls. Any elation he should have felt was choked by his grief and he carefully lay the old man down on the steps.

"I will be back, old friend," he whispered softly in the old man's ears. Rising up, he held his bloodied hands up before him and shuddered. Clenching his fists, he looked towards the broken opening above him and strode up to claim his freedom.

Cornelius could not feel the stone beneath him as his body was numb. He was having to fight for each breath now and every wheezing cough lessened his success as he struggled to cling onto his senses. He moaned, his eyes fluttering as his head lolled dreamily. Was it his imagination, or did his failing sight see the light of day above him? As he strained to see, a swift spasm of pain ripped through his heart and he felt the blood spilling down his chin. The sounds of a struggle above him touched his ears briefly and then the breeze stole it away again.

Fighting with all his might, the old man drew in a deep, painful breath. Fresh air! He grinned as darkness closed in around him and he thought that his time had come.

"Cornelius?" It was the Redani. His words were full of worry and he heard the stonemason sigh in relief as he forced one weak eye open to look at him. The strong black face that looked down at him was a bloody tapestry of welts, bruises and cuts. A deep gash had been opened up on his bearded chin and blood dripped freely from it.

"Are we free?" Cornelius whispered and the stonemason nodded his head, tears spilling down his cheeks. Without a word, the Redani gathered him up into his strong arms and carried him up the remaining steps into the light.

A cooling breeze touched gently at the old man's

face and his eyes blinked rapidly as he looked in momentary wonderment about his surroundings.

"Just my bloody luck," he cackled, a bubble of blood bursting on his lips.

Khadazin followed the old man's dull eyes around their surroundings and shook his head sadly. They were standing in a forest clearing, choked by a tangled undergrowth of tall grasses and twisting thorns. A thick forest surrounded them on all sides and as Khadazin spun around to show Cornelius their surroundings, he could see his head straining to look up at the dark, morose sky overhead. A light rain wept down upon them in sympathy as the old man chortled ironically.

"S-someone up there is having a good laugh," he managed, chasing the air blowing tantalisingly past his reaching gasps. The stonemason nodded grimly. Even now, after all those years, the old man would still not get to see his blue sky.

The dark opening behind them fronted the skeletal remnants of what might have once been a keep. Broken walls and crumbling outbuildings reached above the choking onslaught of nature, as if begging to be free and magnificent once again. The hooded guard Khadazin had fought desperately with moments ago lay beyond the opening, killed by his own blade in the end and now half-concealed by the undergrowth.

"Where are we?" Khadazin wondered aloud to himself.

Cornelius coughed up more blood and when he was able to speak again, his voice was faint and distant.

"Probably W-westhold," he whispered. "Western Woods."

Khadazin lay the old man down and fretted over him, as he cradled him in his arms once more. The

318

Western Woods were several miles to the South-west of Karick and beyond that, the stonemason knew little about them. He looked up at the dark skies above him and could not see the sun to confirm the old man's guess.

"F-find my girl for me," Cornelius said suddenly, coughing up his words. "Tell her I nearly made it back to her..."

Khadazin nodded his head dumbly as tears spilled unchecked down his cheeks. "I will find her for you my friend, I promise."

Cornelius fought for each breath now and he did not respond. Khadazin looked down at the old man and brushed the wild, wispy hair from his eyes as he focused unseeingly up at the sky above him.

"We did it," Khadazin told him. "We escaped."

Cornelius's eyes flickered in response and he attempted a smile. Suddenly his body began to convulse, snapped taut and went rigid. A thin skeletal hand clutched vainly at Khadazin's robes and the stonemason held onto him as the old man snarled, fighting desperately to keep hold of the life slipping away from him.

"My friend," Cornelius murmured weakly, his breath fading away as he slipped down limply in the stonemason's arms.

CHAPTER FIFTEEN

Unexpected Discovery

Cassana shifted nervously in her saddle and eased her discomfort by staring about her surroundings in wonderment. Beautiful meadows of multi-coloured wild flower enticed her down the steep grassy incline into the serene valley below, caught in the gentle swirling breeze that cooled her burning face and soothed her apprehension. Shafts of brilliant sunlight knifed through the sparse cloud cover overhead and the natural carpet of colour beneath her shimmered iridescently. Brushing an unruly strand of hair from her eyes Cassana sighed. Arillion had already started his descent down the twisting trail and he guided his mount on with soft assurances and a confidence that underlined his excellent horsemanship.

It was mid-morning of their second day since leaving the tangled protection of Briar Copse and since their discussion across the fire that night, they had not said more than several words to each other. Arillion had woke her early the next day after he had prepared her a light breakfast. His face was hidden away again and Cassana had felt relieved. She needed to focus on the journey ahead of them and did not need any unnecessary distractions, no matter how pleasing they may or may not have been. Once she had breakfasted and taken care of her mount, a strong chestnut stallion with a white flash on his barrel-chest, Arillion had told her to gather up her belongings. After leaving the copse he had led them silently across the grey, bleak plains towards the north-east. The steady drizzle of the previous day had lessened, and the dark skies above them were subtly lighter. By the end of the sombre day, the silent pair had made good progress, leaving the copse far behind. The Crescent Hills loomed ominously up out of the plains towards the north-west by now and Cassana had felt uneasy. The distant wooded slopes would provide ample protection for anyone looking out for them and although she had chided herself for perhaps putting too much self-importance in her value to them, she was still relieved when the obscured sun had finally set behind the murky hills and they had made their camp beneath the shelter of a solitary old elm. Arillion was reluctant to reveal their path to her and forbade any fire that night. Strangely irritated by Arillion's cold demeanour, Cassana had wrapped herself away in her bedroll, eventually drifting off into a troubled and restless sleep.

Cassana came back to the present as her ears detected the distant call of an eagle. Searching the skies, she smiled as she finally found the large bird, wheeling gracefully away to the east in wide, elegant circles. Her mount snorted in displeasure and tossed his head, eager to follow after his comrade. Turning reluctantly away, Cassana surrendered and gingerly guided the horse down the snaking trail after Arillion. Her heart pounded as she allowed the horse to choose its footing. She did not want to pass on her fear to the impatient stallion, as she felt light-headed under the glare of a rejoicing summer sun and uneasy from the steepness of the brush-choked slope beneath them. Lengthening her grip on the reins, she leant back in her saddle and encouraged her mount on with soothing whispers for him and words of comfort to herself.

It took longer than she had hoped, but they eventually joined Arillion and his mount in the shelter of the valley below. The heady scents of the wild flower and the merry chatter of the local wildlife soon steadied her fear, and the warmer air was alive with the buzz of foraging insects and the gentle dance of mating butterflies.

Arillion's hooded head turned slightly as she finally rejoined him and their mounts greeted each other tenderly. Cassana shook her head. Arillion was still clad completely in black and he was probably sweltering under the sun's furious attentions.

"It is so beautiful here!" Cassana observed, daring to speak to him.

Arillion's eyes found hers and they flicked about her features briefly, before sweeping away in disinterest. "I can't say that I noticed, princess."

Nudging his horse's flanks he set off again, leaving Cassana to watch after him, her face twisting with disagreement. Following his lead, she pulled up alongside him again.

"So," she said brightly. "Where are we heading, sir?"

Arillion looked over at her. "Highwater."

Cassana scowled at him. "I know that," she said,

gesturing at their immediate surroundings. "But how do you plan to get me there and by which way?"

Drawing his mount to a stop, he leant on the pommel of his saddle and regarded her intensely as she passed by. "As you can probably tell, princess, we are taking the scenic route through the lowlands for the next few days, while we pass by the Crescent Hills."

Cassana wheeled her mount about as she guided it back to him. He waited for her to rejoin him, before continuing. "We have probably stolen a march on your enemies, but it is better that we err on the side of caution."

"A good idea."

"Of course it is!" Arillion scoffed, ignoring the look Cassana gave him. "With the mining community of Durrant's Field a few miles to the north-west of here, it is best we stay away from all civilisation for as long as we can. If nobody is aware of our passing, then our journey will hopefully be all the more easy."

Cassana smiled at him and was pleased that his eyes glowed in response. The Crescent Hills were heavily protected as the late high duke had commissioned several companies to mine the hills for minerals for him, some decades before. After discovering that there were rich deposits of silver and iron ore in the rock and soils of the hills, the authorities claimed the land for themselves and protected their interests by establishing a garrison of men in the mining settlement of Durrant's Field; named after the first captain of the watch to be charged with the protection of the region.

"So, once we have passed the Crescent Hills, where do we head from there?" Cassana asked, pleased that he seemed willing to engage in conversation with her again.

Arillion's eyes flashed mischievously. "Assuming we are not noticed by any local patrols, we will cross the East Road two days from now and," he paused, perhaps to lick his lips, before continuing. "We will cross the road and enter Greywood Forest!"

Cassana stared at him, not sure that she had heard him correctly. "I am sorry," she said, chuckling nervously. "I must have misheard you, sir! I could have sworn you just said we are going to be travelling through Greywood Forest?"

Arillion nodded, his eyes burning. "I did, and we are."

Cassana coughed, looked away and then snapped her focus back on him.

"Are you mad? That region is crawling with brigands, vagabonds and cut-throats. You are supposed to be keeping me out of danger, sir. Not leading me into it!"

Arillion leant forward to pat his horse's neck and looked up at her, probably grinning. "Give me some credit princess and think about it a moment. Anyone looking for us will not expect you to put yourself in any further danger."

"And they would be right," Cassana cut in, laughing despairingly.

The infamous road from the Northern Crossways was a veritable playground for the brigands under the control of Devlin Hawke, as it was one of the main routes into the East Vales. The prices of goods bought and sold in the east were often higher as the merchants had to cover their costs by hiring guards to protect their wares. The high duke's men that patrolled the East Road did not seem to deter the bandits and even the patrols sent to police the region by Lord Carwell, steward of the East Vales had met with very little success.

"We should be able to pass through the forest without too much problem," Arillion assured her. "I know the region well and I can assure you, my lady, that we will be able to avoid the most dangerous parts of the forest."

Cassana didn't doubt Arillion's familiarity with the brigands for one moment and she swallowed uneasily. "I do not know," she admitted. "I am reluctant to put myself in any unnecessary danger, if I do not have to."

Arillion reached across to her and clasped her left hand briefly, before withdrawing. "I understand that, princess. I really do! But they will not expect this and while they are busy looking elsewhere for you, with a little luck and my expertise to guide us, we should be well on our way without any trouble."

Cassana nodded finally, her focus distracted for a time by his touch. "If you think that this is the best course of action for us, sir, then I concur and promise to follow your lead."

"It is," he replied, nodding in satisfaction. "Despite what you may or may not think of me, my lady, I have been hired to see you home and I would not jeopardise your safety needlessly."

"Or your payment," Cassana said, before she could stop herself.

Arillion threw his head back and bellowed with laughter, his voice echoing about their surroundings. "Come on, lady," he said chuckling. Nudging his horse forward, he rode away, shaking his head ruefully.

As Cassana turned her mount to follow him, his soft voice floated back towards her on a fresh, jovial breeze.

"Feisty indeed!"

Cassana set her supper aside and covered her mouth to stifle a yawn. Arillion had long since finished his supper and had disappeared into the woods they sheltered in for the night to, how did he put it? Water the roses! Using some water from her canteen, Cassana cleaned her plate and sat back on her bedroll, listening to the silence of the evening. Distant creatures called out their warnings to unseen predators and insects strummed their tunes as they investigated the light of the fire.

Hugging herself, Cassana leant closer to the fire and tossed some fresh sticks into the flames. A shower of triumphant glowing embers snapped up into the night and she dusted some settling ash off the toes of her boots. Sighing, Cassana tied her hair back and looked about the shadows outside the protection of their camp. She could feel those shadows watching her and even glimpsed the luminous glowing eyes of a small creature, watching her from the confines of the dark. They blinked curiously for a few moments, before scuttling away to safety. Smiling, Cassana looked up at the clear night sky; an inky-black canvas pricked by a thousand sparkling stars. Despite her predicament and the uncertainty of the next few days, she had to admit that she was starting to enjoy the freedom these events had inadvertently granted her. The guilt of the fallen and the worry for the future was still there, of course! But here, out in the wilds and surrounded by such beauty, Cassana was strangely at peace for once.

Her peace was soon disrupted as Arillion strode back into the camp without a sound and she started inadvertently. Following his supper, his face scarf was now back in place and Cassana questioned herself whether or not that was a good thing.

"That's better," Arillion sighed, sitting down cross-legged before the fire.

"Thank you for sharing that," Cassana said sarcastically.

Arillion chuckled and looked away.

Cassana watched him for a time as he bowed his head and appeared to be sleeping. She quickly realised however that he was awake and listening to the sounds of the world beyond their fire. Every call from the night drew a subtle twitch from him as he focused on the sound. He was never at rest, she decided. Despite how relaxed he always appeared to be.

"Do you mind if I ask you a question, Arillion?"

His hooded head snapped up and his eyes held her attention as he nodded. "If you must?"

Cassana drew in a steadying breath, before proceeding. "Do you like what you do?"

Arillion regarded her curiously. "Do I *like*?"

"Yes," Cassana replied, clasping her hands together nervously in her lap. "You know, your job and the things you have to do to...earn a living?"

He was silent for a while, before leaning forward. "Of course," he said. "I have a talent for doing things that other people would find repulsive and because of this, people are willing to pay me a lot of money to do it."

Cassana could see the mirth in his eyes. He knew she would find his answer disgusting and she could feel his triumph as she looked away.

"Sorry if that upsets you, princess," he said, not meaning it. "But it's a dangerous and filthy world out here and, to get by, you have to get your hands that little bit dirtier than the next man."

"You do not have to," Cassana said, rounding her focus back on him. "There are many honourable ways to earn your coin."

Arillion laughed bitterly. "What, like you do, princess?"

"And what do you mean by that?" Cassana asked testily.

Arillion offered his hands up to the sky. "Well, how do you earn your money?"

Cassana fell silent, realising what he was getting at. She flushed and stabbed the toe of her left boot into the ground.

Arillion sighed. "Look, my lady. I do what I do because I am bloody well good at it. I can make more money in one day than most people can from a year of *honourable* toil."

Cassana looked up at him. "But you do things," she paused, trying to find the right words and failed miserably. She was out of her depth here and wished she hadn't said anything.

"I have killed people, if that's what you are asking me," Arillion guessed, seeing the look that flashed in her eyes. "Does that disgust you?"

Cassana looked away, nodding timidly.

"Well don't let it," Arillion continued affably. "You speak of an honourable living. Well in the world I travel, princess, my word is *my* honour. If I say I am going to do something, I damn well mean it. The day I fail in that, will be the day the crows can have me."

Cassana swallowed down her rising distaste. How could she have even thought anything for him, other than disgust? The man was reprehensible and cocky beyond belief. His ego was bigger than all of the peacocks at her father's court, put together. And that was saying something!

"So, how about you, Cassana?" Arillion said, drawing her startled attention back to him. He had never used her name before and the sound from his lips was annoyingly pleasing to her ears.

"What do you want to do with your life? Where do you see yourself in ten years time?"

She looked at him curiously. "I don't know, sir," she admitted honestly.

"Well, you must have..." he paused, listening to an unheard sound. For a time he was silent, and then he shrugged, continuing. "What do you want to do with your life? Politics? Marriage? A family? There must be some desire bubbling away beneath all of that tempestuous angst you have?"

Cassana chuckled unexpectedly. "I am a bit cantankerous, I must admit!"

Arillion laughed. "A bit?"

Their eyes met again as they laughed together for a time. After a few moments, however, Cassana felt herself falling into the trap of those captivating eyes and she blinked free from his spell.

"This trip was supposed to be the start of my political education," Cassana murmured. "It was my father's first attempt at showing the high duke's court that he had put his faith in me. Faith in the troublesome daughter, ridiculed by idle gossip and tainted by the whispers of disdain and pity."

"Well, it's certainly been an education," Arillion observed. "Perhaps not the one your father intended, but one that will certainly shape you into a stronger, if that's even possible, a stronger woman ready to take on the fools who rule this country."

"Careful, sir," Cassana smiled. "That was very

nearly a compliment."

"Nearly, but not intentional," Arillion replied, winking.

Cassana shook her head. "You are correct, though, when you say that I will be stronger for this. It seems that I must become the woman my father had hoped me to be, a lot sooner than intended. Fate it seems, has other designs on me now!"

Arillion was suddenly angry and spat his distaste into the air. "Fate? Fate is for people with no destiny, princess! Don't sit on your pretty little backside whining about how fate has set you upon this path. Look on it rather as your destiny. If you can separate the two, you'll find that you won't sit about so much, feeling sorry for yourself. Instead, you'll take a hold of your life and spit into the eye of the storm when he comes for you!"

"You really know how to cheer a girl up, don't you" she said, wincing.

"I'm not here to cheer you up, princess," Arillion snapped. "I am here to keep you alive, remember that!"

Cassana looked back at him, her pale face chastised. As she watched him growl away before her, she could feel his anger over the heat of the fire. She decided to keep quiet and made a mental note to steer clear of the subject in the future.

When Arillion spoke again, however, his voice was calm and controlled. "I bet you wish you hadn't asked me now?"

Cassana shook her head. "On the contrary, sir. I thank you for the lesson."

"Lesson?" Arillion asked, confused.

Cassana smiled. "This conversation was supposed to be about you. However, without me even realising it, you managed to skillfully turn its direction towards me."

Arillion nodded his acceptance. "Remember that, princess. You'll need that skill yourself one day, when your adequate looks have failed you and all you have left to turn someone's head is the strength of your promises."

"You really are an incorrigible man," Cassana said, her words free of any meaningful reproach.

Arillion chuckled. "Your pretty words are wasted on me, princess. I wouldn't know what that meant, even if I really cared."

Cassana stepped up for another round of verbal fencing and was surprised to find that she was actually excited at the prospect for a change.

"You lie, sir! I cannot believe that a man with such excellent oratory skills would not know the meaning of a word over three letters."

"You have me there, princess," Arillion said, holding his hands up in mock surrender. "You'd be amazed at what else I can do with my tongue."

Arillion delighted at Cassana's torment. Her face exploded in embarrassment and she wrung her hands nervously, looking about the camp in discomfort. When she finally had the courage to look back at him again, he winked mischievously at her.

"I give up!" she conceded nervously.

"How about you give in as well then, seeing as you are feeling so charitable?"

Cassana screeched in frustration to hide her discomfort. She rose unsteadily, her face deep scarlet and full of uncertainty as she offered her excuses and made her way over to tend to the horses. Arillion watched the movement of her slender curves as she moved by him and as Cassana began to groom her mount, he suddenly found himself certain of what he wanted. The girl, although not instantly compelling to look at, had a certain way about her and he had begun to notice her more now, having spent several days in her company. She was like a wild horse, untamed and cantankerous, strong and unpredictable. It was not what he was supposed to be focusing on and he knew he would certainly get himself into trouble if he managed it. But Arillion loved to live dangerously and it would be fun trying to break down her defences.

Arillion decided to let her be for a while and allowed her to fuss over the horses without another word. Eventually, when the emotions of the day got the better of her, Cassana said good night to the horses and retired for the evening.

"I shall take the first watch tonight, my lady," he announced, as she turned in for the night. "But I will wake you in the early hours before dawn for your watch, if that is okay with you?"

Sensing that she didn't have a choice the shy girl nodded her accord and turned away from him without another word. Grinning, Arillion turned his thoughts reluctantly to the road ahead and the great risk he would soon be taking by leading her through Greywood Forest.

"He's dead!"

The Kestrel watched impassively as Tobin checked the body, laying half-covered by the undergrowth and glanced back towards her, his face a grim mask of uncertainty. Behind her line of sight the other three members of their fellowship shared worried looks as they spread out cautiously, sliding their weapons slowly from sheaths and shoulders.

The Kestrel moved to Tobin's side, confirming what she already knew. The sentry was dead, killed no more than a few hours ago perhaps and his weapon was missing. Tobin rose and frowned.

"Orders?" he asked her.

The Kestrel spun towards the men behind her. "I want a clean sweep of the hold. Search every shadow and corner. Find out what has happened here!"

Farrell, the oldest of the trio nodded his bald head and gripped the slim blade in his hand tightly for reassurance. Motioning for his comrades, the three of them slipped, wordlessly, into shadowy depths below. Tobin watched them leave, before turning to the woman beside him, his forthcoming question already in his eyes.

"If the Redani has escaped," the Kestrel whispered, her pale face twisting with concern, "we are all going to be in a lot of trouble."

Tobin nodded his agreement and headed down the steps after their companions. The Kestrel remained where she was for a few moments more. Drawing in an ominous breath, she looked about her surroundings. Sunlight showered the clearing with a welcoming brilliance and the trees surrounding the ruins watched on quietly, unwilling to reveal what had recently happened here. As she moved to head down the crumbling steps after her men, she noticed the patch of dark blood staining some disturbed ground before her. Kneeling curiously, she dipped a pale finger in the blood. It was still fresh and had not yet dried out. Smiling, she wrapped her cloak tight about her slender frame and passed silently down into the ruins beneath her.

Tobin looked up at the Kestrel and frowned again as she moved down the steps to join him in the long, torch-lit corridor. The upper level of the old keep's dungeons was empty and there was no sign of any of the remaining men assigned to guard the brotherhood's safe house. Down in the lowest level of the dungeons however, things had taken a more sinister turn and the woman joined him, looking down at the corpse with a pensive look on her face.

"Somebody buried that blade deep," he said to her, indicating towards the bloodied sword several feet away.

The Kestrel followed his pointing hand. "Judging by the mess on the wall, it severed the jugular!"

Tobin nodded. "The poker doesn't have blood on it, but there are several splashes of blood and another fallen blade further down the corridor."

"It seems we are in a great deal of trouble then," she sighed, shaking her head. "With the stonemason *and* the girl gone, our plans have been seriously compromised."

Tobin swore and rose. Together, they proceeded urgently down the corridor. As they reached an open door in the wall on their left, a grim faced Farrell stepped out to meet them.

"What have you found?" Tobin asked.

The man shook his head bitterly. "The boys are checking out the rest of the cells, but I found the interrogator just inside."

As he stepped aside, they peered into the corridor beyond and could see the robed corpse inside. His throat had been opened up and the stone floor was dark with his blood. The Kestrel shook her head, snorting in disbelief. How on earth did the Redani manage it on his own?

"Go back upstairs," she told Farrell, her anger beginning to surface. "Search the immediate area for tracks and find out where he went. There is blood on the ground outside, so it would appear that he may have been injured."

The man nodded obediently, hurrying away from them. Tobin watched him leave and leant against the door frame, shaking his head.

"I find it hard to believe that one tortured man could have done all of this!"

"If a person's desire is great enough, they can be capable of achieving many things," she answered, looking distastefully at the dead man again. "That, however, is what happens to you when you are incompetent and weak."

Tobin looked at the dead interrogator and nodded. "Serves him right," he said. "I never could stand the bastard, anyhow! How he was ever put in charge of this place is beyond me."

The Kestrel shrugged her indifference and closed the door. In silence they continued along the long corridor towards the closed door that would lead them to the torture chamber. As they neared the heavy door, they could feel the heat emanating from inside.

"I doubt that Borin would have given up without a fight!" Tobin said quietly as the woman drew a long knife from the sheath in her right boot and kicked the door open. She stood where she was for a few moments as a wave of heat swept from the room, obscuring his view.

"Believe!" the Kestrel hissed. Turning angrily she pushed by him and strode away from the chamber, her face flushing with uncontrolled rage.

Tobin stared after her for a moment as she swept back down the corridor, before turning to enter the chamber. He drew up short in the doorway, gasping for air that was suddenly not available.

Borin was sat before him in a chair, his head bowed and his arms hanging limply at his sides. Tobin barely noticed the blood that dripped from the multitude of wounds covering his huge naked frame or that the fingers were missing from one of his hands, as his attention was compellingly drawn to the mess in the dead man's lap.

Slumping against the door frame Tobin retched as a wave of nausea swept through his entire body. Someone had disemboweled the man and the dark arterial mass of entrails spilled into his lap, thick rivulets dripping down his legs to pool in a bloody mess underneath the chair. Tobin forced his breakfast up and wiped his mouth with the back of one hand. He had seen and done some terrible things before, but he had never had the stomach for torture. He shook his head. Borin, however, had done some nasty things to a lot of people over the years and had made even more enemies. It was surprising that he had lasted in his job as long as he had.

"What goes around, brother..."

As he turned, Tobin noticed that something was written on the dusty stone floor before him. Stepping reluctantly into the chamber he moved close enough to read the letters painted hastily from Borin's own blood.

Payback!

Turning, Tobin hurried from the chamber and closed the door behind him. His legs felt weak and he shuddered. Looking for his mistress, he could see that she had already reached the steps and was heading back up to the next level again. Even from here, he could detect the anger in her body language. Sighing, he forced his legs into action and hurried after her, leaving Borin to the rats that waited patiently in the shadows for him to leave.

The Kestrel turned slightly as he rejoined her back outside. She looked about their surroundings and her arms hung loosely at her sides, still carrying her knife. Tobin studied her cautiously as he stepped up alongside her and was relieved to find that her beautifully cold face was serene once again.

"What a mess," he murmured, staring away into the woods and shielding his eyes from the glaring sun.

The Kestrel licked her lips and said nothing. They stood together for a time, lost within their own thoughts, before Farrell appeared from the tree line to the south.

"I found a set of tracks heading away in a south westerly direction," he called to them as he picked his way through the maze of broken and crumbling walls to rejoin them.

Tobin looked to the Kestrel, but she did not react. Her face remained stoic, until the bald-headed man reached them.

"What else?" she demanded.

"He's losing a lot of blood, my lady," he reported assuredly. "The tracks are no more than several hours old. He won't have managed to get far in his condition!"

The Kestrel tilted her head as she regarded the tracker thoughtfully and then walked away from them without a word. Tobin followed her slender body with hungry eyes and watched patiently as she moved about the clearing, mulling over the thoughts tumbling about in her mind. She held her long knife by the flat of the blade now and slapped the hilt of it into the palm of her other hand. Farrell flicked a quick look at his companion and shrugged his shoulders.

As the men followed the woman as she continued to move about the clearing, the other two members of their party appeared from the depths below and moved over to join them. The Kestrel turned immediately.

"What did you find?" she asked, motioning for them to speak with a beckoning flick of the knife's hilt.

The taller of the two men, one with dark hair tied behind his neck in a long, greasy ponytail stepped forward to give their report. His pock-marked face was stained with worry and his brown eyes blinked rapidly as he tried to overcome his fear.

"Every cell is empty, Kestrel," he said, hesitating. "We found three dead guards, two of them stripped of their robes and two cells that were open and empty."

The Kestrel stopped. "Two cells?" she looked towards Tobin and Farrell briefly, then turned back to the man. "Anything else I should know?"

Both of the newcomers shook their heads in unison and the squat bull of a man with short blonde hair stepped alongside to support his companion.

"Nothing, lady," he said in a voice far too soft for a man of his build. "It would appear that they somehow escaped from their cells and overpowered the guards."

"How very astute," the Kestrel snarled, her words dripping with sarcasm.

"What are your orders, my lady?" Tobin asked as the Kestrel flicked her attention to him.

"A good question, Tobin," she acknowledged, giving herself time to think as she pointed the hilt of the knife towards him. "By sending out word, we have done all we can for now to ensure that the girl is looked out for and our immediate concern is to find the Redani. Farrell?"

"Yes?" the tracker responded.

"Are you sure there is only one set of tracks leading away from here?" she asked him, although she already knew his answer. Farrell was the best tracker she had ever met and his skill was not in question here. There was a joke amongst the men that he was so good, he could track a fart through a thunder storm.

"Yes my lady," Farrell obliged her, his face creased by the unintended insult. "The tracks I found, thanks to the recent rain, are deep enough to follow and at first I assumed it to be because of the man's purported size. But it appears, with the possibility of a second escapee now, that it could be he was carrying someone."

"That might also explain the heavy blood trail," Tobin offered and Farrell nodded in agreement. "Who else was being held here?"

The Kestrel shook her head. "I do not know. The chancellor will, though."

All of the men focused their attention on the woman before them, resisting the urge to look at each other knowingly, as they heard the venom in her words.

"Farrell," she continued, her voice strengthened by sudden purpose. "I want you to take Beren and Arlen with you and track the prisoners."

Farrell nodded and looked towards the men in question. "What do we do when we find him...them?"

The Kestrel's eyes narrowed. "Kill them! Then return home."

The three men nodded. Gathering together they checked their weapons over and adjusted their packs as

Tobin moved closer to the Kestrel.

"What are we going to do?" he asked, his voice tinged with disappointment. She turned her attentions to him and a thin smile creased her lips.

"We are going to return to the city and give the chancellor the good news."

Tobin grinned as she sheathed her knife and turned her attentions back towards their companions.

"One last thing," she said and the men hesitated as they were about to leave.

"Yes, my lady?" Farrell asked, his voice full of foreboding.

The Kestrel meaningfully studied each of them in turn. "Don't bother to come back if you can't find him!"

They shared surreptitious looks, then nodded in silent acceptance of their fate. Wordlessly, they filtered away into the protection of the trees to the south-west and were soon lost from sight. The Kestrel continued to watch the trees long after they were gone, before finally turning to Tobin.

"Let us make haste, my friend," she said, her words lacking any warmth. Tobin nodded and fell in wordlessly behind her as she headed away towards the eastern tree line. He smirked secretly behind her back.

The chancellor had been living on borrowed time for many years now and he sensed that finally, the Kestrel was going to be allowed to take it back.

CHAPTER SIXTEEN

Desperation

Khadazin stumbled and fell sideward, his surroundings spinning wildly around him. The branches of a nearby bush reluctantly steadied him, but claimed their payment for saving him with thirsty thorns that pierced through his robes and flesh. The stonemason barely felt their touch and slowly scrambled away from their clutches. He was exhausted. The wounds he had received during his escape were beginning to take their toll on him now and, as he stumbled blindly through the forest with little regard for his safety, his vision began to fade.

Trying to take a grip on the forest dancing around him, he struggled over to a large tree and sank wearily down against the base of its trunk. Pain tore though his body as the crossbow hanging from his back dug into him and shaking, he moaned feverishly. His body was covered in a sheen of dripping sweat and his clothes were soaked by the blood running from his recent wounds. Closing his one good eye, the other caked and blinded by drying blood, he drew in a faltering breath and bowed his head.

The forest and its inhabitants watched on sympathetically for a few moments, before coming alive again. Khadazin focused on the sounds rising up about him; the songs of the birds, the gentle rushing of the wind stealing through the trees and the chatter of the insects. On any normal day they would have filled him with peace and helped to relax him, but this was no ordinary day. He shook his head, trying to grasp hold of a thought long enough to come to terms with it and lock it away again before his guilt could prise it from him and tease him incessantly with it. The harder he tried, the more he failed. A thousand questions whispered at once in his mind and the pounding of his head drowned out any excuse he could offer them.

You failed him! One question hissed accusingly at him and Khadazin broke down again, swallowed by his own guilt.

"Forgive me, Cornelius," he whispered vainly.

Khadazin listened hopefully for a spectral reply, but there was no response to ease his guilt. Only the wind answered him, accompanied by the sudden snapping of a pigeon's wings, as it propelled itself from the boughs of a tall, nearby tree and glided gracefully away to leave the wounded man to mourn in peace.

Following his death, he had held Cornelius in his arms for many moments, reluctant to let him go. Finally, however, he had gently laid the old man down and went back inside the dungeons. As quick as his ruined body would allow him, he had gathered some meagre supplies in a sack and retrieved the crossbow and some bolts from the man who had killed his friend. Subconsciously touching the wound on his head, he left the dead behind and had staggered back outside again. He should have reacted quicker. If he had, the old man might still be alive! Chased outside by his rising guilt, he had picked up his friend and headed away into the gloom of the woods. He didn't know where he was going and at that point, he hadn't cared. Anywhere was better than where he had been. After a while, when Khadazin felt he was a safe distance from their prison, he had forced himself to stop. Searching the forest he finally found, despite the grimness of the morning, a peaceful, beautiful glade. Under the watchful protection of a willow tree he used the sword he carried and then his hands to dig a shallow grave for his friend. As he hacked and tore at the sodden ground, the guardian tree wept its sorrow for them and by the time he had dug deep enough into the earth to lay the old man to rest, the corpse was covered in a shroud of willow catkin. After Khadazin had filled the grave and covered it with some fallen leaves and branches, he had knelt on the ground beside it, his head bowed in shame and sorrow.

"I promise that I will honour your courage, Cornelius," he had whispered. "I will find your family for you and before we meet again my friend, I shall make the chancellor pay for his crimes!"

Rising up slowly, Khadazin had marked his friend's resting place with the sword. Turning, he had stumbled from the glade and did not look back...

Khadazin's stomach growled, drawing him from his thoughts and he fumbled blindly for the sack on the ground beside him. Pulling out a water skin, he removed the stopper and sipped briefly at the cool liquid inside. Sighing, he replaced the skin's cork stopper, ignoring the desire to quench his thirst further.

If he drank too much he would be sick. His body had been deprived of proper food and water for many days now and he guessed that his stomach would not be able to cope with their own demands straight away. Coughing, he wiped the sweat and blood from his face and pulled forth a stale piece of cheese. Nibbling tentatively at it, he moaned in ecstasy as the taste of the strong cheddar assaulted his senses. Compared to feasting on the raw flesh of rats, it was the most delicious thing he had ever tasted.

Opening his eye, he stared up at the grey skies that peered down through the natural canopy overhead. Cantankerous clouds drifted quickly by and Khadazin watched them for many moments, noticing the subtle change in their density and colour. By the time he felt himself start to drift off into a welcoming sleep, the day had started to brighten and a pastel blue sky had attempted to round up and chase off the roaming clouds. Sighing, he stared down at his feet and the rags he had tied about them for protection. The strips of torn cloth had protected them well enough as he had not been able to find any footwear big enough from the corpses of the men he had killed. He expected that Borin's sandals may have fitted his feet, but the revulsion and the shame of what they had done to the torturer had kept him firmly away from the closed door and the horrific sight that waited within.

It would take him a long time to overcome the guilt of the things they had done to the torturer, in the heat and madness of the moment. He shouldn't have given it a second thought after what the man had done to them, but he was pleased that he was having these feelings of guilt as it showed him that he was a better man, even though it didn't feel like it at the moment.

Shaking his head wearily, Khadazin leant forward and slid the crossbow from his back. Cranking back the weapon's rusty arm, he reloaded it with a bolt and sat back against the tree, resting the crossbow in his lap. If someone came upon him while he rested, he would feel a little better with it close to hand; although he had never actually fired one before! He just needed to rest a little while so he could gather up his wits and find enough strength to be able to continue on his way. He had no idea where he was going and in which direction he was travelling at the moment. But the Western Woods, if Cornelius had been correct, were several miles to the west of Karick. In his current condition he had no desire to head back to the city and with his heritage, he knew he would be spotted immediately. No! He needed to get to safety, somehow. He had not left the city since the day his father had brought him to live there and his memory was vague on the surrounding Valian lands. He had been told once that it was a couple of weeks travel to reach the western port of Ilithia and despite his current predicament, any lingering desire to return to his homeland was not that great, even now. His good eye felt suddenly very heavy as his fatigue weighed down upon him again and stifling a rising yawn, Khadazin licked his dried lips and bowed his head. The desire for sleep quickly overwhelmed him and despite his vulnerability, he succumbed to his body's demands and was soon fast asleep.

He wasn't even aware, sometime later, when a bright red squirrel scampered down the trunk of the tree from above him and stole the remainder of the cheese from out of the sack.

Choking for breath Khadazin lurched awake and

coughed heavily as he reached for fresh air to fill his starving lungs. Panting heavily he breathed in deeply through his mouth, as he quickly discovered that his broken nose was clogged with fresh blood. Coughing, he lay back against the rough trunk and looked about his surroundings. A bloody, early evening sun sent golden shafts of light down through the leafy canopy overhead to pierce the damp ground beneath. All about him the creatures who inhabited the forest scurried and darted about their business as they made the most of the waning day and Khadazin watched quietly as several rabbits darted in and out of their burrows through the trees away to his left. He smiled despite himself and winced as fresh pain shot through his stiff body. He had slept for far too long and as he urgently tried to move again, his body chided him with a reproachful stab of pain to his face and side.

Groaning, Khadazin sank deeper into the soft ground beneath him and battled against his agony. As the roaring and pounding in his head finally began to subside, he detected the nearby sounds of a dog barking. Khadazin sat up, ignoring his body's protests and lifted the crossbow up from his lap. The sound was coming from the trees directly in front of him and as he strained to separate the shadows from the light, he heard another growl, closer this time. Khadazin felt a warning kiss of fear that breathed its concerns on the back of his neck and he levelled the crossbow towards the sound. Someone had followed him, using dogs to track him through the forest. His desperation to get away from his prison and resulting complacency had probably just cost him his life. His stomach knotted painfully and as he drew in a ragged breath, a large hound bounded into view.

Khadazin held his breath as he trained the crossbow on the large, grizzled black hound. The weapon trembled in his hands and as he watched the dog, it bounded over towards the rabbit burrows. Blinking, the stonemason let out his breath slowly and watched as the hound paced about the burrows, sniffing and snarling at the scents left by the rabbits, hiding in the warrens below. As Khadazin lowered his aim slightly, the hound's greying black head lifted up and sniffed tentatively at the fresh scent borne on a stiffening breeze. The hound's amber eyes swung ominously towards him and as Khadazin raised the weapon again, the dog tensed and began growling, the hackles on its back raising menacingly.

"Kayla?" A high-pitched voice cried out suddenly, causing both of them to start and look towards the echoing sound.

"Where are you girl? Come on, come on!" the fresh voice called out again and Khadazin flicked a wary glance at the dog, who did likewise and then lifted its head in sudden excitement as a piping whistle sounded nearby.

As Khadazin looked through the trees across from him, he noticed a young boy wandering through the forest towards him, his sandy hair shining in the sunlight as he searched for the dog.

"Where are you?" he cried out again in exasperation and then let out a sigh of relief as he spied the dog and began making his way over to it.

"You mustn't run off like that," he scolded the dog as he neared it. Khadazin could see that he carried a bundle of wood in his thin arms and the hound wagged its tail furiously as he approached.

"What have you got there girl, eh?" he asked the

dog as he came over to it, a bright smile breaking across his tanned face. The dog turned back, growling towards him and as the boy looked in his direction, Khadazin just about managed to lower the crossbow in time.

The boy's face paled visibly and he dropped the bundle of firewood onto his feet with a strangled gasp of fright. Screeching, he grabbed the dog by the collar and dragged it off through the trees, away from the nightmarish apparition that was watching them.

"Father! Father!" Khadazin heard him shriek, as the boy and hound were soon lost in the maze of shadowy trees.

Shaking his head bitterly, Khadazin struggled to rise. As he dragged himself urgently forward onto his knees his head began to thunder with pain. As he looked about his swaying surroundings, pinpricks of light blotted his fading vision. Moaning, he went to rise and then pitched forward into the arms of a waiting darkness.

The pungent smells of the forest floor roused him sometime later and as he raised his head weakly from the ground, Khadazin could see that the day was no longer in control. With shaking arms, the stonemason managed to push himself onto his knees and he swayed there for a time, rolling his head dreamily as his senses sought to catch up with the forest swirling wildly about him. The forest was unnaturally quiet and Khadazin looked back carefully for his weapon and belongings. They were still there, laying untouched in the shadows of the tree and, sighing thankfully, Khadazin crawled over to them again. As he picked up the sack, curiously covered in fragments of cheese, he detected the distant sounds of a conversation behind him. Grabbing the fallen crossbow, he rose up unsteadily and began to stumble off through the trees, away from the sounds of approach.

Khadazin picked a path blindly through the trees, stumbling and swaying as he ducked under a low-hanging branch. His head began to spin as he rose up on the other side and he staggered on his way, clutching tightly onto the crossbow and his meagre belongings. With his throat dry and his lungs short of breath he hurried on as quickly as he could and just as he thought he had made his escape, he heard a shout of discovery from behind him. Chased by fear the stonemason hurried away from the cries echoing about the forest and he gritted his teeth, hissing angrily as he fled into the unknown. Following his injuries from his ordeals, however, he was soon short of breath and, as he began to shake uncontrollably, he was blinded by the evening sun and was forced to stop, lest he pass out again. Putting the crossbow down, he fished the water skin from the sack and swilled down the cool liquid inside. As he prepared to set off again, he heard fresh shouts from nearby and panicking, he gathered up his weapon and set off again. His mind was shouting incoherently at him as he hurried away from his pursuers and he tripped over an exposed root, his vision fading as he teetered on the cusp of another furious headache. The shouts coming from behind him were close now and as he tried to pick himself up, the weight of a crushing unconsciousness pushed down hard on his shoulders, forcing him back onto his knees.

"No!" he snarled angrily, pounding on the forest floor with his fist. He had come too far to give in. If he was killed now, all that he and Cornelius had suffered would have been for nothing.

As he hauled himself up, he staggered forward into the impenetrable darkness that reached out and dragged him from his dilemma.

"...told you!"

The sound of an indignant voice probed against the blackness of Khadazin's unconsciousness and gently tried to rouse him. His body's demands for rest won out however and as the stonemason fought vainly to cling on to his wits, he slipped away from another voice into a deep sleep.

"Where is he from?" A voice asked sometime later and the youthful pitch to the words filtered through the darkness, nudging Khadazin to pay attention.

"I dunno lad," an older, deeper voice admitted. "But he's not from these parts, as you can tell!"

"Look," the first voice squeaked, as Khadazin stirred. "He's waking."

The blanket of darkness smothering the stonemason's senses began to lift and shifted into shades of swirling grey. He could hear the older voice hiss out a warning and then an almost musical jingle of a chain. Khadazin thrashed in panic as he imagined he was about to be shackled and was almost thankful when he heard a dog snarl.

Willing himself to wake up, Khadazin pushed through the veil of grey and opened his good eye, focusing finally on the blurred branches and leaves of the forest swaying in concern, high above him.

"Help me," he pleaded weakly, as a dark, shadowy face loomed over him.

Cassana shifted in her saddle, trying to move her cramp on to another part of her aching body. Her efforts were in vain and she scowled bitterly, sinking lower into her saddle and sulking. Allowing her horse its freedom and, not for the first time in recent hours, she fixed a narrow gaze on Arillion in front of her and hoped that he was also suffering. Naturally he wasn't and he relaxed in his own saddle with an effortless swagger that only served to boil her blood further. Since their last camp, they had spent a day trekking through the eastern lowlands, passing in silence by the Crescent Hills without any further contact with civilization. Arillion had been pleased with their progress that day and they had spent a quiet evening out in the open plains, huddled close against the cold of the night and as he had pointed out to her, they didn't need a fire as her mood was creating enough heat to keep them warm anyway.

Cassana couldn't put a firm finger on why she was in such a foul mood, but she was sure that a lot of it had to do with her escort and that only seemed to encourage him to irritate her further by talking inanely to her as often as he could. In the end, she just ignored him and Arillion, for once, was wise enough to let her bubble away on her own. The lowland they travelled through the next morning was featureless and swept away to the east from them towards the distant horizon that shimmered occasionally under the glare of a hazy sun. Despite her refusal to speak to him, Arillion had noticed her interest and told her that it was the distant waters of the Crystal River, which flowed through the central part of the eastern vales and finally came to rest in the south-east to form the Great Lake, near the fishing town of Valen. Her curiosity satiated, she had nodded her thanks and turned her attentions back to the pommel of her saddle and the twitching ears of her mount. Cassana had naturally ridden a lot back home, but none of the mounts could compare to the breeding and training of the horse given to her by Savinn Kassaar. She hoped, if...when she made it home safely, that she was allowed to keep him and that Arillion wouldn't take the magnificent steed back to the merchant-thief.

Cassana's mount snorted and tossed his head in disagreement as she returned her attention to the present to find that Arillion had stopped and was looking for her. She drew up alongside him and looked about their surroundings with a mixed sense of wonderment and apprehension. Since the early afternoon Arillion had led them back up to the higher ground, confident that they were safely away from the scrutiny of the hills. Since then, they had spent the better part of the day riding along the ridge of the high ground, towards the darkening sky. Uneasy at the sloping incline to her right, she had guided her mount to surer ground and in the end, Arillion had decided to join her there. The hills were indeed well behind them now and as the hazy sun began to hide from the greying sky, Cassana caught glimpses of a dark and ominous tree line on the horizon to the north.

"There she is," Arillion said proudly, as Cassana drew up alongside him. She followed his pointing arm and puffed her cheeks out nervously. They could see the distant murky tree line that was Greywood Forest clearly now and also the dirt road that stretched along their field of view before it.

"Is that the East Road?" she asked him. Her voice sounded detached, even to herself and Arillion's eyes widened in surprise.

"It speaks!" he chuckled, shaking his head and then swept his pointing arm grandly along the focus of her attention. "Indeed, lady. As I mentioned before, this road joins with the Northern Crossways and is one of the main trade routes into the east for the north and west vales."

Cassana nodded. "It is awfully quiet," she observed. "I expected the highway to be bustling with caravans and patrols."

"Only the merchants who can afford protection use this road now," Arillion replied. "Or those with no sense or anything of value."

Cassana nodded her agreement. She had expected the horizon to be crawling with dark ant-like figures of the highwaymen and brigands, but was relieved to find out that the tales of their activity had been somewhat embellished.

"That doesn't mean that the bandits are not there, my lady," Arillion pointed out, scattering the relief on her pale, weary face.

"Thank you for the confidence boost," Cassana said sarcastically, scowling at him.

"I am not here to make you feel better, princess" Arillion bristled, his eyes narrowing. "I am here to get you home safely, as you well know! Would you rather I lied to you and said *let's go for a jolly good jaunt through the woods, shall we?*"

Cassana's stern mask hardened further before cracking under the strain and she broke into a reluctant laugh. Sniffing in her laughter she shook her head and looked towards the distant forest again.

"No sir," she whispered. "You are right, of course. Forgive me?"

Arillion chuckled. "I guess I can. Does that mean I get a kiss now?"

She flicked a horrified look towards him to find that

he had pulled his mask down under his chin and his lips were ready to claim his prize. Cassana lost herself in his face again for a moment, before blinking free from his clutches.

"I think not!" she said. "As I recall, you are the one who owes *me* an apology."

"Do I?" Arillion frowned. "Not sure why? Ah well, your loss princess!" Grinning, he pulled the scarf back up over his nose. Cassana shook her head and looked away, letting out a silent sigh of relief.

"You cannot see from here," Arillion said. "But the road has several gibbets erected along it, as a warning to the highwaymen."

Cassana swallowed. "I hate hanging," she said. "I prefer a swift blade as a means of execution, if it is necessary at all."

"And that's why they hang them," Arillion responded. "I can assure you, lady, the bandits don't like it either."

Cassana nodded, silently hoping that the threat of a hanging ensured the nooses would be empty when they reached the roadside.

"When will we enter the forest?" Cassana asked, eager to change the subject.

"We probably won't reach there tonight, my lady and it looks like the weather is changing again," Arillion admitted. "So I think it best that we travel another hour or so, find a sheltered place to rest for the eve and then enter the forest at first light."

"A good idea," Cassana agreed. "Would it be possible for me to take the first watch tonight, sir?"

Arillion looked across at her. "If it means that you are in a better mood tomorrow, then yes, of course you can!" Kicking his horse's flanks, Arillion headed away from her before she could bite back.

Cassana watched him for a moment and was surprised that his words did not anger her. She had been woken roughly for her watch the previous night and the broken night's sleep had left her exhausted and...

"Ah," she said in sudden realisation and, smiling, she urged her mount after her protector.

The chancellor looked up from his desk as a light knock rasped against the glass of the wood framed doors of his study. Putting down his quill, he rose up slowly, his heart racing and his face a grim mask of apprehension and flickering shadows. On unsteady legs, he crossed over his dimly lit study to the red velvet drapes, hesitated and then drew in a calming breath. With a dramatic sweep, he pulled apart the drapes and stared blindly out into the moonless night beyond. Shadows gathered at the window momentarily and letting out his breath, he unlocked the door and pulled the left one open, wide enough to allow the Kestrel by him. She slipped past without a word and as he went to close the glass door behind her, another dark shape stepped by him. Swallowing hard, he closed the door behind them and pulled the drapes back into place with shaking hands. Clasping them together before him, he licked his lips nervously and turned to face his guests.

"Welcome lady, Tobin!" he greeted them softly, his eyes blinking away his brimming fear.

Lowering his hood, Tobin nodded in response and sat on the corner of the chancellor's desk. Likewise, the Kestrel lowered her hood and the chancellor fought back his conflicting emotions as she looked disdainfully at him.

"Where are the pieces on our board now, lady?" he asked her and before he could say anything else she was upon him with dazzling speed.

The room spun as she hurled him back across his desk and as he cried out, he felt a pair of rough hands hold his shoulders down from behind. The room was plunged into darkness as the candle was knocked from the desk in the struggle and he felt the Kestrel lean over him.

"You fool," her voice spat in his ear. The chancellor stiffened as he felt the press of a cold knife point against his throat. "The girl is gone, the Redani has escaped and our men are dead."

The chancellor felt his fear sweep the length of his body and he shuddered in cold terror at the implications. He struggled vainly against the hand on his collar and Tobin's rough grip on his shoulders. "P-please, don't kill me!" he begged, clutching at the hand on his collar pleadingly. "I have news, I-,"

"You have one chance to save your miserable life chancellor," the Kestrel hissed, shaking him angrily. "So it had better be good!"

The chancellor felt the pressure from the knife withdraw as the Kestrel stepped away from him. Tobin's grip relinquished and he stooped down to pick up the fallen candle. He placed the sputtering light source back on the desk beside the trembling man's head and watched on grimly as the pathetic specimen before him attempted to free himself from his tangle of robes.

"A wise move," the chancellor gasped, holding up his sweating hands to them as he found his breath. "This is grim news indeed and if I cannot stay your hand with my news, then I will kneel before you and accept my fate willingly."

The Kestrel looked past him towards Tobin and nodded for him to leave the room. Tobin glared at her silently and then backed down as he saw her eyes narrow meaningfully. He strode towards the drapes, cast a withering look towards the chancellor and then stepped out into the night once again. The Kestrel closed the drapes behind him and then turned back to the chancellor, gesturing for him to speak with a flick of her knife.

Fidgeting nervously, Relan Valus smoothed down his crumpled robes and beckoned for the Kestrel to take a seat. She accepted silently and positioned herself across from him as he picked up his chair and sat at his desk again.

"Now that civility has been restored," he said boldly, "perhaps I could hear from the prosecution, before I offer you my defence?"

The Kestrel leant forward on the desk and placed her knife on the paper-strewn mess between them. She was just about to speak when an urgent knock sounded at the study door, forcing both of them to look towards it in shock.

"My lord?" a concerned, muffled voice asked. "I heard a shout, are you well?"

The Kestrel's eyes flicked to the chancellor and she picked up her knife. Relan Valus waved her away and put a shaking finger to his lips.

"Yes William," he called out, rising up and moving swiftly to the door. The Kestrel rose and slipped silently by the chancellor to position herself on the opposite side of the door. As the door was opened and light from the hallway beyond spilled into the study, the chancellor stepped into view and peered at the guard who stood there, a worried look on his youthful face and a hand on the hilt of his sword.

"I stumbled and cracked my knee in the dark," Relan explained, a little embarrassed. "I should have paid a bit more attention to my candle, rather than my paperwork."

William removed his hand from his sword and smiled. "Forgive me for disturbing you, my lord!" he said, bowing.

"Not to worry, not to worry," the chancellor placated him, smiling sweetly as he waved him away. "Now if you would excuse me, I must return to my work."

Explanation and conversation seemingly over, the guard turned brusquely on his heels and retreated back to his position further down the hallway. Letting out a gentle sigh, the chancellor closed the door and flicked a nervous glance at the Kestrel who nodded to him.

"It's a good job that all of your guards are not as diligent as he is," she observed softly as they returned to their seats. "If anyone else wanted to kill you, they would find it very easy to slip into your estate."

"Forget about my security, or evident lack of it," the chancellor glowered. "Tell me what happened."

The Kestrel paused for as long as she dared and then spoke, just as he was about to explode with frustration.

"As I said before," she hissed. "The Redani escaped from the hold and somehow managed to kill all of our men on his way out!"

The chancellor's composure crumbled before her glittering eyes and she took a long, lingering moment to revel in his discomfort before she leant swiftly across the desk and slapped him hard across one cheek, before he could react and move out of harm's way.

"W-where is he now?" the chancellor asked in desperation, hanging his head in shame. "Did you manage to find him?"

"We have his trail," the Kestrel conceded. "My best tracker and two other men are following him, so if they can't find and kill him, no one can."

"Why didn't you go after him," the chancellor asked, seriously losing his wits now. "What if he manages to tell someone about me, what-,"

"Calm yourself Relan," she growled dangerously. "How can you be of any use to us, if you are of no use to yourself? Steady a breath and tell me what your news is before I decide what to do with you. Your continuing incompetence has cost us many lives and you had better satisfy me, or that deep breath you have just taken will be your last!"

The chancellor shuddered as the woman sat back down and began cleaning the dirt from under her nails with the tip of her knife. His cheek still stung and he trembled uncontrollably. He was a man used to being in control and her news had stolen any strength he had left from him.

"All right," he whispered, holding up his shaking hands in surrender again. "As I said before you left, I was to meet with the high duke to explain what has been happening since the threats against him were first made. This meeting took place as arranged and as you can imagine, the high duke's priority now is to conduct his own investigations into the threats, the disappearance of the Byron girl and the involvement of Madam Grey in all of this."

"Go on," the Kestrel ordered, as the chancellor paused for breath.

Spreading his hands on the table before him, he nodded and then proceeded. The tone of his voice was strained at first, before his confidence and composure returned with every word that passed his thin lips.

"With all that has happened, the high duke is keen to resolve this problem and restore confidence in his rule as soon as he can. To ensure this, he has already questioned all of my staff and especially the girl Dia that I spoke of."

The Kestrel didn't try to hide her contempt, but allowed him to continue.

"She unwittingly played her part to perfection and her innocence in this matter has managed to divert any seeds of doubt about my involvement with the girl's disappearance over to Madam Grey, who of course is most likely dead and unable to testify against me!"

"You are sure about this?" the Kestrel pressed, idly playing with the lobe of her left ear.

"I am," the chancellor replied, conviction restored to his voice. "In fact, in two days time I am to report directly to the high duke to aid his office with their investigations. The high duke is also about to address *his* people with a speech designed to show that he is not afraid of these aggressors and will not hide away from them. A speech, ironically, that he has asked me to help him with!"

The Kestrel blinked in surprise and sat back in her seat as the chancellor, not for the first time, looked across at her with satisfaction in his gloating, beady eyes.

"It seems that the high duke has offered me his hand of support, a hand which naturally I will gratefully accept," he continued, his position of power restored in his own eyes. "Am I to assume, lady, that because you haven't leapt across the desk to cut my throat from me, I have also managed to stay your hand for the moment?"

"Perhaps," she replied, hiding her disappointment from him. "But do not be too quick to assume that you have managed to wriggle free of my hook, just yet, Relan. We still have much to do if we are going to take full advantage of this unexpected turn of events and right the wrongs of your last few weeks."

The chancellor nodded his agreement and smiled. "For once, it seems, we are in agreement with each other then. What do you propose?"

The Kestrel chewed her lip thoughtfully for a while and then smiled. "With the Byron girl out of our reach for now, but perhaps not going to make it home, we must turn our attentions to more important matters."

"Indeed," the chancellor cut in excitedly. "I will soon be in an excellent position for our lord to set the pendulum in motion. If that is indeed his wish, then our plans will quickly fall into place and with my careful orchestration our dream may yet come to be realised."

For once, even the Kestrel felt her emotions stir at the prospect and her pale face flushed with excitement as she allowed herself to be carried along by his enthusiasm. The chancellor detected this and smiled, reaching out a tentative hand to her. She accepted it briefly and then recoiled, shuddering at his clammy touch.

"It seems that you still have luck on your side, chancellor," she pointed out, rising slowly. "Your skin must be stretching pretty thin across your hide, by now?"

"Perhaps," the snake of a man replied, shrugging off his indifference. "So what are your plans now?"

The Kestrel looked down at him for a moment, holding his steely gaze with a piercing riposte of her own. "I must return and report what has happened to our lord. There is not another full moon for a couple of weeks yet and it will be quicker for me to report in person."

"And then?" the chancellor prompted.

"They will no doubt contact you with further instructions. For now, all I will suggest is that you play your part well. There will be no further chances for you, Relan!"

"I understand," came his hollow reply. "Are you sure the girl will be found?"

The Kestrel ignored his question and moved to the drapes. Pulling them apart, she motioned Tobin back into the room and then turned back to him.

"I cannot be certain either way, but we have certainly sent enough birds out to those who will be able to look for her." The Kestrel shrugged. "I do not know what else we can do at this stage, as we do not know who has taken her or when she will even attempt to return home."

"If the Redani is silenced, the girl's testimony would only point the finger of blame at Madam Grey and, if our plans succeed, it will not matter by then, anyhow," the chancellor mused thoughtfully, as Tobin stepped back into the dark study.

"My lady?" he enquired, failing to hide his disappointment at the fact that the chancellor was still alive.

Sheathing her knife, the Kestrel clapped her hands together and turned to him with a guarded look on her face. "I am going to return to our brethren and report all that has happened here."

"What about me?" Tobin asked ominously.

"I want you to ride as hard as you can to the Northern Crossways, Tobin," she responded, offering him a bright smile. "Get our man there to assist you in organising a hunting party!"

Tobin grinned, his tension slipping from his face. Their mission had been an abject failure so far and he sensed that things were finally about to get interesting for him. Satisfied, the Kestrel turned to the chancellor who was watching them both curiously and asked him for a map of the Four Vales. Nodding obediently, he rose and moved to the tall cabinet in the far corner of his study. Opening up a long drawer, he produced a rolled piece of parchment and moved back to the desk. Rolling out the parchment, he smoothed its creases down and spread it wide across his desk for them to see.

"I want you to take the hunting party and wait for the girl," she said softly to Tobin as they gathered around the map.

"Wait? Where?" Tobin asked, straining to see the map in the dying candlelight.

"Here," said the Kestrel, tapping a long finger absently on the map.

Tobin flicked a glance at the chancellor, who returned his look with the same amount of confusion mirrored in his own eyes.

"Why there?" the chancellor asked, as Tobin looked back down at the map and scanned the parchment again.

"Because that is the way I would go if I was attempting to get back into Highwater without being noticed," the Kestrel replied, a wicked smile spreading across her cold, beautiful face.

CHAPTER SEVENTEEN

Greywood Forest

It was in the early stirrings of dawn that Arillion and Cassana crossed the East Road into the misty gloom of Greywood Forest. Although the land was dank and the skies above them were grey and sullen, the air was at least fresh with promise for the new day. Cassana followed Arillion into the shelter of the forest, relieved to be undercover and away from the exposure of the open plains at last. They had spent the night in silence and yet again without the comfort of a fire to warm her apprehension. For what seemed an eternity, she had sat in the dark, listening to the night and counting the hours before she could wake Arillion for his watch. When she finally did, she crawled into her bedroll and was quickly asleep.

"Dismount," Arillion ordered her quietly and Cassana swung her right leg over the pommel of her saddle and slid from her mount. With the reins in one hand, she lowered her hood with the other and ran it through her lank tangled locks that curled like wet snakes in the misty morning air. She felt filthy and her need for a bath was overwhelming. Sighing, she led her mount along the bridle path, choked by the heavy undergrowth. The forest was silent, the dewy foliage and trees cloaked in a carpet of early morning mist that hung over the land like a preying spectre. As Arillion led them away from the fringes of the forest, Cassana caught fleeting glimpses of the local wildlife, as they stirred from their sleep. Ahead of them, Arillion drew her attention to the ghostly shapes of several deer and they watched them silently for a time as they grazed and made their way through the huddling trunks of the tall, grey birch trees.

"On a day like today, I can quite easily see how this forest got its name," Cassana whispered, as one of the deer tested the air before her and the other three in the herd stiffened. Before Arillion could reply, the lead doe coughed a low warning and as one, the deer sprang over bushes and bounded quickly away into the mist.

"There goes breakfast," he complained, looking back at her in irritation as his eyes roamed wistfully over the bow strapped to the back of her saddle.

Cassana dealt him a look of reproach. "We have plenty of rations left, we do not have the need to hunt deer and you have enough apples on you to last the year!"

"True, princess," he replied, chuckling.

As they followed the winding path through the forest, Cassana cast a final look back the way they had come. The trees appeared to have closed in behind them, as if trying to hide their passing and she sighed, her breath clouding on the cool air before her. She wouldn't admit it to Arillion, but despite the threat posed by the outlaws who resided in the forest, she was already starting to feel a lot safer, hidden away from the world in the one place where, hopefully, no one would think to look for her. She had kept her eyes fixed firmly on Arillion's back as they crossed the road, as Arillion had decided to enter the forest at the exact spot where the only gibbet with a corpse hanging from it was. She knew he had done it on purpose, but she was too scared and repulsed at the sight and smell of the bloated, swinging body to say anything appropriate to him.

"How long do you think it will take us to travel through the forest?" she asked him, banishing the image from her mind.

"If all goes well, we should be free in three or four days, my lady," Arillion replied, his eyes sweeping the gloom ahead of them.

"That long?" Cassana said. She realised that the forest covered a vast swathe of land, but had been expecting no more than a couple of days travel. It was huge in size compared to the Moonglade Forest, although if the fine summer weather was to return, she guessed that it would look equally as beautiful. Despite the eerie, haunting beauty to the forest at the moment, Cassana would have preferred a better day to help take the edge off her fear.

"I am afraid so," Arillion said, flicking an apologetic look back at her. "This forest is the second largest in the Four Vales, next to the Old Forest in the south. But as long as we manage to keep ourselves to ourselves, we should get through it without any problems."

Cassana dealt him a look that betrayed her thoughts and he looked away without commenting. High above them in the treetops, an argument suddenly broke out between the hundreds of crows roosting there and the grey skies were soon filled with the angry debate and cawing of the cantankerous birds, as they squawked and settled their differences on the wing. Arillion cast an angry look up at the black shapes, blotting out what little light there was to the day so far.

"Noisy bastards," he snarled, leading his mount on through the maze of trees as quickly as he could.

Cassana suddenly recalled her first meeting with the woodsman and lengthened her strides to keep pace with him. Then, the crows had alerted them to the presence of her pursuers. This time, though, they may have inadvertently alerted any unsavoury characters in the region to her own presence in the forest.

Fortunately for them, however the next couple of hours of travel through the forest passed without any signs of trouble and by then, Greywood Forest was alive with the day. Cassana listened in wonder to the multitude of different bird songs and passed her time searching high and low through the scattering mist, in search of the woodland creatures that would also wake to their songs. By the time Arillion called them to rest, some hours later, she had spotted another herd of deer, seemingly hundreds of birds; from the boisterous robin to the sleek sparrowhawk and an almost constant appearance from the rabbits who played and lived in the long, wet grasses of the forest.

"Here," Arillion said, tossing her an apple from his sack.

Cassana caught it deftly and rubbed a shine on its rosy skin before taking a hungry bite into it. Delighting at the taste again, she sat on the trunk of a fallen tree and watched the horses, as they grazed away under the shade of an old chestnut tree away to her left. They had tended to their mounts before their own needs and had now both settled onto the trunk to rest. Sunlight, much to Cassana's joy had started to filter through the thick leafy canopy overhead and as the midday heat rose, she got the feeling that summer had finally won its battle over the recent bad weather. Well, she hoped so anyway.

Arillion passed her a chunk of cheese to go with her apple and placed a water skin on the dying wood between them. She accepted both with relish and after she had quelled her hunger and thirst, she stretched the weariness from her body and breathed in the intoxicating smells of her surroundings. Although she was in the domain of Devlin Hawke, she was not as exhausted as she was the last time she was in a forest and she was determined to try and enjoy the journey this time, if she was allowed to!

When she turned to ask Arillion more about the forest, she caught him watching her again.

"You are staring again, sir," she snapped, feeling uncomfortable under his gaze.

"I know I am," he said, his eyes flashing wolfishly. "Don't pretend that you don't like it?"

"I am not pretending," Cassana said tersely. Flushing, she rose swiftly and drew herself away from him by moving over to tend to the horses.

Arillion watched her walk away and grinned, his eyes wandering up her slender legs to her buttocks and ranging over the rest of her body. Despite her bedraggled appearance, he was really starting to enjoy waking up to her each morning and occasionally he sensed that she liked it too. Toying with the idea of removing his scarf once and for all, he chided himself and turned his attentions elsewhere. First and foremost, he still had a job to do and he shouldn't lose sight of that. It appeared that there was far too much at stake, not to mention the credibility of his reputation and anything else beyond that was a bonus. And besides, he needed to keep alert and focus on the next few days ahead of them. They were in dangerous territory here and despite his bravado and assurances to the girl, he was on edge and worried. He had not made many friends the last time he had travelled through the forest and if he wasn't careful, he might end up running into some old and unwanted acquaintances.

"Another five minutes, my lady," he told her, almost missing her barely perceptible nod of acknowledgement. Smiling roguishly, he pulled down his scarf and took a long, needed pull on his water skin. At least, he would be guaranteed a couple more hours of peace and quiet now!

Arillion's plans for a few hours of peace actually turned out to be the rest of the day. By the time they left the trail to set camp for the coming night, the only thing that had slightly improved was the weather. Cassana's foul mood had returned and as they travelled safely through the forest, she listened quietly when he imparted any knowledge about their surroundings, or drew her attentions to the identity of a cry from the local wildlife. Cassana spent her time observing these surroundings, hoping to take the edge off her frustration and anger. For a time she succeeded, but after several hours of looking at the numerous species of trees and listening to Arillion drone on about how clever he was, she was back in the depths of her mood and spent the remainder of her time watching her escort for signs of what was actually going on. She was no fool. She could read most people very well and although he kept up the pretence that they should be fine, she quickly realised that he was trying to mask his own concerns to make her feel at ease. Arillion's eyes strayed as often to the trail, as they did their surroundings and although the bridle path appeared overgrown and unused for some time, Cassana sensed a different story, suggesting that he was expecting company.

When they finally stopped for the day, Arillion gently broke the bad news about the need for another fireless night to her and watched quietly as Cassana scowled at him and took herself off to tend to the horses. Sighing, he set about preparing their supper and shook his head. He had to remember the girl's feelings from now on. As much as he enjoyed playing with her emotions, she was still young and had been placed in an impossible situation to cope with, because of the whims and desires of others. He had to be mindful of this, or she would probably make the rest of the journey in truculent silence.

As with most of her moods, however, and following some food and water, she had calmed down enough to afford him a response, when he said he would take most of the watch tonight and wake her for the last couple of hours before dawn. For a brief moment she looked as if she would argue with him, then bit her lip, nodded and thanked him. Smiling, Arillion watched her turn in for the night and let out a quiet sigh of relief.

Cassana woke with a start and listened to the screams. For a time she lay in stiff silence, listening to the still of the night and the beating of her heart. Had she been dreaming? She hoped she had, as the mournful wail sounded like someone was being attacked, or worse...

A hair-raising scream suddenly echoed through the night again and gasping, Cassana sat up in fright and looked about her black surroundings. Blinded by the moonless night she fumbled vainly for her sword, as another deathly scream pierced the silence.

"Calm yourself, lady," Arillion's voice whispered, away to her right.

"What is happening?" Cassana hissed nervously, searching the blackness for him.

"It is a terrible sound, is it not?"

Cassana nodded, even though she couldn't see him. ""Yes," she stammered. "It is horrible. What is it?"

"It is a vixen, a female fox," Arillion explained. "She is in, well by now she would be in late season. They make that sound when a male is near to them."

"How romantic," Cassana shuddered. "It sounds like a woman is being murdered!"

"Indeed it does, my lady," Arillion agreed quietly.

Cassana's eyes were beginning to separate the different shades of black now and as the vixen continued her chilling wails, she managed to locate Arillion. He was sat with his back against the trunk of a tree and across from her, the horses fidgeted on their tethers and tossed their tails nervously.

"Do you mind if I ask you a question, sir?"

"Not really," Arillion replied. "What's on your mind, princess?"

"How is it that you know so much about the wilds?" Cassana asked him softly. "I thought that your line of work kept you in the city."

Arillion chuckled. "I go wherever the coin shines brightest. In my line of work, you have to know as much as you can about everything. Not everyone sits at home and waits for me to come calling, some people even have the audacity to try and flee whatever they have done to earn my attention, before it's too late!"

"So you study?" Cassana asked him, not sure if she was liking the way the conversation was going.

"A little," Arillion conceded. "There is only so much you can learn from a book. The best way to truly know about something is to hear it, or experience it for yourself."

Cassana raised an eyebrow and nodded in surprise agreement. It was true, if she thought about it. She had studied many books on all manner of subjects growing up and since all of this had happened to her, she had learnt ten times more about the world and herself, more than she ever had in over a decade of study.

"Well I certainly will not forget the sound of a vixen in season again," Cassana agreed, listening as the scream sounded again, more distant this time.

"There was this one time," Arillion recounted wistfully, leaning forward in eagerness. "I was tracking this guy who had fled the capital, he made for the Western Woods, made a pretty good chase of it, too-," Cassana coughed meaningfully and Arillion chuckled.

"You don't really want to hear about that, do you?"

"No I do not!" Cassana responded, her face aghast.

Leaning back, Arillion snorted with laughter and folded his arms across his chest.

Cassana settled back down into the warmth of her bedroll and then looked back for Arillion. "Will you wake me when it is time for my watch, please sir?"

Arillion nodded and waited for her to get comfortable. When it appeared that she was, he stood up and stretched.

"Your watch, princess!" he announced, yawning

sleepily.

Cassana looked back at him, her bright eyes flashing furiously. Before she could bite, she laughed away her anger and dragged herself out from her bedroll.

"I suspect that there is something I should call you right about now," she said smirking, watching him as he swaggered over to his bedroll. "But as a lady, I shall refrain from such vulgarities and simply bid you goodnight, sir!"

Arillion looked back at her. Pulling down his scarf, he grinned and then dropped down onto his bed with a sleepy yawn. Shaking her head, Cassana chose a suitable sentry position of her own and settled down for the remainder of the night, listening to the cries of the fox with interest, rather than fear this time.

The still dawn that broke over the forest the following morning was in stark contrast to the previous day and the searching tendrils of sun in an early bright blue sky filtered down to the forest floor, warming the chill and dampness from Cassana's body and clothing. Following a meagre breakfast, Arillion led them back to the bridle path once again and they set off into the tangled forest with renewed enthusiasm and a spring in their step. The continuing density of the forest and the fluctuating elevation of the land ensured that the remainder of the morning was spent on foot as Arillion led them along the twisting path. By the time they stopped for rest, the forest was bright with an intense sun that showered the storm-kissed lands with warming caresses that left the travellers fatigued and drenched in sweat. Cassana soon packed her cloak away, but to her astonishment, Arillion maintained the mystery of his image and remained wrapped in his hood and cloak.

The forest finally relinquished its grip on the path later that afternoon, allowing them to mount their steeds for a while. As they guided their horses along the path Arillion explained that there were many twisting paths like the one they were using, that crossed like veins through the forest, allowing people to traverse the leafy labyrinth in relative peace and obscurity. Cassana smiled at him as he looked back at her. She did not believe a word he was saying but just as she was about to offer her thoughts on the matter, a pheasant burst from the long grasses at the side of the path in a shower of feathers with its screeching double cry of warning startling Arillion's horse.

Cassana brought her own startled mount quickly under control and watched at first in concern and then in admiration as Arillion expertly brought his rearing mount under his command again. As he turned his horse back to face the right way along the path, he patted him on the neck and whispered soft words into his twitching ears.

"Bloody pheasants," he cursed as he straightened in his saddle and glared in the same direction the brightly coloured bird had fled.

Cassana smiled wryly. She had hunted with her father and his associates many times before in the High Forest back home and the birds had unseated several riders in similar circumstances over the years.

"You are an accomplished rider," she pointed out as she urged her mount closer behind him.

"Yes," Arillion replied, focusing on the path ahead of him. "I am!"

"Where did you learn to ride with such skill?" she asked him curiously.

Arillion was silent for a time and then his hooded

head turned slightly. "I used to steal a lot of horses when I was younger for a gang master in Carwell," he explained. "If I hadn't learnt to ride as quick as I did, we probably wouldn't be having this chat now."

Cassana didn't doubt that for a second. "Is there no end to your talents, sir?"

"I have lots of skills, my lady. Some of which you may be lucky enough to experience first-hand one day," Arillion answered her, ignoring the sarcasm dripping from her words.

"I cannot wait," Cassana said evenly. "So where are we heading, exactly? You appear to know this forest very well?" she asked, eager to divert the direction this conversation was now taking.

"I have been here before, yes," Arillion admitted. "The land is always the same here, so my knowledge is sound. It's just the people who change!"

"Meaning?"

"We are on a path that will eventually lead us to a natural spring," Arillion offered. "It has always been there. What is in question, however, is whether or not there will be anyone else there. Hopefully the area around the pool will be deserted, but who can tell."

"You sound as if you are not so certain," Cassana observed.

Arillion looked back at her again, his eyes flashing in the sun. "I am not. There are several outlaw groups operating out of the forest now and there is no telling where they make their camps."

"Several?" Cassana baulked. "I thought Devlin Hawke controlled the forest?"

"He did," Arillion replied. "But he only controls the south of the forest now. I heard tell that many of his band were disenchanted with his methods and the notoriety he was getting. Like most things, envy is a poisonous draught and some sought to increase their own infamy by less honourable means."

"I hardly think Devlin Hawke to be an honourable man," Cassana offered. "I know he is reported to be a gentleman-thief, but he is still a thief, nonetheless!"

Arillion nodded his agreement. "True, my lady. But compared to some of the other outlaw groups, he is noble indeed!"

Cassana said nothing and they continued on in silence for some time. Was that his admission that they were in danger? Or was it something else? She couldn't tell, but she could scratch the itch of worry that was starting to form in the back of her mind again. It wasn't until late afternoon, when her doubts would surface again. They were deep into the forest and the day now, when Arillion slowed his horse to a stop and slid from his saddle. Dropping the reins he strode forward and knelt on one knee to study the trail before them. Cassana remained in her saddle and patted her horses sweating neck.

"What have you found?" she whispered, her voice dry and choked by worry.

Arillion ignored her as he swept a steely gaze about their immediate surroundings and then turned his attentions back to the trail.

"Just some deer tracks, princess," he announced finally, standing and brushing the earth from his knee.

Cassana let out an audible sigh of relief. "May I see?" she asked him.

Arillion glanced back at her as he took back the reins and climbed back into his saddle. "There'll be time for a nature lesson when we are free of this forest, lady."

Chastised, Cassana wiped the sweat from her brow and followed Arillion as he started to lead them on again. He suddenly stopped, turning in his saddle to look at her.

"Do you like me, princess?" he asked her quietly.

Cassana frowned, perplexed at the peculiar question. "Like?" she asked. "You are the most infuriating and annoying man I have ever met, sir!"

Arillion's eyes flashed dangerously.

"But that is not to say that you are not without some qualities!" she added hastily.

Arillion nodded thoughtfully for a time and looked away down the path.

"Follow me," he commanded suddenly, sliding from his saddle again. Cassana copied him and followed him from the path into the dense cover of the forest to their left.

"I do not understand, sir?" she said, confused.

Arillion glanced back quickly as he picked a path through the trees for them. "Do you trust me?"

Trust me? Like me? What was wrong with him? Was the sun boiling his senses? Cassana was too confused to worry at the moment.

"I trust you!" she admitted, more to herself than in answer to his question.

"Good," he nodded, satisfied. "Then trust me and do not ask me again!"

Cassana blinked her answer to him and nodded subtly. Turning, Arillion focused on the forest and led them into a splitting curtain of brilliant sunshine, his head shaking furiously. Cassana followed him, unsure of what had just happened and uncertain now on what was to come...

"Leave us alone!"

Cassana's eyes widened as a piercing female voice rose up above the chatter of the wildlife and echoed around the forest. She flicked a terrified look at Arillion, who had maintained a brooding silence for the last few hours and continued on his chosen route through the trees into an early evening sun, away from the cry.

Distant laughter floated from out of the choke of trees and undergrowth up a rising slope away to the north-east and the youthful female voice rose up in protest again. Cassana hurried to Arillion's side, dragging her mount forward with her.

"Someone is in trouble, sir!" she pointed out to him, certain that he was well aware of the fact already.

"There is always someone in trouble here, lady. You had best not concern yourself with it!" Arillion replied stoically, his eyes avoiding her.

"Leave him alone!" the female cried out again, dragging Cassana's attention away towards the sound and the accompanying mocking cries of fear that rose up.

Cassana planted her feet in the ground and Arillion stopped several paces after, looking back towards her with a dark look in his captivating eyes.

"This is not our business, princess," he hissed quietly.

Cassana let go of her reins and strode up to him boldly. "Well I am making it my business," she stated stubbornly. "You said I had to toughen up if I was to survive through this, well now I am. I would not be here now if someone had not come to help me when I needed it most, so I am not about to turn away when someone needs my help!"

Arillion regarded Cassana curiously, his eyes widening. He blinked as she shook with rage and determination before him and then shook his head.

"We cannot risk getting involved," he said softly.

"You cannot, or will not?" Cassana hissed, prodding him in the chest. "Don't you care?"

Arillion shook his head, swatting her hand away. "Why should I? Getting involved can get you killed and as things stand, there is far too much at stake!"

Cassana laughed sarcastically and turned away in disgust. "Too much money at stake, more like!"

Arillion snarled and grabbed her by one wrist. "We are not getting involved, and that's the end of it princess."

Cassana tried to free herself, but his grip was too strong and he started to drag her away from the rising commotion coming from the north-east.

"I order you to let go of me now, sir," she said, her voice rising.

"Order?" Arillion laughed, dragging her on. "You are not the one in charge here, princess. I am!"

Cassana kicked him in one shin and he grabbed her roughly, holding her before him at arms length.

"You are hurting me. Let go of me, or I will scream!" she promised, missing with another kick.

"Will you shut up," he growled, shaking her. "Listen to yourself. Are you willing to jeopardise all you have gone through, for a complete stranger?"

Cassana nodded, tears in her eyes. "I am willing to try. Everyone has helped *me* these last few weeks, now it is my turn!"

Arillion shook his head. "It's too dangerous, I won't-,"

"It seems you are quite willing to risk your life for

money," Cassana accused him. "So I will pay you one thousand gold crowns to investigate what is happening."

Arillion held her searching eyes and found only the truth there. Frowning, he let go of her and stepped back, shaking his head in wonderment.

"Women!" he chuckled, holding up his hands in exasperation. "All right then princess, if that's the way you want to play it?"

He tethered his horse to a nearby thorn bush and ordered her to do the same. Cassana hurried back to her mount, her legs heavy and her body trembling with emotion. With shaking hands she tethered her mount to the low branch of a tree and unstrapped her bow.

"Stay here!" Arillion ordered her, suddenly at her side. Cassana nearly dropped her quiver of arrows and she flushed, slinging them over her shoulder.

"I can help you," she stated, her eyes narrowing.

Arillion shook his head firmly. "I am only going to have a look, that's all!"

"And I am coming with you," Cassana hissed. "I can shoot the bow, you may need my help."

"Yeah, sure," Arillion snorted dismissively, shaking his head. "Stay well behind me, then. If I need your help, I'll wave you to me, agreed?" Cassana nodded, her eyes bright with fear and trepidation.

Sighing, Arillion headed up the rising slope towards the sounds of laughter drawing him inexorably through the trees to the north-east. Cassana followed him moments later, her heart racing and her body coursing with adrenalin.

"He's just an old man, leave him be!"

Cassana waited further down the slope, as Arillion

picked his way silently towards the sounds from above them. The palm of the hand gripping her bow was sweaty and she wiped it on her waistcoat as she crept up behind her protector. More laughter spilled over the edge and she grimaced.

Arillion reached the crest of the incline and peered cautiously through the forest before him. Some way through the tall screen of ancient trunks, he could make out another path, cutting across the forest to the east and west. Just off the path, on his side of the forest, he could see a small clearing where four men, dressed in woodland garb and cloaks spread out before a pair of travellers. One of the travellers was an old man, who stood protectively before a donkey and a young girl, brandishing a pathetic stick at his antagonisers. The young girl had long, strikingly deep reddish brown hair and she held onto the beast of burden as she wailed her protests at the outlaws. As he crept to the cover of the next tree, he saw Cassana appear behind him and he waved for her to get out of sight. She glared at him and moved across to a tree on her left. Turning his attention back on events before him, Arillion took in the scene and made for the cover of the next tree as one of the outlaws walked up to the old man and shoved him back before he could bring his stick to bear.

"Come on old man," the outlaw laughed, snatching the futile weapon from his hand. He held onto the frail man and tossed the stick back to his companions.

"We don't want to hurt you," he continued, not even trying to cover his lie. "You obviously have nothing else of value, so perhaps we can take our payment some other way?"

He looked back over his shoulder at his comrades, who shared knowing looks and fixed their eyes hungrily on the girl, who was no more than twelve summers old. The girl shrank from their attentions and the old man bristled, shoving the outlaw away from him.

"You will not lay a finger on her," he screeched at them, his ancient voice snapping with concern and anger.

"It's not a finger I am going to touch her with," one of the other outlaws promised and his friends bellowed with laughter.

As Arillion came closer, he could tell that the young girl was terrified now and she sobbed pitifully, her wails drowning out her pleads for them to leave them be. A twig snapped behind him and Arillion flicked his attention back to Cassana who was shadowing his route several trees behind him and not making a very good job of it, either. He pulled his scarf down and drew her attention to him with a wave.

Stay! He ordered her. Pulling his scarf back into place he turned back to the confrontation.

The outlaws were still unaware they were being watched and none of them had their weapons to hand. They were complacent in their confidence that an old man and a young girl would pose them little problem and had inadvertently let their guard down. Arillion smiled through his disgust. They were not Devlin Hawke's men. The Hawke did not allow his men to pick on the elderly or children. These brigands however were bullies and not very good ones either; picking on the weak to make themselves feel bigger men.

"I fought against the Reven alongside the high duke," the old man snapped angrily. "What did your grandfathers do other than spawn a line of imbeciles and cowards!"

Arillion nodded in respect. Nice! But stupid...

The crack of a fist against the old man's chin confirmed Arillion's fears and the frail man fell back into the reaching arms of the girl. They both collapsed to the floor and the outlaws laughed.

"Come on," one of them growled to the lead aggressor. "I am bursting here!"

The outlaw who had thrown the punch turned back, his bearded face splitting into a dangerous grin. "Wait your turn Alden, there should be enough field there for us all to sow our seeds."

Arillion rose and strode towards the small clearing.

Cassana watched in surprise and then astonishment as Arillion rose up and started walking casually towards the commotion. Her skin crawled at what was happening before her eyes and gripping her bow, she raced towards the tree Arillion had just vacated. Panting nervously, she positioned herself on the left of the tree, reaching back for the nearest feathered shaft in her quiver.

"Good evening," Arillion greeted as he strode into the clearing. The demeanour of the men before him changed immediately and the outlaws became alert, reaching for the swords hanging at their sides.

"Piss off," the leader snarled, letting go of the old man he had been dragging off the girl. "Find your own spoils."

Arillion reached up and lowered his hood. "Well, that's not very hospitable is it?" he said, running a hand through his long hair.

"Move on stranger," the one called Alden snarled, sliding his short blade from the sheath on his hip. "There's nothing here for you."

Arillion puffed his concealed cheeks out and

shrugged. "Fair enough lads, I'll be on my way then."

The girl squealed. "Please, help us!"

Arillion started to head off and then stopped, turning back again. "I promise I'll leave you to it after he has apologised," he stated, pointing at the bearded outlaw.

"Apologise? What for?" the man in question laughed. "Arr, did I hurt your feelings when I swore at you?"

Arillion shook his head. "No, I want you to apologise to the old man and the girl, before you walk away from this."

The four outlaws shared looks between themselves and then burst into laughter. Before they could gather their wits Arillion shrugged the cloak from his shoulders in one fluid motion and leapt towards the bearded outlaw, drawing his twin blades from his back as he moved.

The clearing erupted into shouts of anger as Arillion stepped quickly up to the outlaw before he could react and slashed both blades across the man's face. As the bearded man fell away, his gargling screams of terror escaping from several openings in his bloodied face, Arillion spun and stepped under a horizontal slash aimed at his head. Rising up he buried his right blade deep into the exposed armpit of his attacker and moved past the man as he also fell.

The remaining two outlaws converged on him and Arillion smoothly parried Alden's low thrust, spinning past his attacker with ease to elbow him in the side of the head and then slash him across the back of the neck as he stumbled by. With crossed blades he then turned aside the other man's unskilled attack and kicked him away, as the ringing clash of steel reverberated around the clearing.

"You have three seconds to make your next move," Arillion said, barely out of breath. He lowered his bloodied blades to his sides. "One-,"

The outlaw stiffened as a feathered shaft appeared through his right shoulder. Screaming in agony, he spun away and ran straight into the second arrow that buried deep in his chest. Dropping to his knees, the outlaw's blade slipped from his limp hand and he slumped forward onto the leafy ground, twitching as his blood stained the forest floor.

Arillion frowned and looked through the trees to find Cassana. She stood on the fringes of the clearing, her bow held before her and her hand hovering over her quiver.

"I told you to stay!" he growled, seeing the fear in her eyes.

Shouldering her bow, Cassana staggered into the clearing on weak legs and little breath. Her body was shaking and her rushing blood roared its fury in her ears. She hadn't seen or even heard what Arillion had said, but she could guess. As Arillion stooped to clean his blades on one of the corpses and then move back towards the old man and girl, Cassana looked about the clearing and was nearly sick. She had taken another person's life again, but not in self-defence this time. As she stumbled over to join Arillion, she gritted her chattering teeth. The outlaws were brigands and the atrocity they were about to commit needed to be stopped! Now wasn't the time to wrap herself up in the tangle of guilt, nor was it time to reflect on how quickly the battle had been finished. It reminded her of the fight with the Reven at the brook and Arillion's skill with the sword was also reminiscent of the woodsman's own ability, and mystery...

"Gather your wits," Arillion snapped at her, as he stooped down to help the old man up. He looked at Cassana and motioned for her to see to the terrified girl.

"Hush, hush," Cassana soothed, as the wailing girl threw herself into her reaching arms. "You are safe now!"

"Thank you, thank you," the girl sobbed into her shoulder, clinging onto her for dear life. Cassana stroked her head and held her tightly, looking over at Arillion as he checked the old man over to see if he was injured.

"What are you doing out here?" Arillion demanded, keeping a comforting hand on the old man's shoulder. "Have you lost your mind? Bringing a young girl into the forest, without so much as a blade to protect you both?"

The old man looked up at him through opaque eyes, cocking his head at the sound of his voice. Arillion raised his eyebrows and looked across at Cassana, silently conveying his respect for the old man to her. Blind and frail, he had defended the girl with only a stick.

"Did we beat them back, sir?" the old man asked, drool dribbling down his white bearded face.

"Err, yes, we did, soldier," Arillion responded, confused. The old man nodded happily, his thinning, white, wispy hair covering his sightless eyes.

"Where are you travelling to?" Cassana asked the girl softly, as she continued to cling onto her. The girl sniffed, her tears still spilling unchecked from her brilliant emerald eyes as she pulled back from Cassana and wiped her running nose on the back of her hand.

She was a slim thing, no more or less of a waif than Cassana was at that age and she was dressed in a fraying, yellow, knee-length dress and white sandals. Her beautiful, long, red hair was tied back into a ponytail and her freckled face broke into a bright smile as she attempted to overcome her fear.

"We are heading to the village of Colden, to the west," the girl explained and the old man's head snapped around at the sound of her voice.

"Come to me girl," he called, weeping as he reached out for her. Cassana let her go and Arillion stepped back, watching as they embraced and wept together.

Cassana rose and looked briefly towards her protector, scowling as she caught him looking skyward for some assistance.

"It's all right grandfather," the girl sobbed, wiping the dribble from his face and soothing his ramblings. "The brave man and lady saved us from the bad men!"

Arillion groaned and wandered away to pick up his cloak. Shaking it clean, he swung it gracefully back about his shoulders and pulled his hood up over his head. With a sly look towards his charge, he dragged the corpses away from them and began searching their pockets and belongings for anything of interest. Cassana watched him briefly, disgust blazing in her eyes.

"Damned Reven," the old man spat. "They get everywhere these days."

Cassana frowned as the girl looked back at her. "Please forgive grandpa," she apologised. "He drifts in and out of the past quite a lot these days."

Cassana hugged herself and offered the girl a sympathetic smile. "If you do not mind me asking child, where are you from? What are your names?"

The girl hushed her grandfather as he began asking for his captain. "My name is Karlina Roe and this is my grandfather Galen," she said, smiling merrily. "We are from the village of Willow Ford on the northern fringes of the Burning Marsh, several miles east of the forest."

Cassana smiled in greeting. Willow Ford was well known to most in the northern vales. A decade ago a terrible fever had blighted the region, claiming the lives of many of the people who lived there. Those that were lucky enough to survive had spent these last few terrible years trying to rebuild their lives and attract back the trade that people had taken elsewhere from the doomed village. The marshland to the south of the decimated community had been so-named because the fever left the sufferer with burning skin that eventually blistered and killed the person within a terrible, agonising week. In a show of compassion, the high duke sent his best physicians to help the village, but there was little they could do by the time they arrived and the villagers had been left alone, quarantined and prevented from leaving their homes so that they could not spread the killer disease. A month later the Burning Fever, as it came to be known, died out on its own accord, having taken three-quarters of the occupants of Willow Ford with it. Karlina must have been an infant at the time and Cassana swallowed down the lump in her throat as she wondered where the girl's parents were.

"My grandfather has raised me on his own, ever since my parents died," the girl explained answering the question, her eyes still shining with tears. "But he has not been well these last few years, becoming more absent minded and only recently blind. We have no family alive to help us anymore, so I care for him now!" Cassana's heart nearly broke and she offered the girl a smile of encouragement as she felt her own tears arrive. "You are a brave girl, standing up to those brigands the way you did!"

Karlina smiled shyly. "Thank you, miss," she mumbled. "I must get it from my grandfather."

Cassana looked at the old man and nodded her agreement. She looked round as Arillion returned to find that he was stuffing something into his pockets. She glared at him vehemently.

"Hey there, freckles," he greeted the girl, lowering his scarf and smiling.

The girl looked up at him and smiled. "Hello and thank you, sir."

Arillion offered her a slight bow. "At your service-,"

"Don't call her freckles," the old man piped up, fixing his sightless gaze on Arillion. "Her name's Karlina, squirrel to her friends!"

"Squirrel?" Arillion said, failing to hide the amusement in his voice as he looked at the girl. "Because of your hair?"

"Partly," she replied. "And the fact I am good at climbing trees!"

"Fair enough, then," he said, looking away. Arillion was clearly bored and his impatience was starting to show.

"I fought against the Reven," the old man stated, proudly puffing out his chest.

Arillion shook his head, blowing out his exasperation. Cassana glared at him.

"That is fantastic, Galen," Cassana said, kneeling before the old man. "You protected your granddaughter bravely and you saved the day."

"I did, didn't I!" he beamed merrily, ignorant to the fresh dribble running down his chin again.

"Why were you heading to Colden?" Cassana asked, as Karlina tended to her grandfather once more.

"There is an apo... apofac...," the girl began, fumbling her words.

"An apothecary?" Cassana offered.

"Yes," Karlina said, blushing. "We have been selling eggs at the market for two years now so that we could buy some medicine to help grandfather feel better! The outlaws took it from us when they jumped out onto the path!"

Cassana reached forward and patted the girl on one of her bony shoulders, looking round at Arillion.

"Sir?" she prompted him, with a meaningful tilt of her head towards his pockets.

Arillion's eyes narrowed as he fished through his pockets, pulling out a worn leather purse.

"Here you are, red," he said, tossing it to her. The girl caught it and pulled apart the drawstrings.

"We didn't have this much!" she exclaimed, looking up and squeaking in excitement.

"Just a little apology from the outlaws," Arillion answered, his voice full of contempt and tinged with regret.

"Thank you both so much," Karlina cried, turning to her grandfather in excitement. As she started chattering to the old man, Cassana rose and drew Arillion to one side.

"That was a brave thing you did, sir," she admitted, laying a hand on his chest.

Arillion looked past her, his eyes devoid of any emotion. "It's in my contract, don't forget!" he said, flicking his eyes back to her meaningfully.

Cassana stiffened and withdrew her hand.

"Do not fear, you will get paid when I am safely

home," she said evenly, her eyes betraying her anger. Turning, she strode back to the old man and girl.

"The forest is a dangerous place," she began, hesitating. "Would you like to accompany us, there is safety in-,"

"Hold on a second," Arillion cut in angrily, grabbing Cassana by her left arm. "Have you forgotten something, princess?"

"Princess?" Karlina piped up in excitement, before Cassana could reply.

"She's not a princess," Arillion snapped furiously, rounding on the focus of his wrath.

Cassana wrenched her arm from his grasp and stepped back from him. "This forest is clearly dangerous, sir," she observed, looking pointedly at the nearby corpses. "I am only suggesting that we see them safely to the fringes of the forest, before we continue on our way."

"No! No way!" Arillion growled angrily. "I have far too much to do already trying to keep your nose clean, without taking on a scrawny rat and some old goat who soils himself."

"Show some respect," Cassana snapped furiously.

Karlina shrank away from their argument as her grandfather pulled her protectively into his arms. Arillion turned and stalked away, Cassana following him like an annoying wasp.

"We cannot just abandon them," she buzzed in his ear.

"Just watch me," Arillion snarled, rounding on her. "I knew this would happen, I knew you wouldn't be able to just walk away!"

Cassana scowled. "Is that such a terrible thing? If it is, then perhaps you should have asked for more money then, sir!"

Arillion glared at her and started to turn away, before hesitating. Taking a deep breath he rubbed his left eye and sighed.

"Look," he whispered, looking past her at the couple. "Those men were not part of Devlin Hawke's band. When they don't come back, their brothers will come looking for them."

"Which means they will be looking for us," Cassana sighed, finishing off his sentence for him.

"Exactly," Arillion said, sighing with relief. "We have enough worries already princess, without adding any more enemies to our list and besides, if I do not get you home safely, I will never be able to show my face in the capital again."

Cassana looked away for a few moments, before turning back. "Can we not at least see them safely to the edge of the forest?" There was desperation in her voice now and she held onto his hands pleadingly.

"By the storms, princess," Arillion hissed, shaking her hands free. "Do you know how much they will slow us down? We will be taking an unnecessary risk, if we do."

Cassana nodded sheepishly. "I know," she admitted, bowing her head in defeat. "But it is a risk I am willing to take! How much more will it cost me if we do, sir?"

Arillion laughed. "Carry on like this lady, and you won't have any money left to attract a suitor with!"

"How much?"

Arillion shook his head again and his eyes flashed mischievously. "A thousand more to the edge of the forest, then we are done with them!"

Cassana straightened and then nodded her head.

"Settled then," she said haughtily.

Arillion watched as she turned and walked back to the old man and gave him the good news in hushed tones.

"Stubborn," he muttered, shaking his head with reluctant admiration.

The young girl cried out happily at the news and Arillion grimaced as her piercing cry cut through the tranquillity of the evening. Swearing under his breath Arillion walked over to join them, wishing that he had stayed in the Moon Gardens and ignored Savinn Kassaar's summons.

CHAPTER EIGHTEEN

Lifelines

Khadazin dragged himself reluctantly from the icy depths of his unconsciousness and looked in bewilderment about his surroundings. He was no longer lying on the floor of the Western Woods, instead he was tucked up safely in a soft bed that was far too small for him and in the back of what appeared to be a small hard-roofed wagon. Thin shafts of sunlight knifed through the tattered curtains to either side of him like vain fingers of light that reached out tantalisingly towards him as they tried to show him more of his surroundings.

"Where am I?" he whispered feebly. His throat was raw and his words cracked like dry tinder on a virgin flame. As he took a hold of his senses he could tell that the wagon was moving, as it jostled slowly along a bumpy road in tandem to the jingle of harnesses and the muffled sounds of hooves and cautious conversation.

Panicking, Khadazin tried to move from under the

linen bed sheet but found that his naked body was far too weak and ignorant to his commands. As he slumped back down into the comfort of the soft straw-filled pillow that cradled his head, he felt every bruise and wound on his body stiffen in protest. He was not in prison, that was something. And someone had gone through the trouble to put him to bed. Not the usual methods of someone wishing him harm. Khadazin let out a hopeful sigh. Had his fortunes finally started to turn in his favour?

For the next few hours Khadazin tried to relax, drifting in and out of a wary sleep that offered him some respite. From time to time he could hear the whisper of guarded conversation coming from the other side of the wooden wall behind him and he would strain to listen to any words he could perceive. There was little clue to his hosts, but he was sure he heard a child speak at one stage. Had the boy's father taken pity on him? Or had they handed him over to somebody else? Khadazin fretted over his predicament for many hours and by the time the last fingers of daylight had withdrawn for the night, a pounding, tense headache had replaced them.

Khadazin snapped awake as he felt the wagon lurch into a reluctant stop and blinked the dryness from his eyes. It was strange, but in the grip of night he could now see his surroundings a little better and could tell that he was in the back of what appeared to be someone's home. Shelves lined the cluttered walls, heaving with all manner of implements and belongings. The curving roof above him was no different and Khadazin could see several strings of onions, ropes and a cold oil lantern swinging in the last throes of motion above and before him. With his nose broken Khadazin hadn't been able to smell the onions, which was probably for the better at the moment anyhow and at the far end of the wagon, he could just about make out the faint outline of a windowless door. As he listened, Khadazin detected the sound of movement from behind him and licked his lips nervously as he tracked the shuffling footsteps that moved down the side of the wagon on his right and came to stand before the wagon's door. Khadazin struggled to sit up as he noticed the light stealing into his dark domain through the cracks in the wood and before he could discover the strength he needed, the door was hauled open and he was blinded by the lantern light that spilled into the wagon and hungrily devoured the shadows.

"You are awake, I see," a man said, climbing into the back of the wagon.

"That's good, very good!" he continued, breathing heavily as he reached up and hung the lantern from a hook in the roof.

Khadazin nodded weakly, peering through the fingers of the hand covering his eyes as the hazy figure shuffled along the side of the bed to sit on a stool to his right.

"How are you feeling?" the man asked, his voice short of breath. "Better for a sleep, I am sure?"

"Yes," Khadazin managed, blinking his eyes into focus. "Thank you."

Khadazin propped himself up on his right elbow and ignored the pain that shot through his arm as he studied the man taking shape before him. The man was hidden beneath the shadows of a heavy grey, hooded cloak and was dressed in a long-sleeved woollen tunic and worn leather breeches. Aware of his guest's scrutiny, the man subconsciously pulled back on his seat and drew the cloak tight about his frame with hands already hidden away beneath the grey cloth.

"I am sure you have just as many questions for me, as I do for you, stranger?" the man asked, pausing for breath.

"Yes," Khadazin answered, trying to form a smile on his stiff face. "I do, but I would ask them as a friend. My name is Khadazin Sahr!"

The hooded head nodded in greeting, but as Khadazin reached out with his left hand to seal his acquaintance, the man rose swiftly.

"Well met, Redani," he said nervously, stepping away. "I am Sam Geddles. Forgive me for my apparent lack of courtesy, but I must leave you. I will send my son with some broth and herbal tea for you once he has a fire going, perhaps we can talk further afterwards?"

Khadazin nodded in confusion as he withdrew his hand and watched his mysterious host hurry from the wagon as fast as his wheezing frame would allow him. As he left, the man reached up and took down the cold lantern, stepping from the back of the wagon before the stonemason could force his tongue into action and offer him his thanks again. Perplexed, Khadazin slumped back on the bed and shook his head.

"Now what have you gotten yourself into, Redani?" he asked himself, but there was no immediate answer forthcoming to satiate his growing curiosity.

Khadazin did his best to relax for the next hour, as he drifted in and out of a troubled sleep. With light from the lantern now, he was amazed to find that some of his wounds had been cleansed. His tortured side was also bandaged and the itching scabs underneath felt cool, as if someone had applied a poultice to it. Thankful for the care he had already received, the stonemason rested as he listened to the distant chatter outside and, after a while, he could hear the crackling of a fire and the sounds of clashing utensils. As the evening outside progressed, the stonemason finally began to smell food and his mouth began to water in anticipation. Finally, when he could bear the smell no longer, he heard movement outside and the handle to the wagon turned slowly.

Light spilled into the darkness outside, filling up the shadows and the young face that peered nervously into the wagon. Khadazin tried his broadest smile, but it only served to frighten the lad who hesitated and backed away slightly.

"I won't harm you," Khadazin promised, waving him inside. He didn't have any strength left, even if he had wanted to.

The boy steeled himself bravely and stepped timidly inside, trying to smile. He moved nervously over to the bedside and held out a steaming bowl of broth towards him.

"Me pa said you would be hungry," he said, his slim arms shaking. "Here, sir!"

Khadazin struggled to sit up, reaching out gratefully to take the steaming bowl of broth and the rattling spoon from the lad's shaking hands.

"My thanks to you and your father, young man," Khadazin said graciously. His stomach rumbled as the smell of boiled meat and onions wafted up his nose, forcing him to lick his lips hungrily. "This smells delicious!"

The boy stood silently, wide-eyed and transfixed as the stonemason took a tentative sip at the broth and then withdrew from the stinging heat that burnt his dry, cracked lips.

"Phew, hot," Khadazin smiled, wiping his bearded face. "I am Khadazin."

The boy stared at the huge hand being offered to him and was about to shake it when he noticed that all of the nails were missing from the fingers. Khadazin withdrew it apologetically, cursing himself. There was so much pain elsewhere in his body that he had completely forgotten about his hands.

"My name's James," the boy said, tearing his blue eyes away from Khadazin's hand. "I have to tend to father now, and then I'll be back with some bread and tea for you, sir."

"Thank you James," Khadazin said, watching as the boy hurried away and leapt from the back of the wagon. Smiling, Khadazin's hunger won out and he tucked heartily into the piping broth.

By the time James had returned with a large chunk of bread and a cup of herbal tea for him, Khadazin had already devoured the broth. Fortunately his stomach had managed to keep the contents of the bowl down and he settled it further by wiping the bowl clean with the bread.

"My compliments, young man," Khadazin said, allowing the boy to take the empty bowl from him as he passed him the tea.

"Thank you, sir," the boy beamed, perching on the seat next to the bed. "I make a good broth, my pa always says."

Khadazin raised an eyebrow and smiled, sipping at the tea. "You certainly do, it is the best broth I have ever tasted!"

James grinned proudly. "My pa says that the tea will

help to settle you and give you a good night's sleep. Also, that he will speak to you in the morning now, as he is tired and needs to rest."

"Please pass on my thanks for me," Khadazin replied, disguising his curiosity. "I am so very grateful for everything you have done for me!"

"It was nothing, mister Khadazin," the boy said shyly. "It was Kayla who found you, not me!"

"Your dog?"

"Yes," James said, his eyes bright with pride. "She's the best dog we have ever had and the best hunter."

"She certainly is," Khadazin admitted. "I bet she even caught the rabbit I tasted in the broth?"

The boy nodded, swinging his legs on his seat. "I had better go now!" he said, his youthful voice tinged with disappointment. Any of the fear he may have had earlier was now gone and he seemed completely at ease in the company of the dark-skinned, injured mess before him.

"I'll see you in the morning," he said rising from his seat, as he moved towards the door. "Goodnight, sir."

Khadazin smiled. "Goodnight, James."

Sipping at the hot tea, Khadazin watched as the boy closed the door and announced to his father that he was back to help him. Closing his eyes, the stonemason rested his head against the cold wood behind him and raised his cup towards the roof of the wagon.

"To you Cornelius," he whispered sadly, toasting his friend. "May you watch over me a little while longer, until our work is done."

Draining the tea, Khadazin placed the empty cup on the seat beside the bed and slid down onto the soft mattress with a deep groan of pleasure. By the time he slipped away into a welcome sleep, a bright moon was already high in the dark, cloudless night sky, showering the tiny wagon with rays of silver as it sheltered safely under the protection of a large elm tree at the side of a dusty road that twisted away into the darkness towards the south.

Khadazin woke the next morning to find James sat on the seat again, watching him. As the stonemason blinked the sleep from his eyes, he turned towards him and smiled.

"Good morning."

"Did you sleep well, sir?" the boy asked him, smiling.

Khadazin nodded and struggled to rise. "Honestly? The best sleep I have had for many, many days, young man."

That seemed to please the boy and he sprung up, grinning. "Father asks if you would like to join him for lunch, if you think you can manage it, sir?"

"Lunch?" Khadazin spluttered, looking towards the bright sunlight glowing from behind the closed curtains of the wagon.

James chuckled. "Yes, you slept all through the night and this morning's travel."

Khadazin shook his head and grinned back. "I have to admit, I really needed it."

"Father said that you kept him awake all night again, with your snoring though," the boy giggled and Khadazin laughed, ignoring the pain that ignited in his face.

"Hold on a moment," Khadazin said, confusion in his eyes. "Did you say again, James?"

"Yes, sir," the boy answered. "We found you two days ago now, last eve."

Khadazin scratched his head and then smiled. "Well it's lucky for me that you did. Please could you tell your father that I will join him as soon as I can?"

The boy nodded happily. "Your robes are folded up on that table there, sir," he said, pointing towards the small dressing table along the wall to his left.

Khadazin followed the boy's pointing finger and nodded. As the boy left, skipping from the wagon, he called out to him.

"Call me Khadazin," he told him. "I am a simple man, Master James!"

"Okay, sir!" the boy called back, leaving the stonemason to chuckle away to himself.

"Welcome back," James' father greeted him softly, as Khadazin finally emerged from the back of the wagon on weak legs and an uneasy sense of balance.

"Thank you, my friend!"

With one hand, Khadazin shielded his eyes from the high sun overhead and stumbled over to the hooded man, and the small camp fire he sat before. It was an incredible day, any evidence of the recent storms were now gone and they were surrounded by rolling flatlands of long grass and a cacophony of jubilant wildlife. A clear, brilliant blue sky framed the horizon tenderly, showing the stonemason distant wooded hills and the faint scar of a road, far away to his right. Nodding in weary greeting, the stonemason eased himself gingerly down beside the fire and looked back towards the small wagon. It was a traditional wayfarer's wagon, painted garishly red with a sloping green roof, pulled by a single draft horse that currently grazed away on the lush green grasses surrounding the wagon. More of the family's belongings hung from the side of the wagon and Khadazin could also see a hammock suspended from two hooks in the eaves.

"Here," Sam said, passing him a plate of food. He was still cloaked heavily in grey, but as he reached across, the stonemason could see that his hand was wrapped tightly in fresh bandages.

"Thank you," Khadazin said again, taking the plate from him that was full of boiled potatoes, two sizzling sausages and a fried egg. He made no comment as his host withdrew his shaking hand and instead, licked his lips hungrily. His appetite was apparently returning, even if his health and strength wasn't.

"My son has treated your wounds as best he can, Redani," the man wheezed from beneath his hood. "But you are still very weak and in desperate need of proper care and medicine."

Khadazin nodded absently as he bit into a sausage, delighting at its taste. His body was still wreathed in agony and he was already starting to feel light-headed again.

"You have saved my life, Sam," he said, pulling the hood of his own robes up over his sweating head. "If your son had not found me..."

Sam's head nodded slightly, in agreement. "We have much to thank him for, it seems. I am too weak and you too much of a giant for me to have got you back to the wagon, alone."

Khadazin tore his eyes away from some butterflies that had briefly garnered his attention and he leant closer. "How *did* you manage to get me back?"

"Well, after you ran the breath from yourself and we caught up with you," came his chuckling response. "I stayed with you, while James put his plan into action and came back to the wagon to fetch the horse. Using an old canvas tent we have, we attached it to the horse's harness and put you in it. The horse did the rest!"

"Clever lad," Khadazin admitted. "How old is he?"

"Nine summers old by two weeks," Sam replied proudly.

Khadazin smiled. Smart for his age! "Where is he?" he asked, looking about their surroundings.

"He has taken Kayla hunting," Sam replied. "We will need more meat for our broth, now that we have an extra mouth to feed."

Khadazin swallowed down his humility and popped a potato into his mouth to take his mind off his worry for the boy. Was it safe for him to go off on his own?

"Where are we now, Sam?" he asked instead, chewing his food between words.

"We are many miles south of the woods we found you in," Sam began, pausing as he coughed heavily. "After finding you, I thought it best that we put as much distance as we could between those woods and whatever danger you were fleeing from!"

Khadazin bowed his head, rallying against the memories that rose up immediately to haunt him again. "Very wise," he whispered, fighting back the tears welling up in his eyes.

They fell silent for a time, both alone with their thoughts as they listened to the distant cries of a hunting bird of prey. After a while, Sam shifted uncomfortably and put his empty plate to one side.

"I can tell, quite obviously, that you have suffered a great deal recently, Redani," he said. "And the fact that you fled from us, even though you were armed and could have easily killed us both, suggests to me that you have no desire to be found again. Am I correct?"

Khadazin raised his head, blinking back his tears.

"Yes, my friend. But only until I am strong enough again to fight back."

Sam cocked his head to one side, regarding his guest curiously with hidden eyes.

"I do not doubt that for a moment, Redani," he said softly. "Perhaps then, with the lady's blessing and protection, we can be of help to each other. If I will tell you a little of myself, would you place your trust in me by allowing us to help you?"

Khadazin searched the shadows of the man's hood, locking onto the piercing blue eyes that held his gaze firmly.

"Yes, my friend," he said finally. "I will! You have shown me great compassion thus far by helping me and I will show you my respect, by telling you all that I can, without endangering you more than I already have."

Sam looked away and nodded, clearly satisfied. Drawing in a rasping breath, he let it out again slowly and turned back to him again.

"Well, we are originally from the village of Saddleford," he paused momentarily to allow Khadazin to register his unfamiliarity with the name, before continuing. "I was, am a leather-worker by trade and our family have owned our premises for over thirty years. I took over from my father fifteen years ago now, when he became too ill to carry on working. Following his death a year later, I married a local girl and together we ran the business."

Khadazin watched uneasily as the man shuddered and coughed away before him, trying to find his breath and wiping his mouth, hidden away by his hood, with the tails of his cloak.

"Please, my friend," Khadazin said. "If it is too painful for you..."

"No, no," Sam placated him, holding up a bandaged hand, requesting a moment. "It does me good to talk to someone. It has been such a long time since, well, since I have had someone older than ten and who is not a dog to talk to!"

Khadazin nodded, ignorant of his desire to rest again he carried on with his breakfast and waited for Sam to gather himself. When he did finally catch hold of his breath, his voice was full of sorrow.

"I lost my wife on the day I gained a son...Cara, she died following the birth, the midwife tried everything she could to save her, but she could not stop her bleeding," Sam paused, coughing up his memories. "Over the next few years, I threw myself into my work, keeping my reputation alive, whilst raising a son. In the end though, I could not cope with the demands of both and I hired some workers to help me. It should have been the end to my problems-,"

"But it was the beginning!" Khadazin predicted sadly.

Sam nodded slowly. "Yes, Redani. I hired two workers, one a local, a friend of mine since childhood, the other a man who had arrived at the village, some months before. The outsider was a revelation, a quiet, loyal worker with a steady hand and a good eye for the trade. It was as if the lady herself had sent him to me, to ease my burdens and save my soul. Sadly, it would transpire that he was most likely sent to me by the Father of Storms."

Khadazin shifted uncomfortably. Sam had obviously waited a long time to share his demons with someone and despite the fact he had many problems of his own, the stonemason owed his host enough to allow him to at least share his burden.

"I will not bore you with a long tale of the hardships that were to befall me, suffice to say that he became ill. Slowly at first, but enough to affect his workmanship and then, finally, more physically," Sam continued, his voice heavy with sadness. He sighed, reaching up with bandaged hands to slowly lower his hood.

Khadazin stared at the man across from him and let out a breath. Sam's face was a twisted, ruined mass of differing skin lesions and pustules. Only his eyes and his thick head of tangled, fair hair was untouched by the deformity of his face. Sam coughed as they held each other's gaze and Khadazin could see the pain flare in the man's eyes.

"You do not flinch, Redani?" Sam observed, wiping the drool from his blistered lips with a shaking hand. "You do not run away, screaming in fear!"

Khadazin nodded sadly. "I have seen leprosy before, my friend. When my father brought me to these shores, we travelled to the city of Karick, to make our home there. With little coin and no sponsor, we were housed in numerous shelters in the slums of the capital, run by kind hearted souls who helped tend to the sick and the needy. As a welcome gift to their dark-skinned visitors, we were housed in a shelter that cared for people who suffered from your disease."

"Then you know first-hand, of some of the disgust and prejudice that would befall me in the coming months, my friend," Sam guessed, shaking his head.

Khadazin nodded. "I do." he said quietly.

"After the man died, people's attitude towards me changed. They regarded me suspiciously, whispering behind my back. My business began to suffer. Fearful of what he may have contracted, my *friend* left me to work alone and for a time I kept the business going...and then I too started to notice that something was wrong with me. In short, I had contracted the disease."

"I am so sorry," Khadazin whispered and Sam's hideous face broke into what may have once been a handsome smile.

"Please, Khadazin, do not pity me. I have come to terms with what happened next, I would not wish you to carry that burden for me."

"Then you do not need to tell me, Sam," Khadazin said, putting his plate aside. Reaching out, he placed a comforting hand on the man's shoulder. He felt the shoulder stiffen under his hand and Sam pulled away.

"What are you doing, Redani?" Sam hissed.

Khadazin retreated. "I lived for two months with the sufferers of your disease and I did not contract it. Neither did my father, or their carers!"

"Nevertheless, my friend," Sam said, his voice troubled. "I do not think you should tempt fate like this."

"Very well," Khadazin said, tilting his head in acceptance. "I have suffered much prejudice over the years from a reported, *civilised* society. I can guess what happened to you next, as I too have felt like an outsider, if in somewhat different circumstances."

"Yes," Sam agreed. "Friends, customers, people I had known since I was a child shunned me, despised me even. In the end, I was banished from my home and given the wagon as a parting gift. 'Lock yourself in there' some said. 'Take your cursed disease from here' others spat. They even started calling me *Mould*!"

"That's outrageous," Khadazin snarled. "Did nobody try to help you?"

Sam chuckled. "There were a few, mainly friends of my father. But they were soon quietened, lest they be accused of having a mind sick with sympathy. The final insult was when they sent my son out to join me, in the nearby woods where I had made my home. Jimmy had not shown any signs of the disease, but he was tainted in their eyes and nobody would care for him. It was the most humiliating moment of my life!"

Khadazin felt his anger returning and it was surprisingly comforting to him. "I cannot understand how people can be so ignorant and cruel. Surely there was something the authorities could have done for you?"

Sam shook his head. "Fear is a terrible thing, my friend. They would not have heard my pleas, even if I was given the opportunity. In fact, it was the local authorities who handed my home and business over to my friend, the one who had deserted me."

"How long ago did all of this happen?" Khadazin asked. He shifted as cramp settled in his lower back again and he rolled the stiffness from his neck.

"Three years ago, now," Sam replied. "My son should have shown symptoms by now."

"I do not know," Khadazin admitted. "The carers at the shelter did all they could to...to ease their suffering, but they knew very little about the origins, or how to treat it."

"And that leads me to the final part of my tale," Sam said, his voice bright with hope. "There was one kind soul in Saddleford, a friend of my family for many years. She would leave parcels of food for us at the edge of the forest, and one day she left me a note. There was a man in the village, a man who carried word of the Lady of the Vales. He spoke of this new religion and of her compassion for those who would seek comfort in her."

"I am not a religious man," Khadazin began.

"And nor was I, Redani," Sam agreed. "How could this benevolent higher power allow such terrible things to befall honest people? Why had my wife never lived long enough to hear her son talk, or watch him walk for the first time? Why had my life shattered in such a terrible, complete way? Where was her compassion for me? What possible reason could she have for allowing this to happen?"

Khadazin shrugged uncomfortably. "I cannot answer these questions, my friend!"

Sam's face split into a hideous grin. "No, and neither could the messenger of this goddess. I met with him, as he left Saddleford, on his way to the next village. He did not run from me however. No, he showed me great compassion and told me only that it is not for mere mortals to question her will, only that we should accept it and take her into our hearts."

"Not very comforting," Khadazin sniffed disdainfully.

"No, I agree. But what he told me next filled me with hope and for that I thank him from the bottom of my heart."

"Go on, what did he tell you?"

Sam leant forward again, his eyes weeping in the sun. "He told me that there is a monastery, dedicated to the worship of the lady, high in the hills that overlook the Low Sea in the South Vales. The monks there offer care to those that would seek it and the pilgrim told me that, should I seek the lady's favour, the brothers there would be able to offer me and my son the sanctuary we need. They have many who suffer the same as I, sheltering within their walls, and he believes that they will be able to offer me comfort... the comfort that I will one day soon, need."

Khadazin smiled supportively, his excitement rising. The brothers at the monastery would surely be able to offer him the sanctuary he needed also, while he convalesced and decided what to do next. The chancellor's men, should they still be looking for him, would not be able to find him there and even if they did, they would probably not be able to get to him. Khadazin was not that naïve to realise how strong and far the brotherhood's grip could reach, but it was the faint strand of hope he had been looking for and he grabbed on to it with both hands.

"I can see in your eyes, Redani, that you understand why I believe we can help each other," Sam said and waited for the stonemason to nod. "I am becoming weaker by the day now and I fear that the time will soon come when I can no longer move about as I do now. Our journey will take us several weeks and I fear by then, I will be of no use to my son. When my son found you in the woods, it was as if the lady had sent you to me herself, it was then that I realised our fates were entwined."

Khadazin rubbed his chin thoughtfully. "Perhaps, it is true that, had such terrible things not befallen you and your son, then we would not have met, I cannot dispute that. But it seems a terrible cruel road to have travelled for our paths to have crossed!"

"I agree," Sam said. "But I have to cling on to the hope that this is my destiny, Redani. I now have the chance to give my son a better life, one that I can no longer give him and in doing so, I have also hopefully given you the chance to escape from your hardships and, judging by the look on your face, the chance for revenge?"

Khadazin grinned darkly. "More than you know, Sam, more than you know!"

By the time James and Kayla returned from their fruitless hunting trip, Khadazin had recounted all that had befallen him since that fateful day in the high duke's gardens. He told the man all that he dared about his ordeal, leaving out only the identity of the chancellor. When he had finally finished his tale, both men were in tears, perhaps from the blazing sun overhead, or maybe from the strange bond that had quickly formed. Both men were tortured by circumstance, persecuted by others for things that were out of their control. It was a comfort to Khadazin that he was no longer alone. He had lost one friend recently and despite the fact that he would eventually lose another, he was spurred on by the fact that he could help this family shake free of its past. Sam was also touched by the stonemason's plight and was even more confident now that it had been the Lady's desire that they meet. Khadazin was not so sure, but he had to admit that it was indeed fortunate that they had.

"Hello," James said brightly as he trudged back through the long grasses to join them under the shade of the wagon's eaves. The large hound at his side wagged its tail in excitement and bounded over to Sam, panting heavily.

"Hello there, girl," Sam greeted her, tickling her ears fondly.

"How are you, Khada, Khada...,"

"Khadazin," the stonemason finished for the lad, as his tongue stumbled over his foreign name. "But you can call me Khad if it's easier...Jimmy?"

The boy nodded. "Yes, please." he said, grinning impishly.

Sam watched as Kayla eyed the stonemason up and then moved closer to his huge, outstretched hand, sniffing at it tentatively.

"There, there girl," Khadazin said, as she licked at his hand. "I am no threat to you, or your masters."

Sam turned to his son, who was watching the scene fondly. "Can you see to the fire and utensils, Jimmy? I must help our friend back to his bed, so that we can make off again."

"Sure, pa," James said without complaint and calling the hound to his side, they both headed away to finish off Khadazin's food. "Come on girl, are you hungry?"

Sam rose stiffly and helped the stonemason rise with him. By the time Khadazin was back in the bed again, both men were exhausted.

"Thank you, Sam," Khadazin said, as the leper turned to leave him to his rest.

"I think we can both thank the lady for that," Sam said, turning back to him. He made to leave again and hesitated.

"May I ask something of you, Redani?"

"Anything."

"There will be a time, perhaps soon, when I will not be around to care for James. When that time comes, will you make sure that my son remains with the monks until he is old enough to decide his own path through life? He has taken everything that has happened to him in his stride, without stopping to ask why. The only thing he has ever complained about was that 'people like us are not allowed to have friends!' Like us? He does not even have the disease. He could leave whenever he wanted to!"

"But he loves you, Sam!" Khadazin answered, swallowing hard. He reached out and quickly took Sam by one of his bandaged hands. "I promise you that I will and should danger ever come calling for me, I will do all that I can to ensure that we reach the sanctuary of the monastery."

"Thank you, my friend," Sam said, withdrawing his hand. "If it does, your weapons are under the bed." Pulling his hood up over his head, he shuffled from the wagon.

Khadazin watched him leave and then settled down to rest. His mind was full of questions, teased with the promise of revenge, and then dashed by the whisper of caution. He faced a long and arduous road, one that would be filled with many more hardships and dangers. But this chance meeting, if indeed it was by chance, had given him the opportunity to exact revenge upon those who had taken his life and his friend away from him. It was a slim chance, but it was a chance nonetheless.

"Be ready, chancellor," he snarled. "Be ready...!"

"The tracks leave the road," Farrell Elais observed, rising from the muddy trail and staring off across the meadows towards the south. The wagon tracks were clear to see as they cut through the long grasses and behind him, his companions shifted nervously.

"I don't like this!"

Farrell looked round as his tall companion voiced his concerns and scratched his pock-marked face nervously. At his side, their squat friend Arlen nodded his agreement.

"I must confess, I find it astonishing how this man

can keep escaping our clutches," Farrell agreed, resting one hand on the hilt of the sword hanging from his belt. "But we have his trail clearly now and if we travel hard and rest light, we should catch up with him in a couple of days."

Arlen snorted his disagreement. "I'm with Beren on this one. Whose helping him now, I wonder?"

Farrell looked away again. He had wondered the same thing, but it didn't matter either way. Once they caught up with the Redani, they would kill him and anyone that was helping him.

"It matters little to the outcome now," Farrell muttered. "We don't have a choice, do we? Unless of course you want to return and tell the Kestrel that we failed?"

Both men shook their heads quickly and Beren spat his disgust onto the ground.

"We wasted a lot of time digging up that old man," he pointed out, not for the first time that day.

Farrell nodded. "Yes we did, but we had to be sure. However, we did make up some of our time with the clear trail whoever is helping him, left behind!"

"So what's the plan?" Arlen asked, looking at the wagon tracks for himself.

"We do whatever it takes," Farrell replied. "No matter how far he gets, no matter where he goes, we follow him until we finally catch up with him."

"And when we do?"

Farrell started off across the meadows.

"We kill the bastard."

Beren looked at Arlen and grinned. Shouldering their concerns, they followed the tracker into the long grass and headed off into the setting sun towards the south.

CHAPTER NINETEEN

The Long and Whining Road

Arillion groaned and looked away angrily as Cassana and the scrawny rat fussed about the old man, trying vainly to help him onto the donkey, again! It was early evening now and they had made very little distance, or nowhere near as much ground as he would have wanted to! The old man was a burden, and he was regretting the fact he hadn't thrown Cassana over his shoulder and left the pair alone in the clearing to fend for themselves. After Arillion had retrieved their mounts, he had led his charges deeper into the forest towards the north for a time, before heading west. He had no desire to tempt fate further by carrying on along the track through the forest towards Colden, as they would have probably ended up running into more outlaws. But that, as it would soon transpire, was the least of his worries. The absent minded old fool stopped constantly, complaining that he needed to rest, take a piss, or get down from the donkey to fight imaginary foes with his stick. In the end, Arillion's patience had worn thin and stalking back to the old man he had snatched the stick from his hands, throwing it away into the trees. Several minutes were wasted as the old man sobbed for the return of his fallen weapon and with barely contained rage, Cassana had banished Arillion to the rear of the tiny procession as she went to retrieve it. And that suited him just fine!

"There you go, Galen," Cassana said encouragingly, as she helped Karlina steady him on the back of the donkey and gave him his stick back.

"Nice ass!" Arillion observed, not looking at the animal.

Cassana looked askance at him and turned away again. Chuckling, Arillion watched as the donkey brayed and nearly bolted off through the trees with Galen on its back. Unfortunately Karlina managed to soothe the beast with soft whispers and gentle strokes of a pale hand. When the donkey was calm, she looked back at Arillion.

"His name is Flotsam," she said testily.

Arillion could tell she was still angry with him for upsetting her grandfather and her green eyes blazed in the evening sun. Two fiery females, just what he needed! If he had known it was going to be this painful, he would have asked for four times the amount of extra coin he had earned so far.

"That figures," Arillion replied drily. The donkey looked nearly as bad as his passenger, but probably had a few less fleas.

Cassana diverted any possibility of further argument by leading the donkey by its reins through the trees, without a word. Karlina fell in beside Cassana like an obedient puppy and as Arillion led their horses after them, he could hear the two females start up their irritating, incessant chatter again. He shook his head. They were getting on famously, talking about absolutely nothing that mattered and the sound of their excited voices floated through the forest, making him wince. It was as if they had both forgotten about what danger they had just faced and would probably face again, if they didn't shut up. For a brief moment he contemplated turning around and heading back to Karick, but there was a small fortune at stake here and he wasn't about to throw that away, no matter how annoying the next few days would be.

And it would be days. At this rate, anyhow! What should have been a simple, hurried journey through the forest, hastened by the threat of pursuit, would probably turn out to be a three day crawl, at this pace. And that worried him! When those men failed to return to their camp later, their comrades would come looking for them. And when they did, they would easily pick up their trail and come after them. There was a blood debt to be repaid, and knowing the way some of these gangs operated, they wouldn't rest until they had found those culpable.

The final few hours of travel that day offered little to improve Arillion's mood, and by the time he called a halt for the night, he was just about ready to throttle the old man.

"No fire, tonight," Arillion said quietly and as he turned to tend to the horses, Galen started fretting.

"What, sir?" he cried out and Arillion turned back impatiently. "No watch fire? How will our reinforcements find us?"

"No fire," Arillion replied, failing to take the edge from his voice. "Our enemies will find us before our men do, and we cannot stand with so little numbers!"

That explanation seemed to settle the old soldier and Arillion's grey eyes found Cassana meaningfully. She was laying out her bedroll on the ground, under the protection of a silver birch tree and she looked over at him, hearing the warning in his voice. She tilted her head questioningly towards him and Arillion nodded his head silently.

Good! Arillion thought, sighing in relief. He could see the fresh worry that creased her face and she turned away, tying her long hair into a ponytail. Satisfied, Arillion unsaddled their mounts and by the time he had fed and watered them both, the sombre camp was settling down for the night with a cold supper.

"Where do you live, Cass?" Karlina asked, as she cleaned the last of her grandfather's supper from his face. She looked over at her new friend, smiling at her merrily.

Cassana settled down against the trunk of her guardian tree and rested her hands in her lap. "I live in Highwater, to the north."

"The big city?" the girl asked in awe, her freckles seemingly dancing across her face. "I have never been to a big city before, what's it like?"

"It's a lovely city, my girl," Galen piped up, before Cassana could respond. His voice was suddenly very lucid and he sat forward, patting Karlina's knee.

"I recall that I spent several weeks there, before and after the war against the Reven," he said, gazing away into the past. "It was a terrible time for all concerned. The threat of the Reven hordes and the danger that their shadow cast across the mountains was never far from our thoughts. But the splendour of that city and the support the high duke's armies received from its

419

people did much to calm the troops, as we waited for the inevitable call to march to war."

"It must have been a terrible thing, the waiting?" Cassana asked.

"Aye, miss, it was," Galen admitted, then grinned. "But we young soldiers had many a distraction to keep our worried minds occupied. In fact, I met and fell in love with one such distraction."

"Grandma?" Karlina asked, her attention fixed upon her grandfather.

Galen sighed, his eyes wet with emotion. "Yes Karli, your grandmother. She said she would wait for me to come back over the mountains, and if I did, that she would marry me!"

"How lovely," Cassana sighed, tears glistening in her lovely eyes.

"Very sweet," Arillion said, laying back on his bedroll with a yawn.

Galen didn't detect the boredom from the dark figure across from him and he smiled in remembrance, holding onto his granddaughter's hand as he recounted his tale.

"Yes, it was," he sighed, smiling wistfully. "I kept my promise, and she kept hers to me!"

Karlina smiled. Gazing at her grandfather lovingly, she reached up and kissed him on one cheek.

"What was the battle against the Reven like?" Cassana asked, causing Arillion to stir with interest.

"Reven?" Galen asked finally, a puzzled expression creasing his face. "What is that?"

"Typical!" Arillion groaned. Laying back down again, he turned his back on the conversation disdainfully.

"It doesn't matter, Galen," Cassana smiled, flicking

an irritated look towards Arillion.

Galen soon forgot about the subject and fussing over him, Karlina helped him to get into his bedroll, draping an extra blanket over him to help fight off the chill in the night air. The two females watched him for a time, before his ragged breathing evened out and he began to snore softly. Smiling, Karlina wandered over and sat down next to Cassana.

"I am sorry to be a burden, Cass," she whispered, casting a nervous look over at the still form of Arillion. "I know we must be slowing you down, but I will never forget what you and your man did for us today!"

Cassana's face paled. "My man?" she asked the girl, quietly horrified.

Karlina blushed and looked away. "Sorry, I thought that you were together."

"We are," Cassana hissed. "But not like *that*!"

They looked at each other seriously for a brief moment, then leaned into each other subconsciously as they laughed quietly.

"He is protecting me on my journey home, Karli," Cassana explained with a guarded whisper, when she finally managed to find a serious breath.

"That is most certainly *all*!"

"Why does he wear a mask then, and hide away under that hood?" Karlina whispered, looking over at the man in question. "He's not that ugly?"

Cassana blushed, as the girl giggled away to herself. "I cannot say that I have noticed either way, really."

"Well he is the best warrior I have ever seen," Karlina said, her eyes wide with admiration. "The way he killed those men..."

"I bet you were scared?" Cassana asked, eager to change the subject. Her cheeks burned for some reason and she kept sending worried looks towards Arillion.

Karlina's face wrinkled in remembrance and she tugged nervously at her hair, twisting a strand of it around a finger. "A little," she admitted. "But I was more worried for my grandfather. He is very sick!"

Cassana put her arm around the girl's shoulder comfortingly. She could feel the fear trembling away beneath the young girl's bravado and she pulled her close to her.

"I thought Devlin Hawke's men never attacked old people," Karlina sniffed, burying her head into Cassana's chest. "I was going to join his band when I was older, he was my hero... but I don't want to now!"

"There, there," Cassana hushed her, stroking the girl's hair as she began to cry.

"It wasn't Devlin's men, Squirrel," Arillion muttered suddenly, rolling over to look at them. Sighing, he sat up and Karlina raised her head quizzically, sniffing back her tears.

"It wasn't his men?"

Arillion shook his head. "No. The Hawke doesn't allow his men to prey on the vulnerable, as you have probably heard. So if that was his men, then they are probably better off dead anyhow!"

Karlina blinked, her eyes flashing in relief. "Then I can still join his band then, one day?"

Cassana frowned and Arillion looked up at the darkening sky, shaking his head.

"It is not a noble thing to be an outlaw," Cassana pointed out. "You should not idolise him Karlina, no matter how honourable or romantic a picture his reputation paints for him."

"But he is *my* hero!" the girl explained defiantly.

"Hero?" Arillion scoffed, scowling. "Let me tell you

something about your beloved hero, shall I, Red?"

"I think not, sir," Cassana jumped in, glaring at him. Karlina had suffered enough already today, without having her childish dreams dashed and the name of her hero besmirched, no matter how juvenile and misplaced they were. "I think that perhaps we have all had enough excitement for one day!"

"Are you sure you have?" Arillion asked her, his voice thick with promise.

Cassana ignored him and gently ordered Karlina off to get some sleep. Reluctantly, the girl detached herself and shuffled back over to her bedroll, beside her grandfather. Sniffing, she bade them goodnight and settled down for the evening, snuggling close to Galen. Arillion watched her for a time and then flicked his attention back to Cassana. She was ignoring him again and he grinned roguishly.

"Get some rest, princess," he told her. She nodded, but did not look at him as she slipped into her bedroll.

"Thank you," she whispered, as she turned her back on him.

"For what?" Arillion asked.

"For saving them."

"I have lived up to my side of the bargain, princess," Arillion said quietly. "Just see to it that you live up to yours!"

Cassana did not answer him and settled down to try and get some rest.

The crows roosting high in the branches of the trees noisily heralded the arrival of dawn the next morning and woke Cassana from her sleep. Shuddering, she gasped and looked in fright about the forest, realisation catching a hold of her and shaking her accusingly.

She had fallen asleep when she was supposed to be keeping watch.

Looking about her surroundings she could see Galen and his granddaughter, cuddled up in the dewy grass, sheltered from any prying eyes by the huddle of the misty, grey forest. The horses were awake, feeding like ghostly apparitions away to her left and nearby, Flotsam munched lazily on a bramble bush, across from her. Reluctantly, she looked towards Arillion and startled herself with her own shock. He was gone!

Rising up hastily from her bedding, she looked forlornly about her immediate surroundings, searching through the early dawn shadows and mist for him. He was nowhere to be seen. Her heart began to race and she paced about worriedly. *Why had he left her? Where could he be?* Despite their fractious relationship, she had to admit she felt safe in his company and the way he had dealt with those outlaws had only served to reinforce her feelings. But if he had left her, what would happen to her? She began to tremble as she wandered over to his empty bedding. He had taken the rest of his belongings with him and she stooped down on one knee to feel the bedroll, hoping to deduce how long he had been gone. The bedroll was cold and Cassana suddenly felt very alone, and very afraid.

Minutes stretched away like hours for Cassana and still Arillion did not return. Tearing at her hair in frustration, Cassana moved away from their camp and looked through the early morning gloom for any signs of her protector. The tall trees offered little hope for her as she scanned the grey morning around her and she hugged herself tightly, angry that her insistence to help Karlina and her grandfather to safety had probably jeopardised her own. Kicking at the dead leaves on the ground before her, she gasped in fright as she turned back.

"What are you looking at?" Arillion asked, staring away into the trees behind her. His face was masked and his breath seeped through the cloth, clouding before him.

Cassana failed to hide her relief and she scowled as she noticed the glee stealing into his captivating eyes.

"Don't tell me you were missing me, princess?" he asked, merriment in his voice.

Cassana growled in frustration and tried to punch him on the arm. "You know very well that I was looking for you," she snapped, as he casually leant out the way of her strike.

"So you missed me, then?"

"I did not say that!"

Arillion chuckled. "It's okay, I understand how you feel. I've had it before, I am sure it will happen again."

Cassana snarled and went to move by him. As she did, he grabbed hold of her arm gently.

"Here!"

Cassana stared dumbly at the leather quiver of dark feathered arrows he placed into her hands. She looked blankly at them for a moment, then glanced up at him, worry in her eyes.

"Where did you get these, sir?" she asked reluctantly.

"It doesn't matter now," Arillion said quietly. "All you need to know, princess, is that people are looking for us now and that there will be more of them in the coming days. So you will probably need those!"

Cassana eyes widened and she started twisting the strap of the quiver nervously.

"Who? Not the people behind my attempted

abduction? How did they find us?"

Arillion shook his head. "No, no, my lady. Not them. As before, the path I have taken shields us from their attentions, however-,"

"The outlaws!" Cassana guessed, her pale face frightened and full of shame.

"Yes," Arillion whispered, laying a comforting hand on her left shoulder, "I know it's not his fault, but the old man is slowing us down. When the owner of that quiver doesn't return either, they will know which part of the forest we are in, after that, well I am afraid it is only a matter of time..."

Cassana felt her heart race at his touch and she swallowed nervously. "But we had to help them, it was the right thing to do! We cannot just abandon them, not now."

Arillion moved in front of her, his hand still on her shoulder. With his other hand he reached up and gently caressed her face, wiping away the tears that began to run down her cheeks. Cassana shuddered at his touch and her breath formed nervously in the air between them.

"I know that, Cassana," Arillion whispered huskily. "And I am not about to try and persuade you otherwise. But can I give you some advice, while we are being serious with each other?"

Cassana sniffed and slipped away from his touch. Drawing in a faltering breath, she composed herself and nodded her head slightly.

"Please do, sir," she said, rubbing her left eye with the back of her hand.

"Very well," Arillion said, dropping his hands to his sides as he drew in a resigned breath.

"Your sense of duty and devotion to others, no

matter how well intended, may one day cost you your life, or one close to you; if you do not lose that stubborn streak."

Cassana's eyes narrowed as she fought back her anger and before she could snap at him, Arillion continued.

"I imagine that you will become a powerful woman one day, princess, and when that time comes, you will have to think with your head more than you will your heart."

"What do you mean by that?" Cassana said, barely controlling her anger. "Can I not think with my heart, as well as my head?"

"Perhaps," Arillion conceded. "But you are still young, impetuous even and there will be times when the right thing to do, is not necessarily the kindest thing to do!"

"So you are saying that I was wrong to help them," Cassana sighed, looking away.

"Honestly, princess? Yes," Arillion offered. "I can see why you would want to help them, but with everything that's happened recently, you did not look at the broader picture and by doing that, you put yourself in unnecessary danger!"

"I let my heart rule my head," Cassana stated, looking back at him. Arillion held her eyes and nodded.

"Don't get me wrong, princess," he said soothingly. "From the streets I come from, I admire that, I really do and especially as I care about nobody but myself."

"Really? I had never noticed that about you," Cassana cut in sarcastically.

Arillion ignored her. "You will just have to remember in future that you cannot help everyone. Nobody in this world can and-," he paused, choosing his words carefully. "not all people will be helping you because of their honour, or sense of loyalty!"

"Like you, you mean, sir?"

"Grow up," Arillion snapped, turning to leave, then hesitating. "You know exactly what my agenda is. I am doing this for the money, only...but have you ever stopped to think why Savinn Kassaar may have helped you?"

Cassana chewed on her bottom lip. "I, well, I guess because he heard I was in trouble and that he was the only person with the connections to help me."

"Don't be so narrow minded, princess," Arillion laughed, shaking his head. "He didn't risk getting involved in your affairs through any sense of decency. He did it for himself and nothing more."

"I do not understand," Cassana admitted, confused. "He must have risked a great deal to help me, and a lot of money, I would expect! Why would he do that, if he is a man of no honour?"

"Think about it," Arillion replied. "Savinn is a loyal supporter of the high duke, as is your father. Our merchant friend has become *very* rich over the last decade or so, because of his loyalty to the high duke. If anything was to ever happen to him, Savinn's lifestyle and standing may well suffer. There are many prominent members at the high duke's table who do not share in his love for peace, or agree with his proposal to trade with the Reven. Added to that, there are many more of them, who dislike the power that Savinn holds in the Four Vales."

Cassana stared blankly at Arillion for a time, finally blinking the realisation from her eyes. "So Savinn only helped me, so that I might return home and help maintain the strong support that my father gives to the high duke?"

Arillion nodded. "I would guess so! Whoever tried to kidnap you, and subsequently ordered your incarceration at the high duke's keep, probably wanted to use you as leverage, so that they could control your father in whatever storm there is coming!"

Cassana sighed, her mind drifting away to another time and place.

"You are not the first person to suggest that to me, sir," she said, before she could stop herself.

"My lady?" Arillion prompted curiously, as Cassana's mouth opened in shock.

Cassana shook her head and quickly changed the direction the conversation was taking. "So all of this, everything that has happened to me, and to that poor stonemason, is because of the political designs and ambitions of others?"

"I believe so, yes," Arillion said, deciding not to pursue the matter. "But I feel this may only be the beginning of it all."

Cassana shook her head incredulously. "I cannot believe what is happening to these lands, it is all too much for me to take in."

"I can understand that, princess," Arillion said with feeling. "Since the Reven War, the Four Vales have prospered peacefully. Why would anyone look to throw a rock into the water, or even want to?"

Cassana frowned. "I do not know, sir. My father may be able to offer his thoughts on the matter, but-,"

Arillion's eyes flashed mischievously as Cassana stopped in mid-sentence and stood looking at him with her mouth open.

"Which takes our serious little chat full circle, I believe, princess," Arillion said, bowing mockingly.

"Listen to your head, not your heart!"

Cassana clasped her hands before her, wringing them nervously. She studied Arillion for a time, watching as he straightened and paraded before her like a proud stag.

"I have done you a disservice, sir," she said finally. "I have taken you for a mercenary, a man without a thought beyond yourself and your own pocket!"

"And you were right," Arillion chuckled, nodding his head in proud agreement.

"Perhaps," Cassana said. "But there is more to you than meets the eye, Arillion. You see the world differently and more clearly than I ever will. I apologise if I have insulted you with my petulance and harsh words."

"Think nothing of it, my lady," Arillion said, shrugging his indifference. "We are from different sides of the coin, you and I, so it is to be expected."

He started walking back towards the camp, the conversation clearly over in his mind, then he stopped again and looked back.

"And thanks to you, I will soon, if we live long enough, have a lot more of those coins to fill my greedy little pockets with!"

Cassana shook her head in resignation as he walked away from her. She could have almost laughed at his audacity, almost...

If the previous day had been painful for Arillion, then the second day of travel westwards through Greywood Forest was excruciating. In the morning, the small party hardly made any progress, as Galen's condition worsened considerably. He no longer lost himself in the past as he struggled to even grasp hold of the present

430

and his frail body and mind were caught somewhere in between the two. He moaned constantly, having to stop to rest, or refusing to listen to his granddaughter when she hurried him back onto the donkey. As the day wore on, even Cassana's enthusiasm to help them to safety was beginning to wane and by late afternoon, she slipped casually back to walk with Arillion, who had remained quietly at the rear again, leading the horses.

"I can see why Karlina wanted to take her grandfather for help," Cassana said quietly, her eyes on the young girl.

Arillion stared at the girl, dutifully walking along at her grandfather's side, through the trees ahead of them. Sunlight spilled brightly through the tree cover today and the land was alive with its thanks. Outwardly, Karlina took everything that was happening to her grandfather with the same calm, smiling enthusiasm that only a devoted and loving granddaughter could. Karlina must have been worried, but she was mature enough and sensible beyond her years to mask her own emotions for him.

"His mind is dead," Arillion whispered, watching as the old man tried to get down off the donkey again. "His body just doesn't know it, yet!"

Cassana nodded her head, running a hand through her loose, tangled hair. She was exhausted again, the events of her ordeal still taking its toll on her. But since Arillion had rescued the girl and old man, she had been able to turn her attentions to someone else's plight, for a change. It had been a welcome distraction, but even the elation of having helped them was now beginning to drain her waning exhilaration.

"How long do you think we can avoid being found?" she dared to ask.

"At this rate, about a day," Arillion replied softly. There was no hint of anger in his voice, only a hint of resignation, as if he had come to terms with the fact.

Cassana moaned softly and touched Arillion's arm nervously. "I am sorry."

Arillion looked at her briefly, his eyes unreadable. He searched her face for a moment and then looked away.

"Don't be, princess," he said. "We have to live by the decisions we make, sometimes however, we also have to die by them."

Cassana's face paled and she removed her trembling hand from his strong arm. As she moved away to help Karlina, Arillion passed her the reins of her horse.

"Here, take this," he ordered her. "That'll give you something else to focus on, princess."

"I have so much to focus on," she said. "I don't know where to start!"

"Stop thinking about what will happen, when, if you get home," he snapped. "You can't do anything about it yet, and we are still a very long way from achieving that!"

"But I have to think about it," Cassana said defensively. "Who is the spy in my father's camp? How will I find out who it is? I do not know where to even start!"

Arillion did not respond, chastised by the fact that she *did* have a valid point. It was going to be someone close to her father, someone whose words spoke loud enough in his ear for him to listen. They picked separate paths down a heavily choked slope onto lower ground for a time, before joining back up with each other.

"Can I ask you something, sir?" Cassana asked him.

"If you must!"

She took in a deep breath. "May I acquire your services sir, when we reach Highwater?"

"Services?" Arillion enquired, raising one eyebrow curiously. "What kind of service did you want me for?"

"Well, it is delicate, I, it is, I mean to say," she looked away, cursing herself.

"You don't have to pay me anything for that," Arillion grinned, watching expectantly as she rounded angrily on him.

"You know very well I was not eluding to anything that you might be suggesting, sir," she said, putting enough emphasis and scorn on the word, *sir*.

"Of course I do," Arillion chuckled. "You really need to relax a bit, princess. You don't want any wrinkles at your age."

"Well, forgive me if I am a little bit tense at the moment," Cassana retorted sarcastically.

"I can take your mind off it for a while, if you like?"

Cassana screamed in silent frustration and led her horse away from him. She stomped after the girl and her grandfather, her body shaking angrily.

"I'll help you find out who's behind all this, but it'll cost you," Arillion called after her, sighing.

She turned back, surprise etched onto her tired face. "But how did you know what I would ask you, sir?"

"It was pretty obvious, really," Arillion admitted.

"Hmm," Cassana replied, flushing. "Am I that easy to read?"

"Only your front cover!" Arillion said, his eyes wandering over her body.

Cassana stiffened with embarrassment and looked away.

"Look, princess," Arillion said quickly, not wishing

another fight. "I know a lot of people you don't, in *your* city. If we get there eventually, and I emphasise *if*, I'll see what I can find out for you. But once I get you home, we cannot be seen together, do you understand?"

Cassana nodded dutifully. "Thank you, Arillion."

Arillion pulled down his scarf and grinned at her. "Don't thank me yet, my lady. We haven't discussed my fee, yet!"

Cassana nodded curtly and left him alone quickly, lest she lose herself in his face again.

Arillion tensed as he crouched low behind the protection of a tree and stared out into the unnerving darkness of the forest. It was now night and the meagre moonlight overhead filtered down through the thick canopy of the forest, revealing phantom images of his surroundings and the occasional glimpse of a night creature, as it darted hungrily about its dark domain. Somewhere off into the darkness, a pair of night birds called out to each other and a multitude of insects chattered noisily away, adding further discomfort to his watch. He couldn't put a finger on it, but something was wrong.

They had made camp early that day, when the old man became too ill to continue, without rest. Scouting ahead, Arillion found a tiny glade, surrounded by thick bushes and a dense huddle of oaks, that would provide suitable protection for the night. Everyone was exhausted from the drain of the day's events, and after a quiet, cold supper, they had all crawled onto their bedrolls and under blankets to sleep. Arillion had accepted the responsibility to take most of the watch that night, assuring Cassana that he would wake her before dawn. He was used to having little sleep, but even he was beginning to feel the effects of their journey and if he didn't get some rest, he would not be able to face what was inevitably coming.

Away into the darkness, one of the night birds called out in warning and its mate echoed its cry. Arillion remained still, listening to night as more and more warning cries rose up from the inhabitants of the forest. Bowing his head, Arillion slowly slid his swords from the sheaths on his back, and planted them blade-deep in the ground before him. As time crept on, the sound of the forest slipped away into silence, as its inhabitants scuttled and darted away to safety. Something was coming...

Arillion turned his hooded head and looked back at his companions. All slept soundly and if they were to survive the night, they would hopefully remain that way. The animals were also sleeping and he let out a slow, comforting breath in relief. He had chosen their campsite well, and it was quite possible that whatever was stalking them through the night could very well pass by their hiding place, without knowing they were even there. It was impossible to be tracked at night without torchlight and any hunting party worth their salt would not use light to give away their presence.

For what would have seemed an eternity to most, time slipped away agonizingly, as Arillion stared out into the night. As he had said to Cassana before, he was a patient man and it mattered little to him how long it took for him to locate what was out there, lurking in the blackness, looking for them.

Eventually, Arillion's patience was rewarded, as his keen ears detected a subtle shift in the silence of his immediate surroundings. Closing his eyes, he drew in the silence, filtering through it to pick out the sound of careful, distant footfalls. Drawn by the sounds, he opened his eyes and looked towards the south-east. The haunting darkness before him offered him little clue for many minutes, as he searched the forest for signs of their pursuers and just when he thought he was mistaken, he spotted two dark forms, picking their way silently through the night, thirty feet or so away from his sentry position.

Arillion followed them as they moved closer and as he reached out to touch the hilts of his weapons, they stopped, bending low to confer. He could hear the faint whisper of conversation, as they shared their thoughts, and then they rose and came closer still. Sliding his hands slowly around to grasp the hilts, Arillion could tell now that they were heavily cloaked and carried bows. As he watched them, Arillion became aware of the steady sounds of approach and he looked towards the south. There was nothing there and he flicked his eyes back to the two dark shapes, twenty feet away. Again he heard a noise and he suddenly realised that it was actually the beating of his own heart, pounding away worriedly in his chest. He was normally in firm control of his emotions and the strange sensation caught him off guard as he almost forgot about the imminent danger.

Damn you woman, he snarled angrily. He had someone other than himself to worry about now and until that moment, he had not realised how much she had gotten under his skin. Or how much the thought of anything happening to her actually affected him.

This strange, new fear increased as the two shapes began to move past his hiding place towards the north-west. As they passed quietly by him, Arillion became aware of two more dark shapes, following through the darkness after them. The party of four passed by slowly, completely oblivious to his presence and yet assured and familiar with the terrain they travelled through. As they passed by, their quiet footfalls in time to his own fear, Arillion looked back towards his camp. As if prompted by the Father of Storms, Galen shifted in his sleep.

Arillion held his breath and turned reluctantly back. Their pursuers carried on their way, having apparently not heard and Arillion let out a silent prayer of thanks. As the four black shapes were slowly lost to the night, Arillion contemplated following them. He could take the two at the back down, before the others even realised it. But was it worth the risk? As he chewed over his dilemma, he felt his senses prick with worry again and to his horror, he soon detected four more dark shapes, creeping through the night on the other side of their camp. Pulling his blades from the earth, Arillion hid them under his cloak and padded silently over to the far side of the camp to observe them. They were further away than the other group had been and he viewed their passing with some relief. His caution for Cassana's safety and his promised payment had stayed his hand. If he had decided to attack the first group, he would have quickly found himself outnumbered.

Sighing in relief, he remained where he was until the forest wildlife returned to calm his fears. Arillion trudged back to his original sentry position and slid down the trunk of the tree to rest. They had been extremely fortunate! A few feet more and they would have found the camp. The thought terrified him, and he wasn't afraid to admit it. Every footstep they had come closer, was like someone reaching into the purse of his reward to take out another handful of coins.

Arillion scowled and looked over at the sleeping bundle that was Cassana. He sighed and shook his head. Why did he like her so much? They had nothing in common and probably never would. For years now, he had guarded himself against his emotions, cloaking himself in shadows, to hide away from himself. He had only ever had feelings before for one person and she had shattered his heart with her betrayal. Since that day, he had closed his emotions down, hiding them away behind his mask. If possible, he had become more ruthless after that; taking what and who he could, without thought of his actions. He had taken any job he could, throwing himself into his work and enforcing his reputation. After his heart was broken, he had paid coin to be with women, so that he did not become emotionally attached to anyone. He could release his urges then, without having to make any commitment or small talk afterwards. He had chosen this path and was comfortable with who and what he had become... that was until Savinn had asked him to rescue Cassana.

He shook his head, listening to the cold fear that squeezed his heart. Nothing good would come of this. Fate seemed to stalk him through his life, snatching anything that meant something to him away from him before he could find happiness. Perhaps he should just get her home, and then disappear. It would be better for her as she, it seemed at least, had some purpose in her life. The sudden image of the outlaws descending on them filled his mind and he shuddered as he saw one of them drive a blade deep into Cassana's breast. Scowling, he banished that dark image from his mind and looked up at the new moon, obscured by the branches of the trees and the dark clouds that sped past, caressing its luminous beauty. They had been lucky this time, but Arillion knew that if they carried on towards Colden, they would be found.

Sighing deeply, he rose purposefully and looked about the camp. Everyone and thing was sound asleep and he let his breath out. Stepping through his misty breath he crossed silently over to where Karlina and Galen slept beside each other. The pretty girl was buried deep under her blanket and the only evidence she was there, was the wild tangle of her beautiful deep red hair, snaking out from underneath. Galen, however, was thrashing slowly now, moaning at the demons plaguing his dreams.

Kneeling down beside the old man, Arillion reached out with his right hand and tenderly brushed his wispy hair from out of his eyes. The old man stirred at his gentle touch and subconsciously turned away from him in his sleep.

"Forgive me," Arillion whispered softly, covering the old man's mouth and nose with his hands.

CHAPTER TWENTY

Defiance

The elegant study was cloaked in oppressive shadows that drowned the magnificence of the room in a heavy, brooding silence. A silver candelabra rested on one corner of the huge writing desk in the centre of the room, its flickering candlelights choked by the dark night outside that appeared to reach through an open window to extinguish them. Defiant in the meagre draught that stole occasionally into the room and attempted to gather up the parchments scattered across the desk's surface, the flames sputtered angrily, casting fresh life into the dark corners of the study.

The man sat forward at the noise, laying the parchment in his large hand onto the polished cedar wood. Sighing deeply, he slumped back in the high-backed chair and stared into the dancing flames of the candles. Shaking his head, he closed his eyes and searched his mind for answers, having not found any yet that he cared to listen to. Resting his left elbow on the arm of the chair, he groaned and massaged his temples with his hand. He could feel the start of yet another headache and he tried to blank it out by thinking of the coming day, no more than several hours away now.

For many years as the Voice of the Valian Council and presiding ruler of the Four Vales, he had striven to keep a firm grip on the legacy of peace that he had inherited from his late father and his allies. Their sacrifices that fateful day, nearly fifty years ago now, had ensured that any threat of invasion from the united Reven clans was snuffed out; crushed beneath the determined boots of the Valian forces that smashed the fragile unity of the surviving clans and scattered them to the hills and mountains they had marched so confidently down from.

Since then, the Four Vales had prospered. Its people had thrived and a long period of peace had ensued. Trade with the Redani people had also begun and the wealth of the capital's coffers had increased. Taxes, previously raised to fund the campaign against the Reven, had been halved and with more coin to put food into their bellies, the Valian people basked in the safety and harmony of this new era. On his death bed his father, Valan Stromn, had warned his son that there would be those who would seek to test his mettle, probing at the walls of his resolve for a continuance of peace with their neighbours across the mountains. He warned his son that they would whisper cautious words in his ear, hoping to lend credence towards their argument to raise an army and finish off the Reven people once and for all. His father had resisted those very calls from the same hard-liners, following their victory, saying "We have split them asunder this day and taught them a lesson they will never forget. We have defended our homeland honourably – I will not force them to defend theirs and lessen our achievements."

That had settled any open challenges to his father's decision, but he had known, even back then, that they would come again - once their greed and boredom turned their heads northwards towards the rich minerals, laying dormant in the hills and mountains of the Reven lands. His father had warned him so, and after he succeeded his father, they had indeed tested his mettle. Naturally, the new high duke had refused their counsel, honouring his father's wishes and ultimately sharing in his beliefs. The Reven people were clearly beaten. A broken nation, divided by their civil war, as the clans fought for the remnants of Reven Skarl's table. They would not unite again in his lifetime, could not whilst the chieftains fought for a power that was no longer there to control. And while they fought amongst themselves, their people starved and the land suffered.

As his stewardship continued, the newly appointed high duke had gained the respect and devotion of his people. His popularity and reputation for fairness was also a sign of his underlying strength. Those who chose to break the law would be punished, those who led an honest life would be cherished by the authorities and protected. Taxes were kept low to allow people to raise themselves above the poverty line and in doing so, the high duke had managed to increase his standing with the majority of citizens. He had even managed to silence the dissenting voices on the council and as some of the older, more robust members died from old age, he had managed to appoint people to the table, whom he hoped would share a common interest in his desire for peace.

"Where did I go wrong then?" the high duke asked himself, as he continued to massage his head.

Opening his eyes, he reached out with his other hand and picked up the parchment again, reading the words written there for the third time. Chancellor Valus had penned an excellent speech for him, the tone concise and yet laced with a defiant message to those who would seek to threaten his family. Ever since the threat was received, two days before the next Valian Council was scheduled to meet, he had hidden himself away at a secure location. It was the first declaration of hostility against his rule in over twenty years, and it had been a chastening experience for him. His initial, understandable desire to protect his wife and two children had now been replaced by a controlled anger that hardened his resolve to find the people responsible and bring them to swift justice.

His fears had been confirmed soon after, when the chancellor had come to him with the grim news about the initial plot to kidnap Lord Byron's daughter, Cassana. Not only had an attempt been made to abduct her on her journey to the capital, but it transpired, more worryingly, that there were those within his own walls, that sought to aid in the plot. Before her mysterious disappearance, the young lady had reported to the chancellor that the Reven had tried to abduct her. Reven? It was sobering, worrying news, that, should word ever get out into the public arena, would leave his proposed plans to trade with the Reven people, in tatters. Although the girl was missing, and three members of the chancellor's own staff appeared to be colluding with them, Relan Valus had remained strong. Despite concern for his own safety, the chancellor had promised that any news about the Reven involvement in the plot, would be kept a secret. As far as the other members of the council were concerned, the threat against them all was from a group of anarchists, who sought only to destabilise the peace and prosperity of the Four Vales. The speech the chancellor had written for him made it eloquently clear that nothing would be gained from this dishonourable threat made against him and his council members. Resolute, they would stand firm against them and when the people behind this threat were eventually caught, they would be publicly hanged as a warning for all to see.

Of course, they still had no tangible intelligence to suggest who was actually aiding these Reven insurgents, other than the three people who went missing with Lady Byron. But this woman, Madam Grey seemed to be the one behind the second, and apparently, successful abduction and, until the group made their demands clear, their anonymity would remain intact. Whilst they retained their ominous silence, his men would continue with their covert investigations, as they sought to locate and rescue the girl.

The high duke shook his head sadly. Alion Byron had put great faith in his daughter by sending her to the capital, in his stead. Some of the council members had thought it a foolhardy decision, but the high duke had already known this day would come. His friend had confided to him at their last meeting that he wished for his child to take over his council duties for him, one day soon. He fully expected Lord Byron to arrive in the city within the next few weeks, once the personal letters he had sent to him had arrived. The high duke swallowed down his sadness and closed his eyes. Alion Byron was his strongest ally, and his closest friend had never really recovered from the death of his wife. If he had also lost his daughter, he would never be able to forgive himself. Images of the high duke's own daughter flashed vividly before his eyes and the thought of losing her wrenched the heart from his chest and strengthened his resolve to get to the bottom of this mess.

A knock on the door of his study roused him from his morose thoughts and he straightened in his seat.

"Come," he commanded, his voice echoing across the cold room.

The door opened obediently and Chancellor Valus slipped from the light of the hallway beyond and past the guard who granted him entry into the study.

"My lord," the chancellor greeted him, as the guard closed the door behind him. His sandaled feet scraped across the marble floor, silenced briefly by a large bearskin rug, as he crossed the room to stand before him.

"Relan, my friend," the high duke responded, directing him to sit in one of the chairs across the desk from him.

The chancellor thanked him and sat in the chair with a deep sigh. He looked exhausted! His face was lined with worry and the strain of recent events was clearly starting to take its toll on him. The familiar blue robes of his office hung from his sharp shoulders and his gaunt frame looked thinner than the last time he had seen him.

"A fine speech, Relan," the high duke said, tossing the parchment back on the desk. "It conveys my desire and determination with eloquent efficiency."

"Thank you, my lord," the chancellor replied, bowing his head humbly. "The plans for your public address are already in place, as you requested. You will go before the masses at noon tomorrow, my lord."

"Excellent work, chancellor," the high duke said with a thin smile. He reached out a huge hand across the table and Relan accepted it graciously. "Has Captain Varl organised the security, as I asked him to?"

"Yes, my lord," the chancellor replied. "Low key and yet strong in their numbers. We will have a small detachment of guards around the podium, but the main contingent of his men will be in the crowd, dressed as citizens."

"Good, good," the high duke mused, stroking his broad unshaven chin thoughtfully. "Have him sent up to me, once we are done, would you?"

"As you wish, my lord," the chancellor acknowledged, watching as the large man across from him reached down into one of the desk's cabinet doors and produced a decanter of brandy and two glasses.

"No thank you, my lord," Relan said quickly. "I must rest on a clear head, as I fear tomorrow will prove to be a long day for us all."

The high duke stared at the glasses in his hands and nodded his head. "You are right, as always my friend. I seek to dull my headache with brandy, when I should be conserving my strength."

"If you would permit me, my lord?" the chancellor began, smiling nervously as he waited for the high duke to nod his accord. "You look exhausted, and your staff tell me that you have not slept well this last week? If this is true, I think you should try to put aside your concerns for several hours, so that you can at least take some rest and be ready for tomorrow."

The high duke smiled. "What would I do without you, Relan? You are right, of course."

"My lord, you are too kind," the chancellor responded modestly.

The high duke shook his head in disagreement. "I know there is still much we have to do, but, in this state, I will be of no use to anyone, especially Alion's daughter."

Relan Valus swallowed and twisted his hands nervously under the desk. "Understandable, my lord. And, for my part, I am still ashamed that such an affront should occur unnoticed before my own, unseeing eyes. It may sound callous, but we can do no more for her at the moment. There have been no demands made, no word of why they even took her. Until that time comes, we must allow Captain Varl's men to do their work and see what transpires."

"I know, Relan, I know," the high duke sighed reluctantly, waving away the chancellor's apology. "Do not seek to blame yourself, none of us could have foreseen this and we should only attribute blame to those responsible."

"My lord is too kind," Relan replied, his eyes lowering in gratitude. Under the desk he wrung his hands tightly. "With your wife and children safely moved, perhaps I can offer you something that might help you relax and take a good night's sleep?"

The high duke watched him curiously. "Go on."

"I, too have been worried for the safety of my family," the chancellor began, his thin face gaunt and troubled. "But I have been drinking a herbal tea before going to sleep at night, I have found it to be a very good aid for sleeping and it also helps to curb my anxiety, at this most stressful of times."

The high duke regarded him thoughtfully and Relan shrank under the scrutiny of his piercing, deep green eyes.

"My mother passed down the recipe from her

grandfather," Relan added hastily. "She said it helped her to cope with my brother and I, when we were growing up."

Despite the well documented shame brought upon the Valus family name by Relan's estranged brother and the chancellor's uneasiness whenever he mentioned him, the high duke still managed a laugh, shaking off some of his sombreness with a firm nod of his head.

"It sounds like just what I need, my friend," he said, smiling. "Could you have some sent up to me, before you retire for the night?"

"Of course, my lord," the chancellor said, smiling. "In fact, I will see to it personally for you."

"You are too kind," the high duke said, waving him away. "Bring some to me, if you would? I am suddenly keen for my bed. We can discuss the re-arrangement of the council meeting another time."

Chancellor Valus rose, bowing slightly. "I will send for Captain Varl and bring you your tea, before you retire, my lord!"

"Wait," the high duke said, staying the chancellor with the tone in his voice, as he turned to leave.

Relan Valus turned, regarding the tall man sat in the chair before him. His proud, strong face betrayed the weakness his current predicament placed him in and his long dark hair looked unkempt, peculiar for a man who was usually so immaculately presented. He was dressed in a luxurious, silk night gown of the darkest green, the same one he had been wearing when the chancellor had delivered his speech to him that morning, and his usually broad shoulders hung low under the pressure that was weighing down heavily upon him. The chancellor barely managed to stop the triumph from stealing into his own eyes. Everything was working out perfectly for him. It hadn't felt like it a couple of days ago, but it appeared that the Father of Storms had turned his head towards him, once again.

"My lord?"

The high duke scratched his large, sloping nose. "Send a message of regret to Captain Varl for me, would you? Please apologise in advance for me and ask him to attend to me in the morning instead, if you would be so kind?"

"Of course, my lord," the chancellor replied, turning away to hide his grin.

The high duke watched the chancellor leave and when the door had closed softly behind him, he sighed deeply, burying his head in his hands. His exhaustion was threatening to overcome him now and he couldn't think past his last thought, let alone consider the possibilities of the speech tomorrow. It was a show of defiance, one that needed to be taken and, with his family being protected at a secret location now, he could devote all of his time to re-establishing his control. The marble halls and corridors of the keep were awash with idle gossip and misplaced speculation. He needed to silence these rumours before they got out of hand and undermined his efforts to get to the truth of the matter. The high duke had even tried to spend some time alone in the Moon Tower, hoping that the solace of the restricted structure would allow him the peace he needed to think and reflect on what the best course of action would be. Even there however, the sounds of the city below had called up to him, dragging his attention away from his heavy thoughts...

Against his better judgement, he poured himself a quick glass of brandy and downed it before the chancellor returned. Hopefully this tea would, indeed, take the edge off his anxiety and help him to get a good night's sleep. He certainly needed it! Relan had been an invaluable ally to him down the years and his assistance in the past few days had kept him focused, helping him to steady his mind. He would have to remember this, once the dust had settled. He owed the chancellor a great debt of gratitude and he knew that it was one the modest Chancellor Valus would not wish to claim. For now, the best way he could repay Relan was to remain strong. He could think of a way to repay him for his loyalty at a later, calmer stage. His captain, the loyal and dutiful Lucien Varl, had served him tirelessly the last few years, and had proved his worth the last week, above and beyond the call of duty. He, too, would have to be rewarded for his loyal service, and, although he had been vocal in his dislike for the chancellor on several occasions, the two of them had worked well together recently, surprisingly putting aside their rivalry for the time being. When *all* of the dust had finally settled, perhaps the two of them could put their differences to bed, once and for all.

Relan Valus was also thinking of the erstwhile captain, as his messenger headed down the long hall, away from him, bearing the sarcastic message that he knew would infuriate the young upstart. From the moment he had taken over from the last captain of the high duke's personal guard, Lucien Varl had opposed him whenever he could. The man was a fool, lost in the trappings of a forgotten age, his every breath guided by his misplaced sense of honour and duty. An ambitious politician and a dutiful captain! They had disliked each other immediately and Relan had promised himself that when his master's plans came to fruition, the captain would be the first to die.

Smiling at the thought, the chancellor quickly headed down to the keep's main kitchens, gathering together a small teapot and the necessary herbs and ingredients for the high duke's tea. It was late and the kitchens were empty now, the silence of the keep broken occasionally by the laughter resonating from the nearby staff quarters. Boiling some water on a wood-burning stove, the chancellor added his ingredients to the brew. Stirring it vigorously for several minutes, he added some chamomile leaves to finish it off. Sniffing deeply, he sighed in contentment, before looking around the deserted kitchens guardedly.

Satisfied he was alone, the chancellor lifted the green gemstone up off the gold ring he wore on his right forefinger. There was a tiny compartment under the stone and it contained some yellow powder. Grinning, he took a very small pinch of the powder and stirred it slowly into the herbal tea. Putting the gemstone back into place he picked up a silver tray, placing the teapot and a cup upon it. Turning, the chancellor made his way back to the high duke's private study, an eager purpose to his steps. The powder would not have any noticeable effects upon him at first, but given the same dosage over a period of weeks, the high duke's anxiety would actually start to increase, making him more paranoid about the events that would, by then, be unfolding around him. The Kestrel would be furious that he had taken these decisive steps without waiting to consult their brethren, but he was sure that they would understand the importance of this opportunity.

Relan Valus smiled. The storm was finally coming and he was about to set the pendulum into motion...

CHAPTER TWENTY ONE

To Those We Leave Behind

Cassana yawned as she attempted to rub the sleep from her eyes. It was a futile attempt that only served to remind her how tired she really was and of how disgusting she felt. Her hair felt terrible and she was sure that once they were finally free of the cursed forest and its smells, she would discover that she too, smelled terrible. Used to taking daily baths back home, it was a galling thought and she made a mental note to question Arillion about their proposed route when he woke. She just wanted to get home now and the thought of another couple of weeks, traipsing about the Four Vales, left her cold. She looked for the man in question and could see that he was still asleep, lost in the shadows and mist of the tree that he had chosen for the night. He was wrapped tightly in his dark cloak and his hooded head was bowed, as he rested with his back against the trunk. He had woke her quietly for her watch, deep into the night and had slipped away to catch some rest without a word to her.

Cassana's thoughts were disturbed as she heard Squirrel stir. She looked for her through the early dawn light and smiled, as she saw the tangled red mess of hair raise up briefly and then slump back down again with a groan. Finally however, the girl remembered her responsibilities and she lifted up her head again, looking about her surroundings with bleary eyes that lolled heavily.

"Good morning," Cassana greeted her softly.

"Uh, yes, hello," Karlina responded, moaning as she struggled to sit up. They shared a smile and Cassana watched fondly as the girl turned and placed a gentle hand on her grandfather's shoulder.

"Grandpa," she whispered in his ear, shaking him gently.

Cassana had seen the old man start in panic the previous morning, when Arillion had roused him from his sleep with an impatient clap in his ear. Galen had been confused and terrified by the sudden noise and it had taken them a long time to calm him down. Arillion had glared at her as he stalked by, muttering away to himself angrily.

"Grandfather?" Karlina said again, shaking him a little bit harder this time. "We have to get ready, we should reach Colden today! Come on, up you get."

The girl looked towards Cassana, a puzzled look on her face as she shook the old man again.

"Wake up!"

Cassana rose worriedly and crossed over to the couple, a cold chill working its way up her spine. Was it her, or had the morning suddenly become colder? Karlina was starting to panic now and she looked up at Cassana, her eyes wide with worry.

"Keep it down there, Red," Arillion growled,

stretching the night from his body. Both women ignored him and Cassana knelt hurriedly beside the old man. He looked asleep and he had a serene expression on his gnarled features.

"Galen," she said, as she reached out to touch his face. She shuddered, an involuntary gasp escaping her lips, as she withdrew her hand quickly.

His skin was ice-cold...

"Arillion," Cassana called out.

"What's up with him now?" he complained bitterly, as he wandered over to stand behind her.

Cassana looked round at him, her eyes filled with fear and worry. She shook her head and looked quickly at Karlina. The girl was watching her, searching her face for answers.

"No," she begged her, shaking her head in disbelief. "No, please, not now!"

Karlina looked down at her grandfather and shuddered, throwing herself upon him. Sobbing heavily, she wailed as her emotions overcame her. Cassana tried to comfort her, but Karlina ignored her, shrugging her off angrily as she buried her head in the old man's chest.

"Grandfather," she cried. "Don't leave me."

Arillion winced, looking worriedly at the forest around him. The outlaws' who had passed the camp, late last night, were probably far away now, waiting for them on the western fringes of the forest. But if they were still nearby, they would be drawn to their hiding place like flies around...

Arillion shook his head. Perhaps he should have done them both? He quickly dismissed that idea. The girl was a bright young thing, with the fire and attitude to match her hair. She deserved more in life and by getting rid of the old man, he had also released the girl from a heavy burden. She might not feel like thanking him now, but in a few years time, when she was being courted by every hot-blooded male in her village, she would not want an old man dribbling and drooling away, distracting her. Arillion watched as Cassana pulled the hysterical girl off her grandfather's body.

Actually, he thought. *Come back in a few years time Red and I might be interested, too!*

"Get her to calm down, princess," he hissed, glaring at the girl, as she sniffed and choked on her emotions, sobbing into Cassana's shoulder.

Cassana looked up at him and nodded, tears running freely down her own cheeks. Shepherding the girl away, Arillion knelt beside the old man again and bowed his head. There was no stain of guilt on his conscience, no remnant of sorrow for his actions. In fact, he had done everyone here a service, especially the old man. Arillion touched the old man's throat to show that he was checking what he already knew, and then made a show of shaking his head. The old man must have been suffering terribly. Stuck in a mind lost in the past and trying to keep up with the present. It was a horrible way for a man to end his days, where was the justice in that? Shaking his head, Arillion rose and looked down at the old man.

"I will not see your age," Arillion suspected, sighing. "Be at peace, Galen Roe!"

Cassana watched as she held on dearly to the struggling girl in her arms. Arillion looked genuinely saddened by the old man's death and she felt touched, as she watched him kneel again, to pull a blanket up over the body.

"Is he really dead?" Karlina sniffed, raising her head

to look at Cassana, her eyes reddened and her face streaked by tears.

"Yes, Karlina," Cassana replied gently. "I am so sorry!"

Karlina broke down again and Cassana pulled her into her arms, stroking her hair as she soothed her with soft words. Arillion watched them for a moment, his eyes narrowed with thought, before he began to start packing up their camp. When he was finished, he tended to the horses. Afterwards, he moved over to the two females and crouched beside them both.

"My lady?" Arillion said, touching her on one shoulder.

Cassana looked back at him. "What will happen now?"

Arillion shrugged. "We must be going, we are vulnerable and in danger here."

"What about my grandfather?" Karlina asked. She looked at Arillion with defiant eyes and anger in her voice.

"He is at peace now, Red," Arillion replied. "We have to leave though, we cannot take the time to bury him, so you must say your goodbyes."

Karlina looked blankly at him and he could see the fire burning in her eyes. She rose up from Cassana's embrace and walked timidly over to her grandfather. Cassana stood up with Arillion and they watched as the girl knelt down and pulled the blanket off her grandfather. Whispering soft, private words, Karlina leant down and kissed her grandfather's forehead.

"She has spirit, that one," Arillion observed, as they looked respectfully away.

Cassana wiped her eyes and nodded. "What will happen to her now, Arillion?" she asked hesitantly.

"She has no family now, and nowhere to go except back home."

"Well we are not turning back, princess," Arillion promised her.

"I know that," Cassana growled. "So what do you suggest?"

"We cannot carry on towards the west," Arillion whispered. "Last night the outlaws' passed by our camp and it is a miracle that we are not all dead this morning, like the old man."

"How many of them were there?" Cassana dared to ask.

"Eight," Arillion responded grimly.

Cassana gasped and looked about her surroundings worriedly. They could not fight them all with their small numbers and her immediate concern, above the worry for her own safety, was for Karlina.

She cursed herself angrily. Arillion had been right about everything, as usual.

"I will pay you another two thousand crowns, if you allow her to come with us, sir?" she said softly.

Arillion shook his head. "Not a chance!"

Cassana glared at him. "We cannot send her home, and you yourself have said that the outlaws are nearby. So she has to come with us now!"

"Did you not listen to a word I said to you?" Arillion demanded.

Cassana stood up to him and nodded. "Yes, I did. But this *is* the right thing to do as she has nobody left. I am taking her with me sir, if you still wish to protect me and claim your reward, then you must accept my decision."

"Oh," Arillion chuckled. "Must I now?"

"Yes, you must," Cassana growled, hands on her

hips.

Arillion searched her eyes, losing himself in them for a time. He scowled for a moment, then shook his head ruefully. "Very well, princess," he sighed. "But I want that extra two thousand."

"And you shall have it, sir," Cassana acknowledged triumphantly.

"I hope you have a lot of money hidden away, princess," Arillion said evenly. "At this rate, by the time this journey is done, you will owe me a small fortune."

"Do not concern yourself with my affairs, sir," Cassana hissed. "I have enough wealth to honour our agreement, be sure of that!"

"That's good enough for me, princess," Arillion winked. "How about a kiss to seal the agreement?"

Cassana shook her head and walked away from him. Arillion watched her body hungrily as she strode away and listened impatiently as Cassana told the girl the *good* news.

"I can come with you?" Karlina asked in disbelief. "With you, to the city?"

Cassana reached across to wipe tears from the girl's cheeks and smiled. "Yes, Karli. You can come and stay with me, if you like?"

Karlina blinked in disbelief, looking down at her grandfather. "But what about grandfather? We can't just leave him here?"

Cassana nodded, looking for their protector. "Arillion?"

Arillion strode across to stand with them. "I will lay your grandfather in the woods for you, girl," he said gently. "I'll cover his body as best I can."

Karlina nodded, fresh tears spilling down her cheeks. She kissed the old man on the cheek and allowed Cassana to lead her away.

"I love you, grandpa," she sobbed. "I am going to miss you! Thank you for looking after me...and Flotsam says goodbye, too!"

Arillion left the females to weep amongst themselves as he swept the old man up into his arms. He carried him from the camp and headed west into the woods, finding a suitable spot amongst the thick, dense undergrowth. Using the crescent blade, he cut down several branches and covered the blanketed body with them, before scattering fallen leaves over the top.

"No hard feelings, grandpa," he said softly, laying the old man's stick on his grave. Turning, he hurried back through the early dawn light to try and make up for lost time.

After a hurried, cold breakfast, Arillion led his charges towards the north-east for the better part of the morning. By the time the dense forest was warm from the high sun overhead, they had made more progress in those few short hours, than they had made during the entire travel of the previous day. Compared to the last few days, Arillion's mood had improved drastically and despite his building anxiety, he was confident that they would put any danger they may have once faced far behind them.

Arillion quietly led his horse through the twisting tangle of trees, angrily swatting away the black flies that constantly circled about his head. In front of him, Cassana led them through the thick forest, Karlina following dutifully behind, riding Flotsam and lost deep within her own grief. The girl had said nothing all morning, which pleased Arillion immensely as it meant that their journey was made in absolute silence, free from any irksome chatter. Occasionally, Cassana would enquire on how she was holding up and the red-haired youth would simply nod, sniffing out words that Arillion could not hear.

As he swept his gaze around his surroundings, Cassana dropped back to walk alongside him, their mounts tossing their heads in greeting to one another.

"It is getting warm, is it not?" Cassana observed, her face glistening with sweat.

"Summer is finally here," Arillion said, flicking a swift look at her. "What's on your mind, princess?"

Cassana frowned. "What makes you think I was going to ask you anything, sir?"

"Because you have had all morning to talk about the weather," Arillion observed, looking away. "So?"

Cassana scowled at him. "Why can you never make things easy for me?"

"Because that would be boring," Arillion chuckled.

Cassana sighed and fell silent for a moment, before turning her attention back to him again. "Where are we heading, once we are free of the forest?"

"I wondered when you would ask me that," Arillion said, swatting some more flies aside.

"And?"

Arillion sighed, realising he would get no peace until he told her the truth. "We are going to head to the north-east for the next couple of days, before turning north!"

Cassana searched her mind for a mental image of their route. "So that would take us, let me see, across the Crystal River, just to the north of the Sunset Hills?"

"Very good," Arillion said, his voice condescending.

Cassana glared at him. "A simple yes would have sufficed, sir!"

Arillion shrugged as they were separated by the forest for a few moments. "We will cross the river and head, for the next few days, towards the foothills of the Great Divide. From there, we will take a little known trail up into the mountains, known to scoundrels like me as Smuggler's Gap."

"The mountains?" Cassana said, worry in her voice.

Arillion glanced at her and then lifted his eyes towards the sky. "Uh oh, I forgot you are scared of heights."

"Can we not just head along the foothills, towards Highwater?" she asked hopefully. "We can gain entry into the city, before anything can happen to us!"

Arillion was already shaking his head. "The main routes into the city will be watched, we would be attacked long before we reached the safety of those walls."

"But we do not have any climbing gear," Cassana pointed out, clinging on to anything she could use to back up her protests. The thought of hiking into the mountains left her cold, and if she could persuade Arillion to change his mind, she would feel a lot better for it.

"Smuggler's Gap is a narrow crevice that snakes up through the mountains and comes out near Highwater Lake," Arillion continued. "It has been used for many years now, by people seeking to cross into the Reven lands and by immigrants, hoping to find a better life on this side of the mountains."

"So the trail is enclosed?"

"Ahem, not exactly," Arillion said, smiling to himself. "There is a point for several hundred paces, where the trail comes out onto a narrow ledge. You will have to keep your eyes on your footing for quite some time, as there is a sheer drop on the other side."

Cassana paled visibly beside him and he chuckled, adding some colour quickly back into her cheeks.

"Please do not mock me, sir," Cassana snapped furiously. "I cannot help the way I am! The thought of such a journey fills me with terror. There must be another way we can go?"

"There is," Arillion agreed. "But this will take us into the city, from the north. We will come out onto the Reven Pass, a few miles south of The High Fortress. From there, we can head down the pass and into the city, without being seen. Nobody will be expecting us to journey that way, especially if they are aware of your fear of heights."

Cassana didn't look at all convinced as her mind teased her with images of a treacherous trail that looked out across a misty, perilous chasm and threatened to drop her into the stony jaws of a terrible, certain death with every step she took. She had been to the Highwater Lake, many times before, whilst out hunting with her father. The natural lake could be found deep in the heights of the Great Divide and it was said that its waters were the source of the Crystal and Haven rivers. The Reven Pass was the main route north from the city, which led up into the mountains towards the great fortress that had been built to protect the Four Vales from the threat of Reven invasion, some fifty years before. Surrounded on all sides by hundreds of feet of sheer, solid rock, Cassana could make the journey to the lake, without ever experiencing her fear of falling. But this way, the way Arillion was suggesting they take, sounded frightful.

Arillion read the turmoil in her eyes and placed a comforting hand on her shoulder. "Trust me, my lady.

It will be worth the trek. The less people that know you have returned home, the easier it will be for us to find the traitor in your father's camp."

"My arrival in Karick was fairly inconspicuous," Cassana pointed out. "And we both know what happened there, do we not?"

"Point taken," Arillion conceded, squeezing her shoulder sympathetically.

Cassana felt her heart race at his continuing touch and the fear that had cooled her sweating body, was quickly replaced by the warmth of a different sensation. Arillion removed his hand and looked ahead, watching Squirrel as she bounced up and down on the back of Flotsam. He sighed.

"I just ask that you trust me on this one, princess," Arillion said quietly. "I have had many dealings with the type of people who may be behind all of this, and I also know the lengths that they will be prepared to go to. There is no telling how deep this poisonous plot runs and we should do all that we can to avoid its bite, again!"

Cassana listened to her pounding heart for a while, before wiping her sweating brow. "Very well, sir," she said reluctantly. "I will trust your judgement and do all I can to conquer my fears."

"Good girl," Arillion said happily. "I'll be there to help you, so don't worry your pretty little head. You can hold onto me as tightly as you like!"

Cassana blushed and looked away again, listening to the excitement of her heart. "Thank you, Arillion."

The dark figure beside her paused suddenly, and Cassana wandered on for a few moments, before realising he had stopped. She looked back to find that he was staring back through the trees behind them, his head cocked to one side as he scanned the forest cautiously.

"What is-,"

Arillion's head snapped round as he held a finger to his masked face, his eyes blazing away furiously at her. Turning his attentions back to their surroundings, he listened for many moments, his head bowed in concentration. Finally, when Cassana could not bear the tension any longer, he turned and led his horse quickly back to her again.

"I think we are being followed," he whispered, his eyes narrowed with concern.

Cassana glanced worriedly into the trees behind them, before looking hastily for Karlina. They could hardly see her now and as they both hurried to catch her up, they began to notice the ominous silence that had descended upon an expectant forest.

"RIDE!" Arillion hissed suddenly, as he pulled himself up into his saddle.

Cassana leapt swiftly into her saddle and kicking her heels into her mount's flanks, she hurried off through the treacherous forest after Karlina. Arillion turned his horse full circle to look back through the tall trees, before quickly giving chase.

Behind Arillion, several dark shapes slipped suddenly into view and raced swiftly through the forest after him.

Karlina allowed Flotsam to bear her through the forest without any guidance, as her mind reeled from the shock of her grandfather's death. It was a terrible thing for her to have to cope with and any thoughts she could muster were numb with fear and ravaged by her enormous sense of loss. Galen was everything to her.

He had cared for her when her parents had died and over the coming years, as she matured, her grandfather had been there to help her cope with her loss and sense of loneliness. He was like a father to her, the one person she could run to when she was feeling scared, or listen to when she was in need of advice. He had been strong for her all these years, caring and providing for her until the time came when his illness required that his granddaughter return the favour. Karlina had done so out of devotion and without question. She hadn't cared that her friends played outside, whilst she was stuck indoors, caring and cleaning up after her frail grandfather. She loved him dearly. He was the mother and father that her mind was beginning to forget, as she grew older and lost a hold on her childhood memories.

It was because of this, that her fragile mind was plagued by conflicting emotions. There was a deep hole yawning in the pit of her stomach, one that no amount of sorrow and tears could fill. But even as she mourned the loss of her grandfather, another strange and guilty sensation overcame her. She actually felt alive again, as if someone had lifted a terrible weight from her young shoulders. Until this morning, she had not realised that the weight of responsibility was even there...

Karlina wiped the fresh tears from her eyes and swallowed her guilt. Her grandfather was at peace now and he would not want her to feel sad for him. He was finally with grandmother again and the two of them could now spend the rest of their days in eternity together.

"I will never forget you, grandfather," she said softly, her throat dry.

Flotsam brayed impatiently and she chuckled, ruffling his ears. "I'm sorry, boy. I didn't mean to ignore your feelings. I am sure you are missing grandpa, too!"

Flotsam kept his thoughts to himself and she idly turned her attentions to her sun-drenched surroundings. Birds flitted through the branches of the trees around her and the warm summer air was filled with swarming insects. Bees foraged the wild flowers for pollen, whilst beautiful butterflies danced on a gentle breeze before her. She sighed, marvelling at their myriad of colours and did not realise something was not quite right, until Cassana reined her horse to a sudden stop, alongside her.

"What's wrong, Cass?" she asked nervously, seeing the look in the woman's eyes.

"We have to go, now!" Cassana said, quickly looking over her left shoulder as Arillion rode up behind them. Her mount dragged a front hoof impatiently over the ground to emphasise the point.

"Get that flea-ridden thing moving, Red" Arillion shouted angrily. "NOW!"

Karlina dug her heels into Flotsam's sides and with a wail of protest, he trotted off through the forest. Behind her, she could hear a swift, panicked discussion and the outcome of it was that she was to follow Cassana, while Arillion dropped behind to protect them. Although nobody had actually told her what was going on, Karlina was smart enough to guess that the outlaws had probably found them. Her heart missed a beat as images of her last encounter with their ilk flooded her mind and she banished them quickly away as she steered Flotsam through the thick undergrowth, after Cassana.

As one, the three of them raced madly through the forest, ducking under low branches and turning their steeds at sharp angles, as they navigated a safe path through the dense terrain and grasping thorn bushes. Flotsam actually managed to keep pace with Cassana's mount, as the stout donkey could take sharper turns, ensuring that he didn't have to slow quite as often as the horses did.

Arillion followed quite some way behind the other two, slowing his flight enough to draw any danger away from them. Behind him, he could hear distant, echoing shouts of discovery and as he turned his hooded head, he caught fleeting glimpses of a hooded figure chasing him through the forest. Answering cries rose up from other locations behind him and bending low over his mount's neck, he urged the beast on wildly through the trees. Swaying low in his saddle, he narrowly avoided being plucked from his mount by a low reaching branch and as he straightened again, Arillion heard the tell-tale snap of a bowstring. Far behind him, he heard the scratching of wood, as the arrow caught tamely in the tree canopy and he grinned, thankfully, hoping that none of the outlaws had crossbows. With the distance he was from his pursuers, it would take an extremely lucky shot to hit a moving target, through this densely wooded environment. Several other vain attempts also fell short behind him and he chuckled as he heard a distant *thunk*, as an arrow found the heart of a sturdy tree.

"As long as that's all you manage to hit," he said, turning his horse between two tall silver birches.

Cassana led the way, steering her mount expertly through the forest. Occasional glances over her shoulder revealed that Karlina was keeping pace with her and she breathed a sigh of relief. If the worst came to the worst, they would have to abandon Flotsam and Karlina would have to ride with her. The girl had already lost her grandfather and she doubted Squirrel would be able to cope if she lost the only other thing dear to her, in the same day.

For the next few minutes, Cassana led them down a gradual incline, onto lower ground. The forest was slightly thinner here and as she let her mount have its head, she could hear Karlina behind her, crying out for her to slow down. Cassana glanced apologetically over her shoulder and then turned her attention back in time to take a low branch across her face.

The force of the collision sent her reeling and as her mount carried on, she gripped his flanks with her thighs, as she felt herself being dragged from the saddle. Finally, however, the tree reluctantly relinquished its grip on her and Cassana reined her mount to a harsh stop. Blinking the tears from her eyes, she steadied herself with a slow, calming breath and spat the taste of bark from her mouth. A sharp pain stiffened her left cheek and after she had reached up gingerly to touch it, her hand came away with bright blood on her trembling fingers. The branch had cut her deep and she could feel fresh blood running down her face, to drip down her neck. Her top lip felt numb as well and her teeth ached from the force of the impact.

Karlina's eyes were wide with fright as Flotsam trotted up to her. "What happened? Are you okay, Cass?"

"I just got careless, that is all," Cassana smiled comfortingly. "Come on, we had better carry on."

Without checking for Arillion, they set off again at a steadier pace, Cassana reluctant to take any more unnecessary risks. What would have happened to them, if she had struck her head? Shaking herself free of any self-reproach, Cassana urged them on through the thinning tree line, her face wet with blood and her heart thundering with uncontrollable fear.

By the time Arillion reached the top of the incline, he just about managed to locate his charges, as they disappeared from view towards the north. Casting a wary look behind, he pulled down his face scarf and grinned. The outlaws were some way behind them now and confident they wouldn't catch them, he guided his mount down the slope.

"Come on girl," he said, urging his mount into a gallop, as he guided her high over a fallen tree. They landed safely on the other side and he spurred her on through the trees, leaving a trail of flying clods behind them.

The only thing that bothered him, as he began to close in on the two females, was how the outlaws had managed to locate them. He had been fairly confident that they would have headed for the western fringes of the forest. What had changed to turn them back? Had Squirrel's incessant wailing revealed their location? Or had their pursuers spread their net a little wider over the forest. He felt the kiss of fear on his neck, as he realised that there were probably only six at best, after them now. What and where were the other two? Scowling, he looked ahead through the blur of trees, his breath catching in his throat as he realised that they were probably riding into an ambush...

"Hold on there, ladies," Arillion called out as he thundered up to them, his cloak billowing wildly about him. Cassana and Karlina drew their mounts to an obedient halt, as the black garbed man's horse slid to a stop alongside them.

"What in the storms have you been up to?" Arillion asked, his eyebrows raising in confusion as he saw the blood on Cassana's face.

"I was not paying attention," she responded, looking down at her saddle in embarrassment.

"Worried about me, were you, princess?"

"Actually, Cassana was looking for me," Karlina piped up and Arillion glanced at her, frowning in annoyance.

"Have we lost them?" Cassana asked him, her breathing laboured.

Arillion frowned, shaking his head. "For the moment, yes. But I have a feeling we are riding into an ambush."

Karlina looked worriedly at Cassana, then flicked her wide, staring eyes back towards Arillion. He looked at her thoughtfully for a time, and then leant over in his saddle, towards her.

"Here, Red. Take this," he said reluctantly, passing her the crescent blade from the belt at his waist.

Karlina's eyes almost popped out of their sockets as she held the gleaming blade up in both hands before her. "Can I keep it?"

"No you bloody well can't," he snapped. "You can borrow it, until we are free of this forest. Until that time, if anyone comes at you, stick that in them and twist the blade."

Cassana glared at Arillion, as she saw the awe in Karlina's eyes. The girl nodded and stuffed the blade into the ties on the front of her dress.

"Don't lose it," Arillion groaned, as the blade fell out onto the forest floor. Karlina grinned impishly and

470

slid off Flotsam's back to retrieve it. As she straightened, she screamed in fright and pointed with the blade, back behind them.

Arillion twisted in his saddle, quickly picking out the two dark figures, racing through the trees towards them, bows in hand.

Cassana was off before anyone could cry out and as Squirrel turned to jump on Flotsam's back, Arillion bent low in his saddle and plucked her into the air. The girl screamed, as Arillion draped her over the saddle in front of him and kicked his mount into motion.

"No," Squirrel screamed, as they were borne away. Something sped past them, glancing off a nearby tree and as Arillion turned his mount to the left, an arrow cut through the space they had just vacated, embedding deep into the ground.

Squirrel continued to scream, as she bounced up and down on the saddle. The momentum of the horse joggled her vision and as she looked back through the trees, she could see the two green-garbed figures moving around Flotsam, who kicked out in fright and looked forlornly after her.

"Flotsam," she screamed, tears spilling down her face. She felt herself sliding off the saddle and not caring any more, she let go of her grip.

A rough hand grabbed her.

"Don't be stupid," Arillion hissed in her ear, as he bent low over the saddle and took his blade back, before she could drop it again.

Sobbing, she looked back through the blurred landscape behind her. The two outlaws were reaching back for the quivers hanging off their backs and the last thing she saw, before Arillion steered his horse away from harm's way, was the sight of Flotsam, standing in the forest, alone and confused.

Flotsam, she sobbed silently, burying her head deep into the leather of the saddle.

CHAPTER TWENTY TWO

Together We Stand

The two horses broke from the cover of the forest and thundered through the lush grasses of the plains that stretched away from them as far as the eye could see. Chased by fear their riders did not stop to look behind them, or allow their labouring mounts any respite, until they were certain they were safely out of range from the bows of their pursuers.

Arillion called out for Cassana to halt as he reined in his own mount. Karlina was still draped across the saddle in front of him, sobbing, kicking and screaming madly as she fought to slide from the sweating horse and be away from Arillion's clutches.

"Shut up," Arillion shouted, cuffing her roughly about the side of the head. The girl recoiled in startled shock and fell silent for a brief moment, as he turned their mount back to face the forest.

The tall trees watched them stoically as Arillion noticed the two cloaked figures, watching them from the shadows of the thicket. Grinning broadly, he bowed low in his saddle and waved mockingly at them.

Cassana's eyes were blazing with unconstrained fury as she guided her steed alongside him. "How dare you strike her," she fumed, shaking with rage. To enforce the fact that he was apparently in the wrong, Karlina began to sob again.

Arillion groaned.

"You take her then," he hissed bitterly, allowing the girl to slip unchallenged from the horse. He watched dispassionately as the girl rushed over to Cassana, who pulled her up into the saddle in front of her. Both females turned their attention back to Arillion and he could feel the strength of their wrath bear down upon him.

"It was just a stupid donkey," he pointed out defensively, but from the looks he received, it appeared they were not in a charitable mood.

"No he wasn't," Karlina shouted, pointing a shaking finger at him accusingly. "He was Flotsam, and he was my friend!"

Arillion scowled as the girl began to sob again. Duped by her theatrics, Cassana glared across at him, the cut on her face still running freely with blood. "She has been through a lot today already and you are not helping matters. You should go easy on her, sir!" she said, barely managing to control the disappointment in her voice.

"Fine," Arillion sighed, flicking an irritated look at the girl. "I'll buy you a pony, once we get to Highwater, Red!"

"Will you?" Karlina asked in excitement, quickly blinking away her tears.

"No, of course I won't," Arillion snapped. "Now get a grip of yourself and let's get going before those two try for a lucky shot!"

Ignoring the girl's fresh bout of sobbing, Arillion pulled the scarf back up over his face. Kicking his horse's flanks he moved by the two females, shaking his head.

"I hate him," Karlina sniffed a little too loudly, as she glared openly at the dark figure and horse cantering slowly away from them.

"Hush there, now," Cassana soothed, hugging her from behind. "Flotsam will be fine, he will find a nice home. He is a clever donkey!"

Karlina looked back over her shoulder, sniffing through a tangled veil of her striking hair. "That's very sweet of you, Cass," she said, attempting a smile as she wiped the tears from her eyes. "But I am not that young and gullible not to realise that he won't survive on his own in the forest."

"I am sure that someone will find him a new home," Arillion called back to them. "And perhaps some potatoes and a few vegetables to go with him?"

"Arillion," Cassana screeched in disbelief, cutting him a venomous look. Karlina turned away, burying her head in Cassana's shoulder as she broke down again.

Chuckling, Arillion set the pace through the long grass, forcing Cassana to shut up for once and give chase, lest he leave them both behind.

For the next couple of hours Arillion led them towards the north-east. By then, the hot sun was beginning to calm down for the evening and the clear, settling skies were brushed with beautiful strokes of red and purple. Having finally managed to calm her wild emotions, Cassana drew her mount alongside Arillion and tightened her grip around Karlina's slim waist. The girl was exhausted from her ordeal and had fallen asleep in her arms.

"At least she's quiet, for once," Arillion observed, pulling his scarf down under his chin.

"No thanks to you," Cassana replied disdainfully.

Sighing, Arillion looked to the hilly horizon before them and shrugged. "I did her a favour, if you ask me! She would be dead by now, if I hadn't taken her with me."

"True enough," Cassana was forced to admit. "But you really need to work on your diplomatic skills."

Arillion grinned and looked away. The Sunset Hills were still many miles away and they would not make them before nightfall. Looking back again, he caught Cassana staring wistfully away to the west.

"What are you looking at?" he asked her, shielding his eyes with his hand as he squinted under the last desperate light of the fading sun.

Cassana sighed. "I was just thinking about Havensdale. We could find shelter and help there, if we asked for it!"

It was probably no more than a couple of hours ride westwards that would see them safely to the gates of the fortified town.

"We've been through this with you before, princess," Arillion said, shaking his head. "It's too dangerous! They will know of your friendship with the captain and will expect you to head there."

"I know," Cassana replied, growling her frustration. "It is just...ah, just look at me, will you? I am a complete mess, and I feel terrible."

Arillion gratefully accepted her invitation as he allowed his eyes to wander over Cassana's body, before letting them come to rest on those beautiful, if currently angry, blue eyes. Her face was filthy, streaked by dried tears, blood and framed by her wild tangle of long, black hair. The cut to her face had finally stopped bleeding now and was congealed and visibly sore. The blouse and waistcoat she wore were also ruined and she looked as if she was just about ready to fall out of her saddle. He sucked in a breath. She had never looked more beautiful...

"Will you please stop staring at me," Cassana demanded softly, looking away in embarrassment rather than anger.

"Fair enough, my lady!" Arillion answered, smiling triumphantly. "How about I see to that cut for you, once we stop for the night?"

"That would be most welcome. Thank you, sir," Cassana said, reluctant to look back at him. Karlina stirred in her arms and started snoring softly.

"Come on then, princess," Arillion whispered, flicking his reins. "We need to put as much distance as we can between us and the forest, before the night falls."

Cassana nodded obediently as he rode by her. Breathing out a soft sigh to herself, she cast a final, wistful look towards the west before following after him.

"Marek is not going to like this," the giant woodsman said, frowning as he stared down at the two bodies on the bloodstained leafy ground before him. "He has lost quite a few of his men in the last day, or so!"

His companion nodded, pulling a feathered shaft from the neck of one corpse. Cleaning the steel arrowhead on the dead man's clothing, he nodded with satisfaction and slipped it back into the cloth quiver, hanging from his right hip. The man straightened, massaging his back as he looked through the trees towards the rolling plains beyond and shook his head.

"Marek will just have to remember that I am still lord of this forest," the man said, pulling his hood back over his head. He wrapped his long cloak about his rangy frame and turned to the large woodsman.

"He should not allow his men to attack the old or the young. I told him that when he was with us, but he never listened!"

"Well they picked on the wrong people this time," the big man said.

"Gather the men, Trell, and have them meet me back at the den!"

"Where are you going, boss?" the big man asked, a puzzled expression creasing his bearded face. "Marek's men may still be in the area, we only killed five of them!"

The man grinned, his face flashing with mischief. "I can disappear in this forest, don't worry about me, old friend."

"But," Trell began, before the man waved away his concerns.

"But nothing. Do as I command."

"Sure thing, boss." Trell said, crestfallen. "So why do you think he changed his mind and never turned up at the meeting place?"

The man shrugged his shoulders nonchalantly. "Arillion never was one for the conventional, was he? Despite the fact that this gesture would have gone a long way to allowing us to put our differences behind us, it now appears that he has his own agenda. We must forget about the vast sums of coin we would have all made by ransoming her."

"Yes," Trell said bitterly. "But what about our contact in the city?"

"Leave Cullen to me," the man said quietly. "I will have some questions for him, when we next meet!"

Trell turned as they both heard a swift, high-pitched whistle echo through the forest. As they watched the thicket, three hooded figures ghosted into view and stopped, panting to catch their breaths.

"Well?" the man asked them, resting his left hand on the hilt of his Valian long sword.

"One of them got away, Devlin," the first man to catch his breath panted, as he fought for each word. "But Col winged him, so he won't get too far!"

The tall man nodded, looking at Trell. "Go find the others," he ordered him softly. "I'll be back before sunset."

The four woodsmen watched as their leader shouldered his longbow and began heading west through the forest.

"One last thing, boss," one of the newcomers called after him, waiting for him to turn back. "There's a donkey with some belongings on it, back through yonder trees! What shall we do with it?"

Devlin Hawke scratched his dark, forked beard and grinned. "Take it back to camp with you, we can fatten it up for winter!"

Once the notorious outlaw was gone, the men gathered together.

"Where's he going?" one of the outlaws asked Trell. "He'll never catch the girl now!"

"He's not bothered about her," Trell whispered. "Truth be told, I don't think he ever was!"

"But all of that coin would have been really useful for our cause." one man pointed out.

"True enough," Trell admitted, nodding. "But maybe it's for the best. We have enough enemies, without pissing off the lord of Highwater as well!"

All four men rumbled their agreement. "So why mess about with all of this, in the first place then?"

"Who knows with him, the boss has his own reasons for everything, best let him get on with it! All we need to worry about is that we do as he says," Trell said impatiently. "He has been good to all of us and we had better not forget it, like Marek did!"

"Fair enough," one of them said, sensing that Trell's infamous dark mood was returning. "So where has he gone now then, if not after the girl?"

Trell shrugged. "My guess is that he has gone to pay Marek a visit."

"What? Alone?"

"Aye," Trell said. "And not before time, either. It's about time that little bastard learnt his place again."

"Poor bugger," one of the men said and chuckling amongst themselves, the four outlaws headed back through the trees to find the donkey...

"Ouch," Cassana hissed, wincing in pain as Arillion gently cleansed her cut face with a damp cloth.

"Stop whining," Arillion said tenderly, dabbing at the cut again. "You'll have to deal with a lot worse if you ever have any children!"

Cassana's face paled at the thought and her breath escaped her. "I can assure you, sir, that starting a family is the last thing on my mind at this present moment in time!"

Arillion started to say something pithy, but thought better of it for once, and nodded instead. "Very wise, princess. There are going to be some dark days ahead and I fear that this would not be the best time to bring another snivelling rat into the world."

Cassana chose to ignore him as he glanced over at Karlina and smirked. They had decided to make their camp in a small valley that night, hoping to have some shelter from the chilly air that was beginning to steal across the open plains. Karlina had been charged with the task of tending to the horses for them, whilst Arillion dealt with Cassana's cut. Afterwards, by way of an unspoken apology to the girl, he had promised them they could sit around a camp fire tonight and share the lovely hot meal he was graciously going to allow Cassana to prepare for them.

Arillion poured some more water from his flask onto the bloodied cloth and continued to clean Cassana's wound. She reacted instinctively to the fresh pain and looked up at the dark sky above them, through watering eyes. She felt the hairs on her arms rise at his continuing closeness to her and could feel his breath upon her face and neck, each time he spoke.

"Almost finished," Arillion reported, taking her trembling for cramp or impatience. "Just one more...there, all done!"

Using his thumb he quickly wiped away the tear that trickled down her face, before it could sting her cut and smiled broadly. Cassana drew in a steadying breath and smiled her thanks. Arillion had not replaced his scarf for a few hours now and she was becoming accustomed to the distraction and loss of words that his handsome face was drawing from her. She felt her anger return however, as she saw him grin roguishly and look away. Was there nothing that he missed?

Fortunately for Cassana, any continuing emotional turmoil was distracted by Karlina's return. The slim girl looked pale and weary, but her face lit up with a smile as she slumped on the ground beside her.

"That looks really sore, Cassana." she observed, leaning close to scrutinise Arillion's handiwork.

"It is," Cassana admitted, reaching out to brush a loose eyelash from the girl's left cheek. She blew the lash into the night and pulled the girl into a warm embrace. "But I do feel much better, now that Arillion has cleansed it for me!"

"Uh, huh," Karlina murmured sleepily, settling down into the comfort of the hug.

Cassana ruffled her hair and looked across at Arillion. He was watching them both, but looked hurriedly away as she caught him looking at her. Was that a smile or embarrassment she had noticed on his face?

Arillion hastily packed away the bloody cloth and flask, before rising. Brushing down his clothes, he moved away and began unpacking the cooking utensils. Damn if that girl wasn't addling his mind. He pinched his own arm and revelled at the painful distraction. He had to focus on their surroundings and not lose sight of the game. He couldn't allow himself to be dragged off guard, smiling away to himself like a gibbering imbecile, as he observed the tenderness that she was showing to the girl.

Despite all that, he had to admit she would probably make a wonderful mother someday. He just wondered if she knew that perhaps she had already become one, without even realising it!

It was in the early hours of the following morning and an hour after Arillion had rudely awoken her, when Cassana was finally allowed to be alone with her thoughts. Lost in the harrowing events of the previous day, she stared up thoughtfully at the crescent moon in the dark night sky above her which was obscured by a band of ragged clouds and hugged herself against the cold. It wasn't really that cold, it was just that now she was alone, she could appreciate just how lucky they had been. Sighing, Cassana stared into the glowing embers of the dying fire. It had been good to have hot food again, and although she had protested fiercely at first, even Karlina had managed to tear herself away from her sorrow long enough to have something to eat. Thankfully, for sanity's sake, the remainder of the evening had passed by quietly. Karlina was perfectly happy to withdraw into herself and Arillion, for once, seemed sensible enough to keep his thoughts to himself. There was no further teasing from him, or any more of his sly remarks, directed towards either of them. In fact he had, for the better part of the evening, said nothing to them at all. Cassana assumed that her protector was mulling over what had happened, trying to fathom how they had been found. Despite the calm expression on his bared face, Cassana could tell from his eyes, that he also thought they had been lucky. Cassana's own worry, despite the pain from her injuries, had been generally focused towards Karlina. Until now, Cassana had not really been able to think clearly about her own feelings as all of her concerns had been for the safety of the young lady she had decided to protect.

Cassana rose and wandered carefully about the darkness, leaving Karlina wrapped in the bedroll they had shared. It had been an instinctive, natural reaction to want to care for the girl. Despite the fact she had no idea what would happen to her, once they got to the city, Cassana was determined that she would do all she could to give her the life she deserved. Stretching the cramp from her calves, Cassana tied her hair back behind her neck and drew in a deep, refreshing breath. If they continued to hold their course and maintain their pace, by the evening they should have crossed the Crystal River and were then but a mere two days ride from the mountains. Ignoring her fears, Cassana smiled. A further day's travel through the mountains would see her home. *Home!*

Cassana felt her emotions rage inside of her. Her heart ached with her desperation to be home and see her father again. Her head, however, warned her that her problems would not be over and that she may not find the safety there that she was yearning for. Closing her eyes, she kneaded her temples with her fingers, hoping to ease the conflict in her head. It had little effect and, sighing again, she moved back to her sentry position beside Squirrel and sat down again.

Smiling to himself, Arillion closed his eyes as she moved by him and focused his thoughts on something else.

The travel that morning for the tiny fellowship was made quietly under a blazing sun and a brilliant, blue sky. The landscape they journeyed across was a beautiful tapestry of differing terrains, woven breathtakingly with nature's colours, and the further they got away from the forest, the better their morale became. After stopping for lunch to allow the horses some respite, they carried on through the meadows and plains, drawn towards the glistening waters of the Crystal River and the Sunset Hills that guarded its eastern shores.

By the time they began to near the sparkling waters

of the aptly named river, they began to notice the distant, misty peaks of the mountains, that stretched across the horizon before them.

"We still have a couple of days travel yet," Arillion said, noticing Squirrel's interest in them. "Firstly, we have to cross the river and pass by the hills."

"How are we going to cross the river?" Cassana asked him, her own attention captured by the hills and the sheep she could see, grazing on them.

"About an hour's journey to the north, we will find The Old Bridge," Arillion revealed, scanning the distant hills cautiously. "We can cross there and follow the river around the hills towards the north."

"Why is it called The Old Bridge?" Squirrel asked, the first thing she had really said all morning.

"Because it is *old*," Arillion said sarcastically, shaking his head in disbelief.

"Is there a community near here, sir?" Cassana asked hastily, as she felt Karlina tense in the saddle, before her. Arillion dragged his disdainful glare away from the girl, to look back at the hills.

"There are a few secluded farmsteads in the region," Arillion answered. "Mainly cattle farmers, who use the hills and grasslands to fatten up their stock, before selling them at the town of Fallow Downs, found ten miles west of here!"

"The shepherds must feel quite exposed on the hillside?" Cassana imagined, looking subconsciously behind them. "Do they not fear the outlaws?"

Arillion chuckled. "Hardly, my lady. A great deal of their business is actually conducted *with* Devlin Hawke and his men. It's always better to deal with their kind, than alienate them!"

"What? Like we have done, you mean?" Cassana

said before she could stop herself.

Arillion laughed and ran a hand through his long hair. "Exactly so, princess. I fear it may be a while before we can set foot in Greywood Forest again!"

Squirrel shifted uncomfortably in the saddle. "I will go back there one day," she promised them, her eyes blazing with determination. "I will give grandfather a proper burial and find Flotsam, too!"

"Yeah, of course you will, Red," Arillion said, smiling to himself. "And I suppose, while you are there, you can also call in and say hello to your *hero*!"

Cassana scowled across at him and shook her head angrily. Arillion caught her hard stare and sighed in resignation.

"My advice to you, young lady," Arillion said evenly. "Is that you let me look out for err, the donkey, on my way back home to Karick. I'll also see to it that your grandpa gets a proper burial, for you."

Providing the old goat hasn't been eaten by then, anyhow, Arillion chuckled silently to himself.

"Would you, Arillion?" Squirrel asked, excitement on her face and hope in her voice. "Would you do that for me?"

"Sure thing, Red," Arillion smiled. "As long as you promise to keep out of trouble and let Cassana take care of you!"

Squirrel was already nodding vigorously. "I promise, I promise!"

"Great," Arillion said, boredom claiming his handsome face. "That's all settled then! Thank the storms."

He guided his mount alongside them and reached out a hand. Karlina looked at it briefly for a moment and then smiled, shaking it happily.

"Friends?" Arillion asked her, grinning expectantly.

"Friends!" Karlina replied, her freckles bouncing merrily across her face.

Cassana caught the surreptitious look Arillion sent her way and mouthed her own silent thanks to him. Nodding, Arillion turned his horse with a motion for them to follow him as they continued on with their journey towards the glistening Crystal River.

"Now I can see why they call it The Old Bridge," Cassana observed, frowning as she studied the rickety wooden bridge that stretched over the fast-moving waters of the Crystal River. Arillion nodded, scanning their surroundings for signs of danger.

"It may look like it's about to fall into the river, princess, but I can assure you that it is perfectly safe," he said, letting his gaze fall on the slopes of the Sunset Hills. Sheep still roamed freely on the grassy hills, grazing lazily on the brush and long grasses. There was no sign of the watchful shepherds, who may have been sheltering from the ferocious sun under the trees on the summit of the hills, but there was still the sense that they were not alone and, perhaps, were being watched.

Arillion subconsciously adjusted his leather forearm guards and led them across the bridge. As their mount's iron-clad hooves clopped across the sturdy wood, Cassana noticed a river bird on the choppy water. Startled by their presence, the black bird with a white stripe on its head powered across the river, almost running on the water as it fled from them.

"That's a Riverwidth," Arillion disclosed, noting her interest.

"What a strange name," Cassana said, watching as the bird disappeared into the reeds on the western bank of the river.

"Not really," Arillion replied. "It spends all of its time going back and forth across the river, so you can kind of understand how it got its name!"

Cassana was forced to agree and nodded as they rode from the bridge onto the eastern bank. A worn trail twisted away around the hills to the south and Arillion led them through the unspoilt grasses to the north.

For the rest of the day they followed the snaking river northwards through the lush and unspoilt land, encountering only fleeting glimpses of the local wildlife. By the time the sun had set, the darkening skies had also begun to cloud over, offering some respite to Squirrel. The pale girl had been suffering under the sun's glare and had spent most of the afternoon under the hood of the cloak Cassana had leant to her. That evening they camped on the banks of the river and after a hot meal, they settled down for the night. Cassana, in need of an unbroken night's sleep, volunteered for the first watch and spent most of her time gazing towards the looming mountains, dark and menacing under the eerie moonlight that filtered through the cloud cover. Cassana chewed her bottom lip. She would soon be home and despite her previous excitement at the prospect, part of her was beginning to regret the fact. Once she was home, Arillion had said they would not have any contact, whilst he began his investigations and although his work was imperative, she had to admit that she was going to miss him. She had never thought to meet someone who was so compelling and irritating as he was, and the closer the moment of their separation came, the more she wished it would not. Not for the first time of late, she sighed to herself as her conflicting emotions argued away inside of her. Rising, she tossed some more twigs onto the hungry fire and went to wake Arillion.

The next morning, the clear skies had returned and by midday, the small party had left the banks of the Crystal River, as it turned away to the northwest. Under an unforgiving sun, they carried on through the long grass towards the distant mountains and made good progress that day. Arillion set them a furious pace and they stopped twice more than they had the previous day, to rest their mounts. Such was their progress, Cassana, grudgingly, had to admit that they probably would have only just reached The Old Bridge, if they still had Flotsam with them. That afternoon Arillion's decision to abandon Flotsam was strengthened further as they had travelled enough miles now that they could see the wooded slopes of the Great Divide's foothills. The looming mountain ranges on the horizon were crested by hazy, snow-capped peaks and as Arillion picked out where they needed to be heading for now, Cassana swallowed her rising fear. By tomorrow morning, they would probably be in the foothills, ready to head up into the mountains. She shook her head and looked towards Arillion. He was watching her thoughtfully and smiled encouragingly at her. She felt her heart race and her spirits lift momentarily, before her attention was drawn inexorably back to the mountains again.

"We'll travel a few more miles today and then rest for the night," Arillion told them. "If we head up into the foothills at first light, we should be through the pass and at the lake by early afternoon. We are going to have to set the horses free however, as Smuggler's Pass will be too dangerous for them, so it will be a hard day for you both, I am afraid."

Cassana's mouth was wide open from her shock. "But the horses are thoroughbreds, sir! We cannot just let them roam free, they belong to Savinn."

"Who's Savinn?" Squirrel asked.

"Never you mind who he is," Arillion growled, seeing the curiosity light up in her eyes. He looked at Cassana. "Don't worry about Savinn, he can afford it!"

"But they are magnificent beasts," Cassana pointed out, shaking her head in disagreement. "We cannot just leave them on their own."

"We left Flotsam," Squirrel muttered glumly.

Arillion groaned as Cassana started fussing over the girl. "They won't be on their own for long, someone is bound to find them."

Cassana clearly disagreed, but Arillion didn't care. Dealing her a look that suggested the matter was now closed, he spurred his mount away from them. Squirrel leant back in the saddle to rest against Cassana.

"He doesn't care, does he?" she asked quietly.

"Only about himself, Squirrel," Cassana whispered sadly. "But we must abide by what he says as he is our protector, and, at this moment in time, we need him more than he needs us."

"He cares about you, though," Squirrel said, grinning mischievously as she looked back over her shoulder.

"No he does not," Cassana mumbled, blushing.

"He does so," Squirrel said firmly. "I have seen the way he looks at you sometimes!"

Cassana looked away, her heart racing. "I think we had better get going, or he will leave us *both* behind." She flicked the reins and their mount bore them after Arillion, Squirrel's giggles echoing in their wake.

By the time dawn broke the next morning, Arillion had already woken his charges and broken up their camp. In the early morning mist, they set out across the rising ground towards the intimidating mountains. A cool breeze ruffled hair and filled cloaks as they made their way towards the wooded slopes and the closer they came, the more Cassana felt her apprehension rise. Was it her imagination playing tricks on her mind again, or did it feel like something was wrong? She looked at Arillion. He stared ahead, his eyes scanning the impressive range before them and his face a fixed mask of concentration.

"What's that?" Squirrel asked suddenly, diverting her thoughts away from him.

Cassana followed her pointing hand towards the west and stared through the mist at the shapes forming on the horizon. She squinted, trying to discern what it was, but at this distance, she couldn't quite tell.

Arillion looked to the west and studied the horizon for a few moments. As Cassana watched him, his face went pale and his eyes quickly found hers. Cassana began to shake. There was genuine fear in his eyes.

"Head for the hills," he screamed at them. "Follow me!"

Without waiting, he kicked his horse's flanks and galloped madly away. Cassana gave chase, looking towards the west as they fled. As she looked, the dark shapes began to take form. She gasped in fright and Squirrel tensed in her arms.

"Who are they?" she shouted at Arillion.

"I have no idea," Arillion sent back. "But there are enough of them there to make me worry."

Squirrel stared through the mist as he spoke and felt

her chest tighten with fear. She could see what they were now and it frightened her to the core. There were at least twenty riders coming their way. Twenty riders who had just turned their horses on a course to intercept them.

Arillion bent low over the neck of his mount as the land and mist swept by him. As the foothills drew tantalisingly close, he looked towards the riders and growled angrily. They had found them! But how, by the storms did they know they would come this way? Arillion had not told anyone about his plans to get Cassana into Highwater and yet they had still been found. He rode his mount on with urgent cries of encouragement and looked back for Cassana. She was close behind him now and was looking nearly as pale as Squirrel. Dictating the pace, he guided them on towards the foothills, aware that the riders would not reach them before they made the safety of the tree line. Thankful that Squirrel had been more vigilant than he had, Arillion focused on their destination and dismissed the doubts that had surfaced in his mind. He would not allow them to take her, no matter what the cost and if they could get into the pass before getting caught, they would have given themselves a fighting chance of survival.

The chase was in full flight now and Arillion let out an audible sigh of relief as he rode into the forest, Cassana close behind him. Ducking low under a branch, he steered his mount through the tangle of trees and guided him up the gradually rising slope. The dark grey of the misty morning hung over the forest like a spectre and as his mount bore him up into foothills, his keen ears detected the sounds of approach.

Looking to his left he saw two figures racing through the trees to intercept them.

"Look out," he cried, as Cassana rode up behind him.

A loud snap echoed through the silence of the morning as one of the men fired the crossbow he carried. The bolt took Arillion's mount in the left flank and the horse screamed in pain, rearing in fright. As it panicked, the horse lost its footing and fell back down the slope, spilling Arillion from his saddle. Cassana steered her mount past them and held her breath as the tangle of man and beast tumbled past them. Arillion leapt aside, just as his mount threatened to roll over him and he crashed heavily into the base of a nearby tree. Cassana winced and was about to rein her mount in, when Arillion rose up, his eyes narrowing angrily.

"Get away from here," he yelled, pointing directly up the slope. He pulled the hood up over his head and dragged the scarf over his face again. As soon as Cassana spurred her mount away, he drew his left sword and dispatched his horse with a regretful slash across its throat. The stallion had broken a hind leg and was thrashing in pain. Ignoring his belongings, tied to the saddle, he began running up through the trees after them.

Dodging round a thorn bush, Arillion picked out another three cloaked figures, away through the trees to his right as well now. His fear was palpable as he realised they had ridden straight into a trap and putting his head down, he sprinted after the horse and riders, disappearing from view through the trees above him. Shouts of discovery rose up all around him now and he grimaced as the crossbowman came close again. He needed to get into the pass. That was his first goal, survive that long and he could start to fight back.

As he ran on, he noticed that a cloaked figure was rushing through the trees away to his left, to cut him off. The man was apparently alone and carried a long blade in one hand. Drawing both of his blades, Arillion headed for the man and as they came together, he could see that his attacker was dressed in studded armour. Arillion parried the man's confident attack with his left blade and slashed the other blade through his neck as he ran by him. He didn't even slow his ascent as the man clutched vainly at his throat and fell away down the slope. More shouts rose up behind him and, scowling, Arillion turned his thoughts to Cassana. If they were separated now, there would be nothing more he could do for her. It was a harrowing thought and one that he was determined to make sure didn't happen.

Cassana and Squirrel's flight up into the wooded foothills of the mountains was also a desperate one. Chased by fear and followed by danger, they rode hard into the unknown, worried about what was going to happen to them and fearful of what had become of Arillion. At one point Cassana stopped herself looking over her shoulder, mindful of what had happened the last time she did that. Instead, she focused all of her attention on the forest before them and the terrified girl in the saddle in front of her.

"What will happen to us?" Squirrel sobbed overcome by fear and unable to control her emotions.

Another bolt whipped across the forest in front of them, before Cassana could answer her and looking to her right, she could see that a lone crossbowman was racing through the trees to intercept them. Screaming, Cassana kicked her horse's flanks and put as many trees between them and their assailant as she could.

Arillion's body was aching and his thighs were burning as he carried on up through the forested maze before him. He knew where he was going, of course, but his charges had no idea. Cursing the crossbowman, he heard distant shouts below him and allowed himself a smile. He had managed to lose those chasing him, for now, but his keen ears had started to detect the distant rumble of thunder, which meant that the riders had reached the foothills and were coming for them. Holding his left side, injured from his fall, he headed up a precarious looking rise and as it levelled out for a few hundred paces, he noticed the hoofed tracks on the ground before him. Sighing in relief, he drew in a lungful of fresh air and hurried after them. They were still heading in the general direction of the pass and he needed to get to them, before they were diverted.

By the time Arillion heard the faint rumble of a horse ahead of him, he caught the fleeting glimpses of a lone figure hurrying through the bleak mist away to his left. Scowling, he fell in behind the hooded figure and watched helplessly as it raised a crossbow and aimed it up through the trees. The weapon jerked as the bolt sped off through the early gloom of the day, accompanied soon after by a cry of fright from further up ahead. Putting his head down, Arillion pumped his legs as he sprinted up behind the hooded figure. The man was desperately trying to reload his weapon and he spun worriedly at Arillion's swift approach. Seeing the two blades in his attacker's hands, the man threw aside his crossbow and fumbled for the short blade hanging from a sheath off his hip.

"Too slow," Arillion hissed, as he buried both

blades into the man's chest. The man groaned, a dull gasp escaping his twitching lips, as Arillion turned him round on his swords and sent him tumbling away from him as he dragged his blades from his body. Ignoring the blood on his hands, Arillion found the man's crossbow and smashed it to pieces with several stamps from his booted heel. He didn't want anyone else using it on them and in the confines of a narrow pass, a crossbow would finish them off in no time.

"Cassana," he roared out, as he started his ascent again.

"Cassana."

Arillion's voice called out from behind them and both of the females gasped in relief. Reining in their mount, Cassana stared down through the trees beneath them and held onto her breath for several moments as she scanned the mist, searching for him. Squirrel was the first to notice him and let out a cheer as she spotted him hurrying through the forest towards them. Arillion had his bloodied swords in his hands and as he caught up with them, he was wheezing from the strain of his climb.

"Are you okay?" Cassana asked him, her eyes filled with worry. Arillion nodded his head as he bent over, trying to find his breath.

"I am fine," he said finally, pulling the words from the depths of his exhaustion. He looked by them, scanning the forest ahead. He could see the comforting sign of the towering rock face now and dragging in more air, he straightened, beckoning for them to follow him.

Several long minutes passed, before they were finally at the base of the mountains. They stood silently

496

for a few moments, each lost within their own thoughts and silenced by the magnificence and size of the rock, rising up into the clouds before them. Arillion recovered his wits first and looked away to his left, spying the narrow opening he was looking for, a hundred or so yards away from them. Considering the situation, they had been lucky to come out this close to their intended destination.

"There," Arillion said, pointing towards the gap in the rock wall.

They made their way as quickly as they could over the undulating, rocky ground to the narrow opening. Cassana stared up into the shadows of the twisting, treacherous Smuggler's Gap and gulped. It would be like walking into the mouth of a giant beast, and looked like a death trap. If their attackers already had men in the pass, they would be caught between the two and killed in moments.

Arillion helped them both from the saddle and they quickly divided out the supplies. As he sent the horse away with a slap across its rump, he sheathed one of his blades and passed Squirrel the crescent shaped knife again.

"Don't lose it this time," he said cantankerously.

Squirrel held the weapon in her trembling hands and nodded dumbly. She was about to offer a reply, when they heard the distant sounds of approach and started to notice the ominous rumble of approaching horses.

"They are coming," Arillion said grimly. Hurrying away, he led them up the rising slope into the shadows of the pass known as Smuggler's Gap.

For several nervous minutes, Arillion led them around the twisting turns of the rough pass, as it snaked up into the mountains. Cassana trailed at the rear, her chest tight with fear as they hastily climbed higher, her legs heavy with worry. The pass appeared to become narrower with each faltering step that she took and Cassana sent worried glances up at the pale sky above them, trying to escape her fear and the choking, claustrophobic grip of her stony confines. As they climbed, Squirrel slipped on some loose shale, scraping her bared knees on the rocky ground. Wincing, she accepted Arillion's hand as he helped her up and showed him that she had still managed to hold onto knife. Arillion nodded his head and winked.

"Good lass," he said, looking back for Cassana. "Come on, princess. Keep up!"

Cassana glared at him as she reached them, her split lips parting as she made to offer him some choice words. What she was about to say was lost forever though, as they heard the faint sounds of booted feet on the rocky path below them.

"Hurry," Arillion said urgently.

Turning, they scrambled up the pass, eager to leave their pursuers behind. But after a few minutes, it was clear that they would not be able to outrun them. Their attackers were relentless in their determination and with their massing numbers, they had strength over them as both Squirrel and Cassana had run the breath from their bodies. Touching the tips of his blades to both sides of the pass and scraping the steel along the rock walls, Arillion drew them to a halt moments later, as he finally reached the spot on the trail he had been trying to reach.

"Right, listen to me," he hissed, his eyes flicking between the two of them as they gathered round him. "Just around this corner, the pass widens slightly. I will position myself from view and attack them as they come round the corner!"

"Is that-," Arillion whipped up one of his blades, silencing Cassana's question.

"The pass rises up steeply here," he continued. "So I want you two at the top of the slope. As soon as they come for me, I will break off and head back to you. I need you to cover me with your bow!"

He looked at Cassana, his eyes steeling as he silently conveyed how important this was to him. Cassana licked her lips and nodded her head unconvincingly.

"Good," Arillion whispered. "Come on then."

The pass did indeed rise up steeply and Arillion stepped off the trail to position himself against a natural alcove. He watched as the two females struggled their way up the rise and when they reached the top of the trail, Cassana turned, her eyes flashing with worry as she slid the bow from her shoulder. Arillion watched as she slipped an arrow from one of her quivers with a shaking hand and fitted it to the string of her bow. She paused for a brief moment, then moved from view.

Arillion sighed, resting his head on the rocky wall behind him. His heart was pounding in his chest and he closed his eyes as he heard the rising roar of the booted feet on the trail beneath him. Bowing his head, he held both blades up before him and drew in a deep, steadying breath.

CHAPTER TWENTY THREE

...Divided We Fall

Arillion tensed as he heard their pursuers approach. The multiple sounds of heavily booted footfalls reverberated about the pass, seemingly shaking the rock with every step that brought them closer. He opened his eyes to look up the narrow slope again and was thankful that Cassana and Karlina were still hidden from view. Closing his eyes once more, he listened to the rumbling approach, visualising their whereabouts on the trail. They were close now, he could tell and Arillion counted their steps as they came closer...closer...closer...

The first man to appear around the corner stared down in disbelief at the deep wound that appeared in his chest and looked up, just in time to see the second blade, as it flashed into his eyes. As the man screamed and collapsed to the ground Arillion leapt over him, his blades cutting into the next man on the trail. The fools were bunched too tightly together on the narrow pass and as they tried to recover their wits, Arillion killed a third man, slashing his blades across the burly man's chest and left knee. Sparks spat from the rock on either side of the pass as Arillion pulled his blades away from the man and stepped back over the twitching bodies at his feet. Screams of anger and terror rose up from the massing ranks and leaping away, Arillion ran for the slope, aware of the large number of heavily armoured attackers about to chase after him.

"Cassana!" he roared, and as he sprinted up the rocky trail, she appeared above him, wincing as she sent an arrow arching over his head into the throng behind him. Arillion turned briefly, as he reached her, just in time to see a man take her second arrow in the right shoulder.

"Come on," he yelled waving her on, as several mercenaries slipped by the fallen in single file and began charging bravely up the slope towards them.

They fled together, catching up with the terrified Squirrel, who stood with the crescent-shaped knife in her hand and then fled along the narrowing trail before them. The pass levelled out here for a time, turning from view to the right, some distance away. Half way along the trail, Arillion slowed and turned again.

"Keep moving," he told them, as he spun the blades deftly in his hands. "Cover me again and keep an eye out for any crossbowmen. Take them down first, or at least give them something else to worry about instead of me!"

Cassana nodded and led Karlina quickly away from Arillion. Her breathing was ragged and her hands were shaking as she fitted another arrow to her bowstring. Drawing back the string, she pressed the shaft against her cheek and waited for the first attacker to appear.

"Here they come," Karlina screamed, her high-pitched voice echoing along the trail.

Cassana held her breath and released the string of her bow. With a snap the arrow arched towards the lead warrior, a tall and heavily cloaked figure wielding a long-handled axe. The man ducked as the shaft passed by him to shatter on the rock wall to his right. As he charged towards Arillion, Cassana sent another arrow towards the men who appeared behind him. A second man somehow dodged out of the way, but his companion behind was not so lucky and he screamed, pawing vainly at the feathered shaft that had suddenly appeared in his left eye. The warriors who followed behind him slowed their advance, mindful of the prowess of the dark-haired archer. Cassana smoothly pulled another arrow from the quiver on her back and sent it on its way before she had even drawn breath.

Arillion leapt back as the axeman swung a murderous vertical cut towards him. Before the man could recover, he stepped in close, cutting him deep across his right hamstring. The man shrieked in pain as his leg gave way beneath him and before he could bring his axe up to protect himself, Arillion drove his other sword deep into the man's stomach. Dragging the blade free, he spun, barely reacting in time to turn aside the next man's attack. The clash of steel rose up from within the resulting sparks and bounded gleefully away to touch at the ears of the men, gathering on the slope below. Arillion easily parried the next strike from his attacker and hammered the hilt of his free blade into the man's face. As the man staggered back, Arillion cut the hand from his sword arm and kicked him back into the embrace of the rock wall.

Turning, Arillion fled as the next wave of men

stumbled over the injured to reach him. The man he had just defeated thrashed around on the ground, screaming gutturally as he tried to stem the flow of blood, pumping from his wrist. Sometimes it was better to leave the wounded behind you, to guard your escape!

Arillion's plan was short-lived however, as the next man to move by the wounded warrior, drove one of his knives into the dying man's back, shoving him to the ground as he hurried by. Panting, Arillion turned to face the knife wielder, gauging his expertise as he came confidently towards him. The man appeared well-trained and was dressed in light leathers. Good weapons to carry in these narrow confines, he brandished a knife in each hand and as the bald-headed man strode forward, Arillion initially thought that he had forgettable features; that was until he looked deep into his brown eyes. There was a steely confidence there, flashing with menace and the promise of some of the things he was capable of. Arillion crouched low, his blades hovering defensively before him. This warrior would be dangerous, he had met his kind before. Ruthless killers with no fear of death and a skill to match his own.

"Ready to die then, swordsman?" the man snarled, his knives weaving before him as he leapt forward.

Arillion nodded, killing him within seconds...

"Fight a good fight," Arillion hissed, as he saw the life fading from the eyes of the man, hanging off his swords. Ripping the blades from the man's right armpit and groin, Arillion turned to face the next man.

He counted another six heads fighting for view on the trail before him and the first man in the line hesitated, having just witnessed the ruthless way in which Arillion had dispatched the knife man. He was a young warrior, his face barely covered by skin, let alone a beard and as he paused, an arrow struck the ground before him. He backed away.

Sensing the advantage, Arillion stalked confidently towards them, his bloodied swords hanging casually at his sides. Gulping, the blonde-haired warrior turned and tried to shove past the men behind him. They held out at first, but then swept up in their comrades terror, they turned and fled back along the trail. Arillion had bought himself enough time now and turning, he raced along the trail.

Cassana watched as Arillion came towards her, holding her breath in awe as their attackers regrouped on the cusp of the slope. Arillion was fearless and had the cunning skill to match. Her heart gathered momentum as he came back to her and she didn't even react as the tails of Arillion's cloak caught on the grasping rock walls and tore as he angrily snatched it back. Reaching her side, he beckoned for her to follow him. Karlina was already at the abrupt turn in the trail and her bright eyes were wide with astonishment now, rather than fear.

"You are amazing," she squeaked, staring at him in awe.

"Yes, I am," Arillion said wearily as Cassana grabbed the girl by one hand and dragged her along the pass with them.

The trail began to rise steeply again, as Arillion led them up into the mountains. They could hear the sounds of hurried approach behind them again and Arillion was sure that they would have called for a crossbowman to help them by now. They followed the twisting trail for several more minutes, sometimes having to turn sidewards to step through gaps in the narrow rock, before Arillion found his next point of defence. Again, the trail turned sharply, allowing him the chance to ambush their pursuers and even further up the trail, there was a perfect spot from where Cassana could cover his retreat. Arillion knew this would be the last point on the trail where they could make a stand, before they came out onto the open path, where Cassana's courage would probably fail her. Giving Cassana her orders, he turned back again, listening to the sounds of approach.

Make it count, he ordered himself calmly. He knew his own limitations and was aware that he had probably reached his summit. His injured side was really starting to hamper his movements now and his muscles burned with fatigue. He had to buy them some more time, somehow!

Sensibly, the young warrior had now decided to let someone else go first and the old warrior who had taken the responsibility, died before he could use his buckler to turn aside Arillion's attack. The trail was still very narrow here and the warriors were again forced to fight Arillion one at a time. The second man in the line put up a valiant show, before falling to the swordsman's blades and as his comrades surged forward to avenge him, Arillion spied the crossbowman, trying to get a line of sight on him.

Arillion backed away, dodging an attack from the next foe he faced. The heavily armoured man fought with a large mace and hid himself behind a large, battered shield. Testing the man's defences, Arillion was unable to get through as half of his concentration was spent trying to avoid the crossbowman, whilst attempting to fall back. Crouching low, the man aimed a vicious blow towards Arillion's shins, whilst covering his head and torso with his shield. Arillion jumped back as the weapon smashed into the ground, sending shards of rock into the air, then leapt forwards again, throwing himself against the shield. The man was still off-balance, having leant forward to strike and as he fell back, Arillion cut him across the inside of one thigh. As his opponent cried out in pain and fell backwards, covering himself with his shield, Arillion found himself staring down the length of the crossbow that was trained on him.

The crossbow rocked in the man's hands as Arillion dropped to his knees and the wicked bolt sailed harmlessly over his head. Springing up, Arillion leapt off the raised shield before him and raced headlong towards the crossbowman. The man's face twisted with fear as the black-garbed swordsman bore down on him and he fumbled vainly to try and reload his weapon. Arillion disdainfully cut the weapon from his hands and slashed the other blade across his stomach. As the man fell, Arillion turned to find himself trapped. The warrior with the mace and shield had recovered his wits and was rising up sluggishly to block his escape. Growling, Arillion rushed forward as he heard the next man come up behind him.

Cassana paled as she realised the predicament Arillion was in. Why hadn't he fallen back, allowing her to drive off the shield bearer with her arrows? As she deliberated, Squirrel picked up a rock and ran forward, hurling it towards the fray. The tiny projectile spun through the air and fell short, bouncing across the ground. Blinking free of her shock, Cassana could see that Arillion had positioned himself so that he could fight off both of his attackers at the same time.

Swallowing hard, she raised her bow and sent an arrow towards them.

Arillion twisted desperately, barely avoiding the mace that brushed past his head. Turning away from his attacker, he dropped to one knee and with crossed blades he parried a sword thrust, before pushing upwards to hurl his attacker away from him. As Arillion turned to face the shield bearer, the man straightened and staggered towards him, a blank expression staining his face. His shield slipped from his arm and he dropped to his knees, slumping forward to reveal the feathered shaft in his back.

Spinning away from his relief, Arillion sidestepped his onrushing opponent and slashed both blades across his back as he stumbled by. With his heart racing, Arillion leapt over his fallen opponents and ran straight into the stone Squirrel had just thrown.

"Oops!" Karlina said, clapping a hand over her mouth in shock.

Arillion stumbled slightly, as the stone struck him on his left shoulder, but he still carried on towards them. With the pass getting narrower with each step Cassana was becoming more and more uncertain about her skill with the bow. Drawing in a steadying breath she reluctantly sent two shafts down the slope, missing wildly with the first, but finding a target with the second, deep in the groin of the lead pursuer. As the oddly screaming man went down, the man behind tripped over him. Cassana sent one last shaft towards them, but turned to follow Arillion up the trail before she could see if it found a mark.

"Watch where you are throwing those rocks," Arillion growled, leading them up the slope.

"Sorry, Arillion," Squirrel mumbled, her free hand

still clamped over her mouth to hide her shock.

Behind them now, their pursuers had regained their footing and were beginning to give chase, once again. Fitting an arrow to her bowstring, Cassana covered their escape as they rushed higher into the mountains.

Cassana slowed her ascent and almost came to a stop when she saw that the trail levelled out ahead of her and stretched away into the lifting brightness of an early summer morning. As she reluctantly edged forward, she could see that the rock wall to her right suddenly fell away, as the narrow trail twisted up into the mist to her left. Arillion glanced back expectantly and his eyes were almost apologetic, as he motioned her forward with a beckoning flick of a sword.

"Come on, princess," he said urgently.

Cassana edged forward, enjoying the cool rushing air that caressed her face. With her eyes firmly fixed on the narrow trail before her, she edged forward tentatively.

"Look up," Arillion commanded her as she neared him. Steeling her nerves, Cassana obeyed and lifted her head.

"Oh my," she breathed, lost for further words.

The ledge ran up along the west side of a huge canyon that was ringed by towering peaks of the jagged mountain range. It was still very early and the breathtaking scene before her was framed by an opaque sky and complemented by the distant, elegant shapes of two circling eagles. Below her, a vast canyon was thankfully filled by a thick carpet of fog, which meant that her fear only had to cope with several feet of dizziness, which was just as well! On the obscured rocky slopes across from her, she could just about make out the tops of some deciduous trees, hinting at a large forest in the basin of the canyon.

"Now you can see why I was keen to start early," Arillion said. "Another couple of hours and you would be staring a couple of hundred feet down into an abyss."

Cassana shuddered at the thought as the three of them stood, mesmerised by the impressive sight for a few more moments, before the sounds of approach crudely bought them to their senses.

"Head for that small outcropping," Arillion shouted, pointing with a bloody blade towards a small plateau, halfway up the narrow trail. He shoved Squirrel on as she stood gawking at the canyon below and growled impatiently.

Cassana followed after Squirrel, edging carefully by Arillion, who forced her to walk near the edge of the trail. Her legs almost gave way as she pictured herself falling to her death and she moved tentatively after the young girl, who coaxed her on with comforting words. Arillion shook his head as he turned to block the entrance.

The first attacker to reach him moments later blocked Arillion's vicious lunge and sent a riposte back that nearly tore Arillion's other blade from his bloodied hand. Jilting his stance, Arillion ducked low under his opponent's arcing sweep and drove his left blade deep into the man's right boot. As the man roared in pain, Arillion rose up, dragging his other blade up the length of the man's abdomen and chest, opening up a deep and gory wound there. As the warrior swayed before him, Arillion planted his second blade into his right shoulder and kicked him back into his following comrades.

Roars of anger rose up as they swept over the dying man and as Arillion retreated, he sidestepped the pathetic lunge from his next opponent and shoulder-barged him off the ledge. The man hung suspended in mid-air for a brief second, desperately clawing for something to hold onto, before falling to his death, his screams trailing after him. Arillion offered him a sarcastic wave and engaged the next man to attack him.

Cassana watched the ensuing combat with her heart in her mouth, from the safety of the wider part of the ledge. Once, twice, a third time, Arillion danced through his opponents, opening up a wound here, before finishing them off with a thrust there. His dance of death took him perilously close to the edge of no return on several occasions and each time, both she and Karlina closed their eyes and winced. Arillion had been forced back halfway along the trail to them now and Cassana counted at least ten more attackers on the ledge. As she drew back her bow string, she noticed a crossbowman, lining up impatiently in the massing throng and she sent two arrows in rapid succession towards him. The first shaft punched into the man in front of him, hurling him back into the rock face of the towering peak above them and as the crossbowman swung his weapon towards her, the second shaft struck her intended target in the left arm. The man still fired his crossbow as he flinched in pain, but the bolt fell short, disappearing into the murky depths below. Sensing her advantage, Cassana sent several more shafts in his direction and watched as he clutched at one of the arrows, as it buried in his chest. As he stumbled about, clinging onto his fleeing lifeblood, the man behind, fed up of being in the firing line, pitched his dying companion from the ledge.

Cassana scowled. These men had no honour, treating a comrade like that and their actions showed them to be the mercenaries they clearly were. Hired men had no morals or honour, only the desire for coin and riches – it was probably the reason why they were losing the fight at this stage, as their desire for money was not as great as her own desire for survival.

It was all going so well, that was until Arillion slipped on the bloody floor beneath him and his opponent slashed his sword across the swordsman's chest.

"NO!" Squirrel screamed, as Cassana's heart stuck in her throat.

Arillion stumbled back, barely defending himself as he retreated. Sensing his moment, the aggressor pressed forward, aiming a furious succession of powerful blows down upon the wounded figure before him. Panicking, Cassana drew another feathered shaft and fitted it swiftly to her bowstring. It was a risky shot, but if she didn't take it...

The string hummed ominously as the arrow sped towards the fight before her. But her worry for Arillion forced her aim high and the shaft clattered above the duelling swordsmen. Again Arillion slipped and Squirrel screamed as the man towered over him, his sword raised high.

Yelling, Karlina dashed along the ledge, waving her knife angrily above her head as she screamed madly. Before she reached them, Arillion sprung back up, driving both of his blades up under the man's chin, before yanking them away to the left and right. The warrior died instantly, his blade falling from his lifeless hands, behind his head. Arillion dropped onto one knee again, his swords poised defensively before him.

Cassana sent another shaft over Arillion, plucking the next mercenary from the ledge and she watched with a strange sense of detachment as he flailed and spiralled away from sight, down through the fog. The remaining warriors paused, seeing what Arillion had done to their companion. As they hesitated, Arillion turned and stumbled back along the trail. Squealing, Squirrel skidded to a halt and turned, fleeing back to rejoin Cassana. Arillion reached them moments later, his leather tunic running freely with blood.

"That was very brave, Red," Arillion gasped, his eyes narrowed from the pain.

Cassana's heart was thundering in her chest and as she trained her bow on the mercenaries, her eyes flicked to Arillion. She tried to say something, but her fear stayed her tongue.

"Why don't you give up the woman, swordsman?" one of the warriors called out suddenly, as they edged cautiously along the ledge. Cassana shook her bow meaningfully at them and they stopped their approach again.

"You have fought bravely here today," the man continued. "However, no amount of coin will compensate for what we will do to you if you don't!"

Arillion shook his hooded head firmly.

"Last chance," the man growled, his words echoing out across the canyon. "Turn her over and we'll double what you are getting paid!"

"Yeah," Arillion chuckled sarcastically. "Of course you will."

He cocked his head briefly to one side, as if considering the offer and his eyes flicked over the two females beside him.

Squirrel gasped in horror. "Don't you dare!"

"Well?" the man cried out, demanding his answer.

Arillion winked at her and turned his attentions back to the men before them. "When they come for me," he whispered. "Flee along the ledge, I'll join up with you as soon as I can."

Cassana's bow shook in her hands as she heard the tone in Arillion's voice. He would join them, yes! But it sounded as if he wasn't sure that he could...

"My answer is no!" Arillion snarled.

The men roared out their battle cries and surged up the trail. As they came, Arillion moved to intercept them, allowing Cassana and Squirrel time to flee. As she ran after Karlina, Cassana turned, her body shaking with cold fear. Arillion sent one opponent to his death as the next man stepped up to take his place. Turning, she hurried away, praying that the lady would see fit to protect Arillion this day.

Arillion's valiant defence of the narrow ledge was proving to be a costly one. His body was in agony and for the price of three more lives, he now had a deep cut to his left shoulder. As his next opponent stepped forward cautiously, he rolled the fingers of his left hand along the hilt of his sword and winced as pain shot down his arm. His next opponent was a woman and her long dark hair fluttered in the grip of a breeze. Her face twisted as she screamed a battle cry and surged forward to obligingly plant herself on Arillion's swords. Shoving her to the ground, he pulled his blades free and swayed, as his vision faded momentarily. He found focus, just as the next mercenary came for him, swinging his sword before him in wild, sweeping arcs. Arillion stepped back defensively, his head following the blade as he learnt the man's simple and predictable series of moves.

"Far too easy," Arillion hissed, stepping in as the man swung his sword behind his head.

As the man fell to his knees, Arillion looked over him to see that only one man remained now. Well, man was being a little too generous. It was the young man, who had backed away from combat earlier. His eyes were even wider with fear now though, as he watched Arillion slash a blade across the throat of the man kneeling before him and start to come towards him.

The young warrior almost fled, but he somehow found his courage and stood firm, waiting for death with his blade held nervously before him. He aimed a clumsy blow towards Arillion's head and stepping round the attack, Arillion easily disarmed the lad and pressed the point of his other sword to the trembling warrior's throat.

"Make your choice, boy," Arillion hissed, grimacing. "Live, or die today?"

The boy shuddered as his bowels loosened and he blinked rapidly, too afraid to move.

"L-live," he blurted, tears in his wild, furtive eyes.

"Good choice," Arillion said, nodding. He lowered his blade. "Tell whoever is in charge of this, to stop sending boys to their deaths and have the courage to come up here and do his own dirty work."

"Y-yes, sir!" the young warrior nodded, shaking. Arillion stepped back. "Off you go then, before I change my mind!"

The young man turned and stumbled his way down through the line of dead and dying on the ledge before him. Arillion watched him for a few more moments and then went to find Cassana, leaving a bloody trail on the rocky path behind him.

Karlina spotted Arillion first and they watched worriedly, as he staggered up the trail to join them. Cassana had led them from the ledge by now and she was relieved, if somewhat perversely, that she felt relatively secure again. Arillion sheathed both of his swords before he reached them and sagged against the rock wall, breathing heavily. Shouldering her bow, Cassana rushed to his side and wrapped an arm around his waist to support him.

"Ouch!" Arillion winced, as she gently opened his tunic to inspect his chest wound. She shuddered as her hand came away, covered with thick blood. She looked up into his eyes and gasped. The cut had gone through to the breastbone.

"I'll be fine, princess" he winced.

Cassana shuddered as she saw the look he gave her and called Squirrel over to help her.

Between them both, they managed to help Arillion up the increasingly perilous trail for several more minutes, until he had regained enough strength and confidence to stand on his own. Ignoring his protests as she opened his tunic wide, Cassana tore strips of cloth from Arillion's cloak and bandaged his wounds. His upper body was covered in blood and growling angrily, he pulled his tunic together.

"That's enough fussing," he said, swatting their concerned hands aside. "There'll be plenty of time for you to get my clothes off me later, princess."

Squirrel giggled as Cassana looked away in embarrassment.

"Come on," Arillion said, waving them away. "We aren't free of this yet!"

Cassana turned her worried eyes away and looked

up the trail. She listened to her thrumming heart for a moment, thinking that she was in the throat of a stone beast. Tarry for but a moment and she would be quickly swallowed down to its belly. The early morning gloom was starting to lift finally and she hoped that it was a sign that their fortunes were also going to improve. Clenching her fists, she drew her sword and led them up into the unknown.

Tobin patted his stallion's broad neck and watched as the young warrior Balan came rushing down the trail towards him. Darned be, if the Kestrel hadn't got it right again! He was about to ask for the good news, until he saw the look on the young man's face.

"What, by the storms," he roared, "are you all doing up there? Chasing clouds?"

The young warrior tripped at his feet and Tobin pushed his mount away as he helped the lad up. "Well? Out with it?"

Balan shook his head. "We couldn't reach the girl," he stammered, unable to meet his leader's eyes.

Tobin frowned. "What do you mean, *couldn't*?"

"There is a swordsman," Balan explained. "He fights like no man I have ever seen, sir. We couldn't get by him."

Tobin punched him hard in the face and watched dispassionately as the young man crumpled to the ground before him.

"So, the others have sent you down to make their excuses for them, have they?" he growled, tempted to draw his blade and exact his own kind of justice.

"No, no," Balan sobbed. "They are dead, all dead!"

Tobin stayed his hand. "Dead? If they are all dead, then why are you still breathing?"

Balan looked up and grinned through his bloodied teeth. "He sent me back to tell you to have the courage to come up and do your own dirty work."

Balan tensed as he saw an angry mask burn itself onto Tobin's face and then relaxed, as his master threw his head back and roared with laughter. Tobin looked over his shoulder at the three men, stood listening behind him in the misty forest. They joined him in his mirth, chuckling nervously as they looked after the mounts of their absent brethren.

"Nicely done," Tobin admitted, nodding his head grudgingly as he turned his attentions back to the young warrior. "Did you recognise this *master* swordsman?"

"No, sir," Balan said, shaking his head. "He was, he was hooded, a-and cloaked all in black. He wore a scarf over his face, so I could only see his eyes."

"So you had the courage at least for that, eh?" Tobin laughed.

"Yes, sir," Balan replied, shuddering. "His eyes were grey, I was terrified!"

Tobin's laughter died in his throat. "Grey, you say? Like flint?"

Balan nodded vigorously. "Yes, sir. And he fights with twin blades."

"I can't believe it," Tobin breathed, shaking his head in disbelief.

"Sir?" Balan asked, watching the astonishment fade from his master's face.

Tobin shook his head ruefully and turned to his other men. "Leave the horses here and follow me!" he ordered them.

"He was injured, though, sir," Balan reported, hoping to regain some favour.

"And so he bloody well should be," Tobin snapped.

"I sent twenty men up there!"

Motioning to his men, the four warriors strode into Smuggler's Gap, without another word to the young warrior.

"What about me?" Balan asked.

Tobin paused, turning slightly. "If you can find a crossbow, follow us. If not, then don't ever let me see you again!"

Tobin turned and led his men into the mountains, grinning. The Kestrel would have been proud of that one. He shook his head and smiled. If he could bring her back the girl and his head, she would most surely take him back into her bed. As he strode up the narrow trail, he felt his adrenalin and lust stir.

One thing at a time, he cautioned himself. He would have plenty of time to claim his reward between her milky thighs, once the hard work was done, once and for all...

Higher they climbed, following the twisting trail as it led them up into the mountains stony embrace. Their progress was hampered however, as Arillion's injuries slowed them down and Cassana was constantly looking back worriedly for their pursuers. Where were they? As she looked down the trail again, over the head of Arillion, he slowed, placing a steadying hand on the rocky wall to his left.

"Are you okay?" she asked, feeling immediately foolish. Surprisingly though, he didn't have any sarcastic barbs to hurl her way. Instead he nodded his head slowly.

"Cass...," he whispered, collapsing to the ground.

Squirrel and Cassana screamed out his name in unison and rushed to his side, kneeling worriedly beside him.

He was kneeling, his head bowed before him.

"Arillion?" Cassana asked softly, her hands trembling as she reached out to touch him.

Arillion raised his head weakly and Cassana sighed with relief. "Do not scare me like that!" she scolded him gently, as their eyes met.

"Never," Arillion whispered, his head lolling.

Squirrel watched their exchange, trembling with worry. She wasn't sure what to do or say and looked away, down the trail. She started to cry as she noticed how much blood Arillion had left behind him.

"I can't go on," Arillion snarled suddenly, drawing her attention back.

"No!" Cassana pleaded, shaking her head as she looked down. "You have too! You can't leave me, not like this!"

Arillion reached out and tilted her face back up to look at him. "I am too weak, my lady. I have lost a lot of blood and the altitude is crippling me. I can barely concentrate on my own words!"

Cassana started sobbing uncontrollably and Arillion cupped her face gently in his hands. "Don't cry," he whispered. "I will buy you both enough time to get away."

Cassana shook her head, holding his wrists. "No," she pleaded desperately. "We can fight them together, we can all survive this!"

Arillion shook his head. "If I go any higher, I will pass out. How will you get to safety then, my lady?" When Cassana couldn't answer, Arillion continued. "I need to get to lower ground, if I am to survive. I promise you this though, I will find a way to get back to you."

Cassana reached up and pulled down Arillion's

scarf. He smiled at her as Cassana's stomach cramped and her chest tightened around her beating heart.

"This is long overdue," he grinned, his eyes sparkling roguishly. "But I am sorry, princess!"

Cassana began sobbing and smiling at the same time. Caressing his face with a trembling hand, she leant in close and kissed him gently on the lips.

"Yucky!" Squirrel said, looking away as they began to kiss each other passionately.

Arillion finally pulled himself away to look at Cassana. She still had her eyes closed and he quickly licked his lips.

"I must think up something else to warrant another apology, some day," he chuckled, grinning.

Cassana opened her eyes and blushed furiously, her heart racing with her freed emotions. Arillion smiled longingly at her, but decided not to tell her about all of the blood he had left on her face.

"Go," he told her.

Cassana's eyes burned defiantly and she shook her head.

"Go on, get," Arillion snapped, pushing her away gently.

"I will not leave you," Cassana stated defiantly.

Arillion growled, looking up at the brightening sky. "You will. You are too important to die on this mountain and you have a destiny to fulfil."

"But I cannot do it, not without you!"

"You can, and you must!" Arillion said softly.

Cassana fell silent, as they subconsciously held hands.

"Go on now," Arillion said. "And get that tree rat to safety, will you?"

"Hey!" Squirrel protested, wiping her eyes.

Arillion focused his attention on her, smiling. "Keep a hold of that knife, freckles," he said, grinning. "I'll be back for that, one day soon!"

Squirrel clutched the weapon to her chest and nodded.

"And make sure Cassana doesn't come back, promise me?"

"I promise," Karlina sobbed, nodding her head.

Arillion rose, taking Cassana with him. They held onto each other for a few more moments, before he pushed her away, holding onto her hand at arms length.

"Come back to me," Cassana said softly, as their fingers slipped apart.

"Of course, princess," Arillion grinned, bowing stiffly. "You still owe me a small fortune!"

Cassana laughed sadly and shook her head, as Arillion shooed Squirrel up the trail in front of her.

"You really are the most annoying man I have ever met!" she whispered, turning to follow the young girl. She could barely put one foot in front of the other, but she had too, she knew that now.

As she left, Arillion moved forward to slap her across the backside. Cassana leapt in the air and scowled back at him.

"I will expect your apology in due course, sir," she cried, hurrying away from him.

Arillion watched as the two females ran up the trail away from him. They soon reached the top of the rise and before they were out of sight, Cassana turned slowly and waved down to him.

Drawing one sword, Arillion kissed the bloody blade and raised it to her in salute. She smiled through her tears and then hurried from view.

Arillion bowed his head for a time and then turning

abruptly, he stumbled back down the steep trail to fulfil his own destiny.

"Please, help me," the man screamed, as he lay with his back against the rocky wall and clamped his bloodied hands over his stomach, trying to keep its contents in.

Tobin swept by him, ignoring the man's pleading screams and carried on up the steep trail. Behind him, his men followed his example, looking away from the dying man as they hurried by. Finally, at the rear and clutching a crossbow to his chest, came Balan. Blood still stained his mouth and he stumbled around his wounded comrade, bowing his head in shame. He wanted to help the man, but if he angered Tobin any more today...

Further up the trail Tobin stepped out onto the narrow ledge and stared about in wonderment at the sight that greeted him. Bodies lay strewn across his path, blocking his way up the steep rise to a wider outcropping. To his right, the huge expanse of the canyon filled his shallow heart with mild disinterest, other than the fact that a weak sun was starting to burn itself into dominance over the cold and bleak morning. Shaking his head in disbelief at the carnage before him, he ran a hand through his long dark hair and grinned at the ridiculous notion that one man could have done all of this.

"Come on," he growled, leading his men on.

As they picked their way over the carpet of dead and steadied their feet on the slick ground, Tobin thought he saw movement, far up the trail ahead of them.

"Well I'll be," he whispered, shielding his eyes with a hand. "I didn't expect that from you!"

Arillion lowered the hood from off his head and shrugged the cloak from his aching shoulders, as he noticed the group of men on the trail below him. Closing his eyes, he felt the cool wind rush over him and allowed it to calm his nerves and soothe his pain. Moments later his mind was clear and his eyes snapped open, focusing on the small group of warriors coming towards him.

Five of them? Arillion felt his hopes rise slightly. Was that all that was left? Shaking his head ruefully he began staggering down the slope towards them. If he had known that, he would have waited for them. His body was on fire and his eyes were rolling in and out of focus. To have come this far, to have found so much, when he had expected nothing. He smiled faintly, picturing Cassana's face. Head before heart, he had scolded her.

What a hypocrite!

He stumbled, but managed to steady himself. He needed to hurry, get past the outcropping before they reached it and overwhelmed him. He needed to get there now, before his wounded shoulder forced him to completely lose all feeling in his numb arm. As it turned out, the two groups would reach the rocky plateau at the same time and stood facing each other warily.

"You always were on the wrong side," Tobin said, grinning at him.

Arillion stared in disbelief and then shook his head, laughing. "You bastard!" he spat. "If I had known it was you behind all of this, I would have followed the lad down and cut your head off myself."

Tobin spread his arms wide and turned round slowly, laughing. "Well here's your chance now, swordsman!" he spat his own distaste at the bloodied man across from him. "*Swordsman*? That's far too flattering a title for a man who is nothing but a liar, a thief and a murderer!"

Arillion flicked away the blood, running from his fingers. "Compliments, at this hour of the day, Tobin? Don't tell me you are warming to me finally?"

Tobin laughed. "Still quick with your tongue, I see?"

"Always," Arillion grinned, his hair blowing across his eyes.

"Well, no matter now," Tobin growled, his eyes narrowing. "You were never as fast as me with the blade, even when you were fit. So this should be easy...oh, and don't worry, I promise to make your last moments in this life as slow and as painful as possible!"

Arillion nodded his head gratefully, watching as Tobin drew his Valian Longsword and cut the air around him with graceful, sweeping arcs.

"He's mine," Tobin shouted to his men, as they also drew their own blades. It was then that Arillion saw the young warrior, further down the trail. Balan met his piercing gaze and looked away, almost dropping the crossbow he held.

"If you want to shoot him," Arillion chuckled, pointing towards Tobin. "Make sure you hit him in the arse."

Tobin roared with laughter and turned briefly to his men, shaking his head. He turned back to the swordsman, his eyes narrowing.

"You were always the fool, Arillion. Never the king!"

"So how is she?" Arillion asked, instantly cutting the laughter from his throat.

"Blissfully unaware that you are still alive," Tobin said finally, his eyes dark with anger. "But don't worry about her, she'll soon know of your final demise, when I drop your head in her lap."

Arillion drew his blades, letting them hang at his sides. "Well come on then, come and get it!"

As Tobin tested the air a few more times, Arillion sighed and stared out across the canyon. The sun was sending its warmth out across the land now and the beautiful surroundings stole his breath away. He smiled, as he heard the cries of an eagle somewhere high overhead and turned back to his opponent.

"To the death," he hissed, raising his blades in salute.

"That's the general idea," Tobin snarled, spitting on the rock between them.

They began to circle each other warily, like lions stalking their prey. All fell silent as the land and the men watched on. A cool breeze blew over them, ruffling their hair. Suddenly, the eagle called out again, as if demanding they begin and Tobin sprang forward, his blade flashing in the sunlight.

Arillion parried the snaking attack before it hit his face, but Tobin danced away from him before his other blade could draw his blood. Tobin circled him, watching as Arillion turned on the spot.

"You are weak," he laughed, attacking before Arillion could respond.

Their blades clashed and sang out again across the canyon, as Arillion spun into the attack, cutting through Tobin's side as he moved away.

"Good," Tobin said, clamping his hand over his wound. He withdrew it again and shrugged nonchalantly when he saw the blood on his palm. "But not good enough!"

They came together again and Tobin feigned a thrust, reversing his stroke to pierce Arillion in his injured shoulder. Arillion snarled in agony and fell back, his sword slipping from his useless hand. He panted heavily, glaring at Tobin with unconstrained hatred.

"One down," Tobin observed mockingly.

Arillion sighed, feeling the breeze kiss his face. He smiled, as he recounted the taste of Cassana's soft lips.

Cassana! He had always lived his life without any regrets, until today...

Growling, Arillion charged forward and feinted left, before spinning right. He felt a deep cut open up on his left cheek, but it didn't matter, as he turned back inside Tobin's reach and slammed into his opponent. They crashed together heavily, Arillion's momentum forcing them back towards the precipice. Tobin panicked as Arillion dropped his other sword and wrapped his arms about his waist.

"I don't need my sword to kill you," Arillion hissed as he forced Tobin back and bore him from the ledge into the canyon below...

EPILOGUE

Cassana raced up into the mountains, her eyes blinded by her tears and any fears of her surroundings forgotten. She ran on for her love alone, carried upwards by her desire to obey his last wishes, even if it meant that she would not see him again. She came to a halt as she hit a wall of realisation and collapsed, her emotions spent and her body exhausted. Squirrel collapsed onto the trail beside her, sobbing and panting uncontrollably.

"We have to go back," Cassana said, touching her shoulder.

Squirrel looked up at her, confusion in her eyes. "But Arillion said...,"

"Hush," Cassana said, silencing her with a trembling finger to her lips.

Squirrel pulled back, glaring at her. "Don't do this, Cass."

"But I have to," Cassana snapped, tears sliding down her cheeks.

"No, you have to get home to fulfil your density," Squirrel retorted defiantly. "He made me promise that you would."

"You are too young," Cassana replied, shaking her head. "You do not understand these things."

"Oh, don't I?" Squirrel snarled angrily. "Well I may not have all the pretty words like you do, but I know what I know, and what I know is that you should do as he says."

"But he will die," Cassana said, moaning.

"No he won't," Squirrel said, smiling. "He is the greatest swordsman I have ever seen. He will come back, he has too. I have his knife, see?"

She held the crescent blade up before them and the sunlight flashed along the blade as the girl turned it in her slender hand.

Cassana broke down, drawing the girl into a hug. They hung off each other for some time, before Cassana pulled back. Her face was pale and her features haggard, but she wiped her eyes and rose, straightening her clothes and picking up her fallen sword.

"I am sorry," Cassana told the girl. "I would needlessly put you in danger, when a brave man has given us both the chance of escape!"

Karlina rose up sluggishly on tired legs and came over to her. "I won't leave you!" she promised, slipping a small hand inside of hers.

Cassana laughed fondly, allowing her tears to fall again. Looking behind her down the trail, she smiled.

"Thank you," she whispered.

Turning, she gripped Karlina's hand tightly and followed her head up the winding trail.

To be continued...

528

About the Author

Anthony has always loved writing stories and after many years of enjoying other authors' works, he has finally decided to try and give something back to the literary world. From an early age, since reading The Lord of the Rings, he has been inspired to write his own stories. He states that his favourite author is David Gemmell and his style of writing has been inspired by the sadly missed author. Anthony lives in Wales with his fiancée Amy and their cat Bruce. He is currently working on 'Shadows of a Storm', the sequel to his first novel.